murder

A Sinful Secrets Romance

Mariana —
much ♡!
Thanks for your
support!

Ella M

murder

A Sinful Secrets Romance

E L L A   J A M E S

This book is a work of fiction. Any resemblance to actual events or persons, living or dead, is entirely coincidental.

"Murder: A Sinful Secrets Romance," by Ella James.

ISBN-10: 1535315342
ISBN-13: 9781535315340

part one

He takes her in his arms
He wants to say *I love you, nothing can hurt you*
But he thinks this is a lie, so he says in the end
You're dead, nothing can hurt you
Which seems to him
A more promising beginning, more true.

—Louise Gluck, from "A Myth of Devotion"

prologue

The night is dark. The road is white. The snow-caked trees that crowd the shoulder dangle icicles that click as wind dives down the famous ski slopes, somewhere in the pinkish clouds above us.

The weather radio said the snow will keep on through tomorrow night. A New Year's blizzard, maybe twenty inches. This is Breckenridge in winter. Frozen to a crackle. Cloaked in white.

Gwenna's breath and mine plume silver in the velvet dark that hangs like a stage curtain over the curved road. Snow is falling fast now, caking our jacket hoods and freezing in a sheen of sparkles. Her coat is the color of a plum—or blood. The thick down softens her form. She reminds me of an animal: one sweet and small, in need of shelter.

I must be more head-fucked than I thought, because she turns around, her cheeks red, her lashes wet with snowflakes, and I realize she's about twenty feet ahead of me.

"Bear?"

Her large brown eyes are widened slightly—in affection or alarm? Her mouth twitches, then presses into a small, red line. She doesn't speak, and there's no need. I know her so well. I can see the worry on her face, the burden of her fear and grief a notch between her brows.

"Come walk by me and hold my hand." She pulls her left glove off and reaches for me.

I oblige her. Anything she wants. With two long strides, I've closed the space between us. My hands are ungloved. I told her I forgot my gloves, but that's a lie. I need to feel the sting.

Her hand folds around mine and Gwen gasps.

"Barrett! Brr, I need to warm you up…" She pulls my hand into her jacket sleeve, gripping it tightly. "Crazy man."

She laughs, despite the somberness of our affair. Her eyes, wet ink in the moonlight, shine with love—for me.

"Hang on." With her right hand, she unzips her jacket. "Come here…"

She takes my hands and pulls them into her jacket, pressing them atop her sweater, underneath which I can feel her heart beat.

Her face tilts up to mine, despite the driving snow. "You can't be leaving gloves at home. It's so cold. You'll get frostbite." Behind her words, there is a smile—a small, lopsided smile she gives me almost all the time. A dreamy smile I love more than life.

I try my best to return it.

Her boots shuffle in the snow as she tries to step closer to me. "It's so freaking cold. Even with a-all these layers." She shivers, and I pull a hand out of her coat, tucking her close to me and rubbing my hand over her back.

"Better?"

"Yes!" Her voice trembles with cold.

I press her hood over her head and rub behind her neck, down to her shoulder blades, right where she likes.

"I love you." Her eyes peek out from behind the faux-fur lining her big hood. I see them crinkle with another smile.

"I love you too." I pull her close again, and God, I'd like to keep her here forever, locked against me like a splint.

"My Bear," she whispers.

I swallow. We're not there yet, but I'm starting to feel frozen—on the inside. A deep breath does nothing to thaw me. She rubs my arms through my jacket and smiles at me again. This smile is curious. Perhaps concerned.

"Your nose is red," she croons.

Her sweet voice doesn't thaw me either, but I still smile. "Yours too." I hug her close once more, but even that can't pierce the ice that's thick inside me.

We walk on, along the road's edge, through a deep snowdrift I worry will spill into her boots.

Somewhere miles away, I hear a lone firework.

She takes my hand again, searches my face as we walk slowly. "I'm glad you came with me. I'm feeling better than I ever have before. Just knowing that I'm not alone, you know? Jamie used to come with me, but you're different. I feel...healed or something."

My jaw clenches. I force my lips to curve up at the corners. "Good." I know my eyes on hers are earnest. "That's good," I murmur.

She comes closer to me. We are leg to leg, shoulder to shoulder. I'm walking off the road, so she seems as tall as I am.

"Bear?"

"Yeah?"

"Are you okay?"

I blink. "Of course." I stroke her hand. "I'm supposed to ask you that."

She smiles a little, tight and sad. "I am."

We're almost to the bend where the road curves into a copse of trees when pops like mortar sound above us. The clouds are too thick to see the fireworks. They glow faintly—green, pink, gold, purple, blue.

Gwen's face looks delicate and beautiful in the changing light. Her eyes hold mine, and she smiles.

"This is kind of nice."

I nod. Her gaze shifts upward, and I struggle to swallow. Fuck.

I shut my eyes. I think about her under me tonight, about the way she leaned up when we both finished and wrapped her arms around me, bringing me down on her.

"Sweet Bear. Something's bugging you. I'm going to find out. Unless you decide to tell me. Hmm?"

A snowflake melts on my temple, and I can feel the ghost burn of her lips there.

"I love you. You know that, right? You're mine—and you will always be mine. Just because I said so."

"Bear?" Her voice is high and sharp. Her hand is on my arm.

I keep my eyes shut, even as the moisture freezes on my cheeks.

"What's wrong?" Her voice is softer now. Inviting. Understanding.

I inhale, and I can't feel my frozen chest. I still can't look at her.

"Hey..." She wraps her arms around my waist.

Don't do that.

"Is it the noise?"

I squeeze my eyes shut tighter. Shake my head.

"What is it then?"

She strokes my shoulders. I can barely feel it through my jacket. But my hands are free. My hands are free to reach into my pocket.

"It's okay, baby." She wraps her arms around my neck and pulls me lower. Her lips touch my face—ice cold. I feel her stand down off her tiptoes.

"Is it me?" She whispers. "I've been feeling like it's triggering for you. Something about this. Coming here?"

She knows me, this girl. Gwenna misses nothing.

It's an effort to open my eyes. To look at her face. Gwenna, whom I love. Gwen for whom I've waited my whole life.

That I have to do this...

That this is the end. It hurts so much. I ease my hand into my pocket, wrap my fingers around the gun grip. I look into her lovely eyes, although it almost kills me.

"Gwen..."

chapter one

Gwenna
October 20, 2015

"Shit!"

I smack the mouse with my whole palm, making my giant iMac monitor quiver on my desk. Then I lean in, squinting at the frozen image of the woods inside the bear enclosure.

"Ugh."

Just like the last two times, I'm pretty sure that right beside that tree—right *there*, near the upper right-hand corner of the screen—is…something. The ground and limbs and leaves don't match up right. I can't explain it. It's as if a ghost is there, making things almost imperceptibly blurry. Someone in a Harry Potter-style invisibility cloak. Someone in the universe's best camouflage.

I seem destined to go crazy, though, because each time such a thing has caught my eye on one of the bear cams, it's been impossible to tell for sure.

The first time I saw something funny in the footage was two weeks ago, Cam 2, at 4:45 a.m. The blur looked man-sized. I could have sworn I saw an arm swinging, the shadow of an arm, with the rest of the body behind a tree. But it was too dark, and the image therefore too grainy, to say for sure.

Then last week, last Wednesday I believe it was, I was following Aimee from Cam 4's view to Cam 3's, trying to be sure he didn't try to bash his new tracker anklet against that freaking rock like last time, when I saw it again: a funny blurriness on the screen, right up against the bottom of a pine tree trunk. The cameras film in color, but not infrared, so all I could manage to identify was a smudge.

I froze the frames, getting down into the milliseconds, looking for the subtle differences between the frames—and there *were* subtle differences. As if someone was moving: a semi-invisible form, moving between two trees. But it was dusk. Again, I couldn't quite be sure.

And then today—right about the time I finished kicking some punching bag ass in the clearing and started heading down the hill behind my cabin, which is situated at one corner of the 300-acre Bear Inc. enclosure, I heard this weird noise. It sounded like two people wrestling in the leaves.

I booked it home and reviewed the footage from Cams 1 and 2, the ones closest to where I was walking. And I found this. This—person. I swear it is! A person in some kind of top-notch camo—or a ghost. I can only see the back and maybe a bent head, but it totally looks like a person.

...A person-like blur.

Would I swear on it in court?

Well, no.

Can I be one-hundred percent sure where the person's outline ends and the thick woods begin again? Not exactly. But it seems like something. Seriously it does.

And if it *is* something, I need to know. If it's someone, I have to be cautious. With all the ruckus going on around here lately, it could be anything. Maybe evil Haywood has some asshole spying on me. Maybe there's a serial killer in the area, one who gets off on victimizing girls with disabilities. The likelihood he would have an invisibility cloak seems slim, but you never know. It could be really good camouflage. They make some patterns that blend in really well with the woods inside the Smoky Mountain National Forest. My property backs right up to it.

I tilt my head to the side, as if that will help my eyes focus. Then I let out a long sigh, rewind and view the footage one last time, and click the red button on the upper left-hand corner of my Safari window.

The computer's clock says it's 5:15 p.m., which means I need to get moving.

I let out my version of a bear moan. Living alone, I'm free to be as dramatic as I want on any given day. With no pets or people, just me here in the forest and the bears—various distances away from me, in the enclosure behind the cabin—it's not like my shouting, cursing, singing, dancing, or moaning is going to upset anyone. The house next door is empty. That evil bastard Haywood.

I've still got to get a shower, but first…

I hustle from my office into the living room, then through the half-wall opening between den to kitchen. There, inside the cabinet underneath my big, trough-style sink, I keep a bottle of Emile Pernot "Vieux Pontarlier" Absinthe for just such an occasion as this.

I twist the top off, bring the bottle to my lips, and take the smallest of swigs. The warm, licorice taste coats my throat, leaving behind a tang of bitterness as I shut my mouth. I imagine I feel more relaxed as I put the bottle back under the sink.

Absinthe aficionados would be horrified by my bastardization of their fancy drink, but whatever. Again—no one here but me.

I strip out of my workout clothes as I march toward my bedroom, set my iPhone in the Bose sound system on my dresser, grab the remote, and blast some Florence + The Machine as I quickly scrub my body, wash my hair, and dry it, tilting my head upside down and flinging my long, copper locks around like a '70s rock star. I swipe deodorant underneath my underarms twice, because I know I'll sweat tonight, then apply a faintly blue eyeliner that makes my brown eyes pop, followed by my signature red lipstick. I don't care what anybody says about redheads and the color red. It's bullshit. I can rock the red.

My phone starts playing witchy-sounding music—the theme song from the *Harry Potter* movies—as I shimmy into hunter green leggings, but I can't talk to my bestie Jamie *and* get ready, so I decide I'll call her from the car. After a parting eyebrow arch into the mirror, I drift into my room and spend a second staring longingly at a an oversized gray hoodie picturing the cover of one of my favorite books, *My Antonia*, before tossing it aside and grabbing a boring, cream sweater that hits me about mid-thigh. I have these ridiculously awesome Prada combat boots that would breathe some life into this bleh, but I don't want to draw that kind of attention tonight, so I settle on a pair of brown Tory Burch riding boots that would only look expensive to the most discerning eye.

I shake my head around a few more times, letting my armpit-length auburn waves cascade around my face, before I fasten my hair into a casual French braid. Then I grab my backpack purse, my adorable bear keychain, and my phone out of the Bose dock, and sprint toward the garage door: a trek that takes me through the office that adjoins my room, then the den—where the cabin's front door is—through the kitchen, and into the laundry room beside the breakfast nook. The place reeks of gardenias, which are potted and blooming on every spare surface, including the top of the washing machine. I inhale deeply as I slip out the door and into my garage.

The radio in my Mini Cooper (code-named Anderson) is set to NPR, and after deliberation that lasts about the length of my long, twisty driveway, I decide leave it there, distracting myself with an interesting discussion about transgender elementary schoolers before, about two miles from my destination, I call Jamie.

"Are you thereeee?" she asks, in lieu of a normal greeting.

"Not yet." I sigh.

"Are you ready?" she asks. "Are you still going to do it?" She sounds perhaps skeptical. I can't tell for sure. She's got this thing she does where even I can't read her intonation. Tricky whore.

I sigh again. "I guess maybe. Probably," I modify.

"You can do this."

I sink my nails into the leather of the steering wheel and glare out at the traffic.

"It might help," she says.

"*Might*." I attack the stitching on the wheel's side with one dark purple fingernail and make a turn toward the courthouse.

"I wish I could be there," she says in a sympathetic tone. She's got the weirdest accent—Southern and phonetically proper, all at once—and something about it always reminds me of Scarlett O'Hara.

"It's okay. I know you can't be, and it's no biggie."

Jamie's a publicist for country music stars, and one of her mouthiest, most trouble-making clients is filming an interview with CMT in two hours.

"It'll either go well or it won't. I'm trying to prepare for either way." I sound a lot more chilled out than I feel.

"Keep me posted. I'll say a prayer," she says.

"Thanks."

I roll into the Sevier County Courthouse parking lot five minutes late, but still take the time to reapply my red lipstick before exiting the car. It's an attitude thing. Once I feel as if my 'tude is cemented safely in place, I allow my eyes to linger on the left side of my mouth. I try to see myself the way they'll see me. The way *I* saw me the first day I woke up in the ICU.

I can't, though. Not after this long. I just look like me, and I know that's probably a blessing: that my eyes can't see my face with horror.

I lift my chin and practice what I used to call the duck face, back when I modeled. Eyes slightly wide, lips pressed into a pout so subtle there's no way anyone would actually call it that. The look is requested so often by photographers in shoots because it could be anything: pouty, sexy, innocent.

The look makes me feel pouty and hopefully appear innocent—even slightly victimized—so I hold it as I walk briskly past the Dolly Parton statue in front of the building and up the steps.

I hold my shoulders up straight and even use my model walk as I make my way through the crowd and to the elevator banks.

"Shit."

There's a sheet of paper taped to the closed doors.

"OUT OF ORDER. PLEASE USE STAIRS."

I inhale deeply, keeping my face neutral even though I want to scream. There are people all around me, people I believe are staring at me. Probably because they saw my picture in that newspaper article that ran a little while ago. Judgy people. The Southeastern United States may be beautiful and friendly, too, but people here are judgier than Saint Peter.

Shit. I'm late and now I have to take the stairs.

My mood plummets further when I see how freaking packed the stairwell is. Some guy huffs and puffs behind me, and I swear I feel his greedy eyes on my ass. Kind of makes me want to turn around and snarile at him.

As I'm nearing the door that opens onto the third floor, a white-haired woman lunges out in front of me to get the door.

"Thank you." I smile slightly before stepping through.

"Anything for you, dear. You know, my mother's mother worked in a traveling circus. Dancing bears."

It's a good thing the last few years have trained me not to smile—that would be *snarile*: the one-of-a-kind smile + snarl my paralyzed mouth makes when I try to smile—spontaneously because the way she lifts her brows with circus bear pride makes me want to laugh. Some people are just too clueless.

"Oh?" I say.

Before she can answer, we're crossing a hall and entering a set of open doors, moving into a room that may actually qualify as hell. Hell is other people. This many of them is probably the central zone in the Ninth Circle of Hell, which as you may know happens to be a freezing place. *Shudder*. (I have a special hatred of cold places).

At the far end of the awful, sweat-scented, sardine can known as the county commission meeting room, a short, black-haired girl catches my eye and waves. It's Jenny Lin from the Gatlinburg TV news station. I stretch my mouth open a little—my substitute smile—and hold my hand up in what I hope is a friendly wave.

Jenny is nice. She's on a short list of semi-strangers that, under normal conditions, I'd give my snarile to willingly; unfortunately, this room is just too crowded for such a display.

Besides, I need to save the snarile for effect.

My stomach rolls.

I stand against the whitewashed, cement-block wall at the back of the room as the county commissioners seated at two long desks work their way through the minutes, until at last they start to talk about the zoning subcommittee's recommendation to re-zone Mr. Frank Haywood's property on Blue Moon Road.

My heart jackhammers as the commissioners start thumbing through their notes on this subject. One of them, Nancy Stein, the bitchy owner of a luxury car dealership, gives the crowd a recap.

"Mr. Haywood wants his residential property re-zoned so he can sell it to a developer who would make the home—quite a large home, I believe it is—into a bed and breakfast. That developer, as it happens, is here tonight," the councilwoman says in her crisp, schoolteacher voice. "Her name is Ms. Carolina Burns. From Nashville."

A tall woman with gray-blonde hair rises halfway in her plastic chair near the front of the room, giving a little wave. Bitch.

"The property is eighty acres and a large home," Ms. Stein continues. "It's been for sale since March of this year, following the death of Mrs. Haywood. Mr. Haywood has been unsuccessful in finding a residential buyer. Since he voluntarily re-zoned several years back as a favor to the bear sanctuary next door, he wants the zoning back the way it was before that time."

She clears her throat, as if her high-pitched voice is tired already. "The controversy here—if we may call it that—is that re-zoning the property could put the bear sanctuary in jeopardy. Animal sanctuaries in the state of Tennessee cannot share a property line with commercially zoned properties, even low-traffic ones such as the bed and breakfast would be. The sanctuary's owner—" her eyes flicker to me, cuing the rest of the room to look as well—"would have to make an appeal to the state environmental board, asking that board to make an exception on this requirement. And she—Miss White—has written our commission two letters stating she doesn't think they would agree to let her keep her sanctuary open. Did we research this, Bert?"

The councilwoman shifts her gaze to Bert Hayes, a short, pot-bellied councilman with a shiny head and wire-rimmed glasses, sitting two chairs to her left.

He nods from behind his little microphone. "It is true that Ms. White, the sanctuary owner, could run into trouble. But what we have to consider her," Mr. Hayes says, "is that both Mr. Haywood, the property owner, and Ms. Burns, the potential buyer, have offered to help Miss White with the appeal. Ms. Burns, who owns several Mountain Valley Retreats around the state, has even offered to purchase some land from her would-be neighbor, Gwenna White, the owner of the Bear Hugs Sanctuary."

My stomach drops down to my knees. She *what?*

Mr. Hayes, head of the rezoning subcommittee, gives me an earnest nod.

I want to shriek. *My land isn't for sale!* Not unless I have to shut my doors...

Another woman on the commission who sits beside Mr. Hayes at the long table, a blonde whose name I can't recall, holds her hand up. "What are the particulars of the enviro board situation with the sanctuary? So what I'm asking is, what did they say? Can we read the sanctuary owner's letters corresponding with that board?"

I inhale slowly, deeply, then project my voice. "I'd like to address the commission myself—if that's alright."

Mr. Hayes' face scrunches as his cohort, the nameless blonde—my new bestie—nods enthusiastically. "If we're going to potentially shut down an animal sanctuary, Bert, we need to do it knowingly. And with good reason," she says.

Luvah.

All eyes in the crowded room shift from that angelic blonde to me. I realize, after a second of listening to my pounding heart, that now is the moment I should probably step forward. I draw another deep breath and, with my face schooled into a look of nervousness—one I hardly have to fake—I walk down the small aisle to the dais where the councilmembers' tables sit alongside a battered wooden podium.

I focus on my breathing as I step onto the dais. My boots click on the wooden floor. My head feels heavy and hollow all at once. My left eye twitches. Can I do this? I stand behind the podium and look out at the crowd.

Holy hell, this place is even more crowded than I thought. I spot familiar faces—the Gatlinburg city planner, a man from the city's wildlife club who is supportive but fairly ineffectual, two newspaper reporters and a male TV reporter. For a moment, when I see his big, black camera, my whole body goes ice cold.

Is this being filmed?

I take a big breath through my mouth and blink once. *Steady, Gwenna. Poker face.*

I hold onto the podium with both hands, the way I learned in my college public speaking course.

Then I take a half-second to look from the left side of the room to the right, gathering my thoughts, seeing all the faces. I spend so much time alone…This many people…

I swallow again, and when I hear my own voice, loud and clear, I almost jump.

"My name is Gwenna White, and I'm the owner of the Bear Hugs sanctuary."

It's an effort not to cringe; ever since the accident, I hate the sound of my voice, with its slightly lazy "w"s and "o"s and "q"s.

"First I'd like to say, it's true that it's a firm rule of the state environmental board that animal sanctuaries not be located in direct proximity to commercial property. In my informed opinion, no amount of appealing is going to change that. They want to protect the bears. That's the enviro board's main job. So if the property next door to me is re-zoned, within the next month, the state board will shut me down." My voice goes a little weak on those words, so I stop again. I blink out at the crowd. My eyes land on a tall, broad-shouldered man whose face is shaded by the bill of a dark ball cap. He's too far toward the rear of the room for me to see him well, but I imagine his shadowed face looks sympathetic, so I focus my gaze on one of his shoulders and keep going.

"We do some charitable outreach, Bear Hugs does. We give free teddy bears to kids at St. Jude's and we go there dressed in bear suits to cheer up the ones who are sick or having surgery. We have school groups come out. But other than that, we're pretty quiet. I don't get out as much as I should." I swallow hard. I feel a stinging flush, starting at the crown of my head and sweeping all the way to my feet.

"See—I had an accident in 2012. I injured—a lot of things. My leg, my head." I swallow spastically, then lick my lips. "Before that, I had been a pre-med student. I had done some modeling. My real dream was becoming a singer. I had signed a record deal." My eyes water. *Holy hell, emotions. Really—here?* I blink and carry on. "That accident changed things for me. Big time. My mouth lost some mobility on the left side, so I couldn't speak clearly. For a while, I couldn't. If you listen, you can hear it's still not perfect. But it's better.

"I didn't want to leave my house after I got hurt, but my parents made me. My dad would take me to the zoo early in the morning. After nine or ten o'clock, too many people were there. I was too self-conscious to go when it was crowded." Sweat trickles between my breasts. "When I smile, my mouth doesn't turn up on one side. As a former model and performer, I was embarrassed and ashamed of how I looked. Of course, the animals didn't care." I give the crowd a small snarile. Several people smile back.

THEY ALL SAW.

I inhale slowly. Exhale.

"The reason that I'm telling you this stuff is that I wanted to explain how a place like this, a place that might not seem very special, really can be. After my accident, I bonded with an injured bear. Working with bears gave me a sense of purpose. Animals can do that for a lot of people."

I see a few nods and feel bolstered.

"Caring for injured animals takes a lot of coordination. I have lots of grants. That's how my sanctuary runs. You can't just move the bears without some consequences. I guess all I'm saying is, this is my livelihood. And I guess what bothers me is, there are other plots of land. There are other places this retreat could open."

My pulse races, and I feel my cheeks redden with my strong emotions.

"Mr. Haywood's property has been for sale for less than a year. Not being able to sell it in that time—that's not all that unusual. If the property is rezoned, my business will close. I don't care if someone buys some of the land from me. I won't be able to do what I do for business on the land I own. And why? So a house can sell faster? So a developer can open a new business? That seems so pointless." My eyes sting, but I make sure my voice stays steady. "As humans, it's our job to watch out for animals and help them. Please consider us as you make your decision."

I give one last snarile: calculated; awful. I hold it a second longer than usual, so everyone in the room can see the paralyzed left side of my mouth. So maybe someone will feel pity. At this point, I'll take anything.

I walk quickly back down the aisle, which feels much longer now. I get a few smiles, and some averted faces. A few outright stares. I look for the man wearing the dark hat, but he's gone. Another man—a shorter, sterner one wearing a suit—is standing where the tall one was. His lips tighten as I come to stand against the back wall.

God, I wish I could just go now.

I hear a "bless your heart" from my right and turn my head to see a short, elderly woman with huge, magenta reading glasses hanging off the end of her nose. "You were in that movie. With the retirement community, and the brother-sister duo. *End of Day.*"

I nod.

"You're still a very pretty girl." She pats my forearm.

You asked for this, Gwen. You just asked for pity. Suck it up.

I blink, keeping my face still. "Thank you."

She pats my shoulder and I want to run. Instead, I stay and listen to the developer, Carolina Burns, talk about her plans for Mr. Haywood's land. She swears she won't build anything within two hundred yards of the enclosure. She says if she gets this development up and running, she'll buy some more land in the Gatlinburg area as a thank you to the commission for their "faith" in her.

My awesome blonde councilwoman asks why Ms. Burns can't buy other land now, and she says, "I can't find anything that works. Now is the time I'm looking to buy."

She talks about how she'll put up a new building or two to the right of the Haywood house, on the opposite side from where I am, and prattles on about how she'll hire a staff of "only" ten or twenty.

"This is such a beautiful area," she croons. "And you guys, let me tell you, my clients are the quiet type. They want to relax. They are educated people. They are respectful of the environment and would be more than happy to be located next door to an animal preserve. If it helps, I even know a woman who works in the environment board's office. Based on what I hear from her, I genuinely believe Miss White is wrong. She's nervous, maybe, and I get that, but we would be a very conscientious neighbor."

The discussion drags on, with the commission members squabbling over local precedent, then over what's the "right thing" to do since Mr. Haywood "so kindly" did away with his own plans to make his home next door into a B&B to help "a new person in the community" bring the sanctuary here.

"He did that out of the goodness of his heart," says Mr. Jacobs, an influential African-American realtor who is a friend of Mr. Haywood. "Now he's asking for the same thing. You know his wife died there. Owning the property is painful for him."

I'm contemplating the look on Mr. Jacobs' face after catching one of my jump-front kicks right between his legs when the male TV news reporter with the camera appears in front of me and asks if he can see me outside the room.

"We're using a clip of your speech on the ten o'clock news," he tells me when we're in the hall. "I think it's inspiring, that story you told. Would you want to do an interview with us? To raise awareness? I saw that movie you did...*End of Night*?"

It's *End of Day*. *Middle of Knight* released last year; another redhead played my part.

I can feel my pulse pound in my tight throat. "Thanks for asking, but I don't think so."

He spends the next five minutes trying to sell me on it. I can't help notice, he doesn't once check out my tits or ass. His eyes avoid them just as they avoid my mouth. It's how a lot of guys act toward me now.

I hear the meeting room shush and lean in through the doorway just in time to see the vote. I see several hands raised in favor, but I can't see the blonde woman's, so I'm not sure in favor of what exactly. Then her hand raises, along with another man's. My chest aches.

"The county votes to re-zone the Haywood property 'limited business,' as well as write a special petition to the state enviro board on behalf of Bear Hugs. In the event that the sanctuary should be required to relocate, the developer may offer to buy Miss White's land and the council will do everything it can to help Miss White resettle elsewhere."

Tears well in my eyes. My throat tightens so much, I'm worried I might choke.

A few heads turn to me. I see a woman lean behind her program, whispering to the lady beside her.

Beside me, the TV news reporter looks impassive. He doesn't give a shit about my fate.

I suck a big breath back, then hurry toward the stairs. I manage to keep my face impassive until I round the Dolly Parton statue randomly positioned in front of the court house. Tears glitter in my eyes as I crank Anderson, but I don't let them fall. I don't cry until I'm home. Until I'm in my quiet house under the blankets on my couch. I cry for half an hour, then text Jamie, Mom, and my brother Rett.

That night, for the first time in many months, I dream of snow.

chapter two

Gwenna

I'm sipping Absinthe in a scalding bubble bath, reading from the book of Job via the Bible app on my iPhone, when the thing rings.

"Ooh!" I almost drop it in the mounds of bubbles all around me. Such is my coordination at the moment. I get a split-second glimpse of the screen-saver clock—3:48 p.m.—before a name flashes across the screen: THE HAYWOODS.

"Well, well…"

Do I answer it?

Hell no.

I'm not speaking to that asshole Haywood. He can go sit on a rusty nail. I look down on my iPhone as it stops ringing.

"I dare you to leave a voice mail, monkey fucker."

The phone beeps, just to spite me.

I dry my hand, take a small sip of my drink, and hit the "voice-mail" symbol. I have to bring the towel to my ear before I put the iPhone to it.

Despite my heavy Absinthe cloak, I feel my heart throb in the second before Haywood's voice fills my ear.

"This morning," he rumbles, "I accepted an offer on the house. A residential offer. It was for twenty-thousand dollars *less* than asking price." He pauses briefly, as if to let that sink in. Then his crisp, New Yorker voice continues: "I always cared about your situation, Gwenna. I'm pleased it worked out this way, and I wish you all the best."

I sit there blinking for a minute, dripping bubbles off my bent elbow, my mouth open, my head feeling a little light.

When I get my bearings, I start shrieking. I don't even mean to. It's what my body does instinctively. Make noise. *Make music.*

I pull myself out of the tub and dry my hand and then the phone. Still naked, bubble-soaked and laughing, I flop down on my bed and dial Jamie.

She answers, "Hey, you."

With no prior notice, my mouth opens and a squeal peals out.

Barrett

"Well...let's see. Where is it? Hmm."

The woman's cheeks flush slightly as she rifles through her massive, purple purse. She makes a clucking sound to fill the silence, even though it isn't—silent. A cool breeze drifts through the forest, tousling the pine needles, clicking fallen leaves together in a gentle autumn song that she can't hear because her heart is likely pounding in her ears.

I fold my arms. "No rush." My tone is easy but my stance says otherwise. Intentional. It's automatic. And dickish, I realize as I watch her struggle with her monster purse. Controlling people begins with putting them off balance, that first step on the road to making them beholden to you. I don't need to do that, though, do I? Not now that I've gotten what I wanted.

I unfold my arms and pull my phone out of my pants pocket. I tilt my head down and look at the screen, holding my right eye open for a long second while the phone's OS reads and registers my retina. The screen flares from black to blue a millisecond later.

I'm hoping to pass for just a normal guy and take the pressure off my jittery realtor, but as I hold the phone in front of me, I realize I'm not sure what it is that normal guys are doing when I see them fucking with their phones. I need to get a normal phone. Onto which I can download something normal. Angry Birds? Breck played that sometimes.

The memory bumps the shard of pain embedded in my chest up somewhere between my sternum and my throat.

I use my imposter iPhone to take some pictures of Ms. Pryce's gray, high-heeled boots. The phone is still and silent. Unlike an actual iPhone, it can hold millions of images. It gives no indication that it's taking them. If left alone for enough hours, the phone will activate its own camera and begin sending images to headquarters. Of course, there's no emergency right now. But taking pictures of my realtor while she assumes I'm playing games alleviates my strange anxiety.

Anxiety is what it is, I've realized: the weird feeling in my stomach and the elevated pulse. For the last couple of months, I thought it must be normal. Something I'd just failed to notice while I risked my life in war zones. Now I'm not so sure.

"Ugh." She exhales, puffing out her cheeks. "I need to organize this crazy thing."

"Take your time. I'm checking work email," I lie.

I spent the early morning turning up the charm for one Ms. Mallorie Pryce, a 29-year-old divorcee with C-cup tits, a little too much lipstick, and the kind of bright white smile you only see in first-world countries. She wears her blonde hair in a pretty bun. As she fumbles with her megapurse, a strand escapes and hangs down by her face. With a half-curled hand, she pushes it away. Her tension feels corporeal between us, despite the beauty of the wooded clearing where we stand under a gray sky.

Finally, she exhales loudly and pulls a key ring from her bag.

"Here we go." She gives me a smile that panders with its stiff width and apologetic eyes. "There you are, Mr. Drake." She holds the key ring out, its trio of keys dangling. I slide my phone into my pocket and take it, wrapping it in my fist.

"Thank you, Mallorie. I appreciate this."

"Hey, no problem." She holds out her arms, over-emphasizing her agreeability. Because, even as I'm trying to act "normal," I'm making her uncomfortable. Not enough so that she consciously notices. (In fact, she thinks she likes me; I know because I listened to the phone call she made from her car this morning as she left the showing). Rather, just enough so she's more pliant than she'd be with someone else. Just enough to make her want to bend the rules for me.

"When I asked Mr. Haywood, he didn't have a problem with it," she continues. "His bank expedited the transfer of the cash so it's all in his account now, safe and sound." She winks. "He didn't plan to go into the house again, so why couldn't you go ahead and get the key?"

Her tone is soft and understanding, as if she's advocating for me. When I don't return her friendly smile quite fast enough, hers falters, her plump lips pinching nervously. She smiles again to cover her anxiety.

"The closing should be sometime in the next four to six weeks. Until then, he doesn't want to deal with rent. He's happy knowing the sale went through, with no harm to the bear place next door. You know that was an issue," she says with one eyebrow arched.

I nod.

"Don't worry about her, though." She lowers her voice, as if the woman next door can hear her across the 340 yards between our properties. "The bears are in a very secure enclosure, like I told you earlier. With your background, I'm sure you could handle yourself either way." She winks again and gives a fake laugh.

I smile, hoping to project a tranquil, slightly grateful expression that will prompt her to get going.

"You know, Gwenna White...she keeps to herself." She glances over her shoulder, at the trees. "She got hurt sometime back. No one really knows the details, but she has a limp, and... some, well, facial...differences. When she smiles..."

I feel the smile slip off my own face.

"Very pretty woman, though. And very nice." Again, the soothing tone. Slightly patronizing, really, not that I give two fucks.

I nod. "Thank you again, Mallorie."

Embarrassment stains her cheeks. That she made small talk with me, and I—what? Didn't seem interested enough? All this time learning to blend in, and now I'm living here among the civvies, realizing I don't.

"Any time," she says. "I'll keep you posted as we move toward closing. I know where you live." She shakes her finger.

I offer a tight smile. It was intended to look genuine and kind, but as the circumstances go, the half-grimace seems to be the best that I can do.

Three minutes later, Ms. Pryce's pale blue Buick SUV is rolling down the long driveway, toward Blue Moon Road, an offshoot of a long, scenic road that leads from northeast Gatlinburg, Tennessee, to the stretch of I-40 between Hartford and Newport.

Alone again at last, I turn to face the house and look up at the porch. It's at the top of sixteen thick, stone stairs, and like the rest of the second and third floors, rests atop a tall stone foundation that serves as the external walls of the lowermost level.

The movement of the porch swing catches my eye and snatches a knot of tension in my chest. I'll need to bolt it down. Perhaps even remove it.

It's the little things, I think. I can't control it all, but what I can...

I look around me, at the verdant pine forest, and I allow myself a moment of satisfaction. This was unplanned, but it works out perfectly. Not just for the larger plan, but because I've always loved the cover of a forest. Sure as fuck beats somewhere dry and barren.

I turn back to my new-ish bike, a Harley Wide Glide I parked beside the garage, on the right side of the house. Stashed in the vegetation near the house's stone base is my pack. I throw it over my shoulder, then walk up the stairs and unlock the front door with the only key that's sized to fit a deadbolt.

The slick, mahogany door opens to the house's high-end kitchen. It's got granite, stainless, all the shit people are always crowing about on TV shows like *House Hunters*. The floors are all hardwood, and there's no wall or other dividing line between the kitchen and the cavernous living area.

The living room is done in dark woods and stone, with a two-story ceiling, an enormous, L-shaped couch in a soft, shearling-type material, a weathered leather recliner, a coffee table that looks to have been made of tree limbs, and two thick, cedar rocking chairs.

Across from the couch, on the wall to my right, is an enormous stone fireplace with a mantel that sports what has to be a five-foot-long flatscreen. The back wall of the living area—which also happens to be the rearmost wall of the house—is part slider door. I know from my tour this morning that the door opens to a stilted, second-story deck that overlooks the forest.

To the right of the slider door, nestled into a corner, is a large gun cabinet. My gaze clings to it for a moment. Then I stride through the kitchen, into the den, and hang a left, heading down a staircase that leads to a wine cellar and home gym.

I walk through both dark spaces and into the small bathroom between—clearing the floor. (Some habits never die). Then I go back up to the main floor, carry my pack over to the gun cabinet, and, using a small pick I've got in my pocket, unlock the cabinet door. The keys on the key ring appear to be a garage key and two house keys—one a deadbolt, the other not. No one's mentioned anything about Haywood coming back for the contents of this gun cabinet, so for now I'm going to call it mine. I stash my weathered M-14, my M4 Commando, and my HK MP5 there, but leave my TAC-338 in its hard case.

With my bag over my shoulder and the McMillian case in my right hand, I make a quick pass with my left hand over the butt of the .45 at my hip, then start to climb up to the top floor.

The third floor houses two bedrooms and two bathrooms, plus a library. It's probably 2,000 square feet up there, with maybe 1,000 of those dedicated to the palatial master suite. I feel a jab of want as I remember the rustic-opulent space, with its pale stone fireplace, soft, faux bearskin rug, luxurious-looking king-sized bed, and two big, bay windows facing south.

When I'm halfway up the staircase, I turn and grip the bannister. I'm still getting winded pretty easily, but it's better than it was a few months back. I shut my eyes and fill my lungs and try to focus on being present. Right here, right now.

Fuck, I'm tired.

I climb slowly up the remaining eleven stairs and clear the floor. When I've satisfied my irrational impulse, I return to the master. From the doorway, the fireplace is on the left, a stone behemoth in the middle of a wall of built-in mahogany shelves.

The king-size bed is on the right, between the bay windows. I lay my gun case and my bag on the bed's silky, sage-green spread and unzip the bag. Nestled between shirts and pants, socks and boxer-briefs, are a bunch of cans of Red Bull. I pull the cans out and line them on the night stand to the bed's left.

Then I check my watch.

It's 2:12 p.m.

I pop open a can and take a few warm swallows, then set it back down. My stomach growls. My gun case looks strange there on the elegant bedspread. I want to see the .338, so I take it out. I run the fingers of my right hand over its cool grip. I peer through the Leupold MK4 scope, then stand with the gun in hand.

One small step toward the left bay window, and I turn back toward the bed and lay the heavy gun atop the mattress. I take the scope off and take it with me to the window.

Through the thick woods, I can see the green tin roof of the little cabin next door. I peer through the scope and watch some leaves flutter down onto it. How long until Gwenna White emerges for her afternoon workout?

I stand there waiting—two hours and six minutes. With the quiet precision of my trade, I track her up the hill behind her house, moving from the left window to the one on the right of my new bed. When her small form becomes a long shadow, I walk downstairs.

I stand around the kitchen for a moment, feeling lost. Then I fire up the Keurig and make myself a mug of hot chocolate.

chapter three

Gwenna

The rest of Wednesday passes in a thick haze of relief. Everything seems better now. My cappuccino—stale-tasting the last time I brewed one—tastes delicious this time. The sheets on my bed—just regular, silky sheets—feel outright luscious. My closet—an honest-to-God danger zone—appears before me as a giant stack of lovely things. I'm fortunate to have them. I've got a soft robe, a cozy couch, a beautiful clearing near the top of the hill where I can work out.

Working out is more fun, too, I notice Wednesday evening when I finish, because no longer am I practicing my Taekwondo with the intent of getting a last-ditch job as an instructor. I may still get re-licensed for the fun of it. Because, until I got "discovered" as a model, Taekwondo was one of the biggest parts of my life, and it would be nice to be able to instruct again. Maybe even pro bono. But I don't have to if I don't want to.

I spend Wednesday night packaging the plush black bears I sell on the sanctuary's web site at an $8-per-bear profit, then watching *Doctor Who* (David Tennant) while lounging on the couch, yammering with my mom and Jamie. My brother Rett calls too, letting me know how glad he is that everything worked out with the sanctuary.

When I think I'm finished with my talk-a-thon, my mom calls back to ask me a mundane question, and I can hear the tears in her voice. She doesn't like me to ask outright, nor does she actually want to talk about how she misses Dad, so I just chat with her like normal, tidying up my office as we chat, then, when her lengthy debate—mostly with herself—about what piece to sculpt next starts to melt my brains, I sit at my desk and start reviewing footage from the cams.

Tomorrow is an enclosure day for me, so I need to spend some time figuring out where my bears are tonight, and how they seem to be doing. I track them via their anklets and then, because my mom is still going strong—she's leaning toward a woman mostly covered by a large shawl; *"perhaps really a mourning veil,"* she says excitedly—I check the footage from Cams 1 and 2 around the time I was out practicing.

To my horror, I see something. Something blurry. Something moving. Something man-sized. And then, just when I start to second-guess myself, I see a hand. A real, flesh-colored hand—I'm sure it is!

I stop the footage and hit rewind, and I can finally see. It *is* a person. Holy shit! It's someone wearing camouflage. I would never have realized had I not seen that left hand. He must have taken off his camo gloves.

Oh holy shit, who *is* this person?

The trajectory in which he's moving in the footage points him toward me. He's moving toward me at the time I would have been headed back to the house.

Shiiiiitttt.

"Hey Mom, can I call you back?"

"Of course. Don't worry with it tonight. I feel much better. Thanks for listening, love."

"No prob. It sounds amazing, Mom. I love you."

"Love you too."

I hang up with her and dial Jamie. "It *is* a man! It's a man, it's a man!"

"Whoa there, Squirrel. Your new neighbor?"

"No, the camo ripple ghost thing on the cams. It's totally a man. He took his—I guess camo glove off, I could clearly see a *hand*. Who the hell is it?! He's a murderer! Talk to Niccolo, Jamie! Tell his Mafioso ass to come save me!" I flop back in my desk chair, out of breath and laughing at my own dramatics.

"How much Absinthe did you have this morning?" Jamie asks.

"STFU, whoreface. I mean it, there's a man on the cams and he was out there when I was out there. Tell me that's not creepy as hell."

I keep Jamie on the phone for thirty minutes, running my wild theories by her, forcing her to promise she will call me first thing in the morning, telling her if I'm kidnapped, I'll grab the bag of pistachios from my night stand and drop them in the forest like Hansel and Gretel. In other words, trying to make her laugh.

Say what you will about my dislike of Niccolo—she fell for him in the days after my accident; at one point the police tried to link the accident to his younger brother; BFF-related jealousy; yada yada whatever—but I do have one legitame complaint: he's a boring mofo. She spends too much time with his dreary ass, if you ask me. Right now he's producing a movie in L.A. Since Jamie lives in Nashville, they're only seeing each other two or three times a month, leaving more time for me and actual fun.

I review the camera footage one more time, watching up until the moment the hand, and the blur of the man's body, disappear, sometime after he has turned around, away from me and back toward the hill behind my house.

I take the safety off the .38 I keep in my nightstand drawer, say my prayers, and fall asleep mostly untroubled, having managed to partition off my ax-murderer anxiety and any residual upset about the zoning situation—me talking and snarile-ing at the commission meeting in my pathetic attempt to arouse pity.

In dreamland, I find myself on *that* road, holding a gardenia petal in one hand and a cell phone in the other. I keep hearing the squeak of boots against the fresh powder. Snowflakes fall on my nose and forehead, melting on my skin. When I move, my long hair sways around my hips. When I wake up Thursday morning, I remember that: my hair was long. Down to my ass. Not in real life, but in the dream.

I Google it and read that long hair in dreamland is a sign of strength.

Even so, I grab the .38 and tuck it into the pocket of my sheepskin coat before I slip into the woods.

When I tell people I run a bear sanctuary, I almost always get one of two responses.

"You? Like—just you? Aren't you scared of being EATEN?" Or, *"OMG, what's it like playing with those precious bears?"*

The boring truth is, there is almost zero chance of being "eaten," not just because black bears are almost never aggressive unless provoked, but also because there are lots of common sense precautions.

I don't take food into or around the enclosure. I don't even eat in the moments before I go in, nor do I leave my garbage cans outside. I pull up the tracking app on my phone before I unlock the enclosure's gate, so I know exactly where each of my five bear babies is. Also, I carry bear spray. Not because I think I'll need it, but because it's smart. Just like carrying a small gun is smart, because of poachers and criminals of the human-hunting variety.

As for playing with the bears? No way. Caring for captive bears is all about limiting contact. While occasionally I'll get bears like Aimee and Papa, "lifers," I call them, a lot of my charges are only being rehabbed. They'll be released back into the wild, and if they're going to be successful when they are, I have to try to minimize their reliance on human intervention.

I use a computer program to determine which interventions are worthwhile and helpful. For example, five bears living in a three-hundred-acre enclosure is a lot of bears on not much land, so without some tweaks to make the small environment more nutritionally rich than "regular" nature, my bears might not thrive.

My program calibrates several dozen variables, every factor from the number of years the bears have inhabited the same acreage, to number of bears in the enclosure during each month of the total enclosure time, to number of various types of plants that yield various berries, etc.

Some of my grants require me to keep physical data on the bears, so two to three times a year, they're sedated, and I draw blood. I analyze it for nutrition, among other things, so I can adjust their vitamins accordingly.

Five bears is my max capacity. That includes three long-term inhabitants and two transients.

Harold is the oldest and tamest—a former circus bear who would never survive outside captivity, so I enrolled him in a long-term study on osteo-health conducted by a veterinary school in Alabama. Harold is leery of top hats and petrified of whips and sequins. Which is fine, because I'd look nuts in a top hat, and considering my perma-single status, I'm not really one for whips or sequins.

My second-most-laid back bear bud is Aimee. Aimee is a dude, but his owner—a chain-jewelry-store magnate—didn't know that when she bought him on the black market. When she called me about taking custody of Aimee, the photo she emailed featured Aimee in a purple "ear bow." Whether Aimee could be released into the wild in some capacity isn't clear yet. I've been monitoring him carefully and recording data since he came to me in February.

Brooksie is a former petting zoo captive and a lightning-fast tree climber. Like Aimee, she may be capable of living in the wild, particularly if she's tracked and monitored. Since she's female, releasing her would be particularly gratifying; she would likely reproduce. Until then, I've had to program my tracking software to give me an alert when she and Aimee are in the same area.

Fourth on my roster is Cinnamon, a three-year-old female who's spent all but the last five months in the wild. She's here only because her leg was badly injured in a poacher's trap this summer. She'll hunker down on my land when it gets cold, and next spring she'll be tagged and released.

Last, there's Papa Bear, my secret fave. When a family in rural Virginia found him as a cub, they called him "Boo Boo." For years, this family caged Papa with their four Dobermans. They fed him table scraps and tried to "train" him. By the time I got a call from an Appalachia humane society last December, poor Papa Bear was dangerously thin and so unruly, he was being given sedatives.

I took him in early January, even though I knew it was a risk. The crew who brought him recommended I wear a maim-proof vest and helmet, but I just nodded and told them where to lay his tranquilized body in my isolation pen.

The isolation pen is the acre of the enclosure closest to my house and my stock shed. It's not in play unless I choose to partition the acre off, something I only do for very ill bears or bears like Papa, who have been kept in such tight quarters that releasing them into a large space would frighten them.

Papa expected to be fed and watered regularly. He'd never had food fit for a bear. His coat was dull and thin, his body lean enough that I remember thinking that first day, as I watched him sleep, he almost looked like a tall human in a bear suit.

I watched him wake up and walk around in circles that day, moaning and chuffing. His body shook from the anesthesia required to transport him to my place. His eyes darted around— looking for other animals? He'd spent his entire life with dogs, except the previous three weeks, when he'd been kept at a shelter.

Clinging to my cell phone, with my tracking program zeroed in on Papa's small green dot, I went into my cabin and cried.

Gradually, I started reading more about techniques developed by other caretakers in a similar position. Things that might help Papa.

For the remainder of last winter, I found myself obsessed with him. I started talking to him through an opening in the fence. I started throwing cardboard tubes filled with berries and honey- comb over the fence, teaching him, with the tubes, to do normal bear things, like forage for food. The frozen vitamin ball bombs I threw over the fence got his coat looking shiny. I brought him black cherries and hickory nuts that helped him put on weight.

Then in July, just a few weeks after I opened the isolation pen and granted Papa access to the other bears, he cut his foot on something and got an infection. I called my friend Sam, a large- game vet who works at the Memphis Zoo, and he came out and helped me sedate Papa. He cleaned and wrapped the wound, then left me with antibiotics and promised to return in a few days.

I took the opportunity to sit with my sleeping friend.

To my shock and horror, Papa Bear woke up early. I had my arm around his neck. He raised his head and made a keening sound. I stood slowly. He lumbered up and looked right at me. Shaking, and with glazed eyes, he nuzzled me. All the blood drained from my face. He made a roaring noise, and just as my sweating fingers reached for my bear spray, he nuzzled my arm. Since then, he comes to me and leans against me every time I go into the enclosure. I guess he wants the nurturing he never got.

I'm feeling pretty chipper as I punch my code—010212— into the gate and stride to the stock shed just inside.

The weathered shed came with the property, a relic from an old moonshine operation. I thought it was cute, so I reinforced the worn, wood walls from the inside, laid a cement floor, and installed metal shelving, plus a refrigerator and a tiny sink. I punch the same code into the lock beside its door and pull the door open.

Creak…

I see a swirl of snowflakes that aren't here. I smell gardenias, feel the numb cold seeping through my boots. The clink of tire chains against ice is loud enough to drown out every thought inside my head. A year ago, my next move would have been to crouch under the metal shelves and put my head on my knees. Now I stop and take a breath. I count while I release it, imagining the memory running through me like the white fog of a ghost.

Sometimes certain sounds will bring on a flashback. I've noticed the triggers are often clinks and beeps and creaks—like the creaking of the shed's door just now. Since I don't consciously remember anything like that, I've decided they're probably sounds from the emergency vehicles.

I take a few more deep breaths and close my eyes. *"I'm right here, and I'm completely fine."*

I open the freezer and pull out an ice block of berry mash and vitamins, then pull a wood box off the nearest shelf, lift the lid, and drop the ice block in.

Keeping track of supplies and food is one of the most boring aspects of my job, so I try to liven it up with music. I pull the iPhone band off my upper arm and search my song list for one that fits my mood.

Jason Isbell, "24 Frames." I try to let the singer's voice blot out my troubles while my hands get busy fastening my work belt around my hips and grabbing my clipboard off a nail in the wall.

According to my log, I need to spread some cedar shavings near the pond, sink a box of frozen treats, and toss four vitamin ball bombs into the trees.

I tap my foot against the cement floor and sing along with Jason while I slip the vitamin bombs into the pockets of my belt and pile cedar shavings in the middle of a canvas blanket. I shake my ass as I knot the blanket's four corners, creating a big pouch I sling over my shoulder. Finally I mute my music, tuck the treat box under my arm, and step outside into the filmy morning light.

It's cold today; colder than yesterday, I note, as I trudge toward the pond's edge. I look at the leaves spread over the damp ground, papery jewels of gold, red, orange, and brown. My gaze wanders the dense treeline. Spindly branches and barren-looking trunks, crooked tree fingers curled between the tall, green pines. Autumn's cloak is spread around me. Soon the leaves will rot. It will be winter.

Shut up, Gwen, and focus on the present time.

I kneel beside the pond's soggy fringes, set the box down, and shift the woodchip pouch down to the ground. It feels good to throw the treat-filled box at the water. It lands with a splashy slap and bobs a second before sinking. Soon the bears will smell it and come poke around. Whoever gets it first will enjoy the challenge of opening the lid.

I try to focus on my hands as I spread the woodchips along the water's edge. Black bears love to roll in cedar chips.

When I'm finished, I pull out my phone and check the bears' locations. Hmm, so I've been scented.

I toss a vitamin ball bomb into the trees and exhale slowly as Aimee and Cinnamon stroll out of the woods. Even though I don't come at the same times or on the same days of the week, even though their enclosure is vast, sometimes they still scent me. Which, given that a black bear's nose is seven times more powerful than a bloodhound's, shouldn't surprise me but still does.

I toss two more vitamin ball bombs and am turning to go when I hear the well-timed crunch of leaves. Papa Bear. He stops between a pine tree and a big, old oak and blinks in my direction.

"Hey there, Papa."

Glee spreads through me.

As if he knows, Papa Bear's big, black body shuffles closer to me. He lifts his head, his black eyes peering up at me. I give him a reassuring smile.

"Hey, handsome."

I hold my hand out, palm up, like I'm a waitress preparing to carry a plate. I raise it slowly, then turn my palm over, so it's facing the ground. Papa Bear shifts closer to me. Another lumbering step, and his head is right under my palm. He rises up, and I feel the soft warmth of his head against my hand.

"There ya go," I whisper.

This is what I trained for, what I *live* for.

Papa nuzzles my hand, and I sift my fingers through his coarse fur. He leans slightly against me, almost knocking me over with his weight. It makes me laugh.

He makes his happy noise, a borderline illicit sound that's outright silly. I feel his legs shift as he leans against me.

"You're a good guy. You know that, right?"

Papa nuzzles me with his nose before he waddles off into the trees. I head back toward the gate, feeling elated.

As I'm stepping through it, onto the pebble path that leads back to my porch, I hear a loud *thwak!*

chapter four

Gwenna

A ll my muscles lock up as my face flushes and my heart races.
Thwak!

My hand dives into my pocket, wrapping around the handle of the .38 as my eyes fly around the woods.

Thwak!

The sound is somewhat distant, not right here but not far either.

Thwak!

THWAK!

It sounds like…someone punching a taut piece of material. Or jumping on one of those small, indoor trampolines…

I step forward, hand still in my pocket, wrapped around the gun. Two more *thwak*s confirm the bow noise is coming from a single location.

BOW noise!

Could that be the sound of arrows flying through the air, then hitting something?

Thwak!

The thought ratchets my heart rate up a notch, enough so that I have to take a big breath and let it out slowly before I walk toward the sound.

Thwak!

Thwak!

I point myself at the woods directly behind my house, at the small swatch of forest I own that's not within the walls of the enclosure: the area where, farther up the hill, I do my workout in the clearing. Then I adjust course so I'm walking in a trajectory that will lead me to the property line between my land and Mr. Haywood's.

Thwak!

I swallow hard. Maybe it's not a bow, I tell myself. Maybe someone's chopping down a tree. The new homeowner. But it doesn't really sound like that, and anyway, it couldn't be the new owner. The offer was only just accepted.

Thwak!

I should go home. Instinct tries to tug me that way, but curiosity pulls harder. It's my nature. I walk deeper into the woods, hating the crunch of my boots on the dry leaves. My hand is still in my pocket, because if someone was watching me—and I tell myself they're definitely *not*—I wouldn't want them to know I have a gun on me. Not yet.

Thwak!

I walk about twenty more yards before it's unmistakable: the sound is coming from the land to the right of me, from the Haywood property.

Probably a workman.

Thwak!

The sound is so loud, it rings so clear through the quiet woods, I'm almost sure now: it's a bow. Suddenly I remember I have my monocular. I can feel it up against my middle finger's knuckle, in my pocket by the gun. I use it to bird-watch sometimes.

I lift it to my eye and look around, but I'm not at an angle where I can see the land directly behind the Haywood house; it sits on ground a little higher than my own.

I curve back into the woods before resuming my straight line toward the Haywood place. If someone is shooting arrows at a target, I don't need to get too close.

I stop again and look through the monocular. And there he is. This...man. I stare for a long moment, my lungs emptied of air, my throat tightening with something that feels an awful lot like pain. I don't even blink, so my eyes water a little. But I can't take them off him. It's as if my entire being is holding still while the imprint of him is recorded somewhere deep inside me.

The sensation is uncomfortable. Achy. I draw a deep breath, and my brain seems to un-freeze. My eyes leap into action and start cataloguing details. As soon as my heart releases its grip on me, it's pathetically obvious why I reacted so viscerally to him.

The man is stunning. *Stunning.* I've seen more than my fair share of beautiful men—models for Ralph Lauren, Armani, Versace, Calvin Klein, Abercrombie. I used to shoot alongside them. So I can judge him with authority.

I breathe gently and roll my gaze over him a few times, like a talent scout seeking a flaw. I find nothing, neither in his technique with the bow nor with his aesthetics. I blink a few times, trying to shake off the dazed feeling I have, before I study each fine feature, starting with his hair. It's black—or very dark brown—and it's somewhere on the line between short and long. I think it's curly. Yes, it must be. It's not long enough to be a bona fide mane. The curls are more like cresting waves. They shake a little as he takes an arrow from a small, vertical wood box on the ground beside him. I note a curl that's pasted to his forehead.

His skin is slightly pale, and damp with sweat. My gaze drifts down to his dark brows. They're model eyebrows: thick, strong slashes that command my gaze. Beneath them are a pair of long-lashed eyes that might be gray or blue. They're beautiful and shrewd. No doubt about that. His eyes are in the running for Most Prominent Feature. Below them, he's got a strong, straight nose—actually...it might be ever-so-slightly crooked; I can't tell from here. It's framed by high, stark cheekbones that lend him a slightly feline look. His ultra-light beard—only a little more than a shadow—is just enough to give his jaw delectable definition. And his lips. Dear God. I'm not sure I've ever seen more gorgeous full and sultry lips.

The wavy hair, the piercing eyes, that godly mouth—the way those lovely features contrast with his sharp bones, the straight line of his nose and the cut of his jaw, the roughness of the dark beard and the slight circles underneath his eyes—It's damned impressive. Classic.

Armani? Or maybe he's more Dolce & Gabbana? Definitely not delicate enough for Ralph Lauren. Probably not quite slim enough for Calvin Klein.

He's like a next-gen Peter Badenhop. And wouldn't that be fun? Peter is actually super nice and down to earth.

My gaze lingers on the slight furrow between his brows as he notches the arrow with his right hand and slowly draws the cord back. For a second I'm distracted by the way he holds the bow with his left hand: strangely—his pinkie and ring finger held out straight rather than gripping the curve of the bow. Then his tongue darts over his lower lip, and he lets the arrow fly.

My eyes follow it about thirty yards forward, to a round, red target strapped to the front of an oak tree. The arrow is the latest of many.

My gaze latches back onto his tall, strong form as he looks down into the box, then straightens up, showing off his wide shoulders, which are clad in a dark blue thermal shirt. The pants that move with his long strides toward the arrows are dark charcoal—that or faded black. I look down to his black boots: well-worn. He's tall. Big. He wouldn't make a photographic match for me despite our shared traits of striking eyes, straight noses, and full lips, because he's so much taller.

My heart tumbles and my body freezes.

He wouldn't make a match for you at all, Gwen.

I draw a big breath. In that millisecond all my interest in him, all my admiration of his flawless face and form, curdles.

I watch him pull the arrows from the target with an angry-looking fist. I watch his pretty mouth: so taut and flat, as if he's frustrated. I watch his brow tighten as he grabs the last arrow out, clenching his hand around it. He puts the arrows under his left arm—strange, when he could hold them in his fist—and strides quickly, with lion-like grace, to his spot just behind the home's back deck.

Like a model, his movements are elegant and sparse. Actually, he's probably smoother than most of the ones I knew. I watch his face for one more moment. He's definitely a doppelganger for Peter Badenhop. Except this guy is bigger. Starker. Honestly, more striking.

I sigh softly.

So that's my neighbor. Beautiful McBeautyMan. Who looks amazing with his arm pulled back, the bow in hand.

I watch him shoot, and watch the arrow hit the bull's eye.

Wow. He's good.

I'm sure he has a good ego to match.

I turn and move as quietly as I can back toward my cabin, vowing to myself to stay away from him.

Barrett

My knees slam down against the floor; I grab the toilet seat and barely get my head over the bowl before I'm vomiting.

I know it's Red Bull, but it smells like liquor. Tastes like liquor. Stings like liquor.

My body's numb and heavy. Still, I feel a door beside me, bumping my elbow as my body lurches.

Bluebell grabs my arm. As my body heaves and puke splashes on my lap, I feel a heavy arm around my shoulders.

"Fucking hell, man." Blue's hand comes under my right arm, holding me against him as the car swerves. "Dove, take the road right there. That one!"

"Is that a road?"

"Yes. Take it!"

"Fuck, we're gonna track."

"They'll be gone in half an hour."

I feel Blue shift back against his seat and hear his voice closer to me. "Shit, Bear. Is it just the liquor?"

Between hurling, I rasp, "Yeah."

I wrap my hand around one of the metal rods that lock the headrest of the front passenger's seat into the chair and try to aim toward the floor. Far away, I feel the chaos of anxiety as my teammates buzz and the world riots around me.

"All right," Blue says roughly. "We'll get where we're going and there'll be a shower."

Between gasping, I groan, "I don't care."

That's where it ends. I'm always sick until my throat is raw, my eyes and nose are running, neck and jaw are sore. I grip the toilet, moving between then and now, not sure where I'd rather be when I'm aware enough to monitor what's going on. There with that or here with this.

Breck's gone.

Re-realizing that prolongs my stomach's rebellion. Sounds of retching echo in the bathroom, gasping, gagging, panting...Then it's over and I just want to shower.

With my right arm flung across the toilet seat, I tilt my throbbing head down, looking down at my chest through streaming eyes. The room feels like it's tilting.

You're not drunk, you dumb fuck. Get up.

I wipe my right forearm across my mouth and grab onto the partial wall between the toilet and the countertop. My throat and eyes ache. I squint and blink, then step over to one of the sinks to wash my hands and face.

No shirt, I notice as I blink into the mirror. I must have torn it off while I was dreaming. Sometimes I do that, thinking that there's blood on me.

I look from the shower to the bedroom door. I dry my hands and face with a towel I find under the countertop, then I brush my teeth. Then, with one last look at the shower, I walk into the bedroom.

My gaze rolls over the bed and side tables. Nothing broken. That's good. The first time I fell asleep at this place, right after I came in from trying out one of the bows I found in the gun cabinet, I shattered a porcelain lamp on one of the nightstands.

I look down to the floor beside the bed. All the covers are in a ball, including the blanket I was lying on. I don't see my pillow at all. I look from the pallet to the bathroom door, trying to remember getting up.

I can't. I never can.

I go to the dresser and pull open the top drawer. It's the only one with any contents. The Haywoods left some clothes in their closet, but nothing in the dressers. I pull out a soft, thick, camo button-up my brother's fiancé bought me. If it weren't for her—a sweet, Georgia girl named Cleo, who insisted I needed some camo for my civvie wardrobe—I wouldn't have anything to wear. All my shit is still in the apartment in Fort Bragg—a place I still pay rent for. I don't know if I'll ever go back in it.

A glance at one of the windows shows me it's still mostly dark outside, but the sky has a tinge of color to it.

I peel my sweat-soaked boxer-briefs off, replacing them with clean ones despite the lack of shower, then tug on some dark pants and socks.

Only then do I let myself walk over to the window closest to the bathroom and sit slowly in the armchair I've dragged up to it.

I note two Red Bull cans on the floor against the baseboard. I don't remember leaving them, but that's not too surprising these days. I crunch them both and set them on the nightstand, in the blank space where the lamp sat. Then I lift my scope and bring it to my left eye.

Habit.

I tilt it down toward the trees and blink, trying to see the limbs and tree trunks, the pine needles, and the green rectangle my right eye sees so clearly, plain sight. My left eye sees nothing—a sheet of brown only a little lighter than the black I'd see if the eye was shut.

My fingers tighten on the scope. Dizziness peels through my head. I breathe. I move the scope to my right eye and peer down through the trees at her green roof. I can see half-squares of light through two of the windows, which are the size of Saltine crackers from the third story of this house.

My pulse quickens at the sight. I haven't looked at my phone—knowing the time makes it pass more slowly—but with my pedigree, it's almost impossible not to gauge the time from the sky. I'd put it at about 4:45. Maybe 5 a.m.

This is early for her.

I watch the patches of light bleeding through her windows. I watch the home's front door until it opens. I watch her until the trees and morning fog engulf her. Then I rest my head against the window pane.

chapter five

Gwenna

*I*n the dream, I'm in the bag room: this enormous room of Birkin bags, hundreds of $80,000 bags on shelves from floor to ceiling.

Unlike real life, I dream of being there alone - my body thin and taut, my hipbones sharp under my sheath dress, my coppery hair straight, chopped short to my chin. I've spent my hours with the hair and makeup team, and I'm aware, despite the absence of a mirror, that I look better than I have in all my life. Gone the pudgy little red-haired girl with big front teeth. Gone the awkward girl who curved her shoulders in and wished for winter all year 'round so she could cover up her moon white limbs.

I look like a bombshell, and I know it. It feels fucking good.

So now I need to choose a bag: my takeaway from the job, my gift for gracing Hermes with my face. I stand there, looking up at all the endless shelves, and giggle at the thought. I'm a model. How ridiculous - and how amazing.

Up, up, up the shelves rise. All around me. The shelves twist and separate until they're more like giant stacks of cards. I still see the bags, the Birkin bags in all the colors.

"Pick a bag," my own voice says.

I see the green, the color I DID pick, but I don't reach for it. There are so many other colors. Whites, purples, browns and blacks. I could choose any bag, any bag of all these, and I don't know which one to pick. I'm standing there, my legs cold in the chilly air blowing from the air vents done in bamboo like the smooth, slick floor. My dress flutters against my thighs. I smell the fresh, delicious scent of oiled, crocodile-skin bags.

I can see the snow. Not see it...sense it. I can feel the snow, the cold, cold snow. I choose a white bag and it disappears as soon as I start pulling it toward me.

I whirl around. What's going on here? Am I dreaming?

I go for a purple bag with shaking fingers. Get it now and GO. Time is running out!

I grab the bag and hug it to my chest and then it's gone. Black, brown, green: I grab them all and feel them slip away like ghosts. I try grabbing the green one two more times, aware that it's the right bag, it's the one I really chose. But I can't hold onto it.

The shelves tremble and a bag falls by my feet. And I know, I know right then, I have to run. I can't take a bag, but I can save myself.

I wake up soaked with sweat, feeling both triumphant and bereft...

With my damp, stiff hand, I shut the spiral notebook, set it back on my nightstand. My heart feels tight and heavy. My head aches from clenching my jaw while I was dreaming. I could grab my phone and check the time, but everyone knows that's a losing proposition. Time crawls by when I know exactly how early it is. I can tell by the absence of light through my curtains that it's sometime in the wee hours.

I want to get up and make some hot chocolate or tea, but first I fold my legs into a meditative pose, straighten my back, relax my muscles, and rest my hands on my knees. I shut my eyes and do a thing I learned in therapy.

Shut your eyes. Inhale. Smile inwardly. Exhale.

Smiling inwardly is a weird concept—you just imagine your-self smiling—but the exercise works almost freakishly well. I do that twice, and when I feel more peaceful, I pick the notebook back up, flip to a blank page, and attempt to draft a more favorable version of the nightmare.

I go into the bag room and I get a bag. I do the shoot, and during it, I let myself feel beautiful, not just on the outside, but also inside. I try to treat everyone with respect and love, try even harder than normal. I enjoy the way that heavy necklace feels around my neck and when I close my eyes so they can refresh my makeup, I inhale and try to bottle up the smells inside my brain so I can remember this. It's a once-in-a-lifetime opportunity, one I can always remember fondly. I try to feel peaceful and good during the shoot, and when I leave, I go home, put my Birkin bag inside a plastic bag, and list it for sale online. I put the money in a savings account marked "Bear Hugs Inc."

(It's my daydream. I know what's coming and I'm ready for it. So there).

I shut the notebook and set it on the nightstand. Then I take a long swig of my water and stretch slowly. Still no daylight peeking through the blinds. Not even a hint of blue.

I give in and check my phone. It's 4:02 a.m.

Well, then.

I don't feel sleepy. Not at all. In fact, my brain is churning. I tug my black cotton shorts out from wedgie position and straighten my hot pink sports bra before grabbing my fluffy purple robe from the corner of the headboard. This robe always makes me feel so cozy. It's the little things. That's what I've realized, I think, as I slide down off the bed, aiming my feet at my R2D2 slippers. This house has hardwood, and I'm thrifty, so I keep the heat on 65 at night—meaning it's cold when I get out of bed. Colder if it's 4 a.m. and the sun isn't up.

I walk into my office, which adjoins my bedroom. There I turn on the desk lamp and push the curtains open. I drift into the den, turn on my half-moon lamp—the one that sends small dots of light all over everything, the lamp version of a disco ball—and walk into the kitchen, where I whip up some cranberry oatmeal muffins and make myself some minty green tea.

I spill a long tendril of local honey into my tea and stir, then take a seat at the small, round, wood table I bought at a pawn shop and painted dark powder blue. It's bare except a stack of napkins and a set of squirrel salt and pepper shakers. After the first muffin, I pull my phone out of my pocket and navigate to YouTube, then type Elvie Wesson.

I listen to his latest hit—"Dirt and Girls"—while I polish off another muffin and drain my teacup.

Elvie's voice is everything I remember. Better now, of course, with years more practice, studio polish, and some of the best producers in the country on this last album. I don't hate him anymore, but I'm not happy for him either. Feeling like a knot's been loosened in my chest, I play "24 Frames" by Jason Isbell. Him, I'm happy for.

Robe tied tightly, I make myself another cup of tea and do some dishes. Memories of Elvie and me keep popping up in my brain, so, ironically, I sing. I'm feeling slightly masochistic, so I go with "Hallelujah," the Leonard Cohen song Jeff Buckley covered so famously. It's what I sang for Aaron Tomlin, head of Lighthouse Records, when he saw my stills for *End of Day* and finally listened to the demo my agent had been pushing on him. It's this song, combined with pictures of me in the movie, that got me a record deal.

My post-accident articulation isn't perfect, but in my own house, I don't care. I sing "Hallelujah" with the full force of my pipes, which hasn't diminished much because I still sing almost every day. It's who I am, even if no one wants to pay me for it anymore, or watch my messed up lips move as I do it.

While I sing, I step into the laundry room that adjoins my kitchen to water the gardenias I keep under the fluorescent light there. I've got six plants now, so there's never a time when the laundry room doesn't smell overwhelmingly sweet.

Once upon a time, gardenias were my favorite scent, and then after the accident, I couldn't stand them. And by couldn't stand them, I mean the first time I smelled one, I fainted dead away— and in a downtown Memphis restaurant, no less. My brother Rett loved *that*.

I freaking love gardenias, though, so I powered through. I water them and tend their leaves, and I like feeling busy, so I keep on cleaning. The kitchen is clean enough, so I move into my small living room. I straighten the pillows on my burgundy leather couch, move a pair of boots off my plush, beige rug and over to the shoe rack by the door, and re-fold the turquoise throw blanket over the arm of my khaki and white chevron-patterned armchair.

I grab the dusting brush I keep on the bottom of the wide, horizontal bookshelf that houses my small flatscreen TV and sweep it over the half-dozen frames on the top two shelves, lingering a minute longer than I need to of the image of myself, Rett, and my parents. I'm wearing a graduation robe and cap. My hair is boy-short, and the scar above my left eyebrow is still slightly pink. I'm smiling, happy and relieved. My parents are on either side of me, and Rett is standing by my mom. My eyes rove our four faces, then lock onto Dad's. I feel the stinging heat of tears in my eyes, followed almost instantly by heaviness in my chest: the oddest blend of dread, regret, and want.

I look at Mom. She seems so happy here. So peaceful. With a sigh aimed at my brother's image, I move on to the next framed photo, this one of Jamie and I hugging at Fall Creek Falls. I dust the rest of the shelves, package two stuffed bears in my office, and still feel too wound up for sleep.

I'm a disappointed by the nightmare and my early waking, but I tell myself it's bound to happen sometimes. I did all I could, writing a better scenario in my journal. I've got therapy with Helga this afternoon. I plan to talk about the dream then...and, I realize as I dress in leggings and a light jacket, the guy next door.

I try to analyze my feelings as I step outside and lock the door behind me. I feel annoyed by his presence here. Annoyed and... sad. Living out here in the woods the way I do is isolated. Lonely. I tell myself the benefit is that it's also peaceful. This property is mine. I can be myself and do my own thing. When I'm at home or with the bears, I'm in my comfort zone.

I walk around the corner of the enclosure and veer into the woods. The tall fence rises to my left, climbing up the wooded hill alongside me.

When I'm here, I forget the way I look.

There it is.

As always, I feel superficial. Silly. No one cares how I look. No one but me. And why do I care? The answer whispers to me from the dark hole where I keep it buried.

Because you'll never find someone now that you look like this.

I tell myself that isn't true. I think about what the woman said to me in the meeting Tuesday. I'm still pretty. And I'm smart, and kind, and sometimes funny. I'm fun.

Ooh, fun, my inner bitch mocks.

It's normal that I sometimes have sad days, a kinder me insists.

I sigh loudly enough to drown out all my inner monologue and hike at a punishing pace until I reach the clearing midway up the giant hill. The peak of the foothill is maybe another 300 yards past my workout clearing, but my property doesn't go that far up. Instead it expands southwest for 300 acres, bumping into the Smoky Mountain National Park on the south and west sides, up against my own backyard on the north side, and running about 100 yards from Blue Moon Road on the east side.

Shit. I didn't check the tracking app before I left the house. I look down at my phone, even though I know I don't have service here. Without the cell phone signal booster in my house, I wouldn't have more than a bar there either.

I tell myself the bears will be okay, remind myself I haven't seen anything weird on the cameras since last time, and even then, it could have been a random hunter. Theoretically, at least.

I start stretching in the gauzy gray of early dawn.

I'm midway through my workout, sparring an invisible partner, when I see a dark blot on the web of trees in front of me. Man-sized. Moving. My pulse screeches to a halt, then tumbles into wild staccato. For a sickly long second, my head buzzes and I feel like prey. Then my self-defense training kicks in.

I draw a slow, purposeful breath into my lungs and force my fear-numb limbs to keep on moving through the motions of my workout. My eyes size up the shadow and a bolt of fear shoots through me.

God, he's big. Like Sasquatch big. And shit, still moving toward me. My fear is cold, could freeze me. I refuse to let it. I modify my form, and like a figure skater or a gymnast performing an advanced routine, I work myself into a sparring sequence, each move chosen specifically for its ability to lead into a kick.

I'm whirling so fast I lose track of him for split seconds at a time, but I've always been good at tracking moving targets, so even brief glimpses of him tell me he's still moving my way. Fuck. My body flushes, head to toe.

I'm going to have to nail him and run!

When there are maybe eight feet between us, I pause for half a second, double-checking my left ankle before I jump into a modified roundhouse kick.

He's tall, and I'm not as limber as I once was due to the sur- gerized ankle, but I can still jump pretty high. High enough so my right foot makes a hook over his head, catching him just over his left ear.

It's not until he staggers back, his face twisted, his big hand clawing at the air beside his face, that I notice his hair.

Dark, curly hair; a nice jawline. My heart stutters as I note the dark, thick brows, the luscious lips...

He mutters, "Fuck," and heat pours through me.

My new neighbor.

Holy shit.

chapter six

Gwenna

His fingers sink into his hair, and blood spills down his forehead. His face is screwed into a wince. His eyelids seem to quiver in the bluish light, like someone squinting in the bright sun. As I watch, he pulls them slowly open.

He looks zoned. His hand moves in his hair, and another rivulet spills down his temple, dripping down onto his cheek.

Oh. My. God.

"I am *so* sorry!" My mouth reacts before the rest of me is ready to, so there's this strange half-second where we both seem frozen. I'm too scared to step forward and touch him, and he's not moving my way either.

After just the briefest glance at me, he looks down at his chest, pulls his hand out of his hair, and starts unbuttoning his shirt. A camo shirt. The buttons must be the snap type, because he yanks one side of the shirt, and it gapes open. But it's hung up on...a gun strap?

There's a gun strap slung diagonally across his chest.

He was hunting.

Jesus, Gwen.

I feel slightly nauseated as I watch him lift the strap over his head. Another drop of blood lands on his cheek.

I step forward, arms out, my sweaty, shaking hands turned palms-up. "Can I help?"

His face, still slightly tight, morphs as his lips curve and his stark cheeks round a little. Blue-gray eyes find mine. His smile—or smirk—makes me feel weaker than I do already.

And then he laughs, a low, rough chuckle. "I don't think so, Splinter."

Holy hell, his voice is dark: an earthy rumble I feel like a push to the center of my chest. I inhale to get my balance, but I can't stop the goosebumps on my skin or the pleasant echo I feel low in my belly.

I watch, dumbstruck, as he pulls his right arm from its shirt-sleeve, slings the gun strap over his shoulder, and slips free of the shirt, revealing the vast, tatted expanse of the most chiseled slab of muscle I have ever seen in all my life.

Just the sight of that...*perfection* makes me pulse between my legs. Somewhere, I'm aware that he's balled up his shirt and he is pressing it against his head, but my brain is broken.

My gaze caresses his pecs and shoulders, round and sculpted. Strong. That raised arm is a fucking gun—the bicep is like a rock. A boulder. *Stop it, Gwen.* But I just...can't. My hungry gaze slides down his chest: the curve of heavy pecs, the deep groove at the center of his eight-pack. God, his *hips.* I blink. My eyes jump from his chiseled hips to his happy trail, then back to his hips. They're hewn in marble. Lord. They make that "V"...

I'm lit up like a light bulb when I feel his gaze on my face. *Shit!*

I lift my eyes to his, my cheeks burning with shame, and find a tiny, amused smile. I hold my breath for a half a heartbeat, waiting for the little not-quite-smile to turn into a smirk, but he just stands there, looking like a wounded Mr. Autumn pinup, still impeding my breathing.

"Splinter?" I blink and square my shoulders in hopes of steadying myself.

The corners of his lips twitch. "Yeah."

"The one from *Teenage Mutant Ninja Turtles*."

He nods.

I smile.

Maybe he's not an asshole.

Shut up, Gwen. Who cares?

His hand, holding the wadded shirt, clenches—and I feel ill with embarrassment and guilt.

"Are you okay? I'm so sorry, again." I step a little closer, one hand out, because I want to help but don't know how. "I saw you and I thought...I thought I saw someone on my cameras the other day, so when I saw you I freaked. Is your head okay?"

I have to look up to see his face. He's so tall. I feel small and nervous, like a peasant in the presence of a king. It's a new feeling for me, so foreign that when he speaks again, the feeling plus my throat-throbbing reaction to his rumbly voice make it hard for me to focus.

"I had a scar," he says quietly. "I think it split open."

His face relaxes just a little as he takes a deep breath, but the echo of a wince still clings to his features. I can see the careful, achy squint of his eyes.

"Can I look?"

"It's okay." The words—and all the other ones I've heard from him—have an honest sort of quality, as if he's speaking in a voice that's rough because his throat is tight with big emotion. As if he cares about me in some way, though of course he doesn't.

You're ridiculous.

I swallow hard and stand up straighter. "I am so, so sorry," I say in my best just-a-normal-friendly-and-concerned-neighbor tone.

Then I blink a few times, to dispel the feeling that my eyes are stuck to his like magnets.

"Come to my house," I hear myself tell him. My voice sounds shaky, so I swallow. "Let me look at it. I'll drive you if you need to go somewhere."

I'm pleased; my voice sounds clear and normal. Just an ordinary neighbor. So I'm surprised when his face shutters, his mouth tightens, and he shakes his head: *no*.

"Thanks—but I'll be okay."

His voice sounds rough and tired, and that's the last thought I have before he turns and takes a stride away from me, back toward the Haywood land. *His* land. My eyes, again, get hung up on his body: the broad, strong shoulders and that carved-from-marble back, inked with emblems I can't make out, flexing, tossing shadows as he moves.

Wait!

As if he hears the thought, he turns. "Gwenna?" The word, my name, shoots through me like an arrow.

"Yeah?" I whisper.

His eyes narrow into troubled slits. "Be careful out here."

Unlike his other words, these parting ones seem heated— almost harsh. I don't ponder their meaning until he's disappeared into the trees, and I realize I haven't moved at all.

Shame clots in my chest, thick and aching.

I want more.

I've missed this. God—this feeling.

I should have dragged him with me. I should have followed him to his place. Why'd I let him go?

I'm swamped by hunger—sharp, familiar. Wolf's teeth on my own heart. Want.

I psych myself out, taking breaths so big they start to feel like not enough. I scrub my face with my hands and I look up at the pale blue sky through a web of craggy limbs.

He doesn't need you. You're the problem.
Check on him. You can. You should.

Barrett

I make it almost to the house before the chaos in my head and the echo in my body take me down.

I feel the dirt under my knees. I press the shirt against my head.

"You think you can walk, man?"

Is that Breck? I can't see…

"Bear, get up, we've gotta go!"

The frenzied du-du-du-du-du of small arms fire is everywhere. Low shouting. The pop of metal on metal. I hear something snapping. Something…roaring. Rounds and more rounds. I'm not sure where I am, but it's fucking hot. Not just 'happening' hot. Hot hot, too.

I start to cough. My throat and nostrils sting. Someone is pulling on me. I can't open my eyes. They're clamped shut…with something sticky.

"C'mon, bro—or I'll have to carry your big ass!"

That is Breck. I lift my left arm and try to wipe my eyes but—

"Fuck!" I sag back to the ground, gasping. Something's in my shoulder. My arm… "FUCK!"

I feel his hand rub over my eyes, hear him firing. I can smell smoke… really strong.

"My eyes," I rasp.

"Fuck your giant, heavy ass…" But Breck gets me up. Everything is smeared and there are bright flames. Lots of smoke. Despite its thickness, I feel my head clearing.

I try to reach for my eyes once more, too addled to remember—"Aughh!"

"*Fuck, you've got some shrapnel, man. Don't move your arm! Let's go!*" *I hear gunfire again and feel Breck's arm and realize that I'm walking. He's got me between him and one of the alley's sides, and he's covering for both of us.*

That won't fucking do.

I spit into my right hand, smear it over my eyes, lift my SR25 to my right shoulder, and start firing rightie, since I can't seem to use my left arm. I try to keep up with Breck, who's jogging slow for me. My shoulder hurts like fuck with every step. My head aches, too. I don't know where we are, but that's a problem I don't have time for yet, so I just follow Breck. I've got a fuck ton of ammo on me still, so I spray the fucking alley, aiming upward at the windows.

"*We got a ride?*" *I shout.*

"*Half a block,*" *Breck says.* "*Hey, man…Stop firing for a second. I think that's—No. Okay. Fuck.*" *I hear Breck fire, feel it bump the air against the alley wall beside me. I can't fucking see. My left eye…*

We work onward down the alley. The one I fell into from my spot above Maliha's store—

Don't. *I can't think about that shit. Still, my brain dredges up the image of her crumpled form.*

"*Making it?*" *Breck pants.*

I realize then that I'm groaning. I can't work the SR25 without my left arm helping prop it up. Every movement causes what's in my shoulder to slice deeper.

I can feel my body shaking.

"*Okay—all clear, I think.*" *Breck turns to me, framed by the dark alley.* "*C'mon and run with me. Let's go.*" *Everything's gone blurry but I sort of see him. Maybe not, because I trip then. Breck drags me up. I hear the rat-tat-tat of a semiautomatic, hear Breck curse, then fire. My stomach hurts.* You can't pass out.

I swallow. Move. Don't be a fucking pussy.

"You're gold, man. We're almost there." I hear bullets zing around us. "Fuck!" Breck's body bumping mine; the wall behind me. I can't lift my gun. Fear makes my heart beat so hard.

I hear a groan and then I'm down. The world is tilting. I can't see a fucking thing. Breck grabs my shoulders. I curse as his upper back bumps under my pecs; I feel him lift me up, my torso over his shoulder, my legs dragging behind. Every step he takes is murder on the shoulder and…my head. It's hurt…bad. I feel like I'm going to throw up.

I feel him stop. I hear my teammates' voices. Then I'm being lifted up the ramp, into the Bradley's belly. I feel hands on me. I fall against one of the seats.

Voices…shouting. The Bradley rocks, and for a second, I go deaf. Where is Breck?

Hands are pushing me. My shoulder! I try to sit up but I'm dizzy. And then I hear Breck groaning. Screaming. That sound gets me in the fucking gut. I'm up, turning toward the sound as someone hoists him into the Bradley and he plows into me, clutching at me as he pants and groans. Other groaning, shouting men scramble in behind him. I can only see Breck's face…

The way one eyelid bubbles, sizzling with phosphorus…but he tries to keep his eyes open. The sound of a tooth cracking. Because he's clenched his jaw so hard one of his molars broke. The hard, deep breaths that turn into low moans. He never lets himself break down, even as the chemicals from the Willie Pete round eat through him. My last memory of Breck is his eyes squinted with pain, his round cheeks drawn up, almost like a smile—except it is a grimace. And the sounds. My best friend's awful whimpers, then my name.

"Bear?" I can see his fingers fumble at the wrist of my long-sleeved FORTREX combat shirt.

"Don't…don't dream about me. Okay?"

His brows are knitted low over his eyes.

"Don't be a quitter, motherfucker!"

"Tell...my mom..."

I lean down, fumbling at his shoulders, trying to pick him up. I can see him going and I want to have him up against me so he doesn't feel alone the way I do at night when I'm crying in the snow or watching the Iraqi boy bleed out in the dirt.

Sometime later, tubes...machines. I think my eyes are opening and closing. I'm aware I'm shaking. In the ICU at Landstuhl with my head sliced open and pieced back together.

Breck is gone.

"Don't...don't dream about me. Okay?"

The dirt comes into focus—dark, moist dirt; not desert sand—along with my bent knees. I realize I'm kneeling on the ground—the cold ground—and I look around.

How long was I here?

Something stings, and I remember: my head. Gwenna White. Gwenna kicked me in the head. I didn't block her.

I stand up, cold and shaky, tracking everything a half-second too slow. My body feels stiff and achy as I head toward the basement door, the one punched into the stone foundation, that leads into a wine cellar.

I manage to get it open, even as dark dots swim in my eyes.

"Let me look at it. I'll drive you if you need to go somewhere."

I climb the stairs, telling myself I'm okay. While I'm climbing, I forget to inhale through my mouth. The smell of blood makes my gut clench. Pain moves through me in tight waves.

"Don't...don't dream about me. Okay?"

Fuck, I hate it when I hear things over and over.

I have to climb up the other flight of stairs to my room, where I've got my shit. A first aid kit. I take it to the bathroom and open the box. Maybe I lick my lip. I don't know, but I get blood on my tongue and start to shake again.

I shut my right eye—my only working eye—so I can't see, and bring my mostly numb left hand up to my face. I need to use the Dermabond I have to glue the wound shut.

"Let me look at it. I'll drive you if you need to go somewhere."

This shit with her is fucked up. So fucked up. I put my right hand on the partial wall that separates the toilet from the sinks and shut my eyes.

"My name is John, and I'm from Breckenridge. I heard you're Bear from California. You like vodka? Cause I've got some good shit…"

I wrap my arm around the wall and feel the hard, cool plane of it pressed against my ribs and hip.

I grit my teeth. I'm tired of this shit. Fucking tired.

I take a few slow breaths and lean on the countertop. As I wash my hands, I start reciting the "Pledge of Allegiance." Better than counting, and doesn't make me think of Breck or the team the way "The Lord's Prayer" does.

I find a few small mirrors in a drawer filled with women's makeup and try to get a look at my head. I can't see the wound. It's probably been at least an hour since it happened, and I'm still on my feet, so I figure she didn't give me another epidural hematoma.

I pull out a little stool that slides under the counter. The movement makes my head throb.

"Tell…my mom…"

I can hear Breck's mother sobbing as I try once, twice, three times to get my unsteady fingers to rip open the wrapping on a hospital-grade saline syringe. I start to sweat. My throat feels tight and full.

I have the urge to go to the window and look down at Gwenna's house.

Up close like that…Seeing her…

I rub my forehead.

I'm losing my shit. Going out there like that, near where she was. Then she saw me and I had to go to her. That or leave her thinking someone's watching her.

Someone is watching.

I shoot some saline into the wound and try to keep my breathing steady while I look for a wash cloth to get the blood off my face and neck.

That's when the doorbell rings. And rings. And rings and rings and rings.

I put my head in my hands.

"You can't let her in," I whisper.

Maybe I should stop this watching her. Just wait till the house closes. Then do what I have to do and go.

I can't. Without it…I don't know what.

The doorbell rings some more. My shaking hand manages to get more saline in the wound. I let it sit a second, focus all my senses on the deep, sharp sting.

chapter seven

Gwenna

Oh my God. I killed him. There's no other explanation.

I don't mean to go insane on his poor doorbell, but I realize—belatedly, of course—that I'm punching the damn thing as if every *ding-donnnng* enters me to win the lottery.

"Shit." I take a step back on his porch and inhale slowly. Then I let a long breath out and start ringing again.

I followed him for two reasons: one, to be sure he really is okay, and two, because I want to see him—in a regular setting, now that that first thrall has worn off a little…I want to know how I'll react to him. Because being near him in the woods a little bit ago? It made me feel awkward, and embarrassed, and inadequate, and exposed. But that's so much better than feeling *nothing*.

How long have I been doing this to myself, I wonder frantically. Letting myself get so walled off, I didn't even remember what it's like to feel turned on by a hot guy. I, who spent a year surrounded by the most beautiful of men. When did I forget that feeling: the heart-in-your-throat, fire-in-your-tummy sensation of simple physical desire? Sure, I have a healthy amount of private workouts with my LELO but…I shake my head and punch the bell again. LELO is not a person.

When I hear nothing on the other side of the door, I walk down the porch steps, into the bed of azalea bushes nestled up against the stone base of the house. With a guilty glance left and right, I lift a small, quartz stone and turn it over. Yep—the key's still here. I have my own at home, from when I used to check on this place for the Haywoods, but of course, my key isn't on me.

As I climb back up, I swear the day seems brighter. The birds seem louder, the wind feels cooler. If this is what happens after just being near someone who gets my blood pumping, what would happen if—

I shake my head and slide the key into the lock.

No. Just no. Can't go there.

I've never been able to handle getting my hopes up. I'm so excitable by nature…it's just too much. Which is one of the reasons why what happened after my accident was so difficult to bear.

Hot neighbor guy is probably at the urgent care, I tell myself as I turn the doorknob. I'm such a drama llama. He's not dead.

Nope. Not dead at all.

I step fully inside the house and look around the kitchen and the epically large living room. It looks the same in here as it did last time. High-end rustic. Comfortable and cozy.

Mrs. Haywood died in last fall, on a weekend I was visiting my mom in Memphis. Mr. Haywood didn't want anyone at the house the day or two after—in fact, the door was locked and the lights were off—and after that, he jetted back to New York. I heard he'd put the home for sale a short time later, through the teeny Gatlinburg grapevine. So the last time I was here was over a year ago.

I hold my breath as my eyes scan the open space. Not a single mote of lint seems out of place, making me wonder if he's living here yet.

"Hello?"

I take another small step forward and train my gaze on the left side of the open space, where one set of stairs tilts downward and another flight curves elegantly upward to the third level.

He's probably not here. Guilt churns in me. I should have followed right behind him, rather than pace around the woods for half an hour being nervous and uncertain.

Just when I'm about to turn and go, I hear a creak above me.

Could he upstairs? I can't just go up there…can I? What if he's gone to get patched up and he comes back?

I have a good excuse, I guess.

I walk quietly into the kitchen. It's wrong to snoop in other people's things, but I tell myself this will help me discern whether he's living here. If the refrigerator is empty, there will be no reason to go traipsing around on the third level.

I pull the door open and—Red Bull. Yikes. That's a lot of Red Bull in there. Meaning—he must be living here? Or needs a lot of caffeine while he hunts on his new acreage? I make a face. Red Bull is so gross. The refrigerator also harbors a few apples, some apple jelly, a carton of eggs, and a jug of orange juice.

Okay—so maybe he *is* living here. I'm a super snooper. An interloper. Not just any interloper. One who kicked him in the head and made him bleed. I squeeze my eyes shut. I should go now.

But what if he's upstairs, passed out?

What if?

Didn't that Facebook executive's husband die from falling off a treadmill and hitting his head? I think he did.

I blow my breath out. I'm going to do it. Because I know if I don't, I'll wonder till I drive myself insane. And really, can I embarrass myself any more than I already have by attacking the man in the first place?

I stride into the living area, which smells like leather and firewood.

"Hello?" I call, more loudly than before.

When there's no answer—just a lonely echo—I start up the stairs. My heart begins to pound. Do I remember CPR? Only on bears!

Fuck me.

At the top of the staircase, I hesitate. The stairs lead to the midpoint of a hallway, so I can't see directly down it without taking a few more steps. Which I do, slowly and quietly. From the right side of the hall, I see a crack of light. A crack of light—which means a door is open. Maybe the master bedroom door.

I've come this far. I figure what the hell. If he's up here and not answering my creepy interloper cries, there's probably something wrong. My heart pounds. I hope there's nothing wrong. I walk slowly toward the light, which does indeed turn out to be a door ajar.

I stand just in front of it. "Hello?"

My voice is softer now, because I'm scared of what I'm going to find. I should say something else, but I can barely breathe. I push the door open and—holy master bedroom, Batman! I blink a few times, surprised by the opulence. And the gun. There's a gun on the bed. A really big gun on the—

The hunting rifle. *That's his hunting rifle, Einstein.*

He's been here! Where is he now?

My body goes ice cold, then flaming hot. Fuck me. Fuck fuck fuck me. I walk further inside, so I can check the floor on the opposite side of the bed.

Please let him be okay...

That's when I notice another door. A door through which I can see his gorgeous back and shoulders. I can see he's got his head down on the bathroom counter.

Shit!

I bustle in, and he is up, arms raised, eyes wide, looming over me before I can even blink.

"Whoa…" I wobble back.

"What the fuck?"

I blink a few times, taking in his bloody head and wary eyes. He gives me a long look, then lowers his arms.

"I'm sorry. I thought…" My cheeks sting as I try to remember what exactly I was thinking mere minutes ago. *I wanted you to make me feel the feels.* Not just that, I tell myself defensively. I *did* want to check on him.

"You thought what?" He looks steely. Guarded.

I rub my temple, peeking at him under my curved hand. "I thought maybe you passed out or something." I look down at my feet, then back up—just in time to see him shut his eyes in what looks like exasperation. His jaw tightens. A millisecond later, he opens his eyes. They look blank. Not angry, just…unreadable.

"Where'd you get the key?" His tone and stance are neutral now. As if we're talking about weather.

And still, my stomach flutters with anxiety. "It's the spare one from the flower bed outside."

I watch his face for clues as to how he's feeling, and a drop of blood spills down his brow.

"Oh no! It's still bleeding?" I look him over, wondering if he's grumpy because he's about to keel over. That's when I see the small tube in his hand.

I frown and lean a little closer. "Is that Dermabond?"

"It is."

"You're going to glue it up yourself?"

His hand goes to his forehead, long, strong fingers rubbing at the blood there. "Yes." His eyes burn mine. I get the feeling he's using them to tell me something vitally important, but I can't decipher what.

I say the first thing that pops into my head. "Let me help."

His eyes widen.

"I know, I know. It doesn't seem to make sense, but I have opposing thumbs and I can see it from an angle you can't. And anyway, I did this…so I should fix it."

My throat tightens. My eyes feel hot, and all I can think is someone new moved in, a really pretty guy moved right next door, and what do I do? I go make the worst impression possible!

Holy hell. I cannot *believe* I'm on the verge of crying. *What a lunatic. That's what he thinks, you know that's what he thinks, you're such a freak.* I refrain from blinking, willing the few tears my eyes have brewed to disappear.

His dark brows scrunch, giving him a vaguely eagle-like look. I can see the moment he notices the feelings pooling in my eyes, because his sharp expression gentles.

"What's the matter?"

I cover my face and shake my head. My heart is pounding. *Only you,* I snarl at myself.

I suck a small breath in, rub two fingers over my eyes, and pull my hands down. (Why hide now?) "I'm sorry. This is not my day." I shake my head. "I know it's not yours either. Let me help you fix it. Then I'll go."

He looks mystified. Maybe concerned. I don't know which. He steps closer and I get so hot, I think I might catch fire.

When there's just a foot or two between us, he tilts his head. I force my wet gaze to hold his gorgeous blue-gray one. Which, I can't help noticing, is filled with nothing but what I'm coining *concerned curiosity.*

I have the urge to roll my lips, or cover them with my hand. I'm not sure when I last stood so close to a man who wasn't my brother or Jamie's boyfriend. I sigh. "This whole thing is embarrassing, and unfortunate for you, I realize. I am really sorry. I'm just—I'm your weird new neighbor." I tilt my head back, rolling my eyes at the ceiling. "Heaven help you."

When I dare to look at him again, I find that same kind concern in the press of his lips and the tension at his brow.

"I swear, I'm not always such a nutjob. Sit down—if you want to. I'll do what you tell me to if you're a Dermabond pro." I hold my hand up. "I'm just here to lend a hand."

I wipe my eyes and paste on an apologetic smile.

It occurs to me a half-second too late that I am snarling at him. Perfect. My eyes shut—on their own accord.

I suck a big breath in and hold it in my chest. I'm lonely, I realize. It hits me with gale force as I stand here in my neighbor's bathroom.

I'm so lonely, I could shrivel up and die.

That's when I feel a light touch on my cheek.

chapter eight

Gwenna

I stand painfully still, my eyes shut, my heart throbbing, trying to decide if I'm imagining the touch. Everything but my sore heart is paused mid-furl, awaiting new life. I wait like an idiot—until I hear a little tap a few feet away. I open my eyes and find him seated on the stool.

He's got his right hand around his left one, and he's looking down. The look on his face reminds me of the one I used to see in the mirror at Helga's office in those first months of 2012. When Mom or Dad or Rett would take me and I'd just sit on the couch, occasionally catching a glimpse of myself in the mirror behind her chair.

His jaw is slightly tight. He looks like he's trying to hold onto something: anger, maybe, or sadness.

My own sadness rocks in my chest like an ocean wave, so deep it threatens to choke me.

Of course he didn't touch your cheek. He doesn't even know you.

I really want to turn and run straight home, but that's not what I do. I find my feet stepping over to him, as if we're linked by an invisible cord.

I can't seem to find the nerve to look him in the face—not after how insane I've acted since I got here—so I only guess his eyes are still on his lap. As I stop mere inches from his bare, tattooed back, he reaches into a brown, tin-looking box on the counter and draws out a saline-filled syringe.

For the barest second, our eyes meet in the mirror.

I step over to the sink, where there's a bottle of Dial soap. I wash my hands. My gaze flicks toward him as I rub my soapy hands together. It bumps into his. He's watching me. *Of course he is. You're the only other human in the room, Gwen.*

I dry my hands on a beige towel hanging from a rack that's standing on the counter, oddly comforted by the knowledge that neither of us is going to talk until I take my place behind him again.

When I station myself there, he hands me the syringe. "Have you irrigated a wound before?" His words are low and clipped.

I nod. All signs of tears are gone now. I feel numb inside. I can't find the energy to tell him the wounds I've irrigated were on bears.

With no other words, he shuts his eyes. The stool has no back, so I can see the muscles of his back shift as he relaxes just a little. My gaze catches on his ink, but I don't let myself linger.

I reach for his hair, a nervous fullness in my throat. My body flushes as my fingers sift through his dark curls. All around the wound, his hair is damp, so I can see his scalp with ease. I can see the long scars, making an imperfect pink semi-circle just over his ear.

My stomach twists. "You had a craniotomy?"

His eyes open, and I can feel his back and shoulders stiffen. As if in answer, the wound—along the rightmost side—seeps.

His shrewd blue eyes are blank and maybe hard; I can't tell what he's thinking, so I'm surprised when he says, "Nothing that a little glue can't fix, Miss White."

Despite the sternness of his face, his tone is unmistakably gentle.

I nod. And breathe. Should I tell him that I had one, too? Mine is on the back of my head, safely hidden underneath my hair. I swallow. Then I pull a little on each side of the wound, until it parts and I can gauge the depth.

Seeing that pink skin makes my stomach clench. "Does it hurt?" I whisper.

"No."

I don't believe him, but I rinse the wound with saline, and he doesn't move at all. I'm standing so close to his back that I can feel the heat of him. I'm trying not to look down at his amazing body, so as I let the saline sink in, I let my palm hover over his hair and train my eyes on it.

"I think you can wash your hair, with a washcloth," I say softly, "but not until the Dermabond sets." Of course, he probably knows that. My cheeks warm. I call forth my long-benched acting skills and try to keep my voice casual and steady. "I could maybe wash on the area that's not right by the cut."

We look at each other—me trying to hide the way each sight of his show-stopping face makes my stomach twist; him seeming steady and reserved. Removed.

"Why don't you let me?" I say in my new, faux calm, assertive tone. "I can see the area better than you can. In a minute I can use some gauze to dry around the wound and then I'll glue it and be gone."

He frowns, and I think I see one of his cheeks pull in a little, as if he's biting the inside of it. That draws my attention to his lips. Dear baby Jesus, they look even more plump in the bathroom light. Perfect, succulent, and somehow very masculine, surrounded by that shadow on his chin and cheeks.

His tongue rolls out along the lower lip, and I have to look away. I see a towel on the counter—wet already.

"Is this…" I reach for it, stepping away from him—thank God.

"That one is fine."

I wet it while he sits there, gaze trained on his hands again. I notice blood on his fingers and pass him the towel. "Here—I'll get another one for your hair."

To the right of the long countertop, there's a bank of cabinets. I find a few more towels there and set all but the washcloth on the countertop beside his first aid kit. As I stand back at the sink, waiting for warm water, it strikes me how strange this whole thing is—in addition to awkward, painful, and humiliating.

I don't even know his name. I attacked him. I attacked my brand new neighbor. The neighbor that saved my business by purchasing this place. I kicked him in the head while he was out hunting. Now I've burst into his house and forced my nursing assistance on him. I'm overwhelmed by the company of a male human and worried about ruining my panties because he's so breathtakingly attractive.

I wonder what the hell he thinks of me. *Probably that I'm mentally unstable. Or worse…the pathetic handicapped woman who has nothing else to do but push herself on strangers.*

I can feel his eyes on me as I hold the towel under the warm water, but I don't meet them. I'm far too embarrassed. When my towel is warm and wet, I return to stand beside him. He tilts his head slightly rightward, so I have better access to the gash, and as he does, I notice the thick, pink rope of scar tissue atop his left shoulder blade.

"Mm." I don't mean to make a sound; the murmur escapes me.

His eyes rise to mine in the mirror, his sharp brows notching slightly.

"Sorry." My fingertip hovers over the scar for a moment before I stroke some hair about two inches from his wound, gathering the stiff curls in one hand and using the warm towel to clean them. His head is down again, so I can't see his face.

What is that huge scar from? I break my self-imposed no-looking rule and sneak another peek at it, finding that it actually starts up by his neck and twines over his left shoulder, down his shoulder blade. It's so thick and jagged.

Not your business.

I try to settle my attention on his hair.

"You have really pretty hair," I murmur. I figure the least I can do is be polite and try to put the man at ease. "You know what's funny?" I ask, rubbing the wash cloth over a handful of curls. "I don't think I even know your name."

"Barrett." The word is warm and rumbling. I notice the presence of the "t"s on the end and realize he's not from around here, not from anywhere below the Mason-Dixon Line.

"Anyone ever call you Bear?" I ask him, teasing.

"Yeah."

I release the hair in my left hand and take another section of wet curls, and when it's clear he's not going to expound on his nickname, I say, "I'm sorry I've put you in a position to need Bear rehab. In all my years of doing taekwondo, I've never hurt someone like this. I think—I guess you scared me. Like I said."

He's silent, still, although I feel his shoulders tense. My eyes run down them—I can't seem to help it—and I notice the ink covering most of the right one: a black emblem featuring a sword. It looks military-ish.

Oh Lord. If he got his head injury in the Army, I'm sure all he needs is to have it split open again so he can be reminded of the circumstances.

I blow out the breath I'm holding. *Just get this done and go.* I rake my fingers down his nape. "I think I need to glue the wound now, if you still want me to do it."

His head lifts so our eyes meet in the mirror. His mouth is pressed into a line, and for a long moment, I think he's going to say "no." Instead he says, "I'll hold the right side."

He lifts his right arm and presses on the right side of the wound with his fingertips.

"Hang on," I say softly. "I think I should dab it with some gauze."

He moves his hand out of his hair, handing me a gauze square from the little first aid box. I push his hair out of the way and dab the wound. "Okay."

His fingers come back, pressing the right side of the wound toward the left side: helping hold it closed. My left hand does the same thing, and when the two sides are joined—a jagged, fire-red puzzle piece fitted together—I grab the Dermabond from where I've left it and squeeze the tube to get it going. Then I rub the padded tip from the top of the slash to the bottom. I repeat the process three or four times, then go the other way: from bottom to top. I roll it over the skin a few more times, because I'd rather have too much glue than too little.

"Okay. I think that should be enough." I lift my right hand, still holding the Dermabond. "I can hold the right side if your arm is tired."

He smirks.

I smile. "I was starting to think you might be part statue. Or just hating my guts."

I press my lips together.

Why say that? Do you have to make things awkward?

"The hate would be totally justified," I ramble. Realizing I've almost obligated him to reassure me, I make a frenzied attempt to change the subject: "Hey, are you in the Army or Marines or something?"

This is the new Gwenna: insecure, and trying too hard. *It's no wonder I never spend any time around guys. I'm unfit.*

It takes me a second to notice his eyes on mine in the mirror. They feel warmer this time, just a little.

"Why do you ask?" he says after a beat.

"About the Army? Um, because of your tattoos." The one has a sword in the design, but there are many on his strong, wide back—and even from the brief glance I've gotten, they look like a soldier's ink.

"I am." He blinks. "Was."

His reflection in the mirror looks troubled for a split second before he schools it into its usual blank canvas.

"What branch?" I ask, thinking it's a neutral, polite question.

He looks down at his lap, and then back up at me. "I started in the Army."

I frown. *Started?* I don't get it. "So…what happened after that?"

His fingers let go of his scalp, which seems safely secured now with the Dermabond. He folds his arms over his chest. "I was in the Rangers."

"Oh, wow." I don't know all that much about the Rangers, but since my dad was in the Army, I know the bare essentials. They do special missions, and it's hard to get through the weed-out training. If I remember correctly, only a dozen out of like 200 troops get in every time they open their doors for new members. I trace my fingertip lightly over the tattoo with the sword. "Is this a Ranger symbol?"

"Something like that."

"Is it custom, like, did you design it?"

His brows lift. "Something like that." His lips twitch.

I laugh. "You're evasive. That makes me believe you are—or were—in the special forces."

His eyes burn into mine. His lips linger between smirk and smile. "Is there something that made you apt to disbelieve?"

"Apt to disbelieve?" I laugh. "That's some formal language, soldier. You must have been an officer."

He shakes his head, still smirk-smiling.

I giggle. "Did your face cause a cease-fire?"

His eyebrows scrunch, making him look no less perfect.

"Oh, c'mon." I step out on a limb, grappling for the old Gwen—the one who used to tease guys, second nature. "Don't tell me you've never been teased about your face."

"My face?" He frowns.

"Yes. Your hot face." I laugh and hold my arms out. "I said it. I used to do some modeling with male models and your face? The artists would get them to that point with makeup. Fake lashes and an eyebrow pencil. I would be more likely to believe you did an Army-themed campaign for Armani than you were in the actual Army."

I realize as soon as I finish that what I said was insulting.

"God. I guess that's really rude." I brave a look at him and find his dark head tilted back. A chuckle rises from his throat and he lifts a hand to his head, as if to keep the wound from splitting open. He's grinning ear to ear and holy baby Jesus… "You have dimples." I dip my own head back and slam my hand over my heart. "Slain."

His low, rich laughter is beautiful—and contagious.

"Gwenna…Gwen. Fuck." He lets out another low hoot, then rubs his eyes. "I can't remember the last time I laughed that hard."

His face goes stark so fast I know he must have thought of something painful. He covers it with a radiant, dimpled smile. Pushing my self-consciousness aside, I snarile back.

"Just being honest." I shrug. "I can see some women taking off their burkas for that." I nod at him, an objectifying look that's mean to amuse.

His face goes completely white. He does this weird blink thing—a long blink, like a doll's blink. Like he can clear the windshield of his brain with that blink. I expect him to turn to me and smile or offer some cover for his strange reaction, so when he stares blankly out at nothing, my throat tightens.

"Oh God, wrong thing to say. I'm sorry." I clamp my teeth down on my lip. "Like, really. I'm a moron."

He shakes his head and slowly brings his eyes to me. "No." He sounds a little breathless.

I see his Adam's apple bob along the column of his throat. He tries to smile again, and it's the biggest fail I've ever seen. It has to actually hurt.

His left hand goes up to his temple, and I can see the fingers shaking.

My body flushes with remorse. "I'm so sorry. Really sorry. I should be more careful with my big mouth."

He shuts his eyes again, and I watch his chest rise and fall as he exhales. His gray-blue eyes open.

"I don't get out enough," he starts. His voice is full-on hoarse. He turns to me, his eyes deep wells. "You did...nothing wrong. Don't feel badly."

My throat thickens and my eyes begin to sting. "I'm sorry. I should go now. I don't want to keep on messing things up."

I rush out of the bathroom and hurry through his massive bedroom. As I reach for the doorknob, his hand comes down on my shoulder. The touch is fleeting. As I turn to him, he lets me go.

"Thank you," he says. His face is grave, his body hard and warm beside mine.

I laugh. "The last thing you should do is thank me."

I turn and hurry down his stairs.

When I get home, I find a smudge of blood on my left cheek.

chapter nine

Gwenna

This is stupid. Really stupid. I'm standing on his porch in this long-sleeved Ziggy Stardust t-shirt and a pair of skin-tight jeggings with my favorite casual, retro Jag Timberwolf boots, shivering from cold and nerves and feeling like a moron. It's late, and he's probably asleep.

Either way, I'm hoping this will satisfy Helga, who, yesterday, when I arrived for my weekly appointment, knew something was off with me after maybe thirty seconds. I told her the whole sad and sordid tale of my assault on my new neighbor, followed by my trip to emo land while helping glue his head shut, and she said the first thing I should do is come back over and try to smooth things out.

The first thing *she* did is made me do a mindful breathing exercise. After which we talked about my "evolving self-image," and *then* she said I ought to drop back by here.

Because I'm *sure* he wants to see me.

That's negative self-talk, I tell myself, clutching the Tupperware container to my chest.

I can't help thinking, as I reach my index finger out to ring his doorbell once more, how differently I feel today than two days ago.

Helga says she thinks I'm making progress—whatever that means—and I don't know. Maybe I am. But maybe I'm not. I didn't tell her about the rust-colored spot I found on my cheek. About how I think he *did* touch me after I flashed my freakish-looking snarile. And I'm not telling her that I listened to Radiohead's angsty, angry *OK Computer* album while I made this chocolate-on-chocolate cake: my least favorite kind of cake, as it happens. Because if I'm going to bake an apology cake for him, why should it be *my* favorite kind of cake?

He touched my face. I know he did, because I didn't have blood on my fingers, and when I did, I made sure not to touch my face. He could have HIV for all I know.

But he doesn't.

He can't.

I sigh.

He's nice. I like him. Which is not okay for many reasons. Chief among them: he probably hates me. All I've done is fuck up in his presence, and on top of that, I'm weird looking. A guy who looks like him would never feel attracted to a woman with a smile like mine.

I ring his bell the final time, and the sort of cold that precedes passing out or hyperventilating winds its way through my body.

Why does he affect me this way? Helga theorizes it's because he's the first guy I've had close contact with since the accident. I don't want to think that's it—because that's so pathetic. It's been almost four years, after all. And anyway, I've had close contact with other guys. Say, the check-out guy at my neighborhood grocery store. He's college-aged and cute. Or the priest at my church. I feel at ease around them, don't I?

I let my breath out, long and slow, and try to put a wall between me and my disappointment.

You wanted to see him. You've got a crush.

After I deliver my confectionery apology for being so insensitive the other day, I really need to stay away from him. I should treat this whole thing as a signal to myself that it's time to dip a toe back in the dating waters. Not with Barrett, Gorgeous Army Ranger. But with someone.

Someone old or desperate. Someone I could feel at ease with. Someone around whom, at the very least, I'm not flailing around like Facial Paralysis Muppet.

I prop the Tupperware against a hip and stare at his doorbell.

The last two nights, I dreamed of white, of lying on the ground immobilized. Both times I saw him walking over me: a giant, while I was ant-sized.

I turn away, back toward the steps, rolling my eyes at myself. Self-loathing is a buoyant force inside me, making me feel darkly energetic—like I just might run back through the woods and slam my front door behind myself.

Just about the time I turn around to do that, I hear a whiny creak, and then a soft whoosh.

"Gwenna?"

I turn slowly toward the door to find him standing in it.

His wavy-curly hair is all over the place—as if he's been tugging on it. His shadow is more beard-y, and his chiseled face looks starker underneath this wild crown of dark hair. Where two days ago, his eyes showed just a hint of tiredness, which I thought was pain from taking a kick to the head, now there are obvious circles under his eyes. He blinks, bringing his solemn face to life, but he still looks slightly dazed. Like he just popped a Xanax—or woke up.

"Oh hell, did I wake you up?" I shake my head again as goldfish do synchronized backflips in my stomach. I can feel my cheeks burn as my gaze sweeps over his slouchy jeans and snug-ish white undershirt.

He brings a hand up and pushes at the curls over his left eye. His face is still that quiet neutral.

Silence stretches out between us. I swallow. He blinks, his eyes a little wider.

"No," he says belatedly, as if he's only just now processing. He shakes his head. His lips press together. God, his eyes are serious. Probably because he's wondering what it will take to get rid of me. With one hand on the doorframe, he leans out slightly. "Do you need something?"

"Um, well...I just wanted to swing by and give you—" I hold out the Tupperware box. "Chocolate cake. It's the traditional Southern new neighbor offering. Post-assault, of course."

After a brief hint of confusion in his brows, his mouth lifts slightly on one side. I pass the cake container to him.

He blinks a few times down at it, then looks up at me. His face is serious and stark, as are his words when he says, "Thank you, Gwenna."

I nod. *Now go.* My feet don't move. "How are you doing? I've been thinking of you. In a totally non-stalker way." *Stalker.*

His eyes widen. Is that supposed to be an answer? My hand lifts of its own accord. "Can I see it? Does it look okay?"

He leans his head down. I step closer and push a few curls aside with my unsteady fingers.

"Oh...yeah. It does look like it's healing."

He lifts his head. He smiles, but it looks strained. Or maybe tired. I think of how our last encounter ended and I draw a deep breath of chilly air.

"I wanted to say one thing...about the other day. That is: my dad was in the Army. I have a lot of respect for combat vets. Honestly. I just act like a dolt around you. I was tactless and I'm sorry."

"I don't think I'd say that." He looks down at his left arm, where a watch would be. When he looks back up, his face looks pained. "So your father. Army?"

Awkward. He's trying to make small talk, but he definitely seems uncomfortable now.

I nod. "He was a bomb squad guy." My eyes tear up with zero notice, and I want to give myself a throat-punch.

He nods slowly, as if he's taking that in. "Great guys. He still active duty?"

I swallow, trying desperately to keep my eyes dry. "He passed away last November," I manage with a stiff spine.

I'm puzzled when he turns away from me and takes a step inside. A moment later, he turns back, empty-handed, and then surprises me by stepping out onto the porch.

I eye his plain white undershirt, loose jeans, and bare feet. "Don't come out here. It's cold." I fold my arms over my chest in demonstration.

He smirks. "It's not that cold."

"To me it is." I hug myself.

It's hard not to be aware of how attractive he is when he's standing right in front of me. Attractive, and massive, too. I wonder how long he works out every day.

"You want a jacket?" he asks.

What is this? I swallow. I'm supposed to say, *I need to go now,* but the words get stuck.

I'm looking up at him like a pilgrim at a shrine. I feel him step in closer, then his arm comes heavy around my back.

"Thanks for the cake," he says.

I feel his eyes on me, the hard warmth of his body against mine. I stand there holding my breath, waiting for him to let go of me so my heart can resume beating—but he doesn't. He just stands beside me, his big arm around me, like we've known each other our whole lives and are good friends.

I try and fail to breathe. My stomach sags into my knees.

"You're tall," I manage, awkward as fuck; I dare a glance up at him.

He nods. He lifts his arm off me, but doesn't step away.

I fold my arms around myself and watch his brows scrunch, like I'm a bug and he's a scientist.

"Thanks for the cake," he says again. He puts his hands in his jeans pockets, casual although his eyes on mine feel hot. "I meant to tell you, the kick was good."

I laugh, widening my eyes up at him. "Really?"

I have to struggle not to stare at his muscular arms, showcased by the way he's got his hands in his pockets. We're standing close enough that we could be eighth-graders at a school dance.

He smiles, dimples and all. "You have surprisingly good form, considering your ankle." His smile falters.

I press my lips together. "What about my ankle?"

"You have pins…right?"

I make an "o" of my mouth, *tres dramatique*. "How the hell do you know that?"

He crouches down by my feet and tips his head up, giving me a view of mostly his curls and his eyes. Then he looks down, laying his hand over the outside of my ankle. "Pins and maybe a screw or two on this side?"

"What are you? Some kind of Fucked-Up Ankle Whisperer?"

His hand curls around my leg, making my body burn so hot I worry I may spontaneously combust. Then he stands, shaking his head. "A friend of mine had similar range of motion. Not as good as yours, though. He did one tour after that—after the surgery to put the ankle back together—and that was it. It wouldn't hold. He's an instructor now."

I wonder what that means—what kind of instructor?—but I don't ask. I nod.

"I noticed you as I walked by," he goes on slowly. "I had stopped to watch you, how you moved, and when I saw you saw me, I thought I'd come and introduce myself."

I bring a hand up to my face and nod my head. "That makes sense." My tone sounds sarcastic, even though I'm not. I'm just embarrassed.

He doesn't speak, just looks down at me with one side of his mouth curved in a sympathetic kind of look.

"I'm glad you could appreciate the kick." I step away from him, because my cheeks are burning—*again.*

He shrugs. "I've done some martial arts instructing."

"What? So—wait a second. How'd I get the drop on you?"

He blinks. "I didn't block."

"You what?"

"Your ankle," he says, his dark brows arched. "I didn't know how your landing would be if I threw you backward. You had so much height on the kick…" He lifts his right shoulder.

"You didn't know, so you let me kick you in the head?"

Now he's smirking. But it's not a smirk, is it? He looks maybe embarrassed.

"You've got to be kidding," I say.

"You would have spun back this way." He turns his big body, demonstrating the trajectory. "It would have put a lot of pressure on that plate or whatever scaffolding they put in there."

I smack my forehead, shake my head. "Holy hell. Well, you know how to make a girl feel like an asshole."

"Why are you an asshole? Maybe I'm just nice," he teases.

I look up at him. Hot and nice. Perfect. I nod. "Maybe so." I want to say I think his brains are addled, but I don't know what might set him off, so I keep my mouth shut.

"You should consider supplementing your Taekwondo with some more HTH. Hand-to-hand. To take some pressure off your ankle."

I frown up at him. "Okay." I fold my arms again. "I guess you're going to volunteer to teach me. What kind of martial arts do you know, sensei?"

He shrugs. "A mix."

"Like...?"

"Kali. Krav Maga. Judo, Jiujitsu, Aikido. And Taekwondo. I learned that first, in high school. We focus on a lot of different things for CQC. Close quarters contact. So I know a little of them all."

"Well, shit."

He winks.

"So you're an expert."

He shrugs.

"And you can teach me...what?"

"I can teach you quicker, safer ways to take someone down—yeah. So you don't have to risk your ankle."

"Really? That would be awesome."

He nods, a little on the slow side.

"Well, when can we get started?"

He shrugs. His eyes find the porch floor, then return to mine.

"Now?" I laugh. "Just kidding. What about tomorrow?"

His brows lift. Agreement? I assume so.

"Anytime is probably okay for me, and any day. It doesn't have to be tomorrow. Or ever. You may be busier than I am," I say.

"I doubt that."

"Well tell me when. I'll bake another cake. Then we can trade."

"You don't have to do that."

"Okay, no cake. Would you rather have cinnamon rolls or brownies?"

He looks down at his hands, still in his pockets. He presses his lips together. His eyes return to mine. "What's your favorite?" he asks, looking thoughtful.

"I'm a cupcake person."

"Do that, then."

He steps back toward the door and rakes a hand through his hair.

"Let me give you my phone number," I say. "That way you can text me when you're ready."

"What's your number?"

I rattle it off and wait for him to go inside. Now standing in the doorway, he nods. "Thanks, Gwenna."

"You can remember it?"

Another funny, sideways smile. Or smirk.

"And to think, I had you pegged as just a pretty face." I grin, and hold, despite the way it makes my stomach twist.

He smiles back. "To think."

Inside my chest, something spreads its wings. I start down the steps, still smiling as I call over my shoulder, "Later, sensei."

As I start into the woods between our houses, my heart is pounding in the best possible way.

chapter ten

Barrett

My balls are throbbing so hard I can feel it down the insides of my thighs. My shaft is swollen and hard as a baseball bat, with slick precum oozing out the head, coating my palm, which grips my cock and strokes it up and down.

I lift my hips and drag my loose fist upward from the base, making a ring under the head. My thumb finds the soft notch just underneath the head and strokes there, while my left hand plays support and grips my sac. I close my eyes and roll my balls around until they, too, are taut and aching.

I'm breathing hard. My legs are shaking. I'm leaning back in the armchair—the one by the window. The one where a few hours ago, I dozed off for two hours and woke up screaming so loud I'm surprised Gwenna didn't hear me from next door.

I tighten my fist and stroke faster, up and down my shaft, bouncing when I reach the base, causing my balls to bounce, too. I slide back up and roll my palm over my head and stroke back down, and then back up, until I'm right there on the edge. My head is too sensitive to touch. My cock throbs with my pulse, and my balls have drawn up tight.

I want to come. I need to get off. Jesus Christ, my body needs that hot wash of endorphins or I'll go fucking insane.

I wrap my hand around the base and tug up toward my swollen head. My cock throbs and I try to think of pussy. Wet, pink pussy; plump, slick pussy; fat lips spread, glistening cunt that drips down toward her taint. I imagine tonguing the smooth pearl of Gwenna's clit, the way her cunt tightens and then spasms hard enough to squeeze my shaft. I cup my head. It's warm and smooth and sensitive from being buried deep inside her.

No.

The voice is faint. I can't afford to listen. Not when I'm so close.

Panting now, like a damn dog, I spread my legs and cup my aching balls and grip my shaft, harder than it's ever been, so damn hard it's twitching every time I stroke it.

It's that pussy. Her pussy. I lift my hips as I imagine driving deep inside her, making her bounce atop me…tits swinging. I groan. I can feel cum pulsing in me, filling up my shaft till I'm so full of it, more precum leaks. I spread it all around, tweaking the rim of my head, and feel my balls throb.

"Fuckkk." I spread my legs and press them shut, and spread my legs and jack myself…so hard and fast…I feel it ripple out, sensation building in the core of my cock, radiating outward till my balls clench and my cock jerks and I feel the warmth of cum spill in between my fingers.

Breathing hard, I sag against the chair. Gold stars dance in the blackness behind my eyelids. My head spins—but it feels good. I can breathe now.

That's the last thought I have before I wake up some time later, whimpering and writhing, tugging on my hair so hard there's blood on my fingertips from where I've pulled some of the Dermabond off my busted scar.

My body shakes there on the stretcher as I hear the drill's sharp whine. I can't move my head and neck, my arms and legs. I'm strapped down tightly. I can't seem to summon up the fear I should be feeling. The headache is all-consuming; there's nothing else I can process besides the excruciating pain radiating through my head and face.

I look at the ceiling of the plane. I'm floating there, while lying here. I think I might be dead. Who lies still while someone drills a hole in their skull? Except I feel the scalding bite of the drill bit as it pokes through bone. The airplane's ceiling spins. Bile splashes up over the back of my tongue. Then I feel the headache ease…The pressure in my chest eases. My throbbing eyes go numb…My neck and shoulder—blinding, hot, white pain—are peeled away. My body feels so cold.

"Am I dead?" I slur.

Just kill me. Kill me like I killed her. Kill me like I killed Breck.

I wake up eons later to the sight of my numb lower body, lumpy underneath a blue blanket, framed by thick, beige bed rails. There's a tube or drain in every orifice. My left eye is fucked up. My left hand is fucked up. I can't move or speak. Don't even have the strength to roll over to hide the tears that soon start dripping from my eyes.

I'm aware of nurses easing me over on my side so they can change the dressing on my shoulder. The one that cost me the use of my left hand when Breck needed me. The one that took my gun.

Strange to have them all buzzing around me. Strange, these doctors—caring for the dead…

I shut my eyes and focus on each breath. I'm not dead. I curve my hand over the bleeding, Dermabond-edged wound and lean over so I can prop my arms on the windowsill.

I wrap my arms around my head and draw my legs in close to my chest. My heart is beating fast, but it feels like an echo. Everything, an echo. This place isn't real. I pull my hair again, to feel it sting.

Sometimes…I rub my eyes. My hands tremble. *You can't think about those things.*

I pull my .45 out of its hidden holster and set it on the night-stand. I don't allow myself to look at it before I stand up, turning toward the bathroom. I feel, as I move toward the shower, like there's something I should remember. Something from before I fell asleep. Something I did or thought...

I push the nameless worry away. It could be anything. I chuckle, mirthless, and rub my sore temples. I step into the bath-room and I look into my bloodshot eyes. I rub them. I start the shower, strip out of my sweat-soaked clothes.

As I do, something vibrates. My phone...still in the pocket of my pants. I reach down for it, hold it to my eye, and wait for it to unlock and present the source of the buzzing.

A text—from Dove, of course.

'So? How's it going?'

I wipe the steam off the phone's screen and blink down at the message. Set the phone down on the sink counter.

How's it going? For some reason, the more I think on it, the more I want to laugh. How's it going?

Oh, it's going fucking great.

I think of all the possible replies, and I do laugh.

I'm still laughing as I step under the hot shower, avoiding the stinging spot in my hair, soaping up my body, prodding at sore muscles. As I bathe, my mind wanders: a predictable circuit of pain, weakness, and craving. I tell myself there's nothing wrong with offering to show her some new hand-to-hand.

As if that's all it is.

As if she's just anyone.

As if I'm the guy next door.

Guilt twists in my chest, but I ignore it.

What's the point of guilt on top of guilt? There is no scenario in which I'm what I seem to be. I tell myself it doesn't matter.

So what if I go show her some new moves? It doesn't change a fucking thing.

Gwenna

I get home from speech therapy and the grocery store at 4 p.m., and get a text from Barrett at 4:30.

'*6—your yard?*'

I save his number and reply, unable to keep a silly grin off my face. '*Sounds good.*'

After spooning a dollop of chocolate mousse out of a plastic cup full from the grocery store bakery, I walk into my room and do something ridiculous: I get a long, luxurious shower before donning black leggings, my favorite hot pink sneakers, and a gray long-sleeved shirt. I pull my hair up into a bun so he can't use my long tresses against me. Then I spend a few minutes standing in front of my bathroom mirror.

This is low-key, I tell myself. I lean forward and look into my own brown eyes. Just sparring. No big deal. I try to bunch my lips together, watch the left side of my mouth fail. I put on red lipstick anyway. I put on mascara.

Maybe I have a crush on him. It's not as if it's going to kill me. I can keep my expectations low. Or not.

I blink down at the handwritten notecard taped to the bottom corner of my bathroom mirror. It's a quote attributed to Edgar Allan Poe that reads: "There is no exquisite beauty…without some strangeness in proportions."

Jamie dug the quote up for me on Tumblr, I think, sometime in 2013, right about the time my obsession with "The Raven" flared.

I debate the merits of wearing mascara. If he noticed, he might know I put it on for him. But he probably wouldn't. And if he did? Do I really care? Can I not handle my neighbor knowing I find him attractive? Did I not just call him hot right to his face, playing Old Gwenna for that moment?

I brush on some mascara. Then I sink down onto my fluffy bedroom rug, pull out my fishbowl full of colored marbles, and start stretching.

Don't ask me why, the marbles make this whole thing interesting enough that I can actually do it: stretch. Not just pre-workout, but for fun and relaxation. I read somewhere if you hold something in your left hand—especially if you squeeze—your mind will be less anxious. So when I'm stretching here in my room, I always hold a marble in my fist.

As I stretch, my mind wanders. I can see him standing on his porch in loose jeans and that sexy as fuck undershirt. I can almost feel the firm warmth of his arms. His slightly hair-fuzzed arms. The dimpled smile. The sharp-browed, keen but sleepy eyes.

Classic obsession. I don't even know the guy. *You know he touched your cheek when you were being awkward. Plus, he put his arm around you for no reason.*

I stretch my back and drop my marble back into the bowl. It makes a satisfying *thunk.*

I smooth a palm over the top of my head, tuck the wispy stands of my stray hairs behind my ears. I go to my jewelry box, atop my dresser, and pull out my chunky Michael Kors men's watch, slide it on my arm, and check the time. Hmmm. It's only 5:20. I go into the kitchen and splash some absinthe into my Pontarlier glass. While I'll admit my newfound absinthe obsession is slightly ridiculous, given I don't drink enough to actually get drunk or even buzzed most of the time, and that I drink it neat, without the sugar and water pour, that doesn't stop me from taking the glass to my couch and stretching out with my TV remove in hand.

After a few minutes flipping channels, I call Jamie, who regales me with a tale of one of her chart-topping clients peeing in a bush outside the Grand Ole Opry.

"Do I want to know if he was drunk, or just raised in a barn?"

"He'd been drinking Southern Comfort. From the bottle."

I snort. "Well, that's one way to excuse it."

"Totally." I hear her pop her lips, which probably means she's wearing that overbearing strawberry lip gloss she likes so much. "So is he still coming over?" she asks.

"Yep. At six."

"Are you hyperventilating like the fangirl you are?"

"No." I glower at the phone. Since Jamie's going to be annoying and make fun of me when I'm feeling sensitive and nervous, I decide to go into my office and watch cam footage while we talk. I spend the next ten minutes listening to her talk about Niccolo, and how the movie he's working on is over-budget. When she's finished, she clucks. "I hear your little mouse clicks."

Whoops. "Guilty as charged. No sign of my woodland creeper."

"That's good. I told Nicci you were scared and you wanted his help."

"You did not."

"Yeah. I did. He said he'll get Casper—" Niccolo's creepy older brother, who runs a security company in Denver—"to send you a body guard."

I stand up and stretch. "He better not have." I slip my watch off and leave it on my work desk, go fill a bottle of water, and wander out onto my tiny porch to wait for Barrett. Or Bear.

I interrupt Jamie to ask, "Barrett or Bear? Which one should I call him?"

"What?"

"He told me people sometimes call him Bear."

I can see her perfectly plucked eyebrows raise, in my mind's eye. "Well then, you have to call him Bear. C'mon. That's an easy one."

"I'm not sure if I can without laughing."

"What's wrong with laughing?"

"Oop, I think I hear leaves crunching! Gotta go," I hiss.

"Have fun."

I hang up so quickly, my butterfingers manage to turn on the phone's noise maker. I'm still fumbling to turn that off when his dark, tall form becomes visible through the leafless trees.

As soon as he comes into sight, my stomach lurches roller-coaster hard. I can taste the absinthe in the back of my throat. I swallow reflexively, just to be sure my throat can still manage the maneuver. Because it's knotting up as he moves lithely toward me.

chapter eleven

Gwenna

There's something gloriously sexy about watching a man approach. I have time to admire all my favorite things about him: the curly hair, the striking eyes and luscious lips, the huge shoulders and chest that taper to those sexy hips. His legs are long, I notice, as he steps over brush and a fallen log.

He breaks through the last line of trees before he reaches my small yard—still partitioned into sad sod squares that have never really thrived despite the moisture of the forest.

My eyes roll once more over his gray hoodie, jeans, and nondescript black sneakers. Nike running sneakers, I note, as he saunters up to my porch.

I can't help noticing he looks tired again. Maybe even more tired than last time I saw him. I stand up slowly and smile in welcome, even though I hate to smile. He lifts his eyebrows, looking moody. When he's just a three or four feet away, I step down the porch steps. "Hey, neighbor. Doing okay?"

He nods, folding his arms. "Yeah. Why?" He frowns.

"You look a little tired or something. Sorry. I'm one of those people who says everything I think. It's not one of my selling points. I'll try to keep my commentary to myself. I had a long day, and I'm tired too." I stand up and start stretching my shoulders. He's so inert, with his arms still folded, I'm starting to get nervous.

I'm relieved when he takes my cue and starts stretching his own upper body. "What kind of long day?" he asks. His eyes cling to me for just a moment, then move back to what he's doing with his arm.

"I saw my speech therapist, in downtown Gatlinburg. Her name is Reagan, and she's super hard on me. Which is good," I say, stretching my arms over my head. I feel his eyes on me and lose my train of thought. A quick breath, and I've got it back. "She's the biggest part of why I can speak clearly now, after the accident paralyzed this side of my mouth. I used to go three times a week and—anyway, it's just kind of tiring. I think I still attach stressful feelings to going there, even though she's turned into a friend and I'm almost over all my speech issues now."

I squeeze my eyes shut. God, I'm sure I'm boring him to tears. "Nothing exciting," I summarize. "Just a very tasky day, and now I'm feeling lazy."

"Tasky?" He smirks, and spreads his legs to stretch.

"It should be in Webster's," I say. My cheeks flush at his pose, which is ridiculous, and which I pray to God, Allah, and Moses, that he doesn't notice. "Tell me you've never had a day that's tasky. Boring, lots of mundane stuff to do, and tiring at the end. It's not really tasky," I say, mimicking his stretch, "unless you're totally exhausted at the end and you feel almost no real satisfaction."

He nods.

"So how about your day?"

His pretty eyes lift to meet mine, though his head is still tucked down. He shrugs, bending one knee so he can stretch the muscles on the inside of his thighs.

"Fine," he says simply.

"Oh, c'mon. No exciting tales of blowing bubbles, hunting down organic avocadoes at the grocery store, or flipping through TV channels? Don't tell me my boring, tasky day has got yours beat."

He stands straight up, pulling one leg behind him to stretch his thigh.

"Damn, that's good form," I say, at the same moment he says, "Blowing bubbles?"

"Huh?"

He smiles—a patiently obliging, almost shy-looking smile—and steps over to my porch steps, pulling the toes of his right foot up toward his shin and stretching his calf with the help of my step. "You said you were blowing bubbles?"

"Yeah. At speech." I laugh. Embarrassing.

"What does that help with?"

"Just getting my mouth stronger. Helping my lips re-learn to make an 'o.'" The comment sounds perverted to my sensitive ears. I can feel my cheeks burn. Damn fair skin to hell.

When I brave a look at his face, he's not smirking or cracking jokes. He looks natural and curious.

"Tell me what you mean."

My cheeks sting anew. All this focus on me...I stretch my calves too, my smaller shoe beside his on the stair's edge. "It's just weaker on the left side. I still have a little trouble saying certain words. Anyway, by the time speech therapy is over, I feel like I need a drink or something. Have you ever had absinthe?"

"Once or twice." He nods, and takes a big step from the porch. He moves his big body effortlessly into a flawless side kick. "Mostly French," he says.

I struggle to stay looking natural, versus impressed, which is how I feel after he does a few more flawless-looking kicks.

I do a side-kick of my own, and feel embarrassed. Years ago, my form looked more like his, but—it doesn't matter what he says about my kick—it's nothing anyone would watch admiringly.

"You should come in and have some, sometime. No pressure or anything. I just got a recipe for Death in the Afternoon, which is basically champagne and absinthe, if you didn't know."

Barrett

She sinks into a sparring pose, legs spread wide, knees slightly bent, arms up. I match hers. Her face isn't eager or curious. She could tell I wasn't going to reply. She said what she wanted to say, but she tried to keep me from feeling pressured.

It dawns on me, as I spar with her, focusing on her weak spots and cataloguing responses she could offer with one of the other martial arts, that no one has invited me to do anything in a long time. Not since my team within ACE was stateside and training at Fort Bragg. When was that? Last June?

No one but this girl has sought my presence. Not even Kellan. He's been sick, although he's getting better all the time, so the few times I've seen him and Cleo, it was my idea. I guess that's pretty fucking sad.

I push the thought away and keep on trying Gwenna, testing her to see how much she knows. I'd put her at about a first degree black belt. I still feel impressed with her mobility. Finally, just when my left shoulder has started aching, I stop and show her some new tactics.

I show her a few pressure points I teach sometimes for use in street fights gone wrong: like when you lose a gun, or God forbid, run out of rounds. After I've shown her, I step back and raise my eyebrows. "Try one on me. Your pick."

She presses her lips together, quiet and round-eyed. "I don't want to hurt you."

I arch a brow and give her a smirk.

"Oh—" Her funny smile blooms on her face—"so it's like that, is it?"

Instead of answering, I lunge forward on the balls of my feet and shove her shoulders. She springs toward me, feinting for my neck, but balling up her right fist and striking me in the solar plexus instead. The bundle of nerves, just underneath the sternum, is sensitive as fuck if you hit it right. I know she did because my diaphragm locks up, and I can't get a breath. I clench my jaw to keep from yelling—the natural foil to that maneuver—and I don't step out of her reach until my head is feeling fuzzy. Then I snatch her wrist and twist her elbow so her body follows that motion; she hits the ground with her right side and flops onto her back.

I'm panting over her.

Her eyes are wide. "You're insane!" She laughs, jumps up, and makes a grab for my inner elbow, attempting another new trick. She's a righty, so she goes for my left arm, which doesn't have sensation in that region, so I have to shake her off. She looks pissed. Her eyes cling to my left hand. "How can you keep your balance on that hand? Some of the fingers don't work, right?"

I grin.

"You jerk." She shoves me and I let her, laughing at her energy. She's like one of those little yappy dogs: more show than actual threat, although I'd never tell her that.

"Truce." I swing my hand out, faking a hand-shake, and when she grabs it, I hook a foot around her good ankle so she'll have to use her injured one to fall. I haven't taught her that, and I'm not positive she knows it, so I catch her on her way down, pulling her atop me.

She spins around to face me, her ass rubbing my crotch in such a way that I'm glad when she hops off my lap so she can face me fully. "Holy hell. Are you a gymnast or something?"

I stand, and hold a hand out for her.

"No thanks, mister. I don't think I need your kind of help," she teases. She hops up and brushes her rear end off. I keep my eyes locked on her face. "Barrett, that was seriously impressive. You're acrobatic."

I laugh. I'm breathing a little hard. "Out of practice."

"God, I'm glad." She laughs. "This was awesome! Just enough ass-kicking so it was fun without me feeling totally pathetic."

"Next time I'll show you more target areas around the neck and head."

I swallow. Next time?

Fuck.

She's grinning. She waves me toward her front door. "Come here. Come inside, absinthe or not. I got your cupcakes."

"Serious?"

She beams like Betty fucking Crocker. Little tendrils of auburn hair float around her flushed face as she moves toward her door. "Made them last night—from scratch, by the way." She winks. "Easy peasy."

I decline the absinthe, take another Tupperware box from her, and ask to use her restroom before I go.

That night, when I'm in my chair drinking Red Bull, I navigate to my phone's camera mode. Without opening the lens of the camera in her room, I punch the code for audio and listen to her snore.

chapter twelve

Gwenna

For the next three nights, we meet at 6, at my house. Every
night, I have something for Barrett. Brownies, fudge, colored
rice crispy treats. In exchange for food, he helps me hone my
trachea-crushing skills and learn the groin stomp. Which, mind
you, he doesn't let me practice anywhere near him.

The arrangement is working really well, giving me something
fun to look forward to and something to do when he's not here.
My comfort level around him is evolving, too. After the second
night, I forego my silly pre-workout shower and greet him looking like my regular self.

With some effort, I try to stop overthinking things and focus
more on making him laugh, which I increasingly think he needs.
I'm no expert, but after our second night together, I become
convinced his awkwardness is not so much that, but rather some
kind of fatigue. The more I loosen up around him, the more often
I notice him rubbing his eyes and forehead and pressing on his
temples when he thinks I'm not paying attention.

Always, I want to ask about his service, but I know better. I
gather details like my bears forage for their autumn binge. He's
from the L.A. area. He has a younger brother. He doesn't talk to

his dad much. He was a Ranger for a long time. I learn he's savvy about the caffeine content of chocolate, leading me to wonder if he has sleep issues; he says he doesn't mind food coloring because "there are worse things." Every night, I invite him in for dinner or some wine or absinthe. Every night, he finds a way to politely accept the treats I've made and go straight home.

A comment he made yesterday raised my eyebrows—something about it made it sound like he'd be sitting up all night. So today, after a brief trip into the enclosure, I spend the hours before he's coming over making a chicken pasta casserole, which I leave in the oven, covered with foil.

The second I see him coming through the woods, worry knots my stomach and I know my Pushy Gwenna Dinner Plan is needed. I watch him move through the trees and my pulse actually pounds between my ears. He's wearing dark jeans that I've never seen before and a navy and denim-blue, ringer-style shirt with the same black Nikes that he always wears to spar.

I can tell something is off just by the way he moves. This guy has better balance than anyone I've met—and that includes my childhood Taekwondo instructor, a fourth-degree black belt—but I actually see him reach out and put his hand against a tree trunk one time as he moves—more staggers—through the trees. His hair is sticking up off his forehead on one side, as if he fell asleep face-first on a desk or something. As he pushes limbs out of his way and comes into my yard, he gives me what I think is meant to be a smile, but it's nothing more than a slight twitch of his mouth. His eyelids sag, although as he gets closer to me, I can see him try to pull them open. Dark circles wreath his eyes.

I just want to hug him as I stand up from my porch perch and his long legs close the distance between us. I decide to test my theory. When he gets close enough for me to reach, my hand darts out and toward his cheek. His big hand catches mine before my fingers touch his scruff. His eyes pop open wide as his fingers tighten around mine.

"Gwenna, Gwenna…" He gives me a smile and a slow shake of his head, which morphs into an eyebrows-raised, lips-pursed look of challenge. "You must want the nightly snack to be your sweet ass on a plate."

I can't help giggling like a high-schooler.

"You look tired." I take a swipe at his abs. His hand catches my wrist, squeezing slightly.

"You want to keep that up?" He arches his dark brows again.

I grin, and try to thump his ear. I expect reciprocal behavior, so when he knocks my feet out from under me, sending me flying back, then pulls me by the hand—which, apparently, he grabbed at some point—so when we land, I'm face-down over his lap, I turn my head to look up at him, feeling dazed and stunned.

"You think this is my first time fighting tired?" The look on his face is knowing—and, I think, a little jaded.

I sit up, and put my hands on his thick shoulders. Then I give into a rare pre-accident-Gwenna urge and snuggle up against him. "I think this is your first time coming in for dinner," I say with my cheek against his chest.

I slide one hand down from his neck, over the hard swell of his outer arm, and down to his ribcage. Despite the lack of air in my lungs, I manage to lean back and give him my most charming snarile.

In the moment, I'm counting on my physicality to keep him from seeing this as flirting. The truth is, I really care about his wellbeing. After just a few days of his little smiles and deep chuckles, his smartass comments and his thinly veiled conscientiousness, I feel a surprising depth of affection for my sparring partner.

Which is why I push myself to let my guard down as I lean away from him and smack my hand against his shadowed cheek. "A-hah." I arch my brows. "Gotcha."

He leans back on his arms, looking slightly wide-eyed. I climb off his lap and crouch in front of him.

"You know you're off your game, sensei." I wrap my hand around his forearm. "Come inside with me and have some food. Maybe that will wake you up."

His eyes narrow on me like he's trying to figure out who body-snatched the woman he met last week and replaced her with this assertive lunatic. I snarile—and realize this feels good. I feel so natural tugging on his arm, tipping my head at my porch. "C'mon. Don't pretend you have a better dinner plan or better company."

I smirk. He laughs. He looks a little more awake.

I can see him school his features into a more serious expression as he stands up. "You think you set our agenda?"

"Yes." I put a hand on my hip. "She who wields the spatula has the power."

He grins, dark and Cheshire. His arm darts out so quick, I don't even think of blocking it before his hand is gliding through my hair. He wraps a wavy lock around his hand and tugs lightly.

He smirks. His brows arch over his expressive eyes. "That right?"

I wrap my hand around the arm that's got me by the hair. "Touché." I want to keep the ruse going, but I can't stop myself from laughing.

He smiles back at me, and I feel like I've won the lottery.

He lets me go. I fold my arms. "You gonna shun my company? Am I good enough to fight but not dinner material?" I quirk one brow up in mock challenge. I'm not even really sure what I'm saying. I just plan to tease until he comes inside with me, so I can try to figure out what's up with him.

I feel the strangest blend of pure, 100-proof affection mixed with cheek-staining attraction and a dash of friendly fondness. So I'm not shocked that my heart pounds as I wait for his reply.

His mouth opens slightly. His full lips press together for a moment—in which I wink. "I didn't think so."

I hold out my hand. I'm not sure what I expect of his response. Maybe for him to step inside my outstretched arm and come inside with me, like an animal I'm herding. Instead, he takes my hand and laces his long fingers through mine. His fingers squeeze mine slightly and his hand draws mine a fraction closer to his chest.

I watch his eyebrows notch as he tilts his head, his lips curving just slightly. "You're in a mood today." The words are quiet. His eyes are, as ever, intense, and underscored by his peculiar brand of kind curiosity. Not curiosity about a certain thing but just…interest in me. At least, that's how it feels.

Every time I see him, I feel more and more addicted to it.

Since he's laced our fingers together, I tug him lightly toward my door. "I'm in a giving mood. You look like the zombie version of yourself and I would hate to kick my sensei's ass."

His lips twitch, and I'm pleased to see he can't keep his mouth from blooming into a teasing smile. "You really want to go there?"

"You want to tell me you're all good so your new friend doesn't worry about you?"

As soon as the words fly out, accompanied by what I'm pretty sure is my concerned look, I want to disappear into a sinkhole. *Way to go, Einstein. Start off dinner with a nagging, mother-hen comment.*

My hand tenses in his, but Barrett doesn't let mine go as I push my front door open, looking over my shoulder at him. His mouth is pressed into a line, but the corners twitch a little. "Worried about me?" The words sound light but his eyes are unhappy. Probably embarrassed, since I came on so strong. ARGH.

My hand is sweating, so I let his go and push the door open, waving him in. "Guests first. And no, I'm not really worried," I lie. "I'm that friend who sends presents when it's not a holiday and

ELLA JAMES

gives excessive hugs. Former actress, you know? You seem tired and I skipped dinner, so I thought..." I shrug.

He doesn't answer. His eyes move around my living room, then shift to my own.

"It smells good," he says simply.

I smile. "Thanks."

We walk into the kitchen and I think he seems distracted as he looks around. "Sit down if you want." I pull out a chair. "I'll get our plates. I've got chicken tetrazzini casserole and some seasoned green beans, plus rolls." I keep my gaze away from him as he sits at the table. "What kind of drink do you want? Dr. Pepper? Water? Tea?"

"Water is fine."

I pour him some water, me some sweet tea, and focus on making our plates. "Green beans?" I ask, glancing at him.

"Sure."

Damn, his shoulders look wide in my little chair. His wavy hair, the way it curls around his nape...

I swallow. Have I always been this reactive, or is it because I've subjected myself to such a long dry spell? I press my thighs together. "So what have you been doing over in that lair of yours?" My voice sounds unsteady and husky. Damn. I swallow as he looks over his shoulder. I can see a smile flirt with the corner of his mouth.

"Lair?" he asks as I heat up his plate in the microwave.

"Lair: a secret or private place in which a person seeks seclusion." I infuse my voice with confidence so he won't know my heart is pounding 90 percent of the time that I'm around him.

I bring his plate and glass to the table, sweating slightly, even though it's not hot in here.

"Oopsie, silverware." I take some pieces from the drawer and set them in the correct places on the table. "Sorry I don't have a placemat or anything. I'm pretty low-key these days."

"I am too."

My footsteps on the floor are the only sound as I get my own plate and glass and cutlery together and sit down across from him.

I pluck a napkin from the holder at the middle of the table. I feel painfully shy as I look over at him.

He laughs.

"What?"

He flashes me a dimpled smile. "Your face."

"My *face*?" My tone and countenance are light and teasing, but my body has gone cold.

He nods, forking some pasta. "So expressive." He brings the bite to his mouth and chews, and as he does, his own brows arch up toward his hairline. I laugh at him.

"Speaking of expressive…"

He swallows. His eyes widen. I watch him lick his lips, pretending that it doesn't make me hot. "Shit, this stuff is good."

"You doubted me?"

"Guess not," he murmurs. He swallows some water.

"Thanks for joining me. It's nice to hang out when we're not trying to bash each other's brains in."

He gives me a wondering look.

"Too violent?"

He smirks. "No. You're just…"

I flush.

He looks down at his plate, then up. I see his shoulders sink on an exhale. "You're very welcoming," he says finally. He looks slightly puzzled.

"It's a compulsion. Like early Christmasing. Which by the way is not as bad as people make it seem. It's all about fun, and what's so wrong with fun?"

I watch him biting back a laugh. And then he fails and grins.

"So anyway. My family doesn't live here and neither does my BFF. Mom lives in Memphis, and my older brother Rett is a teacher in Jonesboro, which is South of Nashville. My bestie Jamie lives in Nashville, too. If you're not careful," I warn, getting up to get some wine, "I'll end up adopting you just like any other bear, and you'll get hooked on my cooking."

I grab some white I chilled the other day, plus two glasses, using the bustling to hide my aching awareness that he hasn't answered. I'm coming on too strong. I used to never get a vibe like that from guys, but I guess my looks excused me then.

I sink back into my chair. I sit up straight and cross my ankles underneath the table, determined not to let this dinner devolve into something awkward.

"Where does your family live now?" I ask, pouring some wine. "I don't think you said...Your dad and brother?"

He pauses with his fork almost to his mouth. "They're all in California right now."

I want to ask about his mom. Are his parents married? Is it just the one brother? But I don't want to sound like an interrogator. I wrack my brain for questions that don't seem so pushy.

"So how'd you end up in the Army, if you don't mind my asking?"

He licks his lips and lifts his eyes to mine.

"Here—have some." I push a glass his way. His hand closes around the stem.

"My Dad was in the Navy," he says. He takes a swallow and again, his eyebrows lift. He nods, as if to say *good stuff.* "So Dad joined the Navy to pay for med school," he continues. "I wanted to join the SEALS, but they said I was part colorblind or some shit. Couldn't see all the shades of green and red they wanted. Ended up in the Rangers, and on up, instead."

"On up?"

He looks down at his plate, then back up at me. "I retired from ACE."

"What's ACE?"

"Used to be called Delta Force."

My eyes pop out of my head. "What?"

He nods, forking another bite of pasta. "Yeah, like that show on TV called The Unit."

"So you were in it for a long time? I don't know your age."

"Yeah." He brings his napkin to his mouth.

"Not going to tell me your age?"

"I've almost forgotten," he says with a grin.

"You must have done some secret stuff. A lot of secret stuff?" I laugh at myself. "God. I get excited. Sorry."

His face goes a little pale. Or did it? Did it? Damn. "Feel free to tell me to STFU. I've always been a freak about secrets. I just want to know all the things."

Okay—his face *is* pale. I drop my head into my hands, then lift it, smiling sadly. "I need to be like journalists over in China and North Korea. Just have a censor right beside me, smacking me when I say the wrong things."

He smiles and shakes his head. "You're fine."

We eat in silence for a long moment.

"I suppose now is not the time to ask why you had a craniotomy." I roll my eyes at myself.

He shakes his head, chewing some green beans. Swallows. "Up to you. Ask anything you want."

"I'm asking then. Because I'm curious. If you don't want to talk about it, tell me your favorite singer and I'll take the conversation that way." I wink exaggeratedly, making fun of myself.

He laughs. "Gwenna." It's so nice to see his smile. He rubs his eyes as it fades, then looks right at me. "It was an IED. A bomb." His face washes out a little, and I feel like shit for asking.

"I'm sorry. I probably shouldn't have asked. I don't like to be asked all the time myself—about what happened to me. I thought it might be something like that." I swallow hard. Heat rises in my cheeks. "I have a brain injury myself."

chapter thirteen

Barrett

"I don't want to ask a lot of nosy questions, but I felt a little weird not telling you. So if you ever want to talk or anything…" She leans her head down and I watch her pull her wavy hair into a rubber band that was around her wrist. Then she turns her head to one side, pressing a hand against the back of her head. "Mine is right there. I have a plate there. I had a bad car accident. Hit and cracked that part of my skull."

My mouth goes dry. She sounds so damn matter-of-fact. I swallow as resistance to the idea rises in me. "Do you…still struggle with it?" I ask carefully. "With the brain injury?"

She shrugs and turns to face me fully once more. "Sometimes. If I'm stressed out, I forget dumb things like where the bread is at the grocery store. I think I stay more tired than other people. I need to exercise consistently if I don't want to feel depressed or anxious. But I usually stay on top of it." She lifts a shoulder, like she's mulling my question over. "I had to take anti-seizure meds for a while right after it happened. I hated those. I had to do a lot of physical therapy, but that was more from other injuries than from the traumatic brain injury. Now my only lasting issue is that white looks like pink."

I frown.

"I know. It's weird." She gives a soft laugh. "The color white—it either looks like blue or pink. Usually pink."

I consciously suppress my face's urge to twist in surprise. "My skin?" I ask.

"Well, that's not white." She laughs again, a small, dry sound. "You don't look like some pink alien or anything, if that's what you're worried about. Even eyes are white where they look white. Clouds are blue-gray. But that works for me. Red is red, blue is blue, and sometimes white is white. But like the petals of a gardenia? Snowfall? That stuff is a little pink. I actually like it. Pink happens to be my favorite color."

She grins, and I can't help but chuckle. "You're quite the optimist."

"Actually—" she folds her napkin in half before she looks back up at me—"I'm a pessimistic realist with a calculated good attitude."

I give a little hoot: a sound I've never really made much until I started hanging out with her. My gaze holds her brown one. "That's amazing. Is the accident what happened to your ankle?"

She nods. "Can I ask *you* a question? I don't want to—"

"Ruffle my feathers?"

She smiles, or maybe it's a smirk—though I doubt it. "I'm pretty stalwart."

"What's your rank?"

"I'm a Master Sergeant."

"Nice. So was your head why you left?"

I swallow, deciding what to tell her. It doesn't matter. Nothing I say does. Very soon—probably early next week—I'll put an end to all of this. I nod. "I was in the special forces, like I told you.

The type of anti-terrorism recon...the tasks I did." I shake my head, because no fucking way am I going into detail there. I leave it at, "I'm left-handed," and hope she doesn't have too vivid an imagination.

"Shit. I'm sorry. That must be hard."

I look into her eyes, and all of a sudden, mine sort of sting. I blink. "It's fine."

She tilts her head, and I swear, her eyes are like an X-ray machine. "I can see you're still a badass. But c'mon...I know how it is. It's not a cakewalk, losing everything you know and like about your life."

I blink down at the table.

Suddenly I hate myself for telling her this shit. Because somewhere in the back of my mind—I knew she would do this. I knew she would care. I'm such a sick fuck.

"Has it caused you a lot of trouble? Is that too personal? You seem to be doing so well. But...your scar is pink. When mine was that fresh, I was still using a wheelchair part of the day because I was so tired and weak. I was on all kinds of anxiety meds and sleeping meds and seizure meds. I was a hot mess. You're teaching me fight moves." She arches her brows and leaves them that way, daring me to tell her everything is good with me.

"Sleep," I manage, after pushing past the image of this girl in pain.

"You have trouble sleeping?" The concern in her eyes is almost too damn much. I want to turn away. Somehow I force myself to hold her gaze. I even manage to nod.

"That doesn't shock me completely." She stretches a hand out on the table and starts picking at her purple nail polish before she glances back up. "My dad—you know—he used to have night-mares about the Gulf War. After what happened to me, he helped me find a good therapist for my PTSD. Now I'm—well, not perfect or anything, but it's interfering with my life a lot less." She smiles, looking embarrassed. "You're so quiet all the time. It makes me want to talk!"

I want to tell her I wasn't always like this.

"Oh, hell. Do you need a hand with that?"

She sighs and cradles the bowl against her chest. "I should be able to hold a fishbowl. Even though I am drunk." She rolls her eyes, then blinks a few times, like a bird who just flew into a window.

It's a struggle not to smile at her, she's so fucking cute. "Where are you headed?"

She nods to the corner of the room—to where my crowd is.

"Over there with John and Nic?" I ask her.

Her brown eyes widen. "How'd you know?"

Because there's no other woman in this bar that's a perfect fucking 10. She must be the one Bluebell told me about. I just wink, and leave it at, "They're good guys."

"I'm too drunk to tell." I frown as her eyes fill with—Are those tears? I look her over, wondering if I should pry. Probably not. If she gives me any encouragement, I'm likely to take it and run. And tonight is not the night I need to fuck some sweet, teary-eyed girl. Especially one who knows Breck's people.

I stroke her arm and nod. "Trust me."

I see a drop of water on a strand of hair just over her forehead. Before I think to stop myself, I press my fingertip to it.

"Snowflake," I murmur. Her eyes blink up at mine, so wide and trusting. "What's your name, snowflake?"

"Gwenna."

"Anyway." She brings her hands together in front of her, in a prayer type pose. "Let me close by saying it amazes me—how badass and strong you are. And I'm really happy you're still here, to kick my ass. It's a crappy first year. Are you a year from when it happened yet?" She rests her cheek in her palm, her elbow propped up on the table. "Are you doing better or worse than you expected?"

"I don't know." I have to stifle a laugh at all her frenzied questions. And at the same time, I feel kind of warm and have to swallow.

She lifts a brow. "So…worse."

This girl.

I can't help laughing.

"I'm blunt," she says, "I know. I got more blunt after my wreck. Just less tolerance for bullshit I guess."

"Well, bullshit sucks." I feel a stab of guilt. I push it down.

"Did your brain injury impact your hand?"

I hold it out. "No. I hurt my neck too. The scar you saw? Shrapnel that severed some nerves."

She leans forward in her seat, reaching across the table. I hold my hand out, feeling a weird dip in my belly. I flex my thumb and index finger, showing her they work, although she probably already knows from sparring with me.

"You can't feel anything?" she asks tapping my pinkie.

"Just pressure."

"Yeah…" A thoughtful frown twists her lips. "My face is like that too."

I want to touch it. To look into her eyes and…

I blow my breath out.

Gwenna sinks back into her chair, across the table.

"I'm sorry about your job. Reminds me of my stuff. What I knew how to do wasn't an option anymore. It was really hard. What were you doing before you bought the house? How long had you been stateside?"

I drum my fingers on the table, thinking back. "I was over there in Germany, in the U.S. military hospital, from…mmm, August

2014 to November. Came back over here, was in Virginia from December to February of this year, doing rehab. From then…"

I shrug. I can't tell her the truth. Flailing. Getting unaddicted to Ambien and having nonstop nightmares. Visiting Breck's family. Camping up there near his house for three months in a cabin with no amenities and nothing but the empty sky to keep me company. "Regrouping, I guess. I've got some family…"

I'm veering into bullshit territory, so I'm grateful when she nods enthusiastically. "So, seeing them and stuff? That's good."

Gwenna

His blue eyes rest on my face with preternatural interest, a serene sort of focus that makes me feel like the only person in the world. He's got a fork in his fingers, his right hand hovering near the side of his plate. The denim blue cotton of his shirt stretches across his shoulders, the color of it making his eyes look deep oceans. His dark curls hang over his forehead, messy and delicious. His face is pale. His face is beautiful. His lips and nose and eyes and cheeks and jaw…the features feel familiar. Every time I look at him, I get this weird sensation that I know him, combined with the thrilling shock of coming face-to-face with a breathtaking stranger.

Oh. My. God.

This is *so* not good.

I flex my toes inside my sneakers, trying to keep my cool and not betray my…intense—sort-of obsession with him. We are neighbors. Nothing more. For a thousand reasons, most of them my stupid mouth and lousy self-esteem, but also because I'm pretty sure he's not looking for more.

Any butterflies I might or might not be having—any blushing or heart palpitations or giddiness or desire to take him to my room and jump his bones—all those things are obviously related to me being long overdue for male company.

And that makes sense, I tell myself. I picture Helga telling me it all makes sense. How anyone's feelings about themselves would change if they went through what I did. How by now, anyone would be lonely.

"You should put yourself back out there, though. One toe at a time."

I push her voice away and realize Barrett is staring at me. I blink and drum my fingers on the table. "Zone-out moment! Sorry. I swear I have adult ADD. Among other things." I mime a knock on the side of my head. "So what were we saying? Did I already ask you if I should call you Bear or Barrett?"

He smiles, one side of his mouth first, then spreading to a full-on, lovely, gentle smile.

"Squirrel," he says. "You remind me of a girl I knew in high school we called Squirrel. She was always bouncing around, losing her focus. It was funny." He smiles once more, then brings a hand up to his hair, touching his forehead lightly with the fingers of his right hand as his face takes on a slightly more serious expression. "Yeah." He nods, blinking at his plate. "I got called Bear." He looks at me. I look at him. That's not the question I asked.

He sits back, away from the table, staring at its edge. "Not anymore."

His dark brows draw together, and I wait for his gaze to come to mine. And wait. My throat feels heavy as I read the pain on his face.

"Ohh. So no one calls you that because you're not active duty anymore." I can understand that feeling just a little. Losing your identity overnight. It's hard. It's sad. When he looks up at me, with his lips pressed together and that veil of sadness over his features, my chest aches.

"Were you with them for a long time? The people in your unit...or team or whatever? Or hey," I slap the table lightly, "you know, maybe it's time to get some ice cream and watch *Finding Nemo*."

"*Finding Nemo?*" He does this funny little thing where his face frowns, but his mouth smiles.

I lift my brows. "Could be a really nice distraction."

I'm rewarded for my bumbling awkwardness by the first real laugh I've seen from him tonight.

He grins, shaking his head. "You're funny."

"I try."

I have the urge to tell him more of my story, just to take away some of the isolation I'm sure he must feel. But it only takes me half a second to realize my story is about a wreck that happened on a trip with a friend. His probably involves dead friends, extreme scenarios beyond the imagination of a civilian like me.

"Anyway." I take a deep breath. Let it out. "You should keep in mind that you can use me for advice or referrals and stuff. For PTSD stuff. If you even need it. And you can talk to me, if you ever want some Squirrel help." I give him what I hope and pray is a kind, low-key type smile. "When I say that, I mean it, too. When my thing happened, my people didn't really get it. I was too overwhelmed to explain it to them. I got really depressed and things were bad for a while. You might have more friends. Other vets and all that. But you know, if you need another one."

I salute him, then double over and hold my head, laughing like the lunatic I am. I peek up at him. "Is that offensive? Army equivalent of the Atlanta Braves tomahawk chop? Tell me no. Please."

I look up and find him looking down at me with a surprised look that softens as my heart pounds. "Gwenna." He blinks at me. My stomach flips because he's so serious. I start to sweat because I'm worried I hurt or offended him or made him mad.

Instead, he asks softly, "Are you really this way with everyone?"

I lean away from him, snariling apologetically. "I told you! Yes: insane."

"No."

"Crazy?"

"Kind." The word is low and so soft, for a moment I wonder if I imagined it.

My cheeks go hot. I go to roll my eyes but end up leaning my head back, looking up at the ceiling and giving an awkward little laugh. "I try to be." I wink. "Just so you know, BTW, you've won me over as a friend. I don't feel nervous when I smile around you."

"That's good. You have a lovely smile."

I swallow. "Thank you."

He stares at me for a long moment, so long my heart pounds. Finally, he nods and says, "You're welcome."

I choose that moment to take our dishes to the sink. As I tidy up the kitchen and he tries to help, we touch on the subject of my dad, and how he died of a heart defect no one even knew he had.

Barrett listens, drinking up my words, or seeming to. His eyes never leave my face, not even when we walk into the den. As I curl up with the remotes on one side of the couch, he's leaning into the corner of the other side.

I turn one of the iron lamps on—a sun-shaped one with little holes all in it, creating dozens of tiny dots of light. "Does this bother you?"

His eyelids look a little heavy, but he gives a small smile. "Not at all."

I reach into the basket beside my end of the couch and grab two blankets, a big, fuzzy bear blanket for me and a bigger brown fleece for him.

"You're going to like this movie. I swear. Everyone does."

I'm right—for a little while. He watches *Nemo* with apparent interest. Then, around eight thirty, his eyelids start to sag. I start to shake his shoulder but remember what he said. About his trouble sleeping. I remember how I used to hate to sleep alone. Here at my house, maybe he would sleep more soundly.

Maybe I just want to look at him.

chapter fourteen

Gwenna

I take care of real bears, but I sell plush ones. Right after the sanctuary opened, I used some money from my own savings to buy the two bear suits for visits to St. Jude Children's Hospital. The first time I went—with my brother Rett—I thought about how nice it would be to hand out teddy bears to the kids there. So I reached out to a few toy companies. On sanctuary letterhead, of course.

I asked to buy some bears at half-off, just for distribution at St. Jude. They offered them to me at two-thirds off the regular price, and after a year of seeing happy sick kid pictures, they started donating for free.

When I asked for the half-off price and proposed selling them for twice that on the sanctuary's web site, they again offered them at a two-thirds discount. Which is how it came to be that the large closet in my office and the top two shelves of my bedroom closet are filled with small, stuffed black bears.

I spend fifteen minutes packaging some orders, stepping into the doorway between office and den a few times to watch human Bear. I feel slightly strange about myself for not waking him, for watching quietly as he sags into the corner of my couch, his long legs covered with the blanket, his bearded jaw tipped up as the back of his head rests between the couch's back and arm.

I tell myself I'll wake him up at 10:00 p.m. if he doesn't wake up first. To my kind-of surprise, he doesn't. I package more bears and check some emails in my office, peeking in on him a few times here and there.

Around 10:10, I remember I washed a load of laundry earlier today and never turned it over.

I walk softly from my office toward the laundry room, stopping by the couch to stand there like a creeper. Now he's got an arm around himself. His shoulders seem pulled a little more inward; he's slouched deeper into the corner of the couch. He's so big: long legs stretching across the couch, so his feet reach the couch's other arm. I can't lie to myself: I like him here. It feels deeply right to have a man in my house, covered in one of my blankets, dozing by the TV. It reminds me of my parents. Of my dad.

I watch the gentle thrum of his pulse in his throat for a moment before I make myself go to the laundry room. I happily—albeit a little nuttily—leave the fluorescent light on almost all the time for my pink gardenias, and feed them special fertilizer that I order from Australia. When the laundry room warms with the heat of the dryer, hot, gardenia-scented air spills into the cooler kitchen, so the fragrance wafts into the rest of the house. The moisture from repeated loads of laundry makes the plants happy.

It's weird, I realize, but so am I. At 26, I finally don't care.

I flip the load of laundry over, open the door into the kitchen, and get a thrill when I realize Barrett's still asleep. *If I didn't wake him, would he sleep all night?*

The way my heart pounds makes me feel pathetic.

I hover in the space afforded by the partial wall between kitchen and den. Then I step back into the kitchen and get a chocolate granola bar from the pantry. One of the things I can do for myself, for my battle-scarred body, is treat it well, so I try to eat healthy minus any baking I do.

I mill around the kitchen telling myself that I should wake him up. Instead I decide to unload the dishwasher. I don't think the clinking of plates would twist his dreams in the direction of wartime. Not unless I really bang around—and I'm not going to. Maybe he'd prefer to wake up naturally to me shaking his shoulder.

Yeahhhh. Keep telling yourself that, honey.

I think about that way he looks at me. The quiet, soulful way. I like him. Lots. More than is logical, I would imagine…not that I'm too much in touch with logic.

Why do I like him? I wonder as I peer into the den. His looks—sure. But I never felt this way toward any of the guy models I knew. It's not just his looks. It's his…everything. I like him unconditionally. Which reminds me of a quote by C.S. Lewis: "Love is not an affectionate feeling, but a steady wish for the loved person's ultimate good as far as it can be obtained."

I tell myself that quote is bunk. I don't love Barrett, whom I barely even know. But really—what if he's my person? What if it's fate that he moved in next door?

I roll my eyes and step back over by the table. Still, I'm unable to do anything but stand here rooted to the floor, trying to imagine other nights like this.

I'm lonely. That's all. And he's pretty, mysterious, and nice. He touched my face after I snarled. If he's always been this type of guy, he's probably had women falling at his feet since he was 7.

I catch my lip between my teeth. I pull out my phone and text Jamie.

'Neighbor guy is here. He fell asleep on my couch. I'm feeling all domestic and I want him. Help!'

I see the little bubble, letting me know she's typing. I'm like Pavlov's dog, smiling at the site of it. *'I knew it!'*

'*Fuck you.*' I add one of those adorable new flipping-the-bird icons my iPhone has. '*Fuck HIM,*' I type, adding the laughing face with tears dripping from its little emoticon eyes.

'*You're hopeless,*' she writes back.

'*You love me.*'

I set the phone down on the counter and decide to make some jam out of the blackberries I bought the other day at the farmer's market.

When I've got my little metal and glass food mill, a soup pot, and a bunch of sugar set out on the counter, I take a picture and text it to Jamie, tacking on the little smilie with the half-smile, half-frown face. Then I type, '*#SadSpinster.*'

She sends me a photo reply. I click the picture to enlarge. It's an empty ice-cream carton.

'*#AbandonedGirlfriend.*'

She fires off another text. It's a picture of the Mafioso with a smug smile and a thumbs up. '*Before he left,*' she adds.

'*Cute.*'

"Hashtag sarcasm," I murmur to myself. I pour the blackberries into the pot and start to crush them with a wooden spoon.

That's when I hear it: a low moan like a strong wind moving along the cabin's logs. I stop and swallow. I don't think it's that windy tonight. A whimper reaches my ears and my heart kicks up into my throat.

Barrett

I fumble for my pocket. Many nights, it's the first thing that I do. Go for my medic bag. Because I think the pain is physical. I think I got blown up and need to fix myself.

A few more grains of sand in the hourglass of consciousness, and my mind lights up like a bomb. Regret cuts through me, slicing through my heart, puncturing my lungs so I can't breathe. I can't move, and Breck—he couldn't move.

It all makes sense, a kind of cosmic sense. I never try to fight it. Vaguely aware of something softer than the floor beneath me, I curl over on my side and hold my head. With every cell in my body, I know I deserve this. I lie here and try to take it.

I can't stop the sounds escaping from my mouth. The wordless feelings. They're the black that paints the night inside my head, keeping me lost.

And lost I should be.

I tug my hair because it helps mute the inferno in my chest. I push my face into the pillow and pull air in through its fibers. Until my body is awake enough to sense its own flailing. Until adrenaline starts flowing and I'm lightheaded. Until the shaking starts.

I roll over, wanting to stretch and feel my body. Make sure I'm still here…

Gwenna

"Barrett?"

My voice sounds clipped and breathless, spilling from my throat before I make it around the half wall behind the couch.

When I see him curled up with one arm around his head, the other covering his face, I feel like I just got punched in the gut.

"Barrett?" Softer now, because I'm standing right behind the couch. Sweat prickles my hairline and my heart throbs in my throat.

That's the moment he jerks upright and writhes onto his left side, the left side of his head hitting the arm of my couch hard enough to *thump*.

A hoarse moan rips the silence.

Shit.

It all makes sense. Why he's so tired. He always looks like he's exhausted, even though he seems in physically good shape.

You've got this. Better you than someone else, I tell myself as I hurry around to the front of the couch.

My mom told me when Dad had nightmares, she'd tickle his feet. That way if he came up swinging, he wouldn't hurt her. I peel the blanket off Barrett's lower body, groping around for his soles. I feel...sneakers.

Shit.

My gaze lifts to his face out of habit, but all I can see is the top of his bowed head. I watch, feeling frozen, as his left hand, then his right one, grasps his hair. He breathes in huffs, then whimpers as he rests his head against the couch's back. My throat knots up as he whimpers, then moans. He holds his head as if it hurts, and guilt fillets my insides.

I lean over, my stomach flipping as I grab his shoulder and shake gently.

"Barrett..."

He sinks back down into the corner of the couch, clutching his head. His teeth are bared. His breaths are strained.

A cold sweat prickles through me. What do I do? Even as I wonder, I'm pulling the coffee table over right beside the couch. I sit on its edge. Then I take a deep breath, grab Barrett's elbows gently, and pull his hands down from his face.

His eyes are clamped shut. His face is tight. His posture is coiled, almost cowed.

"Barrett...hey..."

I fold his hands in mine. They're damp and curled, half-fisted and limp at the same time. I lean over closer to him, squeezing gently as I whisper, "Hey—it's Gwenna. You're at my house, remember?" I stroke his knuckles. "We were watching *Finding Nemo* and you fell asleep."

His eyelids flutter and he squints, recoiling like I've got a flashlight in his face. He drops his head back down. I feel a shudder rip through him. "I know," he groans.

I release one of his hands and tap his bicep. "Can you look at me?"

He doesn't lift his head. His shoulders rise, then fall. I hear him suck a deep breath down into his lungs—his shoulders curl a little on the exhale—and then gasp for another one. I can see the cords of tension in his neck. The tightness of his shoulders. He's struggling to breathe. I can't just watch and do nothing.

I move to the couch beside him, hesitating just a second while I find an angle that will work. Then I lean in close and wrap my arms around his wide chest. I press my cheek against the hard swell of his bicep and meld my body to his side.

I feel his torso stiffen. Feel his breathing hitch. A heartbeat later, one big arm encircles me. He crushes me against him, holding on so tight it hurts my ribs.

His mouth is on my hair. I feel him inhale, tickling my scalp. The breath shudders back out. For a heartbeat, I can feel his body lose some of its tension. Then he lets me go and leans away.

"Gwenna?" His eyes stretch wide. His lips part.

"Hey." I stroke his cheek.

His eyes drift shut. There's this little rumble low down in his throat. I think it sounds like someone easing.

Then his eyes open again. They search mine—frantic and confused. He blinks a few times. Stands up. He turns a slow circle.

"I've got to go," he says, and stumbles toward the door. He looks back at me for a long second. Then he turns and slips into the night.

chapter fifteen

Barrett

The steady pitter-patter, the blanket of steam, the blur of streaming water all around me: these things quiet my mind some. It feels good until my eyelids sag shut and my mind slips into darkness. My body jerks as if I'm falling, and I come to slumped against the shower wall, shaky and nauseated from not sleeping.

I keep hearing voices speaking in Pashto. That time the Taliban had us hogtied in that cabin in the Hindu Kush, keeping us awake for six days straight before we shot our way out...

I reach down into a soap dish for my phone. I turn it on, then turn the volume off and turn the camera view on. As it happens, she is in her bedroom. I don't know what time it is. She's in a robe. Is it morning or evening? Details blur together. A black window... a bright window...the moving trees. All the endless hours watching from the chair in the bedroom.

She's wearing her robe. Is she getting ready to leave the house or settling in for the night?

I lean my back against the shower's side and notice her mouth moving and her head tipped back. The way her mouth stretches...

She's singing. I sit up, feeling interested in something for the first time in days.

I turn the volume up slowly, until her rich voice echoes through the shower, drifting in the steam above me. Fuck, her voice is powerful. It's low and sultry. I feel it in the shaking of my hands, in the staccato of my pulse. It settles in the back of my throat, blurring my eyes. I close them, but I can't leave them shut for long. I want to watch her move and sing.

I can't believe it's really her. *That's Gwenna.*

A bolt of pride flares through me as I watch her flip her hair over her shoulder and dance around her room. I watch and listen—a combination I previously did not allow myself because it felt too invasive.

As she sings, she drops the robe. My throat tightens as she turns slightly toward the camera, showing me one milky-white breast. She turns a little more and I see both of them: small, soft globes spilling out of a lacy bra.

Lust surges through me. My dick twitches to life.

She leans over her dresser, toward a mirror hanging over it. I watch the curve of her back, the roundness of her ass.

My hand goes around my dick automatically. I groan and squeeze just under the head. I start to stroke it as she moves about her room, shimmying into and out of various shirts. I watch her ass as she turns circles. I fanaticize about grabbing her hips, stroking my cock until my balls tighten and I think I might come, just watching her.

I grit my teeth and turn the monitoring app off. Then I stand up slowly, with a massive boner. I step out of the shower, check the time and find it's during business hours, and dial Mallorie.

"Barrett. How are you?" That's her answer.

"Doing just fine, and you?"

"I'm good. What can I help you with?"

"When do you think the house will close?"

"Hmm…" I hear nails clicking on some surface. "Earliest? Some time next week. Latest, the week or two after."

My fingers clench the phone. "Thank you."

"How is the house?"

"It's great. I hope you're doing well," I add.

"I am." I can tell she's going to say more, so I beat her to the punch. "I'll be in touch."

When the call is dead, I slam my fist against the countertop. I close my eyes and I can feel her hands in my hair. Her arms around me. I can hear her voice, her pretty, sultry voice that gets into my dick and makes me want her.

I dry off quickly. Roughly. My head feels hollow. My skin hums. My cock presses against my lower belly. Gwenna dances in and out of my mind.

Not okay.

I go to the bed and pull up some porn on my phone. Even as I watch big tits and a gleaming, pink pussy, I feel her palm cupping my face. I imagine her fingers stroking the inside of my thigh. I watch some porn star suck a dick and I imagine Gwenna's lips, my dick.

I squeeze the phone as tightly as I can, then hurl it at the wall. It's because I'm tired. That's all.

I go downstairs and make some coffee, waiting for my dick to deflate as the Keurig coughs and chokes.

Gwenna

Two nights. Two times sparring by myself next to the porch. I rang his doorbell yesterday at 5:30 p.m., but nothing.

I worry. I think anybody would. I clean, and sing, and talk to Mom and Jamie and, once, Rett. Jamie tells me I should use my key if I want to. I don't. I don't have a reason to invade his space. After what happened at my house the other night, he's avoiding me. I wish he wasn't, but I understand. So much more than most people would.

I dress for my lone fight tonight in some brown leggings and a long-sleeved blue shirt featuring the creatures on the children's show *Yo Gabba-Gabba*. Inspired, I go to YouTube and find "Don't Bite Your Friends," a favorite song of the kids I babysit twice a month. I sing it as I lace up my hot pink sneaks.

It's getting dark sooner. Working out at night seems even more depressing than it should. I tell myself if he doesn't show up tonight, I'll start working out in the daytime again, up in the clearing.

As it is, I can't seem to make myself go out. A little after 5:30, I call Jamie and ask if she wants to go to the local hospital tomorrow in the bear suits.

"When do I *not* want to be a bear?"

I laugh. She's weird. It's why we're friends.

"You hanging in there?" she asks.

"Yeah."

"Don't worry about him. It's not your responsibility. You've done everything you can to be a good friend. He won't hide forever. Give him another few days."

"Yeah." I chew my lip, then cut our conversation short and go outside and start to stretch.

And there he comes. I see him at a distance as he walks from his long yard into the woods between our houses, and my heart leaps so high, I swear I feel it get hung in my throat.

Barrett!

He's wearing a green shirt. The sight of him makes me feel like I'm vibrating just a little. I try to gauge his mood from just his movements, but it's impossible, even as he nears me.

I'm straightening up from touching my toes when he steps into my yard, and holy shit. How many times am I going to forget and re-remember how gorgeous this man is?

He steps slowly over to me, stops in front of me, and looks into my eyes for a long moment. Then he runs one of his big hands gently over my hair. I hold my breath while his fingers blaze warm trails atop my scalp, and just when my eyelids droop from the pleasure of this simple touch, he holds a battered-looking leaf in front of my face.

"Thanks." I take it, my fingertips brushing his.

He nods, expressionless although his eyes are still on mine. My spirits plummet.

So this is how it's going to be.

Be patient, I tell myself. I'm reminded, strangely, of Papa Bear—and all the work I've done with him.

You're a patient person.

Still, I'm disappointed when he starts stretching without another word to me. During our workout, he teaches me more about the vulnerable places on the head. He has his fingers threaded through my hair half of the time, rubbing lightly on various pressure points and making my entire body burn. The rest of the time, I'm focused on getting my hands around his neck, or finding the best angle for gouging his overly perfect eyes out.

The few times he demonstrates a move on his own, I let my hungry eyes rove over him. I sift my feelings through the filter of "just friends." How long has it been since I had a guy friend? (College). I feel this warm swell concern for him, this proprietary feeling that he's mine to take care of. And yeah, I also kind of want his body. Is this what it's like to have a male friend?

We touch and talk and orbit each other—acting like nothing happened the other night, like nothing's ever happened between us except just sparring in my yard—and I tell myself that I *can* be his friend. I'd take that in a heartbeat if it was that or nothing. And it is. It's that or nothing, I tell myself sternly.

Entertaining any other option—even for a millisecond—is proof that I'm losing my grip on reality.

We end our workout with some free-form sparring. I can tell he's letting me "win"; I take it anyway, and bow theatrically when we're finished.

As soon as he starts stretching, I feel heat prickle my cheeks. I stretch alongside him until he's bending down toward his toes, and then, when he can't see my face, I say, "I made three different types of cookies. Peanut butter the one night, M&M last night, and chocolate chip today. You want to come in, or want me to run go get them?"

He rises to his full height and spreads his legs, then bends over to the left side. "You don't have to." His voice is soft and low. I have to run his words through my mind twice to convince myself he said them.

Then I smack a hand over my heart. "You don't want my cookies?"

I swear, I think the asshole rolls his eyes.

I sigh and wag a finger at him. "You're grumpy. I had a sense of it, but I couldn't tell for sure while we were sparring. You're pretty good at hiding your emotions, Secret Agent Ranger Guy."

Rising up again to roll his shoulders, he blinks at me.

I nod. "Like that." I shrug, determined not to sink into a sea of insecurity. I whirl around. "I'm going to get the cookies," I call over my shoulder. "Don't run off on me."

I didn't mean to reference the other night, but apparently my big mouth has a mind of its own. Typical me. Typical *pre* me. I feel a rush of warmth at the realization.

He makes me feel like me, I imagine telling Helga. I'm not sure if she'd be glad or appalled. Possibly appalled.

I pile three Ziplock freezer bags full of cookies into my arms and walk back out onto the front porch. I'm surprised to find Barrett sitting on the top step, leaning over his lap with his head in his hands. I drop down beside him on the stair and put the three bags at our feet.

When he shifts his wary eyes to me, I wait for him to say something. Instead he looks back down.

What should I do?

I wish I knew him better.

After a minute staring at the bags of cookies, wondering why I feel such a compulsion to take care of him, I decide it doesn't really matter. I do—and that's the thing. Sometimes people just connect, and this is how I feel toward him. It doesn't have to be a big deal. In that spirit, I pony up and throw an arm around his shoulders.

They're harder, wider than I realized they would be, and once my arm is resting on his strong back, I feel tingles spread through me. I still my body, feeling for movement, but he is frozen too. *It's your move.* I take a deep, slow breath and spread my hand out on a ridge of muscle.

Then I lean my head against his shoulder.

I'm not thinking about our height difference, so I *think* my cheek will press against his shoulder. Instead my forehead bumps against the hard swell of his bicep. It's unyielding. No more receptive to my attempt at comfort than the man himself.

Without meaning to, I laugh, and all the tension in me ebbs. I rub my forehead against his arm, feeling ridiculous.

Eventually, I guess even Barrett gets curious; he lifts his head so he can see my face. "What are you doing?" His face is twisted in a look of total incredulity.

I giggle. "Forehead-humping your arm. Can't you tell?"

"Yeah." He makes this husky, half-breath-half-laugh sound, and I feel a zing of victory.

"I'm trying to un-grouch you through osmosis."

When he cuts his eyes sideways at me, I find his handsome face skeptical. I grin and rub against his arm some more.

Finally—a real laugh from him. "I don't know about you, Gwen."

"I don't know about *you* either. Who refuses homemade cookies?" I arch my brows accusingly.

"Someone who's not hungry."

I hold his gaze as mine softens. My arm around him squeezes. I don't know what to say, so I just sit beside him, looking at his somber face, into his striking eyes, and try to send good vibes.

"You know…" I let my arm slide down his back, so it's looser around him. "After my wreck, I had some terrible nightmares. I don't have them as much now, but I had some in the last week. I find that if I'm stressed out or something shifts in my day-to-day life, sometimes they crop up again. I have this journal where I write them out. And then I go back in and like…re-script them. Change what happens. I know it probably sounds kind of stupid, but it really does help."

With my arm still up against his back, I feel him exhale. After a second during which his body feels completely inert, he turns to me with raised brows and twisted lips.

"Is there a reason you told me that?" His tone is surprisingly sharp.

My pulse pounds in irritation. I give him my best *oh really* look.

"I'm fine," he says. I swear, I think he grits his teeth.

I feel his back knot up under my hand. *Riiight.*

"Okay," I say airily. "You seem tired, that's all."

He looks at me strangely, almost angrily. "Yes, we have established that. I don't see why you give a fuck."

My heart squeezes, making my head feel light and spinny. I move my arm from him and hug myself. "Because we're *friends.*"

"Are we?"

chapter sixteen

Gwenna

I'm not aware of what I do, or what kind of look I give him. I just know it takes a couple of seconds to draw my next breath, and when I do, my pulse gallops and my cheeks feel hot. I jump up and turn around, toward my door.

I feel Barrett's fingers wrap around my arm. "Dammit." This time, it's his eyes seeking mine. I train mine on his green shirt.

"I'm sorry, Gwenna. I'm just..." He scrubs his forehead with his right hand, then lets out a loud sigh. "I'm an asshole."

He looks so contrite, so worried and—indeed—so tired, my anger melts in a few seconds.

I press my lips together, not quite willing to let him know that yet. I sink back down onto the porch step. If he doesn't want to be here anymore tonight, this is his chance to go.

Just go.

Instead he sits beside me, searching my face with his gray-blue eyes. "Gwen..." He tilts his head. "I'm sorry." With no warning, his arm wraps around my back. He pulls me gently to him, so my shoulder and right side come up against his warm chest.

"It's okay." I try to stay still, so I won't touch him more than I have to, and keep my eyes trained on the Ziplock bags. I cut my eyes toward him, so he believes me when I say, "Forgiven."

I wait for him to move his heavy arm. He doesn't. I might not be angry with him, but I'm still embarrassed. I debate wriggling out of his grasp and going into my house, but I'm supposed to be his friend, so I just sit there, wondering what made me think I should put myself out there. What made me even think he wanted that.

Friends? We're neighbors. The only reason we know each other is that I kicked him in the head.

As if he hears my thoughts, his hand flattens on my back and he says, "You're a good friend, Gwenna. Better than I am."

I let a long breath out. I tip my head back, looking at the sky through bare limbs and crinkling leaves.

He shifts his weight a little, moving closer to me, so I'm almost underneath his arm. I still feel the weight of his hand just under my bra strap on the left side of my back.

My throat aches. I just...can't look at him. I keep my head tipped back.

A moment later, his voice rumbles near my ear. "See something up there?"

"Stars." The word is smaller, tighter than intended. It seems, for better or for worse, all I want now is to go inside. I don't understand this weird pseudo-friendship we have, and now I'm not so sure I want to.

"You like the stars?" he asks.

I like his sexy, raspy voice—damn it all. I exhale slowly, so he can't feel it. "Who doesn't?"

There's a beat of silence, in which crackling leaves chase each other across my brownish grass. Then he moves his arm off me and steps down off the porch. He holds a hand out. "C'mon."

"Huh?"

He reaches down and wraps his hands around my waist, under my arms. "C'mon, Gwenna." He lifts me up. "You ever get called Gwen?" He sets me on my feet, then seems to re-evaluate and throws me over his shoulder. The motion is surprisingly controlled and gentle.

After a second of shock at our little plot twist, I shriek and mock-beat his back. "Where are you taking me, you freaking Sasquatch?"

He laughs. "Sasquatch?"

"When I saw you, when I kicked you, I thought you were Sasquatch."

I can feel his laughter in the movement of his shoulders. "That's some funny shit."

"Yeah, you're like…part giant."

His arm around my back tightens. "To answer you," he says as we get into his yard, "it's somewhere good. You'll see."

I think I know where he might be taking me when we start up the stairs to the third floor of his house, but I don't know for sure until he sets me in the second floor hall outside the bedroom doors and reaches for a notch there in the ceiling. He tugs it lightly, pulling a big square of ceiling downward just a little. With his left hand, he pushes me gently back.

He turns to me and smiles, dimpled and panty-melting. "Do you trust me?"

I arch a brow. "Should I?"

He looks stricken.

"Yes." I roll my eyes. "Why wouldn't I? Although I will say," I tell him as he pulls the stairs all the way down, "if you chop me into little pieces, I will haunt your shit so hard…"

He gives a low laugh. "Well, I don't need that."

I smile sweetly. "Then you better treat me like a BFF."

He gives me a funny little look—a kind of long pre-smile in which he somehow, indescribably, just *looks* like he could smile. And then he does.

My heart skips several beats.

"I'll go first. To test the ladder," he says.

As I watch him climb into the attic and turn on a light, I have a strange déjà vu feeling: *high school.* Butterflies and flop sweat and lust, I think as he leans back down over the ladder.

"We're good," that low voice rumbles. "Come on up."

He hovers near the top of the ladder as I climb. I'm watching his face as I step fully up into the attic space, so I see him opening his mouth, seemingly to protest. Then I get a peek at the room behind him and my jaw drops.

The room looks like—it *is*—a little library. It's a rectangular space about the size of a school classroom, with a cedar floor, exposed rafters, and whitewashed walls. Right out in front of me, punched into the wall that forms the top line of the rectangle, there is a quilted, queen-sized bed that folds out of the wall. The long wall to my right is nothing but built-in shelving, packed with books, trinkets, and even a little lantern. To my left, along that long wall, there is an antique desk, a fish-shaped floor lamp beside a cozy leather armchair, and—perhaps the room's most awesome feature—the most giant window seat I've ever seen: about the size of my kitchen table. The window is three giant sheets of glass arranged like the top of a hexagon.

My eyes rove the room again as my hand covers my mouth. "Holy hell, this is beyond adorable."

I turn a circle, noting an antique rocking chair, a circular woven rug, a random gnome statue, and tiny wind chimes hanging from the ceiling near the window seat.

The only thing I've ever heard about the Haywoods' attic was something about a homemade telescope. I search the room for it, and when I don't see it, my gaze boomerangs to Barrett.

He's got his arms folded in front of his chest, and I'm pretty sure the look on his face is a smug one.

"This is fabulous," I say. "I may move in."

He smiles. "Turn to your left."

"That window seat is awesome. I think I should sit in it."

I'm almost to it when I notice the left sheet of glass seems to have a hole at the bottom, near the seat's padding.

Another step and I can it's not a hole; it's a little electronic panel of some kind, looking at first glance like a smaller version of the black Wii U box. One more step, and the low lamplight reveals the box to be a giant, T-Rex-sized pair of goggles. I climb up onto the seat's padding and pull them out of the window—or rather, off a little shelf I can now see they're sitting on—and watch, confused, as they trail a small, plastic-looking tube in from outside the window.

"It's some kind of fiber optics," Barrett says, coming up to stand behind me. "He had it set up so the telescope is on the roof and sends the image through that little tube that runs from tele-scope to goggles."

I blink down at the goggles. "How random. And cool. I want to see."

I turn them over, but I have no clue how to make them work, so when Barrett climbs up onto the padded cushion beside me, I hand them to him.

I watch his brows notch as he looks down at them, pressing a few buttons. He brings them up over his eyes, and I see his lips twitch.

"Nice," he says, passing them to me. "Tell me what you see."

I pull the goggles to my eyes and almost gasp.

"Is that—It looks like…the Milky Way? Like, the whole of it, right?"

It's disconcerting to see such a vast view of the sky while sitting cross-legged on a padded seat. I blink a few times, awe-struck by the lovely spread of stars and soft light against the black of space. Maybe I wobble a little, because I feel Barrett's hands on my shoulders, and I'm aware of being laid down. I pull the goggles off my face and see my head is on a long pillow that lines the bottom of glass pane that juts farthest out.

"I think you're meant to lie down like that." He's right; there's plenty of room for me to rest my head up against the top window pane, my legs out with the knees bent, so my shoes are against the cushion.

My eyes fly from the space beside me to Barrett, and then I put the goggles back over my eyes.

"There's a manual downstairs that I've been thumbing through. When you want to see a different view, just let me know."

I pull the goggles down. "What are my options?"

He takes them from me, punches a few buttons, and passes them back with a funny little smile.

I bring them to my eyes and find a molten-looking image that, though stained dark amber, I am sure must be the sun.

"Please tell me I don't see that thing…moving." I swallow hard, and Barrett laughs.

"You mean the surface of it?"

I struggle not to shudder. "Yes."

I'm tempted to pull the goggles away from my face, because something about seeing the sun's shifting surface makes me want to hurl.

"I think that's supposed to be the fun part." Barrett laughs.

"It's...creepish. It looks kind of like...What are those little lines? It almost looks like geysers shooting up."

"Sun spots? Or solar flares? Haywood had a long monologue written out on cue cards." He laughs again. "Kind of like a tour of space. I guess he would go through it while guests looked through the goggles like you're doing."

I peek out from behind the goggles. "Do you remember any of it?"

"Some."

Or maybe all. I remember how he didn't have to write my phone number down on the porch that night as Barrett gives me what I'm sure must be Haywood's geeky guided solar system tour, verbatim. The wording doesn't sound like his, and sometimes after dropping a hardcore nerdy fact on me, I think I can hear him smirking.

I find myself giggling around Jupiter. A second later, I feel Barrett's big hand on my knee. I draw the goggles away from my eyes and find him looking at me with arched brows and a shaming look.

"Are you laughing at your celestial tour guide?"

I wrap my hand around his. "Maybe."

I'm hoping he'll lie down beside me. Instead he moves his hand and changes my view again, zooming out so I can see the big dipper. About which he knows all the things.

When he's finished unloading more data on me, I smile and hand the goggles to him. "I'm not going to ask how you know that stuff, you dork."

"Nav," he answers. His tongue darts over his lower lip. "Navigating."

So, by constellations, I guess. "Were you a navigator in the Rangers?"

His eyebrows lift, his features making a poker face. "I was a lot of things."

I want to ask—like *really* want to—but I'm not about to pry. There's been enough drama tonight between the two of us, and despite how solicitous he's being now, I don't trust him not to go all moody on me again.

"That fits with my impression of you as a closet geek," I tease.

His hand comes around my thigh, the fingers squeezing gently at a spot that makes me giggle. "You better watch yourself," he teases.

It's my turn to watch him as looks through the goggles for a few minutes, sitting cross-legged beside me. I make him tell me what he's focused on, and this time I get the long, tragic tale of Artemis and Orion—Zeus's daughter and her mortal human lover—and Scorpius, the scorpion Zeus used to kill Orion, who, as a mortal, was not supposed to cavort with royal Artemis.

"The story goes, Artemis flew away with Orion's body and tossed him into the sky—but nowhere near the scorpion that killed him," Barrett finishes.

"Scorpius…"

He brings the goggles down off his eyes. "Yeah."

"Wow. That's impressive storytelling, geek boy."

He sets the glasses on his knee and leans back on his hands, his back to the left panel of glass. I don't expect the heavy sigh that comes from him, nor the way his eyes squeeze shut just briefly before he says, "I haven't told that story in a long time."

"Yeah?" When he just blinks at me, I add softly, "Who'd you tell it to last time?"

I see his chest inflate with breath before he says, "My brothers."

Brothers?

I pull myself up to sit cross-legged to his left, leaning back against a beam between two of the window panes. Once I'm settled in my new position, I blink over at him, but I can't tell shit from his face. After another heartbeat, I venture, "I didn't realize you had two."

He rubs his eyes, looking at me around his hand. "Kellan and Lyon. Twins. Lyon used to love to hear the Leo story." Another deep breath swells his chest, and he looks right at me as he says, "He died a few years back."

My heart squeezes as I look into his carefully blank eyes. "Oh my God, I didn't know."

He lifts his brows. "I didn't tell you."

"I'm so sorry."

When he says nothing, just looks down at the beige and gold paisley cushion under us, I swallow past my dry throat.

"When did it happen? If you don't mind me asking…" My voice is whispered—probably because my throat is tight.

"End of 2011." He rubs the bridge of his nose, eyes on his leg before they slowly lift to mine. "They had leukemia."

I lean into the space between us. "Who did?"

"Ly and Kelly."

I blink. "Both? They *both* did?"

"Yeah." He finger-drums the seat cushion, looking down at his hand as it moves. "Identical twins. I guess it was…" He shakes his head.

My chest feels tight with pain for him. I wrack my brain for what to say. There's nothing…

His eyes lift to meet mine, and his handsome face is hard and still. I can feel the pain behind it, though, the weight of wordless things.

"Barrett—I'm so sorry." I lean over closer to him, wanting very much to touch him but unsure how—or *if*. He shifts positions, I think mostly so he doesn't have to look at me. He's sitting cross-legged with his eyes fixed on his lap. He blinks down at his calves, pushes a curl out of his eyes.

"That must have been so awful," I say in a half-whisper. "I wouldn't know, because my dad died suddenly. And I've never lost a sibling."

He bites the inside of his cheek and lifts his gaze to mine. "*I* wouldn't know," he rasps. "I wasn't there."

He runs a hand into his hair and looks down at the cushion.

Wasn't there? "You were—overseas? Is that what you're saying?"

He laughs, a small, dry sound, and cuts his eyes up at me before pulling them back down, shaking his head. "I don't know why I told you that." His voice is rough.

I almost say "because we're friends," but are we? Maybe we're just really strange acquaintances, able to be unnaturally open with one another because I kicked off our neighbor-ship by bashing his head open, and since then, we've spent something like 10 hours trying to kill each other.

Still—I feel a magnetic sort of pull to him. One that seems to emanate at this moment from the center of my achy chest.

I take a small, fortifying breath and scoot closer to him. When I get there, knee-to-knee with him, my limbs feel heavy with uncertainty. He's looking at his lap, and my heart is pounding like it always does when I'm near him. After holding still a few heartbeats, I press my knee against his.

I lean my head back against the cold glass of the window and I try to think of what makes me feel better...with Dad. And I realize: I like to talk about him. So much more than I would have ever have imagined. It gives me a kind of pride. He was here. He was *my* Dad.

I take a deep, slow breath, and when my eyes feel confidently free of tears, I lean a little closer to him. "So your brothers liked to hear you tell them stories? I'm guessing they must have been younger than you."

There's a long half-second in which I'm scared I said the wrong thing. Then he nods.

"When our mom died—" I watch his Adam's apple bob—"the boys were ten, almost eleven. I was sixteen."

He blinks, as if he was going to say something else but can't remember what. I take a chance and lean my head against his arm. Not because it's comfortable—it's still rock-like—but just for basic human contact. Comfort.

I'm surprised when he shifts, stretching his arm behind my neck—in one smooth motion, scooting closer, so our folded thighs are pressed together and his shoulder hovers over mine. His arm drops down along my upper back.

I blink at his chest, easily accessible to me now. All that's left is for me to snuggle up to him. I wait for some signal that's what he wants, and when he doesn't give one, my back begins to tremble from the effort required to keep my cheek from touching his pec.

"Anyway," he rumbles, sounding normal and relaxed, as if he didn't just put an arm around me, "our dad worked long hours. They had a nanny, but I liked to watch them."

The arm around my shoulders tightens slightly, pressing me against him. My lungs stop working as I lay my cheek against his chest.

I feel the rumble of his chuckle, feel his fingers sifting gently through my hair. I look up and see him smile. It looks both sweet and smug. His eyes find mine, and the scales tip to sweet; almost indulgently so.

"You're tense," he says softly.

"I know." For the second time in the last hour, I feel like a teenager again.

He squeezes me closer, and I feel his big chest rise and fall. "I thought you wanted to be friends," he whispers.

"Is this what friends do?" My words are husky. Charged. I strain my gaze to look up at his face without moving my cheek off his pec. I find his eyes closed.

"I don't know," he answers. His hand strokes my shoulder, and I want to shriek—or rip his pants off. As it is, I feel a little shaky. Like I'm on a roller coaster.

He presses his cheek against the top of my head. I shiver as his scruff tickles my hair.

"You smell good," he murmurs, his arm around me squeezing.

I wrap my arms gently around his chest. "You're nice and warm," I whisper. Underneath my carefully roving fingers, all I feel are ridges of hard muscle. On his back...along his side...

I feel a hot pulse in between my legs and have to take a slow breath so I don't implode.

We stay like that for a brief stretch of time—Barrett leaning on the window, his legs out in front of him; me tucked up against him, unable to move or think.

Every breath he takes is hypnotic. I find I love the feel and smell of him. The strength and size of him.

Why is he doing this?

He's lonely...

So am I.

His fingers stroke my shoulder once more, and my stomach tightens. I can feel him take a long breath—and then he pulls me closer, curving his wrist so the rough, warm fingertips of the hand that's cupping my shoulder straighten out and drift over my neck.

I'm struggling to breathe around the knot in my throat when he pulls his arm out from around me, and shifts so he's kneeling in front of me. His hands cup my elbows, roving up from there. One comes to rest on my collarbone; the other spreads over my throat.

"What do you want with me?" The words are almost groaned. They strike straight to my heart, which stops, then takes off at a gallop.

"What do you mean?" I murmur, looking at his solemn face. His eyes shut.

"What do you mean?" I whisper, gently. I reach a hand out, stroking his warm neck.

His eyes open. His hands frame my face—gently—and I feel his rough cheek brush against mine. His arms encircle me and then his mouth is near my ear. I can hear and feel him take a deep breath; so deep it's almost like a gasp.

I pull him close, his face against my shoulder, his huge torso bowed around me. I find I have to swallow before I speak, and even then, my voice is raspy. "I don't want anything from you, Bear." My hand rubs a circle on his back.

His breath tickles my shoulder. "Why are you so kind?" It's almost groaned.

My heart squeezes painfully. I hold him tighter. "I'm not… that way. I'm just…" I cup his head, shaking mine—because it's all I can manage.

He leans against me, and I take him. With one shoulder pressed against the window, I take all his heavy weight, so I can feel it when he shudders.

"What's the matter?"

"I feel like I'm dreaming. None of this…feels real."

I hold him tightly, aching at the raw pain in his voice. I stroke his nape. "I think you're tired," I whisper.

I kiss his hair. I don't mean to, but here he is—his big, heavy, beautiful body cradled up against me, just the way I've wanted since I met him.

It's such a small kiss, so fast and light, it takes me a long moment to realize that since I pressed my lips against him, I can feel him breathing faster.

"You should go home, Gwenna."

"Why?" I whisper.

He lifts his head and frames my face with his hands, lifting my chin so we're eye to eye—and I can see his heavy-lidded ones. "Because you're right. I'm tired. And I don't have a lot of self-control."

chapter seventeen

Gwenna

My body flares white hot as his words roll through my mind. It's been so long since anyone—I think I haven't heard him right.

Then his forehead presses against mine. His arms encircle me, warm hands stroking up and down along my sides. His dazed eyes cling to mine, and they are more transparent than I've ever seen them. I feel like I can read his whole soul in their smoky depths: want and need, shame, exhaustion.

He doesn't love you, warns an inner voice.

But this feels so good, it feels so right, and I'm so hungry for him, I don't care.

"You're so fucking sweet and soft." His voice is low, and as he speaks, his eyes drift almost shut. Then they peek back open, and I feel the soft burn of his mouth on my throat, so gentle I can't tell if it's his tongue or lips.

"It's okay," I rasp, grasping his hair.

"What do you want with me?"

"I want this…"

My want throbs between my legs, a tsunami building as I tilt my face toward his and our lips meet, the kissing slow and careful, hard and faster, frantic, until I'm shaking. Every time his tongue strokes mine, I feel a pulse of need spread through my core.

Barrett leans me back. I'm lying down. His heavy body comes between my legs, and he's kissing my throat so hard it hurts. But good…

As I pant, the scent of his skin swims through my head; his beard scratches my tender skin; his sturdy weight bears down on me—and it's perfection. A low groan vibrates against my skin as his mouth climbs up my throat and roves along my jaw.

Chills riot over me. I grip his neck, holding him to me. "'S good…"

His palm roves up my neck and cups my cheek. I feel his hot tongue drag over my jaw and try to press my legs together. Instead, my thighs just squeeze his hips, making them buck. I lift my own hips, seeking…

God. I moan. He lifts his mouth off me and breathes hard.

"Gwen…" His hand grips my shoulder. His eyes shout at mine, then squeeze shut. He shifts his hips and my gaze drags between our bodies.

I can see him bulging in his pants. Oh Lord, I have to touch him. Need to see his face and hear his sounds when my hand cups the swell of his erection.

His head rests on my shoulder, warm and heavy. I can feel his hot breath on my neck. His chest presses against my breasts with every inhalation. He moans, a rough, low sound, and I can feel his legs tense.

"Gwen…"

He cups my cheek and with his heavy-lidded eyes on mine, a lost look on his face, he lowers himself slowly down on me and shifts his hips so I can feel him hard and thick against my inner thigh.

He takes a deep, long breath and looks down at where he's got his big bulge pressed against me. His gaze lifts back up to mine. "Is...this okay?" He drags himself along my leg and grinds against me even as he asks.

I press my leg against him, my core throbbing as he grunts and thrusts against my soft thigh.

"Fuck..."

"I love it."

"God," he groans.

I can feel his upper body shake with building tension, and his dick throbs once as if it's desperate for release.

"It's...been...a while," he groans, his eyes squeezed shut. I cup his scratchy cheek and wrap my hand around his shoulder.

"Me too...I just want to feel you."

As he feathers kisses over my temple, I arch my back, lifting my hips and shimmying as my fingers fumble blindly at his abs, reaching lower till my hand covers his bulge. Barrett's breath catches.

I rub him, pressing my palm against his hard length as my fingers find the soft swell of his balls below.

The sound he makes is guttural and wasted.

"Oh God...." Even through his pants, I can feel the outline of his head...the firm ridge of its rim. I rub along his swollen shaft. God, he's big. Long and thick and...God. My pussy clenches as I brush against his balls.

"Don't," he grits.

I draw my hand back, stung. But I can see him in the shadow of the lamplight. See how big he is, how hard he is. He's here with me. He's hard for *me*. I thought I couldn't do this...after. Couldn't let my guard down—but I have.

My excitement turns to frenzy, so intense I can't think straight. Since shifted his hips so I can't touch him with my hands, I bring my leg up so my knee pushes against him there. Heaven help me, I can feel his shaft twitch, feel his balls sway.

I groan and his eyes flip open, dazed and burning. "Gwen."

I move my leg against him and my center throbs, just from the feel of him through his jeans.

I reach down for him again. Before my hungry fingers make their mark, he grabs my wrists, stretching my arms above my head and urging me back down onto the cushion. For a long second, his gaze captures mine. I can see the indecision in his.

I grip his shoulder.

"Barrett—"

"Fuck…"

I feel his body shudder. His eyes shut. His breathing picks up. "Gwen, I need…"

"Me too," I whisper.

He runs his hand under my shirt and thumbs my nipple through my bra.

I groan, hips rolling. "Please…"

He slips his hand beneath my bra and cups my breast. I feel his hips against my leg, his cock against my thigh.

"Your skin…So soft." He moves against me, and I can feel every long inch of him.

I rub my thigh against him, laughing from adrenaline. "You're not."

He leans down over me and bites me through my shirt.

His hand strokes my lower belly as his lips pull one of my nipples into his mouth. As I start to pant and his hand comes to cup me through my leggings, his eyes darken.

"You're beautiful. You want this."

"Yes."

His hand slides into my leggings, smoothing down over my mound. I groan as his fingers part my lips; two calloused fingers drag through my slick and swollen folds. I'm so wet. I need him inside me.

I see his eyes shut as his fingertips roll around my entrance, playing in the moisture there. His breathes loudly, running a finger up and down my slit and skating gently around my clit.

I pant. His head dips back down to my chest; he mouths my nipple once again, then pulls my shirt away, pushes my bra up and drags his tongue around my nipple.

"Barrett!"

He slides a finger into me and I see stars. "Ohhhhh God." I grind against his hand, loving the fullness, the invasion...knowing that's him, it's Barrett's finger in me.

I gasp as he pushes in and pulls his finger slowly out, then surges back inside, prodding until he strokes my G-spot. My whole body jumps. He starts to rub my clit again, and tongue my nipple. I grab his hair and drag him up. I drag him up so I can kiss his mouth, so I can see his handsome, lust-drunk face, but mostly so maybe he will press his hips against me one more time and I can feel his cock against my leg.

It's been so long.

I'm panting when his tongue glides back into my mouth, so strong and smooth. The tip of it explores; our tongues stroke. I can barely even move mine. My whole mind is focused on the pressure building in between my legs. He tries to work another finger into me. I gasp.

"You're tight, baby."

I try to push against his finger.

"I'll be careful..."

"I don't care!"

He works the second finger in—only the tip. I moan as he pumps in, stretching, then pulls his fingers slowly out. He crawls down my throbbing body, peels my leggings down, and looks up at me.

"Jesus Christ, *I have to.*"

He lowers his mouth over me. I can feel the light brush of his lips. Then his tongue touches my clit, and I scream. His fingers delve inside me as he drags his tongue down, stroking between my lips before he comes back up to kiss my clit again. He rubs his lips over it, strokes it with the tip of his tongue.

I'm thrusting at him, panting like I'm on the last mile of a marathon. Inside me, his fingers surge, until I spread my legs; my hand gropes blindly for his dick as I throb underneath his slick tongue. I clench my core against his fingers, raise my leg, trying to find his hardness with my knee.

"Sixty-nine," I rasp.

He laughs. "Enjoy this," he breathes, and lavishes my clit with smooth, soft pressure, his fingers gliding in and pulling slowly out of me. I can't hold off another moment. I cry out and pulse around him as the world goes brilliant gold; sounds fade. Only the weight of him on me remains.

I feel my eyes roll back into my head, but still, I pull him down on top of me. The last thought I have before I drift away is I'm not sure what I like the best: the weight of him atop me, or the way his tongue felt lapping in between my legs.

chapter eighteen

Barrett
2010

The door opens, and one of the cadre members, Bobby, nods toward the room behind him. As usual, his face is blank. As are the faces of Colonel Wentworth, Sergeant Major Luthe, and Sergeant Hamm, sitting in three chairs in the center of the room.

Wentworth, the commander of the unit, is husky and freckled, with a thick, reddish beard and pale blue eyes that narrow on me as I kick off my appearance with a sharp salute.

"Sir! Sergeant Drake reports to the commander!"

Wentworth has me hold my position while he runs those keen eyes up and down me. Finally he returns my salute and tells me to sit down.

Then he lumbers up and shuffles over to me. With his limp and his big frame, he reminds me slightly of a wounded bear. He scowls down at me as the other men watch impassively.

I can see his nostrils flaring with his exhalations, see his belly move under his uniform. When he speaks, his voice is a low boom, like a sports announcer's.

"I was gonna call you in here and tell you you're in." His bushy brows wiggle as he sinks a hand into his pocket. "We want you." He blinks down at me. "Seems like you've got what it takes to be an Operator. To be a sniper. In the Unit, we want the best. Seemed you were the best."

My head hammers. My mouth feels dry as I look up at him, just waiting for the catch.

"Then we found out you're a liar." He jerks something from his pocket. It's a Polaroid picture—one that shows me stopped beside a man who's lying on a winding mountain road beside a banged up motorcycle.

"Do you know this man?"

I blink, my blood rushing in my ears.

"Is this fellow a friend of yours? Someone you had to try and come and help you?" My mouth opens. He grits his teeth and glares down at me, glaring me to interrupt in self-defense.

"You deviated from your assignment on the field navigation test to help this man and even wandered down the way to one of the road's emergency phone booths. You made a call to local law enforcement. A Good Samaritan." Wentworth laughs derisively and shakes his head. The look on his face tells me I'm an idiot, and I don't even know why.

"You didn't do the humane thing, Drake. You didn't stay with him, even though he called behind you as you walked away."

My face must show some quiver of surprise, because his tightens as his neck and cheeks flush deeper red.

"Did you think we weren't watching? You think you can do whatever you want? You were not to deviate from the mission!" Spittle flies down at me. "You think you can jeopardize what you do as an Operator for a stranger? Play Good Samaritan and call for help for the guy? You didn't stay the course! You didn't even stay with him. He was bleeding, and you left him." Shame flares through me. "That motorcyclist you came across—the one you threw the nav test away for—he died. You could have saved him, but you half-assed that, too."

My stomach rolls as he holds his hand up, ticking my sins off on his fingers. "First you leave your course. You use a phone and call police. And then you lack the balls to even follow through and stay with this man as he suffers. He was an innocent civilian, not a war criminal. You have the conscience to help him but you're too big of a pussy to abandon your mission and stay to comfort this man in his time of need." He shakes his head. The guilt I'm feeling lessens as I realize he's rambling. "You have no morals. You're worthless!"

The insult makes my head feel hot, my fists clench up. Instead of jumping up and throttling the asshole, I hold still, the wheels in my head spinning.

"I wouldn't have thought a Ranger would be worthless, but that's what you are, sergeant."

I take a slow breath. Exhale as he scowls down at me.

I get this. They're trying to rattle me. Why else would Wentworth chastise me for not staying with the injured biker I came up on during the nav course? My actual orders were not to deviate for anything, so it makes no sense that I'm being chastised for not sitting with the injured stranger long enough.

I take another deep breath. *Ride it out. This is a test.*

"What do you have to say for yourself?" His voice booms, echoing faintly in the near-to-empty meeting room. "You let a stranger *die* when you have medical training as an Army Ranger. You lied to us—to the cadre members who assumed you had done nothing but chart and travel your route. On top of that, you barely met your check-in time!"

I grit my teeth to keep from barking back. I arrived at the RV in time for check-in, despite having wandered miles out of my way to reach the pay phone that I used to call for help. I made the time cut even though I've got a hairline fracture in my ankle.

I inhale again, then exhale and peer up at him.

"What do you have to say, Drake?" His jaw is tight; his cheeks are ruddy; forehead shining. "You think you're too good to give an answer? Too good to be accountable? You think because you're a sniper for the Rangers you're big shit? Do you?"

"No sir."

"No sir," he sneers. "You sound like such a brownnoser, such a little pansy-ass. I heard you're a real do-gooder, Drake. I heard that about you. Stuck-up brownnoser. Son of a doctor. Little kiss-ass. I heard from your boys in Benning that you're good with a gun but not much else."

I feel my head throb.

"You think because you're a Sergeant, because you've got the best record for a Ranger sniper at this moment in time, that you're better than *me*? That's what you're thinking right now, isn't it? Look at that fat-ass Wentworth, I'm better than him! You think you should be able to determine people's fates yourself, don't you? I heard your mother died when you were just a boy. What happened?"

My mind blanks. I have to struggle to work past my shock at the abrupt change of subject and draw in another breath.

"C'mon, tell me, pussy. You want to be an Operator, you want a spot on one of my teams, you will tell me *anything* I ask."

I'm shaking my head before I realize what I'm doing. "I don't have to talk about that."

"No?" His folds his arms. His upper lip curls. "You do if it's an order."

I look up at him, gritting my teeth. Who the fuck does he think he is, bringing my mom into a fucking test?

"Tell me about your mother, Sergeant Drake. Tell me how she died."

My chest aches, so sharp and deep I have to struggle not to bring a hand up to it. "Cancer," I rasp.

"What kind of cancer?" he sneers.

I shut my eyes. Even though I know I'm being fucked with, it still hurts to say it. "Breast cancer." I force myself to look back up at him, trying to detach my feelings from this moment and place.

"Your dad's a surgeon. What kind of piece of shit doctor can't save his own wife? Tell me about your old man. He a fan of you?"

My stomach twists. My throat tightens.

"Does he like you? Your father. Does your father like you, Drake? It's yes or no."

I blow my breath out. Glare up at him. "No."

"Were you a mama's boy?"

I swallow. My throat actually aches, even though my heart is pounding and I'm getting more and more pissed off.

I grit my teeth. Test or not, this fucker needs to shut up.

"Oh, so a little mama's boy. Mama died, so we want her to be proud, is that it?" I press my lips together. "The way you aborted your mission, got off-track and didn't tell us. Mr. Good Samaritan, wanting to save everybody that he can save."

I clamp my molars on the inside of my cheek. I didn't abort my mission! I stopped for half an hour to help a guy who had a wreck. I grit my teeth again, and Wentworth again jumps subjects.

"We've seen you use restraint as a sniper. You'd never go on a rampage, that's what our white coats tell us. But are you one who might get *over*-sympathetic? Say, if you were assigned a female target. Could you take a woman out?"

I frown, confused. "I have."

"But she was old, probably toothless," he crows. "She had also thrown a bomb that got someone you knew. What if she'd been hot? Someone who looked like Mama. And you watched her for a long time, a little Munich Olympics situation. You watched her shave her legs and watched her cry. You never saw her do anything bad." He sneers. "Could you eliminate a target like that?" He shakes his head, continuing the theatrics. "We don't know about you, Drake. Where your sympathies lie."

"Sir, I'm a sniper for the Rangers." It comes out before I realize I've spoken.

"Aww, so got a kill list. I hear that. I've seen it. Im-press-ive," he says in his Southern drawl. "But only one woman scribbled down there. Not American—and not a sympathetic character. What if she was even hurt or…sick? Then what?"

part two

"There are a thousand things I want.
Each begins with going back in time."

—Jill Alexander Essbaum, from *The Devastation*

chapter one

Barrett
November 3, 2015

I do push-ups in the living room until I can't feel my arms, and the fingers I can feel on my left hand are aching.

I'm interrupted by my phone flashing on the couch's arm. Dove. I answer out of masochism.

"What the hell, dude? Haven't heard from you in two days."

"And?" My voice is tight with fury.

"And…you know. How are things?"

I grit my molars. Fucking Dove in his fucking compound out in nowhere Montana. Probably chopping wood and welding shit all day. Dancing on that peg leg like the happy fucker he's always been.

"Don't you have a wife to nag?" His wife's an author. Thrillers.

"You know I'd rather get at you," he says. "Anyway, Melinda's in Cali. Had to go talk to someone about a script."

I pace around and end up in the kitchen with my back against the refrigerator. I cast my eyes into the living room and lower my voice. "Quit calling every damn day."

"I'm just standing in for my brother. He'd be doing the same thing."

It's true. Breck would. He might even be here with me. I sigh. "Well, you're not him."

"I know, man. But really, what the fuck is going on down there?"

I exhale—away from the phone, so Mr. Happy can't hear it. "I wanted to tie up some loose ends. Do things right so it comes off clean and I have options. Like you claim to want."

I glance down at my pants, where I'm still throbbing and half hard, then squeeze my eyes shut.

I hear Dove sigh. "You know, man…Did I tell you Bluebell's been stateside?"

"No."

"He went to Breck's parents' place, right? I talked to him, happened to mention where you were. That was two days ago. Since then, he just disappeared. I don't know where the fuck he went."

"Except you do." I roll my eyes.

"It's just a guess," Dove says. He doesn't even have to tell me what the guess is: that Bluebell's coming here to interfere with my shit. Working together as long as we all did, I can read his mind, and he mine.

"How long's his leave?" I rub my brow.

"Don't know. But I can't see how any good will come of this. You drawing that shit out with her."

"You don't have to, do you? It's *my* shit."

He doesn't have the balls to argue—even though he could. Because it's not just mine. Because of what I did, it's all of ours.

But Dove feels guilty. He was covering for Breck and me when everything went down in Syria that day. It's probably the only reason he still talks to me. Dove won't blame me for Breck because he blames himself. For Breck, and me as well.

Finally I get him off the phone and walk across the living room. I lean against the slider door that leads onto the back deck, and I look out at the darkness.

I can smell her on me. If I swallow, I can taste her sweetness. I look through the glass, out at the nothing of the night, and I can see her satiated smile. I like her smile. The way the one cheek curves. It doesn't look messed up to me. It looks funny, kind, and sometimes sly.

I bring my hand up near my face and inhale deeply, hoping to imprint the scent of her in my brain.

I'm such a sick fuck. A pathetic fuck.

I pull my right fist back, then punch the glass door. The fucking glass sheet actually cracks. The outer side of my right hand lights up like a blowtorch.

"Fuck me! FUCK!"

I walk over to the couch and sink down onto the rug in front of it. With a quick glance back over my shoulder—stairs are empty, thank fuck—I grab my hair and pull until my breaths are coming slower.

I can do this.

I can do this.

When she wakes up, I'll take her home, and after that, no more.

I look down at my throbbing hand. At least it's not my fucking cock.

It's over.

I'm a fucking Operator. I am not a coward.

Something in me tightens—feels like tugging. When I think about those little squirrel salt and pepper shakers. I can hear her voice say "BFF." Her smile is in my head. It's everywhere.

I tell myself to hate it. Hate her. Because there's not a different outcome. Not for us. There never was.

In the end, I hurt her. That's our fucking fate. This sweet girl with her bears and her little cabin. She's not mine. Not even for a night. Not even for a minute.

I walk upstairs again, and climb the ladder to the attic room. The little library is filled with amber light. There on the window seat, Gwen lies curled on her side, covered by a quilt. I stand there with my feet on the top step of the ladder, longing to go over to her.

I don't even need to touch her. I just want to see her. Not through a windowpane or through a fucking scope.

Of course, I don't go over to her. I head downstairs and pull my phone out of my pocket. Pull up Netflix, brew some coffee, get my .338. I step out onto the deck, leaving the door cracked so I hear her if she walks downstairs.

In the meantime, I can't let this—I can't let Gwenna—die so easy.

I sit on the deck for hours, scouring the internet. Licking her crumbs.

Gwenna White signs with Superior Model Management.
Gwenna White signs on for indie film *End of Day*.

Gwenna White signs with Forward Momentum Records.

"Gwenna White. Gwenna White. Gwenna White." My breaths are clouds that linger longer than I would have thought.

When the cold has set in, when there's nothing that I haven't read and memorized and weaponized, I click on the link from the *Breckenridge County Gazette*, a small news brief dated January 1, 2012.

Gwenna

When I open my eyes, the first thing I think is that I'm obviously still dreaming. I seem to be floating, blinking out over the dark forest. Then I look down at the soft cushion I feel under me, and I remember everything. The window seat. Barrett. *Barrett's mouth.*

I push myself up on one elbow as my eyes dart about the little attic room. He isn't here. What time is it? I turn back to the window, but the night gives nothing. I guess I fell asleep. Guilt wars with glee inside me. After a long moment, I decide to let glee win.

That happened.

Yeah…it happened. I didn't return the favor—damn me! But it happened. Barrett wrapped his arm around me when we were talking about his brothers. He said we were friends, and then I gave him that little kiss—a friendly kiss—and it made him go crazy.

Not just me.

Barrett, too.

I remember his big body stretched over mine. The way he shook. How tight his face was, and him saying it had been a long time.

Glee loses ground to guilt.

I need to find him and return the favor! I can't let this stand.

I toss the quilt off and discover I'm naked from the waist down.

"Damn." I can't stop a grin from spreading across my face as I hop down off the window seat. I shimmy into my leggings, do a little walk around the room, and feel my stomach flip as I look at the ladder.

Go get him!

I start down the ladder, then turn back around for my phone, which I find on the window seat. I check the time and am stunned to find it's almost 1 a.m.

Oh God. I'm a *taker.* Shame heats up my neck and face.

I wasn't even tired. Barrett was. I could see and feel how tired he was. I can't freaking believe I let him get me off and then I fell asleep. I start down the ladder, praying I'll find him asleep in his room. Preferably with his dick in hand.

His room is empty.

My chest feels tight as I descend the stairs. My feet feel heavy. This is so like me. Falling all over myself around him since we met, and then we get together and I screw it up.

I swallow hard as tears well in my eyes.

It's not as if I'm such a catch, either.

That evil part of me…She's hard to argue with.

I step into the den and find dying embers winking in the fireplace. *He wanted me. He wanted me.* I almost say it aloud, but then I notice the dark curtains over to my left. They're drawn over the slider door, the one that leads onto the stilted deck. I've never seen them shut before. I step closer and I feel a rush of cool air.

Because the door is slightly open.

I creep more closely to it, peel the curtain back, and—

"Oh."

It's just a squeak. My hand covers my mouth as I blink at the glass door. Someone hit it. Someone—Barrett—hit it hard enough to dent it. There's a fist-sized circle appearing white from all the little cracks, and all around it, thinner cracks ripple out.

He punched the door. Tonight? I try to remember whether the curtains were shut when we arrived here, but I can't.

Then it doesn't matter. I see movement on the deck: Barrett. He turns his head, and as I wrap my hand around the door handle, he steps over and pushes it open with his big arm, stepping inside in just jeans.

One of his hands is cradling his phone, and he looks somber. Tired.

"Barrett. I can't—I'm *so* sorry. I didn't mean—" Heat stings my cheeks. "I…fell asleep."

He blinks. "I let you sleep." He slides his phone into his back pocket and takes a few steps past me. Then he looks over his shoulder. "I can walk you home now."

"No…" I look into his eyes, expecting them to soften. "I want to…return the favor." I step closer to him, giving him a little smile and reaching for his arm. "I wanted to so much, I can't believe I didn't. You…I was so tired after. I want to do it now, if you want. Then maybe you'll be sleepy too."

His face hardens. I feel like a fish on sand. "I'm sorry. I'm embarrassed. Let's go to your room, and then I can walk home."

He shakes his head, then turns around and starts toward the kitchen. "Don't worry about it. I have some things I need to do."

He glances once again toward me as he reaches his door, and my throat tightens. He looks apathetic. Cold.

I don't notice I've stopped moving until he takes a black jacket off the coat rack beside the door and holds it out. "C'mon."

I move toward him as if underwater. Something changed. What happened? Does he think I'm selfish?

"Barrett…" I reach for his arm, raised as he holds the coat open for me. He flinches back.

Well…shit.

I stand there staring at the jacket. Barrett moves around behind me. "Put your arms in, Gwenna."

He regrets it.

I slide my arms into his sleeves. The jacket melds around me, cool, thin fabric. Some kind of Thinsulate shell thing.

My body pauses, awaiting his touch, so I am stunned to hear him turn a lock. I whirl around and frown.

"Is that a deadbolt?"

"Yes," he says. He sounds almost robotic.

I don't think the Haywoods had a deadbolt. Actually—I know they didn't. Why'd he change the lock?

He steps onto the porch and holds the door. My eyes find his and plead. His shift away. He lets go of the door, and I push through it.

"Cold out here," I murmur.

Maybe he mumbles something. I don't even know. My pulse is pounding; blood is racing through my veins.

He starts down the stairs, a step in front of me. I realize he's still shirtless. The wind blows at us from the direction of my house, and I can see a shudder race across his shoulders.

Sympathy for him. Or empathy. I don't know why. My stupid heart won't close its door.

It's awkward now; I'll have to break the ice again. His shoulders hunch against the wind. I tell myself I'll do that as long as I have to. Break the ice and break the ice, until he's thawed enough that I can always reach him.

When we're halfway down the front porch stairs, I touch his elbow. "Hey…"

His body stiffens as his eyes come reluctantly to mine.

"What's wrong?" I whisper.

"Why would anything be wrong?"

My blood runs cold. Even his voice is different. I feel sweat pop out along my hairline.

I wait a heartbeat for the swell of bravery I always feel around him—that extra little something that makes me feel the way I used to back before the accident, back when I was everything I hoped to be and I had never lost enough to make me second-guess myself. I look into his face and make myself available for when the feeling comes, so I can grab on and I'll know what to say, or what to do. But nothing happens.

He stares at me like I'm no one to him, and all I hear is what he said at my house.

"We're friends."

"Are we?"

I have a split-second memory of my knee rubbing between his legs. His fingers surging inside me. The recollection warms my blood, and brings with that physical sensation a small crest of glee.

I press my lips together and look over at him. His eyes meet mine, but quickly pull away. He keeps on down the stairs.

As I follow behind him, watching his broad shoulders and the sparseness of his movements, I can almost see him on a catwalk. I look down at my ankle. I can't even keep it straight. The foot turns slightly outward, as it has on stairs since the accident.

"Barrett?"

I don't even mean to speak. My voice just reaches out for him.

He turns, his striking brows bunched and his lips pressed flat.

"I wanted to say thank you."

As he nods and turns to step down the last stair, my throat thickens so much I can't breathe.

"What do you mean just Mr. and Mrs. Wesson?"

I watch my parents exchange loaded looks. My mother shifts positions at the foot of my railed bed.

"They weren't invited here," she says to my father. My mother sounds defensive. Angry.

Why?

"Am I not here?" My voice sounds duck-ish—the words all rubbery and cramped. Because my mouth won't work. They think I'm too doped up to notice, but they're wrong. I saw it yesterday when Jamie helped me to the bathroom.

I lick at it and the numbness there spreads to my chest.

"Sit back." My father strides over, his loafers clicking on the shiny tile floor. He puts his hands on my shoulders and looks into my eyes. "You know you're not supposed to get excited, Gwen." He steps back, giving me some space, and again, his eyes catch Mom's.

She looks at me and her spine stiffens. "The Wessons wanted to see you, sweetheart. They flew out on their own. Jamie told us what you told her last night. About not wanting guests. So they're going home. They'll visit later, when they can."

I blink a few times, and the pinkish walls behind my dad's face shift a little. "What about Elvie?"

I look from Mom to Dad, alarmed to see his jaw tighten. "He couldn't make it."

"Why not?"

My mother scoots up closer to me. "He had school," she says.

"Has spring break passed?" Tears pool in my eyes, because I realize I have no idea. I feel like an alien dropped here from Mars. One look down at my left leg, suspended in metal and casting, makes me feel like throwing up.

"It hasn't happened quite yet," Mom says.

My heart seems to lose its rhythm as sweat beads along my neck and hairline. "When did Elvie come?"

"He—" Dad starts.

"You were asleep," my mother says firmly.

Again, the pinkish-tinted ceiling seems to spin.

"Did…Jamie said…Dad, Elvie came here, right?" I draw a breath. My lungs can't seem to hold the right amount of air. My heart throbs as I struggle with my words. "He…came out those first few days," I say. I inhale. Exhale. My ribs ache. "He sat in the waiting room. They wouldn't let him in because…we aren't engaged."

"Yes." My mother's nod is emphatic.

My father blinks and casts his eyes down.

And I know. I know, I know, I fucking know.

"He hasn't come…"

"Gwenna, are you coming?"

I blink up at Barrett's tight-jawed face.

My eyes sting. "Oh," I murmur. "Right…" I step down off the last stair as he turns away from me.

"Italy," I murmur.

He turns. "What?"

I blink. "What?" I echo.

"You said something?"

I arch my eyebrows. "Nope."

But I'm acting. I realize now…I said that out loud.

Perfect.

Hello, PTSD. Nice to see you.

Next time I blink, Barrett's turning back toward me again. His eyes meet mine; they're hard and strangely urgent. He steps into the woods before me, and when I scamper to catch up, hand wraps around my wrist and tugs—as if he can't wait to get me home.

chapter two

Barrett

My fingers, gripping her arm, gentle almost as soon as I latch onto her. Guilt stings somewhere near the base of my throat. I want to wrap my arms around her, hold her close against me so she isn't cold. I want to take her to her room and—

NO.

Never again.

You know you can't. Stop thinking of it.

I lead her through the woods, stopping only to hold back a limb or take her elbow as she moves over a fallen log.

When we reach her porch, she scoops the bags of cookies up and steps up to the door, her hand already holding out the key. I stop at the bottom of her steps and wait.

She unlocks the door first, then turns slowly to me. I watch her gaze drag down my body. I can't miss noting where it lingers. I grit my teeth and fix my eyes on her face.

Say something to her.

The wind blows her hair around her pink cheeks—and she beats me to it. "Barrett?"

I have to open my mouth to get air past the knot in my throat. "Yes?"

"Is it...the way I look?" Her eyes open wide, as if they're filling up with tears and she's trying to keep them from falling.

"What?"

Her eyes glisten. "I think maybe you're just being moody. Hot and cold. Because of...whatever your reasons are. You might be mad because I fell asleep. But I can't help thinking—I should ask...Well, I look...different." She drags air into her lungs, her face a mask of misery. "I guess what I'm saying is, are you bothered by what happened earlier because you aren't really attracted to me? Because I'm...injured?"

Looking up at her, holding those cookies, clad in my huge coat, I feel my own eyes ache with heat and pressure. I can't stop my legs from climbing up her stairs, nor my hand gripping her shoulder.

"Look at me." The words are snarled—much rougher than intended. Her gaze blinks against mine. "That's what you think?" My heart pounds.

She presses her lips together.

My body feels heavy. My head feels light. Inside my veins, my blood runs hotter.

My finger finds the left side of her mouth: so soft. My jaw twitches as I look into her eyes. "Gwen. You think I care about this?"

Her brows arch: an unsure look.

Despite it all, I know I have to make her sure. I speak softly. "You think this—this little part of you—you think it bothers me? Would bother someone else?"

A tear falls down her round cheek, and my chest aches so much, I look down on instinct, checking for a wound. Of course, there's nothing visible.

"Open the door, Gwenna."

She drags her gaze away from mine and turns back to it. I try to inhale, but every part of me is buzzing and I can't slow down.

My eyes rake over her: the shape of her under my coat. I fist my hands as she pushes the door open.

More than anything in all my life, I long to scoop her up and press her up against me. Standing still—not doing that—It makes my chest ache.

You can't. It doesn't matter how you feel.

Gwenna steps inside her living room and turns toward me. Her face flickers with emotion: delicate and fragile. Vulnerable. Because I took what wasn't mine. I sought comfort from her. From day one, I've gotten in too deep with her. Tonight, I did the unforgiveable.

So turn around and go. Your course is set.

I try to tell myself that walking into the cabin behind her will lead to more hurt down the road—for both of us. Logic has no place within me right now, though.

I need to wipe it off her face: that look. And then I'll step away. I could end tonight on a high note, and then fabricate something: a long trip. After which I come back and pay my debt. Tonight, though—I could bowtie all this, leave her feeling beautiful and good.

Isn't that the least that I can do for her?

Gwenna sighs. "I just wish I knew what you were thinking. Earlier…I didn't mean to fall asleep. Or was that even it?" She puts her head in her hands. "I should shut up now. I know. If you don't want things to be—"

I go to her in one long stride and take her arms in my hands.

"Gwen." I look down at her face. "That little mouth…" I run my tongue over my own lips while my heart pounds. "You think I don't want you? That I don't want these lips…on every part of me?" My voice runs ragged. I swallow as I touch the corner of her mouth. Her eyes widen.

I stroke her lower lip, and my cock throbs.

"I could push you up against the wall—" I take her shoulders, turn her toward the nearest wall—"and rip these leggings off." My fingers pluck at the elastic waistband. One delves inside, stroking soft, hot flesh.

"I could kiss those lips and then I'd eat that pussy one more time. Does it have red curls? I know it does. I had wondered; now I know. I could push my cock inside you, Gwen. I'd push in deep—until it almost hurts it feels so fucking good. Until you can't move, and then you're mine to take, you're mine to please."

I wrap a hand around the back of her head, forcing her to look up at me. Her nipples jut against the fabric of her shirt. I twist one, groaning as my dick throbs.

"Do you know how long it's been?" She gasps and starts to pant. "It's been a long time, Gwen." I laugh, the mirthless sound of giving up. "I love this body. When we spar, I watch your tits—" I palm one now—"I watch your soft, round ass and want to sink my fingers into that plump pussy."

I cup her breast and stretch my hand down toward her swollen lips.

Her eyes slip shut, and anger throbs within me. That she'd give herself to me so easily. That she looks so wanton and relaxed. That this is what we could have had. It makes me crazy.

I press my hand against her, willing my probing fingers to be still. I press my mouth against her hair. "You said you trust me earlier. But you don't know me, Gwenna. You don't know if you can trust me." My fingers find her swollen clit, then part her soft, slick lips.

She rocks against me. "Yes," she moans. Her eyes open. They're glossy. Dazed. "I think...I can." She swallows and I prod her hot, wet center. I make her shudder—*just this once.*

I thumb her clit and push inside her with the tip of my finger. Her hips jerk. She makes a little "ahh" that I feel in my balls.

"Does anybody know you're seeing me? Does your best friend know you're taking risks? Because this body needs it so damn much?"

She shoves my hand away, her brown eyes hot. "It's not about me needing sex. You think I'm not embarrassed? Putting myself out there? Because I am." Her eyes glisten again. She jerks my hand out of her pants and takes a step back, until her back touches the wall. "I wish I *didn't* feel like this. You're impossible to read! I'm always off balance." She lets a big breath out and waves at the door. "I don't like games, but I like you and I don't know why. If it's too much or I'm pushing, if it's all me, then you should leave."

This is my out.

Take it.

I step closer. I cup her soft, hot cheek with my right hand and lean down, wanting very much to taste her lips.

"Why are you embarrassed, Gwenna?" I stroke her hair. "You've been kind. Compassionate. You're a good person. And beautiful." I stroke her cheek. "You know that, right? You're pretty. You'd make any man hard." I stroke her lip. I kiss it gently, licking at the left side of her mouth. She trembles, and I take her hand. I drag it down, cupping my hardness. "Feel that?" I rub her hand over my bulge and feel my knees weaken. My voice is rough. "That's all for you."

"Then why be mean?" Her eyes are dark pools. "Why are you taunting me? Come to my room, Barrett. If we both want to…"

She rubs my cock. I swallow back a groan.

"I want you," she whispers. "I don't think I've ever wanted anyone this much. Not just your body." Her hand caresses my erection, curving from my head down to my balls. She trails a finger over them and I moan. Then she presses her body against mine, wrapping her arm around my waist, pressing her cheek against my chest. "Barrett, please…"

"Oh, Gwen." Her fingers encircle the swollen head of me. I thrust lightly against her. "That's…such a bad idea." She rubs me, all the while, looking up at my face. "I can't tell you…what a bad idea it is…for you." I grab her wrist and try to fill my lungs with air. "Listen to me. Let go…and I'll go." Her hand sifts around my balls, playing lightly through my jeans. They draw up instantly, aching so much I start to shake. I can't help groaning as her other hand grabs my head and thumbs the rim.

I step away from her. My legs are shaking.

"What's wrong? I won't believe that you don't want it." She backs me into the wall and when she gets me there, she kisses the inside of my elbow, where I taught her to strike. I lace my left hand through her hair.

She finds my nipple and she nips it through my shirt.

"Barrett…*am* I safe with you?"

My heart stops. My blood whooshes in my head, making the room around her tilt.

"Don't think, just answer. Barrett—would you hurt me?"

She bites my nipple, and I hiss.

"Would you hurt me on purpose?"

Her hand unbuttons my pants and delves inside, right past the elastic of my boxer-briefs, not stopping until her hand is wrapped around my dick. I can't help myself: I rub against her soft hand.

"No. You wouldn't."

"No," I groan. She starts to stroke me.

"I don't care about the rest. Look at me." I do—for just a second— till my eyes shut. "Barrett—I don't care. Come with me to my room and let me make you feel good. Let me make you sleep. Unless you don't want me. Do you want me?"

"Yes," I moan, putting a hand over her hand. "But when I take you—" My jaw clenches. I'm so hard I can't think straight. "I don't know if I can... *Fuck*." I groan again as she encircles my head, feathering her fingertips over the rim, then tightening her grip as she strokes firmly down.

"Don't worry. You're all good." And with that terrible untruth, Gwenna leads me toward her room.

chapter three

Barrett

"Why do you think…I can't sleep?" I manage as we walk through her dark office. I clutch her arm as her hand moves between my legs. "What do you think…I remember?" My voice is hoarse with all my secrets.

Her hand squeezes my shaft. "It doesn't matter, Barrett. Don't push me away." Her free hand lifts my shirt, glides down my abs, and joins the one that's stroking me inside my boxer-briefs. I groan as she starts to work me with both hands, one pumping up and down my shaft, the other gently tugging on my sac.

"Fuck, Gwen—*Ohh.*" My balls draw up and I can feel my cockhead leaking. "You keep that up…" I pant in warning. She pauses in mid-stroke to kiss my bicep, then resumes her stroking, her hand squeezing tighter, stroking faster.

She knows just how I like it…on my dick. I try to catch my breath and find I can't. Her hand…

Gwenna's voice cuts through my heavy breathing. "That's right, baby. Come in my hand." She jerks my cock just right, making my hips tremble and my balls tighten. She fondles me there, lifting up and stroking just behind them.

"Fucking hell…"

Bliss billows through me, hot and potent. I thrust against her hands because I can't help it. I need…

I buck against her. Panic streaks through me, but I can't grasp it. I spread my legs and clench her shoulder. Groan.

"You made me come, so now it's your turn, Barrett. Keep your eyes shut just like that and think about my mouth on you… sucking." Her hand grips me underneath my head. "My tongue would lick just under here…" Her finger strokes around the rim. "Then I'd pull you into my mouth, where it's warm…and soft. I'd stroke my tongue right here—" She fingers the sensitive notch under my head, making my legs tremble. "Then I'd pull you out and lick underneath one more time and…flick my tongue over this little slit." She drags her thumb over it, and my body bucks.

I let out a loud moan.

"You're so big," she whispers. Her palm cups my head, twisting slightly as her other hand tugs on my balls. My shaft throbs, desperate for attention. I can feel my legs move, my weight shifting as I thrust my aching member at her.

"Gwenna…please."

"That's right," she murmurs. The hand around my head moves down my shaft, sliding toward the base. "If you…were in me…" She strokes up and down, making my balls bounce. "It would stretch me. I'd be…tight…around you."

Her hand plays under the rim of my head, stroking so light it should tickle…but instead it makes my legs feel weaker. "Oh fuck, Gwen…I'm gonna *come*…"

"That's right. I want to see you, Barrett…" Her words are whispered, warm against my chest. I feel my cock swell and stiffen further, pleasure building, moving through my belly, down my thighs. Her hand grips tighter, strokes me faster.

"Gwen—"

I think about her pussy, swollen, slick against my mouth. Her hand rolls my balls as the other strokes my head, and I come like a fucking cannon, throbbing once, then blowing in her hands.

A sound that's neither sigh nor groan and maybe part sob burbles from my throat. Then my eyes squeeze shut, heat fills my head, I put a hand over my eyes.

"Oh fuck." I start to tremble, feel the sting of bile in my throat. "Why'd you do that? *Gwen.*" I grip her forearm.

Her eyes find mine. "You didn't like it?"

I laugh. "Holy fucking—*Fuck.*" I pull away from her and hold my head. She grabs a tissue from her desk, and my eyes feast on her. Her cheeks are flushed. Her nipples push against the fabric of my jacket, which is stained from what we just did.

"Fuck." I pull my hair.

She pauses, hands reaching for me. "Are you mad at me?"

Her eyes are wide and innocent.

Because she doesn't know.

I stalk out her office door, and through the den. I hear her voice behind me as I throw her front door open. My legs are so weak, I sink down on her porch stairs, holding my head with both hands.

She doesn't know I can't stop now. I can't stop now. My dick is still hard. I can't breathe.

I feel her come around in front of me. Her little hands cup my knees. She's so gentle. I can feel the kindness emanating from her and it makes me want scream and tear my hair out.

"Barrett? Will you look at me?"

My eyes lift, involuntary.

"What's wrong, Barrett?" She strokes my thigh.

I laugh. I rub my eyes, shielding myself from her warm gaze with my fingers.

"If I went too far...I'm sorry. I thought...You were hard and I—That was the first time since..." I open my eyes and find hers wide, her face gone pale and earnest. "I'm scared with other people," she whispers.

I swear to God, I feel it all fall down around me. My resolve. My desperate barriers and all my longing—dead leaves scattered at her feet.

I stand up. *Walk away! Just walk. You can't stay here. You can't tell her. Don't keep lying. There is nothing you can do, you stupid fucker.*

And still—my gaze finds hers. "It's been that long?" My voice is low and soft, almost unrecognizable.

Her eyes go teary. "Please don't pity me. I just...I don't get out, you know? I'm stubborn, and I have my habits, staying here. I've gotten...bad at taking chances. I think over time it all got worse. I lose my nerve more every day and until you moved here I thought..."

"You thought what?" I rasp.

She blinks. A tear falls. "I don't know." She rubs her eyes. "I'm probably embarrassing myself. I think I did already." She looks down at her—*my*—jacket. Her face reddens, and another tear falls. "This is how I've always been. I get so dumb and reckless. It's been even worse with you." She turns around, her back to me, her face lifting so I think her eyes are on the treetops.

"I'm sorry."

I see her hands clutching her elbows. She's hugging herself.

Before I have to choose—to go to her or not—she turns to face me. "I'm the kind of person who gets carried away. I think tonight I did that and I won't do it again."

She takes my jacket off, then pulls it to her chest.

"I'll wash it," she says, moving toward her door. She turns around and looks me in the eye when she gets on the top step. "Still friends?" she asks.

She gives me a tiny smile, her tongue sweeping over her lower lip as it begins to fade.

This is my out.

This is the moment that I close this door. I tell a lie. My girlfriend died—the Burka-wearing one. Now is the wrong time. I'm a mess. Not well enough to get entangled. *Anything.*

Words are clogging in my throat; the wrong words. I swallow them back. I nod, hoping my eyes don't scream too loudly.

"Always."

chapter four

Barrett
September 20, 2011

Dove is at the highest point in our overwatch formation, on an outcropping above my head, when the call comes through the Porta Phone.

"Pack up shop and go back to the insert point," McVay tells him.

"Uhh...*what?*"

"You heard me." McVay is an asshole. "Get moving."

Over the mountain peak. Back to the field we ID'd back at base as our entry and exit point.

Dove doesn't tell McVay that the highest of all our high-value targets—a top-ranking al-Qaeda officer we've code named Ugly Fuck—has just shown up in the village down below us. Dove himself has not yet noticed this.

We've been waiting on Ugly Fuck for weeks up here in the barren Hindu Kush, a stark, 25,000-foot-elevation mountain range between central Afghanistan and northern Pakistan. Two of our team's best assaulters have been on the ground for the last four days, but we got no warning about Ugly Fuck's appearance, so they clearly didn't have the intel for it.

Ugly Fuck is on a tall camel, fifth in a long caravan of rocket mortar and AK-bearing beasts that's trickling into one of the most Taliban-friendly Pashtun villages.

During the thirty minutes I use to photograph Ugly Fuck's bearded mug and document his location, Dove struggles to signal me. I don't notice the pebbles he's lobbing at my head because my mind is in the game.

I pull some pale, dry-looking faux grass from my pack and stuff it in my camo cloak, then start the slow scuttle to Breck, due west and a little lower down the barren mountain face.

I don't want to risk electronic comm, not yet, and this is how we've planned things.

Dove is at the top left of our square, and I'm at the bottom left. Since Dove has comm on this mission, I'll rendezvous with Breck at the bottom right point of our square. Breck and I will make a plan, which Breck will take up to the square's top right corner—Bluebell—while I go up to Dove. Who, if things go correctly, will make a call to base to coordinate a backup plus withdrawal.

If we're on our game, this should be achievable in less than twenty minutes.

About the time Breck is laughing silently at the big, awkward bush scuttling up to him, Dove, whose sole mission at this point is telling us we have to leave, is finding my spot empty.

After a couple minutes, Breck and I determine a course of action and part ways, me returning to my spot, from which I'll head up to Dove, and Breck picking his way up a cliff face to inform Bluebell of our plans.

The square can work a variety of ways, but in this situation, this is our plan. McVay or not.

As it happens, I'm the last man back to my spot—after hiking up to Dove's spot, where the two of us traded deets. While I get back settled, Dove calls McVay and the rest of the head shed, seeking official permission to take out our HVTs and put in the order for a withdraw. From that point on, the four of us Operators communicate with hand signals.

Unless the group of Taliban in the village square stops logging equipment and something changes, Bluebell will take out Ugly Fuck. Breck ID'd two other high value targets, so Dove's asking the head shed about those guys. If we get permission to eliminate them, Dove will take one and I'll take the other.

I'll fire first, then scramble up toward Dove. He'll fire shortly before I reach him, and we'll head over the mountain's peak toward the withdraw point, while Breck hikes up to Bluebell and the two of them will scurry up behind us.

Three near simultaneous shots from three coordinates should confuse the enemy, and assuming our backup arrives in the prescribed timeframe, those guys can keep Taliban reinforcements from coming up the other side of the peak and spilling down over the summit onto us.

We've got a bunch of backup ready and waiting by a chopper for this very thing back at base, a mere thirty fly minutes away.

As I await Dove's go-ahead and watch Ugly Fuck and Co. unload their weapons, I start thinking about my brothers. I've got this bad feeling that the call Dove got was about one of the twins. They're still fucking teenagers, and both of them have cancer. I haven't seen them since February, right after Kelly was diagnosed. I did a cheek swab test in April to see if I could donate bone marrow to help cure one of them, but I wasn't a match for either of my little brothers.

Now the transplants are done. The boys are hanging in there. I try to call when I can, but we've been out here doing this for coming up on two months now. I asked the head shed for a short pass home, but since both boys are doing okay, they didn't want to grant it yet.

I look down at Ugly Fuck and hope the satisfaction of eliminating such a piece of shit will seem worth it if something happened to either of my brothers.

Dove signals me a few minutes later. Yes—take out the targets. But don't do it right now. Wait twenty-five minutes, unless Ugly Fuck moves out of range (in which case, we shoot and make a messy, risky withdraw).

The twenty-five-minute delay before taking out HVTs is almost unheard of. The reason for it: due to the planned—and now canceled—early withdraw McVay called about, the guys at base aren't ready and waiting in a chopper. So—take out the HVTs in twenty. Backup will, by that time, be twenty minutes away. Not ideal, I think, but not the worst. And then I realize, "Holy fuck."

I told Breck if Dove got the order to *not* eliminate Ugly Fuck immediately, I would let him—Breck—know within thirty minutes. Instead, I've been lying here thinking about my brothers.

By the time my gaffe is realized, Breck's already a third of the way to Bluebell, about to give Blue the order to fire more than half an hour before our backup is in place.

I realize this and I tell Dove. We start to head toward Bluebell.

Right about the time Dove and I near Bluebell and Breck, the camel crew starts moving. Breck is right by Bluebell. They decide to aim for Ugly Fuck—and Bluebell hits him. The camel caravan scatters.

Not five minutes later, as we scramble for the withdraw point, fire starts coming down from the upper ridge of the mountain. Taliban militia from another village. Fuck, they got here *fast*.

By the time our withdraw chopper sets down in a small field on the back side of the peak, the four of us are surrounded on all fucking sides.

Bluebell takes a bullet to the shoulder, but he doesn't let that stop him from taking out a dozen Taliban fighters. Breck gets pinged in the calf and catches some shrapnel in his left forearm, but he never goes light on the trigger either. Dove covers us all and takes out probably fifteen of the fighters on the high ground. I take out another dozen or more before we manage to crest the ridge. At the center of the field in front of us is a bird: a beautiful Black Hawk that is a welcome sight to all of us.

I'm in the rear—it's only fair, since I fucked up this gig—so when one fucker rises from the dead to spray the field with bullets, my brother Operators have already made it to the bird.

I hit the ground, waiting for Breck, who's on a drop rope, to cover me. That's how I get hit in the back. The bullet gets me in the liver.

I'm stabilized at base and flown to Landstuhl Hospital in Germany.

I don't remember much, but according to Breck later, I ask about my brothers every time my eyes are open.

In the Landstuhl ICU twelve hours later, I wake for the first time after surgery.

"My brother. Which one?"

Breck's eyes go red and wet, and through the veil of sedatives, I feel something sharp.

He tells me Lyon died the eighteenth. Unexpected. All the chemo they gave him fucked his heart up.

Breck lifts my IV-laden arm and wraps his hand around it. He leans down and puts his forehead on the mattress, still holding my arm.

Lying there in Landstuhl, watching my best friend's bowed head with blurry eyes, I remember why I failed to get to Breck before he left to give the okay to Bluebell.

I was thinking of my brothers.

The mission went wrong because the call that came summoning us back to base—triggered by the call that informed the base my brother died—got me distracted, worrying about my brother. Worrying about my brother got me shot.

Breck tells me the funeral is the twenty-first. Being shot keeps me from getting there in time.

I try to wrap my head around the fucked up circularity of fate.

I tell no one—certainly not Breck, who brings me fast food and spends hours laughing his ass off as I play Assassins' Creed doped up on opiates—but for the first time in my life, I use pain like a salve.

Action and consequence. Isn't that life?

I should have fought harder to get back stateside. I should have seen Ly. I should be there now with Kelly.

I embrace the gunshot as my punishment.

When, a week later, I'm discharged back to Afghanistan because our guys are getting their asses handed to them by the angry Taliban, I fight like I never have before. For Lyon. For me.

Blood drips down the backdrop of my dreams.

chapter five

Barrett
November 5, 2015

It's not hard to tell myself this is the best thing for her.

I'm still waiting on the house to close. Mallorie the realtor says she thinks it'll be next week. Next week, I'll be glad I did the right thing. Actually, I'll probably still feel guilty. But at least I won't have fucked things up worse than I did already.

Gwenna last touched me on Monday.

Tuesday, I call in a favor and have Bluebell's phone tracked to a little highway in bumfuck Illinois. I get a chuckle when, that night, he spends three hours in a country music bar, then drives his luxury rental car to a nearby roach motel, where he stays for four hours before driving to the next Hampton Inn: the only place stateside where fucking Blue will lay his carefully gelled head.

I wonder when he'll be off leave. I could find out if I answered Dove's calls—but I don't.

Dove and his fucking writer wife.

I spend Wednesday burning all the Polaroids I have of Gwenna in the bedroom fireplace. I keep one in which she's sparring on the foothill behind her house. Most of the days I've been here, that's the way I spent my time: watching her practice her Taekwondo.

She looks pissed off in the shot. She's got her arms out and her hands balled into fists. Her hair is swept up in a ponytail, but much of it has come loose and hangs in her face. In the image, her left ankle looks uncomfortable and stiff. I remember in the moment after I took the picture, she said "shit-fuck" a bunch of times and kicked a stump.

I watch the other pictures burn, and tell myself she won't always have so many shit-fuck moments. I have plans to ease her pain.

In the light of morning—I still watch her lights come on: the bedroom first, study, then den—I can sometimes tell myself I didn't really hurt her. I don't even know her. Or maybe I do know her, but it never was reciprocal. So how much could it really hurt—our two trysts that one night?

I focus on the fact that she felt comfortable with me. Didn't she say that? I was her first since what happened. *First to what*, a small voice mocks. I look down and find myself hard. Always hard now. Never satisfied.

In the wee hours, I'm honest about Gwenna to the point of pain. I know that she will hate me. In that first moment, especially, she'll feel betrayed and maybe even used. She'll never understand. Of course not. I will always be the end of all things good. The grim reaper. I will always be a thief, and she my victim.

I put a coaster over the photo I saved. Looking at it makes me feel like sucking on the barrel of my .38.

Thursday sometime after midnight, I slip into sleep and wake up screaming with an aching boner. My battered mind is full of Gwen and Breck and diapered children bleeding on the dry Iraqi dirt, their mothers wailing as our convoy rolls by. When I wipe my eyes and look outside from where I'm sitting in the armchair, I find it's snowing.

Snow here is a rarity. I can't help but see it as a sign.

Gwenna's bedroom light comes on at 4 a.m. I watch her windows through my scope, unmoving until 6, when she lights up her study, then the den.

I take a shower. As I trim my beard, my mind drifts off the road and tumbles down to what will happen after. After. After.

Dove calls a short time later. He, too, wants to know.

With a towel tucked around my waist, I check my phone and find Blue cutting down toward Kentucky. So he's coming my way. Why would I think any different? Dove told him what was up and Blue will spend his leave time checking up on me, going back to wherever the fuck they are now—North Korea?—with his pretty reassurances. With the illusion of control.

I tell myself there's nothing to do for now besides watch Gwen. When, at lunch time, I give in and jack off to the memory of her hands, I feel almost ill after.

When, in the late afternoon, she treks up the sleet-wet foothill toward the clearing, I feel stricken. The past two nights, she sparred beside her porch a little before 6—waiting for me.

I take my Polaroid and my scope and hurry after her. I tell myself I need to see her face clearly. That's all. I find my old spot on the high ground easily. It's even easier to see her than it was when I arrived in Tennessee; many of the trees are bare now.

I think she looks okay at first. Her forms are strong and forceful, and her face is clenched and angry.

Good.

I can breathe while I watch her. I can almost smell her. Then she folds her body from a kick into a crouch. She brings her hands up to her face and sits down on the slushy ground. She holds her head and sobs.

I watch the whole time.

Gwenna

Thursday night, I go to dinner with Jamie and Niccolo, who's flown to Knoxville for two days to meet with a new movie financier.

Jamie doesn't know what happened between Barrett and I, but she knows something did, because I've been in hiding. The thing about being in hiding is, when she asks what's up, I always tell her nothing.

I'm not sure what she expects from dinner, but as we both listen to Niccolo talk about the movie's budget and I pick at my crab bisque, I get the sense that she's annoyed.

As we drive from the restaurant, in downtown Gatlinburg, and toward my land, I feel guilty. They drove here to take me out to dinner, and I was lousy company.

Near the road to my house, Niccolo gets out to pump some gas and Jamie turns around in the driver's seat.

"You better tell me what happened with Barrett."

My eyes widen; dammit! I un-widen them, but it's too late. It was too late before she even mentioned Barrett. Jamie always knows.

I look down at my boots. "Nothing."

She laughs. "I think you like these theatrics."

I roll my eyes. "Well, duh." I give her my old sad-mysterious look from my modeling days and remain mum, then as Niccolo opens his door, I say, "We messed around. He didn't like it."

Jamie's eyes bug out. "You better call me," she mouths as Niccolo buckles.

When they drop me at my house, I invite them in for wine or absinthe, but they decline, in almost perfect unison. It seems as if they planned it, and although I know they didn't, I go inside feeling rejected.

I've tried so hard to keep my head above water since that night. So hard. And I've…well, I wouldn't say succeeded exactly. But I haven't called any of my people crying. Day-to-day life has proceeded mostly as usual, with the exception of the sob-fest I had the night he left and another meltdown while I was practicing my Taekwondo and HTH alone up in the clearing.

I set my purse down on the couch and drift into my bedroom. I kick my boots off and walk into the bathroom, where I turn on the light and stand there staring at myself.

He isn't wrong. I *am* still pretty. From the right side. If I'm not smiling. Maybe pretty isn't even right. I'm very striking. It's impossible not to know this when you've made a living—even briefly—off your face. My hair is coppery, a little darker than your average red. It's fine but heavy, with a wave that can be straightened or gelled into looking curly. Like Barrett, I think with an ache, I have nice, high cheekbones; striking eyes—amber-brown, with brown brows rather than the pale ones some redheads have; a nondescript nose; smooth skin; and fuller-than-average lips.

I smile and watch the pleasant face in front of me twist garishly. Snarile: it's snarl and smile. Because when I smile and the left side of my mouth hangs down while the right side curves, it looks like a snarl. It looks gross and garish. Beauty lies in a certain type of symmetry. I of all people would know.

I shut my eyes and rub my temples, feeling like a freak. "Why do you even do this?" I hiss into the silence of the small room. "Who even cares about your stupid face?"

But maybe Barrett cares. Maybe that's the problem. He said he didn't mind my mouth, and I concede, as I stare into my own sad eyes, that maybe he doesn't—care about my mouth. But right before he left, wasn't I telling him how long it's been for me?

Maybe he didn't want the responsibility.

Maybe when I jacked him off, he realized it didn't feel right. Maybe he'd been lonely and started lusting after me and the second he indulged, the attraction went *kaput.*

I sigh and drag my sad self to the kitchen, where I drink a third of a bottle of Pinot Grigio alone at my table and remember: his jacket is in the dryer. I'm usually not an emotional drinker, but holding the jacket in my arms makes me feel even sadder than before. I spread the jacket over my legs and pour myself another big glass. I just want to drink until I'm sleepy. Then I'll go crawl into bed. Maybe I won't have dreams tonight.

I've always been a sucker for a really bad idea, so after a few more swigs straight from the bottle, I know what I'm going to do.

I get another bottle from the pantry—this one Pinot Noir— and don his jacket—why not?—then slip into my dark brown Uggs and start off through the woods.

It's cold as hell, which makes my head feel slightly cloudy. I trip on a stump and snag his jacket on a limb.

"Shit!"

But I don't see a tear.

As I drift through the trees, my heavy feet feeling detached from the part of me that's floating, I note how big his jacket is on me and feel the ghost of snow falling around me.

"Oh my God, you're Jessica from End of Day*!" I nod and set my items on the Breckenridge General Store's counter. The cashier, a young girl, turns around, cupping her mouth before she bellows, "Come here, Silas! Jessica from* End of Day *is here, and she's buying one of your dad's gardenias!"*

A high school guy plods up. He's tall, with white-blond Justin Bieber hair. He sticks his thin hands in his pockets, cool and poker-faced, while the short blonde cuts her eyes at him. When he doesn't fall down at my feet, she widens her eyes at him. "Can you believe it?"

Never meeting my eyes, he gives her a sideways smile and murmurs, "No."

It doesn't take an idiot to see this boy has my Abercrombie pool party stuff, or my Burberry nothing-under-the-jacket campaign bookmarked in his spank bank. Which means it's time to change the subject before we all end up embarrassed.

"Your dad grows the gardenias you guys sell?" I ask him, hoping to put everyone at ease, as well as steer the subject away from the movie. I'm a singer, not an actress—although I am proud of the movie.

The guy nods and finally, he looks into my eyes.

"It's a kind of insanity," he says, revealing a retainer than makes his voice sound—well, like he's got something in his mouth. "They won't survive for long in someone's yard. So they're just house plants."

I hover a fingertip over one of the satiny white leaves, mostly so I can break the stare he's now aiming at me. "It's probably insanity to buy one when it's snowing this hard. I'm not even staying at my own house." I smile at them before I realize my publicist would smack my mouth for giving details.

"Jessica," the girl squeals, jumping up and down.

I tug Mr. Madison's big black jacket down around my ankles before reaching in his huge pocket to grab my wallet out.

I stumble back a little, my gaze catching on Barrett's porch light. Whoa…I don't remember climbing up the stairs. I rub my forehead.

"Stupid Gwenna. No drinking with a TBI, you dumbass," I murmur.

People who've had a brain injury are encouraged not to drink, but I've never really heeded those warnings, probably because I don't usually get drunk. I look down at the wine bottle in my right hand.

I should leave.

I blink a few times at the door, and then, as if by my command, it opens.

chapter six

Gwenna

My heart drops straight down to my feet and out my boot soles, and I wobble back a little.

Barrett stands there shirtless in the doorway, looking dazed in rumpled gray sweatpants, like he just rolled out of bed. My eyes wander down his legs before I jerk my gaze up to his face. I blink a few times, just to keep it there.

He blinks back, then frowns, his thick brows pinching. "Gwenna." He sounds slightly hoarse; perhaps surprised.

I swallow. "Hi." I laugh—this awful, awkward sound that's not a laugh at all. I raise my hand but can't manage to follow-through with an actual wave. I just stick it up like I'm taking an oath. I laugh again, a more authentic laugh that's laced with panic and self-loathing. "Hey."

My face is so hot now, I expect to catch on fire at any moment.

Barrett's brows scrunch further as he peers down at me. "Are you okay, Gwenna?"

I nod, although it makes him tilt a little, back and forth, like the needle of a compass.

"I brought wine," I whisper, "but…I think I'm going to go."

The door opens a little more and Barrett steps onto the porch. I feel a dizzying sense of déjà vu. Or maybe I'm just dizzy.

"Why?" He brings a hand up to his eyes, as if the moonlight is too bright.

I cradle the wine closer and frown up at him. Does he think I'm crazy, showing up here unannounced? I blink a few times and notice he looks…weird. Kind of washed out. His cheekbones seem too stark. His dark scruff looks more beardy than normal, and his eyes are wreathed by dark circles.

Worry makes my stomach fizzy. I frown up at him. "Are you sick?"

Instead of answering, he reaches for the wine bottle, and in my buzzed state, I don't notice that I let him have it until he's reading the label.

I stuff my hands in my pockets—his jacket pockets—which reminds me why I came here.

"I came to give your jacket back."

I close my eyes—because really, what the hell was I thinking, coming over here like this?

When I open them, I find him looking at me with his head tilted slightly to one side, his striking features schooled into a kind and understanding look. The one that says whatever's going on with me, he wants to know about it.

"Why don't you come in?" he asks after a moment.

He beckons me toward the door, then steps into the house. For a moment, I debate following, but of course I have no choice. I feel like I can't breathe, but damned if I don't follow him right in. I step over to the island at the center of the kitchen, where he's set my wine bottle, and I look from it to his face.

"You should have some."

"Would you like that?" His eyes cling to mine—so intense I feel almost hypnotized.

I nod, still holding his gaze. I have this distant urge to say more, but my brain and my mouth can't seem to sync up.

Barrett arches his brows in answer, then turns to get two wine glasses out of a cabinet. He sets them by the wine bottle, then turns his back to me again.

I'm aware, as I watch the gorgeous ripple of his back and shoulder muscles, that even though I can't seem to resist his presence, I can still have options. I was once an actress, after all. So I can play this straight, and act the way I feel, and let him see me—the real me, with all my soft spots. Or I can build a wall and let him see me climb behind it—an option I realize isn't good because it would show how much I care.

And I do care, I realize as he walks around the island, opening and closing various drawers. Being in his presence means looking to him, and then away, and back to him, and then away again; every time my eyes land on him anew, my poor heart bursts like a Roman Candle. The feeling is intense. Proprietary. And so, so, so misplaced.

I take a deep breath as he sifts through another drawer, and I decide I'll aim for Gwenna Lite. I'll try to act the same way I always have, but from a couple of steps back.

You can do that.

I stare at the ink on his back and shoulders, trying on the idea of Barrett as my friend. It doesn't fit. It doesn't fit because I'm bursting out of it.

He turns back to the island with a corkscrew and a funny, flat-lipped look for me. I can't quite interpret it. As he grabs the wine bottle with his left hand, hugging it against his chest, and works the corkscrew with his right, I watch his face, but only for a long second. The calculation in that move makes me aware my buzz is fading.

I look away from him, out at the living room, where I notice there's a fire cracking in the big, stone fireplace. I wonder what he did tonight. If it was good. I imagine weeks and months and years of him living next door. Barrett—my friend.

And I realize it was bullshit—me thinking we could just be friends. This is illogical. Intense. Obsession. All the crazy, reckless instalove I thought was for other people...Nope. I guess it's like a lightning strike. Hits hard and fast, and other than the matter of where I place myself—in line of that violent streak or out—there's nothing I can do about it.

My stomach twists and I try not to watch his arms move as he works the cork out of the bottle.

I exhale slowly. I'm not proud of my reaction to him, but now at least I can be honest with myself. I need to try to stay away until my feelings wane.

I feel his gaze on my face and I shift my eyes back to his. *Steady, Gwenna.* I manage it: a steady, neutral look; just friends. I'm holding my breath, waiting for his gaze to shift, to stop pouring electricity through me, but instead his eyes seem to get hung up with mine. Heat races over my face, and when I just can't take it anymore, I jerk my gaze away.

Barrett

It's taking me forever to get the cork out of the bottle. Because my fucking hands are shaking. Fuck me.

One minute I was ranging around the living room, stoking the fire, chasing my racing thoughts, trying to decide whether to clean my McMillan TAC .338 or go outside and have one of the Marlboros I found under an ice pack in the freezer. The next second, I hear heavy footfall through the partially open kitchen window and I look out and see her.

Gwenna in my jacket. Gwenna with a goddamned bottle of wine.

The house hasn't closed. It's not time to make my move. I have nothing for her, nothing but a bunch of shit she doesn't need or deserve. So you might think I'd exercise intelligence. Back up my own decision to take a big step back by not answering the door.

Instead, I heard her footsteps on the porch and started sweating. My head pounded. My throat stung and tightened, and although I circled the couch two times before I went to her, I found I didn't have the willpower for three.

So there is Gwenna. Gwen with wine. Here she is in my kitchen, swallowed by my jacket, glassy-eyed from drinking whatever I could smell on her before she came inside. Her cheeks are tinged with pink, the way they always seem to be, and when she thinks I'm not looking, she's chewing on her lower lip.

Troubled. Plain enough to see.

So why did she come here drunk with wine in hand? Said she should go, then frowned and told me that I look like shit, then came inside and told me I should have some wine.

If I didn't know better, I'd think we'd reversed roles and Gwenna had a mind to take me out.

Well—I might if this fucking cork wasn't stuffed so fucking tightly in the bottle. I look up at her, and as I work the cork out, using my left arm to hold the bottle since my hand won't work, I think of big things stuffed in little spaces, my cock, Gwen's cunt; I wonder what she feels like underneath my jacket, if her skin is warm, if her pants have an elastic waist or button and zipper. I think of hauling her over to the couch and finding out. My tongue sweeping through her sweet, slick, puffy lips, and then—

I'm hard.

Fuck.

I try to think of what I'll have to do to her. I think of Gwen in pain, of that betrayal in her eyes, and...I'm still fucking hard.

Finally, the cork pops free. I pour a glass for each of us and Gwenna takes hers, looking more spooked than I've ever seen her. As if she can hear my thoughts and knows just what a fuck I am, and knows that she should go.

I drain my glass and watch her, daring her to go.

Go now—while you can.

The way I'm looking at her has her flustered. As if I care. I don't. I like it. I let my gaze linger on her pretty face until her soft, smooth skin is cherry red. Until she takes my jacket off, revealing a light green sweater and dark gray pants that, from where I stand, seem to have a button and a zipper.

"I—" she starts.

I pour more wine into my glass, causing her to bite down on her lower lip again. "I'm going to go now." She looks over my shoulder, at the clock, I realize, following her gaze. "It's almost eleven o'clock. I shouldn't have come too late."

Inside my head, it burns and roars. My wants and needs and shoulds; desire and discipline.

Protect her.

Have her.

Soothe her.

Banish her.

I even think of getting on my bike and driving off, just riding far, far, far away until she isn't near enough to touch and smell. Until I'm not so tempted I feel like I can't breathe.

I try to swallow, loosen up my throat. Around my glass's stem, my fingers clench.

My gaze rips up and down her. What's so special about her? Of all the women, why this one?

I try to focus on her mouth: the defect. I look at the left side of her mouth and think of what it represents and how it looks—all things that should repel me. I think about her ankle, about the scars I felt on her silk-soft belly as I ate her pussy. I try to tell myself it's not even *me* she wants. She'd take any company, perhaps.

Or maybe it's my body. I see the way she looks at me. She wants my abs, my chest, these shoulders that are waning every day I don't work out. I can't work out, not for more than an hour or two at a time. I'm so low on sleep, it makes my heart beat fast, and then I think of Ly and end up with my head between my knees.

I conjure an image of myself hugging the toilet bowl—and crying. What woman wants a man who cries every time he falls asleep? What woman wants someone who's seen a child bleed out and walked away, who's choked on smoke that billows up off burning corpses?

I can feel her hugging me at her house, on the couch that night. The night I should have realized I can't do this with her. I can't creep so close to her. The ground begins to crumple and I slip and fall.

"Anyway…" She steps to the counter, lays my jacket on it. Her brows lift as her eyes roll down me. "I hope you have a good rest of your night."

She turns toward the door and takes a small step toward it.

"Hey—wait."

Her feet stop moving and she looks over her shoulder.

"Don't you want to…come sit down?" I motion at the couch and watch the indecision flit across her face.

"Umm, I don't—"

"C'mon." I step toward her, hand out. "Just for a few minutes."

What are you doing?

I close the distance between us, all thoughts silenced by the rush of blood between my ears and my loud heartbeat. Distantly, I hear myself say, "I want to ask you something."

"What?"

"About business property. In downtown Gatlinburg," I lie.

Her brows lift, and she turns a little more toward me. "You're buying something in town?"

I nod. I can feel the pressure in my chest ease as I watch her face…the interest on it. Words pour from my mouth, unplanned and somehow also calculated. "I'm opening a martial arts place, I think. If I can find a good storefront."

I watch her frown, then swallow. She looks stricken. "Oh. I—didn't know."

"It's a new idea," I blather—even though it's not. It was always an option I'd considered, part of the larger plan to get her taken care of. "I don't know the area, but I've looked at a few places. I was hoping you could take a look at a few of the listings and share your thoughts."

Her brows draw even more tightly together. "Right now?"

I nod, and feel the fist just under my throat loosen. "I'm going tomorrow to see more."

She looks at me, then quickly down, licking her lips. "Okay. I guess that would work."

chapter seven

Gwenna

He looks relieved for a long moment, and then puzzled. Maybe I'm giving him a wide-eyed look, because right then he laughs—that chuckle I love, his striking face gone soft and gentle. "Gwenna…I won't bite you."

He holds his hand out. "Come with me."

I look down at his hand. My body starts to sing, and a scared kind of anger simmers in my chest. "You know…you don't owe me anything. Like…hanging out. From my angle, things are fine between us." I take a small step back, away from his hand, and struggle for something to tack on. Something about being neighbors. But I can't think of anything to say to frame our experience in significance.

We sparred. We messed around one night. The end.

It's a painful almost.

I shake my head and look back toward the door. I can't even trust myself to sit on the couch with him. He could spread me on the floor right now and I would let him have me. I have never, ever felt this way—and I'm not sure I like it anymore.

The dazed pain in his eyes is enough to make me take another step back.

"I'm sorry," I whisper.

He shakes his head. His eyes squeeze shut. He bows his head and rubs his forehead with his fingers, letting out a long, unsteady breath.

"I messed things up." His eyes flash briefly up to mine, but they sink quickly to the floor.

"What do you mean?" My stomach feels like someone turned it inside out.

He blows another long breath out and shakes his head again. Through the barrier of his fingers, I can see his eyes are shut.

He turns away from me. I watch his shoulders rise and fall... and rise...and fall. He walks over to the couch and puts his hands on the spine, letting his head hang in between his outstretched arms.

I messed things up. So...he cares? Is that what that means? My heart races. I step closer to him. Whether I'm responding to his obvious distress or creeping closer because I want to be near him—for my own selfish purposes—I can't be sure.

When I get within arms' reach, he turns around, propping his hips against the couch's spine. His eyes on mine are gravely serious. His face is tense.

"What's the worst thing you've ever done?"

My stomach flips. "What do you mean?"

When he doesn't answer, I, too, lean against the couch. I look at him, and find his eyes trained on me. I can't read them, but there is something about his gaze that makes me feel compelled to answer.

I exhale and look from him down to my boots. "My childhood cat. Sugar." I look out in front of me before my gaze gravitates to his. "She lived to be seventeen in human years. Spent most of them very healthy. The day we put her to sleep, I told my parents I had a final exam. I could have gone there...to the vet where they were…" I shake my head. "But at the time, I didn't think I could. Do it." I seek his gaze and find it gentle. "Then my Dad died suddenly, and more than anything on earth, I wished I could say bye to him. It's funny how that works, I think."

When he doesn't answer, just continues looking at me, I swallow. "Why'd you ask?"

He shakes his head. There's something weird about his eyes. Like…he's not blinking. He closes his eyes, his hand clenches, and I can see his shoulders rise, his chest expand, as he tries to inhale. The tendons in his neck stand out. He holds his breath a second, then his Adam's apple bobs.

And it's not rocket science. He doesn't want to look at real estate. I think he just wants me to stay. Instead of alarm bells—the kind that should alert me to protect myself—all I hear is the fast thud of my heart behind my ribs.

Here I am again, I realize. Totally ensnared. *But you could go*, I tell myself.

I look at him. At his pale face. *What do you owe him to be here?* But it's just futile.

I tell myself I won't stay long. Just long enough to see what's going on with him, and then I'll go.

As for right now…I reach out and take his hands—and it feels good. So good I almost shut my eyes to relish it. He shifts our fingers so his hands are cupping mine, then bows his head again.

I stroke his fingers. "Tell me, why'd you ask?"

I watch his shoulders rise as he inhales.

I swallow. "I think I know."

His eyes, so cold and hollow, shift to mine.

"You're having PTSD issues. Is that it?"

He lets a slow breath out, then drops my hands and walks around the couch and sits. I watch him lean over his lap and hold his head, and then I can't stand it anymore. I reach over the couch and lay my palm on his warm back. I feel his muscles twitch under my hand.

"It's okay." I rub in little circles like my mom would do when I was little. I'm rewarded with an easing of the tension in him. My hand trails up his spine and brushes the dark curls at the nape of his neck.

"Why'd you come?" The words sound breathy.

I stroke his neck, my hips digging into the couch's back as I lean over him. "Because I had your jacket. And I wondered how you were," I say quietly. It's not untrue. "I have PTSD too, remember? From my accident. I know it's probably nothing like yours, but I can empathize a little bit at least. I can't stand to think of you feeling that way. Whether we're friends or neighbors or whatever. Whether...anything with us."

The fire crackles in the wake of my soft words, and Barrett leans over his knees, hands in his hair as if he's tugging.

I see his ribcage expand without the rise and fall of his shoulders. I don't know how exactly, but I can tell from the movement that he can't get air into his locked-up lungs. He shifts back, lifting his arms off his knees, resting his head against the couch's spine. Again the low, hollow inhalation. He lets out a little groan and starts to pant a little.

Shit. I come around in front of him and kneel there at his feet. I reach out slowly. Take his hands. I scoot a little closer on my knees, then gather his big hands against my chest, pressing them gently against the warm skin just above my breasts. I wrap one of his hands around my throat and inhale deeply. "Breathe with me, okay? Count to five slowly as you breathe in. Hold it for a second. And then count to eight as you exhale."

chapter eight

Barrett

I can't do it. Not tonight. Maybe not ever.

You can.

You will.

You don't have a choice.

I inhale.

Exhale.

Underneath my hand, I feel her warm, satiny throat move as she does the same. I smell her fruity lotion as I inhale; try to do it slowly.

"That's right." Her right hand holds my larger, half-curled left one tenderly against her collarbone. Despite not looking at her face, I'm pretty sure I feel the kindness of her gaze—just like I always do when I'm with her.

"Just breathe when I count. Okay? Exhale and hold for...one Mississippi, two Mississippi..." She counts to five, and I'm unable to do anything but breathe in time with her words.

"You're Operators now. You have to manage your anxiety. Most of that is in the breathing."

Shame moves through me in a sting of heat. I lose track of her counting, then try to grab a few, more shallow breaths to catch back up. It doesn't work. My lungs feel like they're shrinking. I feel my hands twitch.

"Do you have a paper bag?" her soft voice asks.

I shake my head, hating myself for this.

Her left hand on my right one presses gently. "What about some Xanax?"

I shake it again.

"That's okay." After a moment, she lets my left hand go and joins me on the couch. I feel her small, soft body as she moves in close beside me. Her free hand closes on my shoulder, urging me closer. But…I can't.

Gwenna scoots closer to me, until she's almost in my lap. She wraps a soft, warm hand behind my head and urges me to lean against her. This time, my mind is so fuzzy, my lungs are so damn tight, I can't fight her. My face presses in between her chin and shoulder.

She inhales.

"You feel me breathe?" She wraps an arm around my shoulders—or tries to. I'm too wide for her to get it all the way around me, so she settles, pressing her small palm in the center of my back.

"Relax against me. Listen to my heartbeat. If you were to pass out—not that you will; worst case scenario…I'll just hold you till you wake up."

I manage to get a tiny breath.

"Good," she whispers. She relaxes just a little too; I feel the softness of her chest against my pecs. "Just breathe when I do." Her hand rubs my back.

I squeeze my eyes shut. I feel a wave of pressure build behind them. *This is wrong.* A fast, hard shudder jerks me. Gwenna holds me tighter.

"You can…go now." I inhale with effort. Lift my head and blink, ignoring the hollow feeling behind my eyes. "I just need to sleep, I think."

Her brown eyes are warm pools of concern. Her hand slides from behind my neck up to my shoulder, then strokes down my triceps.

"When's the last time you slept?"

Her hand wanders to the crease inside my elbow, fingers playing so gently, it causes goosebumps on my skin. Sound escapes my throat on a soft exhale.

Fuck. I lean away from her as my dick twitches. My heart is pounding so hard, I can hear the blood whoosh in my head.

"This didn't used to happen," I rasp. I didn't plan to speak, but suddenly it's vital to me that she know.

I feel her nod. "It's okay. It's just anxiety. Something must have built. Bothered you for a while and then snowballed. It can happen to anyone."

I shake my head. I'm not like other people. I'm not *anyone*.

Do it now. This would be the perfect moment.

My eyes throb, then sting.

Her hand touches the side of my neck. "I'm so sorry, Barrett."

I spread my legs and lean down, holding my head.

I try to think about the truth of things between us. It should be more than enough to shut me down, but I'm so fucking tired and weak. Gwenna wraps her arm around my shoulders, and my dick gets harder.

I sit back, shift so that I'm facing her. My hand goes for her breasts, then, at the last minute, slides up her neck, into her hair. My fingers curl into a fist.

"You need to go," I mumble.

"Why?"

With no forethought, my hand snatches hers and drags it in between my legs, pressing her palm against my hard cock.

Pleasure ripples through me, and I hear her soft inhale.

"This is what you do." I push her hand against me as I say it. When she doesn't move—in fact, I think her hand rocks up against my aching length—I pull her arm away and bolt up off the couch.

She looks frozen there, her brown eyes wide, her cheeks afire.

"It's wrong. You don't need this." I can feel the color draining from my face at just the thought of what I could do with her. With Gwenna White. *If I fucked Gwenna White…*

Her lower lip is caught between her teeth. She releases it, licking that succulent lip with the tip of her tongue as my dick throbs and the scene takes on a surreal sheen.

"Maybe I do." She gives a little laugh. "Maybe I need it even worse than you do."

Her words make my heart beat hard: it's like a gong is being hit, and I can feel the vibrations all through me.

I shut my eyes. She doesn't know. She doesn't know that I'm a wolf in lamb's clothes. Touching her would be a sin. Would be a lie. I try to think about her eyes—how they would look when she found out.

I rub my hand over my face and try to remember what she said last. Anything but the insistent pounding in between my legs, and in my head. I push my own raw misery aside and replay her lovely words.

"Maybe I need it even worse than you do."

No.

"With someone else." I let a long breath out, open my eyes. "Not me."

I try to read her face, but it's so still. I can see the fast throb of her jugular in the shifting firelight. "Why not you?" Her voice is tiny.

Gwenna wants *me*.

I see her grinning over me, her hand curled over my face, her legs straddling me in her yard. And then I have this fucking flash of Landstuhl—nauseating Landstuhl and the room is empty, no more Breck; I can feel this deep sting in my head; my scalp is tight; my eye is blind; my hand. I feel, for just a flash, my heavy body; numb and cold and dead. My mouth is dry, but I'm too tired to speak. I think *I'm trapped like Mom was.*

Nurses come in, shift me over on my side. Their eyes flit over me. They talk—English or German?—and I want to stop them but can't get my voice to work. Someone peels the bandage off my back, and I hear words like *shock* and *Ativan* and *poor guy*; days and days and days of white walls and white ceilings, and I think I'm never getting out; but then I do and… why?

I see myself upstairs lying on the floor, the bed skirt in my line of sight, and I can't even close my eyes and find peace there.

I don't feel alone; I just feel dead.

And Gwenna looks up at me. I don't think she's even breathing. *Answer her, you pussy fuck.* My throat thickens. "Because I *can't*."

"But why not? I…don't get it. Not wanting to…I could see…" Her face loses its blush as she shakes her head. "But *can't*?"

My secret snakes through me, it writhes its way around me and it chokes me: dead, the way I'm meant to be.

And I can't say it. Can—but *won't*.

The words come out unplanned. Desperate. Hoped for or dreaded? I don't know what she will say. I don't know why I do;

I throw the only thing at her that I can think of that might work, besides the truth.

"I'm not a Ranger. I'm a killer. I kill…men, women…and even kids sometimes." My voice cracks. "That's what I do. That's why I'm all fucked up. You want a piece of *that*?"

chapter nine

Gwenna

straighten my spine as shock washes through me, starting in my throat and spreading coolly through my stomach.

I frown up at him. He is wide-eyed, with his hands held out in front of him like he might need to fight, or even turn and run.

"I'm a killer…That's why I'm all fucked up."

The rough words echo through my head, but I can't seem to pin them down or assign meaning to them. I blink slowly.

"Like…in combat?"

He shakes his head. He swallows. Nods. "Usually." The word is rasped, so soft I barely hear it over the crackling fire.

Usually…but sometimes not? "What does that mean?"

He stares through me, and I feel a bite of fear. Standing there in just those sweatpants, with his arm around his chest and a hand raised to his bowed head, Barrett looks so broken, I have trouble feeling anything but worry for him—for this man who's slow to laugh and quick to touch me; hard to reach and so easy to want.

I have this memory of him crouching down and touching my ankle. I can feel his finger on my face and hear him telling me I'm beautiful. I almost don't believe he *could* kill. If he did, surely it would have wounded him terribly.

I whisper, "Why?" I don't mean to; the word just comes. I stand up slowly, my heart pounding. "What do you mean?" I shake my head.

His eyes meet mine, and they are haunted.

I want to go to him—to close the distance between us and wrap my arms around him—but I feel heavy.

"I want to get what you're saying. A—do you mean like…an assassin? Like…a sniper?"

His eyes shift so he's looking into mine. He doesn't say it, but can see it in his tight jaw.

So Barrett was a sniper. Okay. I inhale slowly. "In the special forces?"

I can see his throat move as he swallows. His face is impassive; elsewhere.

"I don't judge you." I'm not even sure it's true, but I feel compelled to say it—just to ease him. I step closer. "Barrett…You're my friend. I'm going to be on your side. You know?"

I catch his gaze and try to hold it, willing him to hear the truth in what I'm saying.

I step slowly closer. "I know how wars work. Think about our great-grandparents. Almost everyone had been to war. You think I don't get that everyone comes back from that different? I don't know what it's like personally, but I can imagine. I can sympathize. Of *course* it had an impact on you. God, how could it not?" Another step, and I've closed the distance between us.

Moving slowly, hedging bets, I stretch my hand out, till my fingers touch his elbow. He stiffens. I wrap my hand around it, fingertips prodding gently at the area where he taught me to squeeze.

"Barrett…" I stroke his damp skin, and he shudders. His eyes are peeled wide, red-rimmed and unfocused. He looks skittish. "Look at me."

He does, and I see so much pain there, I can barely breathe.

"It's okay." I hold his anguished gaze. "You're a friend to me, yeah?"

As I speak, I wrap my arms around him, pull his heavy body close. His head is bowed again, eyes shut. My throat feels tight and aching. Underneath my fingers, his skin twitches. My hand caresses his nape; I lead his heavy head down to my shoulder.

"I know." I squeeze him tightly. "You're having a bad time. I know. It's okay. You're going to be okay."

This quiet, kind man—I can't see him poised behind a sniper rifle. I squeeze his shoulders and, despite his strength, I can't imagine him ending a life. My gaze laps at his familiar profile. How handsome he is. I see his small, tight smiles and weary eyes. I shake my head.

"Never think that I would judge you. I'm your friend. I'm so sorry, Barrett."

I can feel his pain. Even in the way he holds his body, tight and still, like someone badly hurt.

He must be having a really hard time. He never sleeps…He said he wasn't hungry. I'm angry with myself—that I didn't realize how troubled he's been.

He lifts his head and he looks down at me with tired eyes; they're insulated by a sort of vacancy.

His thick brows pinch together, making his pale face look vaguely troubled. And it hits me that I've seen this look before. When I opened the front door and I thought he'd just woken up. A time or two when we were sparring.

"I didn't want to lie about it," he says roughly. His gaze shifts to mine. "You would want to know what kind of person…"

I shake my head.

"What kind of person," he continues—

"No." I shake my head again, and move one of my arms from around him so I can touch his neck. "Do you really think that's the best measure of who you are? What you did when you were over in a war zone?"

He shakes his head, blinking slowly. "You don't understand."

"Are you a serial killer, Barrett? Do you force women into things or kidnap kids or take a baseball bat to other cars when you're on the road? What have you been doing since you got back? Taking people out at the mall and Target? Did you hunt down your neighbor and carve her into pieces? Kill a cat? Set a house on fire?"

He watches me without speaking, without moving. I move my hand that's on his neck up to his cheek, trying to make him focus on me; *just* me.

"How did you get into the Army? What made you want to join?"

He blinks, and I can feel him focus more on me. "When my mom—" He shakes his head. "I was 15, but I would drive her. I had missed a lot of school...and they had said they were going to hold me back. I had this plan to join the SEALS. My dad found out. I finished school, but after that..." He blinks into my eyes.

"So you joined when you were...?"

"Eighteen." He drops his gaze, as if he doesn't want to look into my face.

"Were you prepared?"

He frowns.

"You knew what you were getting into? Special forces, sniping? Nightmares, losing people, all the people you would...come in contact with."

"Kill." His voice is flat—but still, he looks at me like he is waiting to hear more.

"Well?" I raise my brows. "Did you knowingly go into it?"

"I tried to get with the SEALs, but it wasn't a time when they were starting a new class. Then I heard about the Rangers."

"And you made it there."

He cuts his eyes my way, not a trace of pride on his pale face.

"Then what?" I press. "You moved on up?"

"Joined ACE. Got a longer kill list. Got hurt. Came home. What are you getting at?"

"You came back, it all seems like it's kind of crashing down. You're by yourself, you're trying to readjust to being out of the Army. You're telling me you can't be with me because you used to be a sniper. Are you trying to punish yourself?"

He takes a step back, out of my grasp. "I want to keep you away from this," he says roughly.

"Away from what?"

He holds his arms out, as if the room around us is the problem. "Who would want to…to invest their time in someone who can barely keep their fucking head above water?"

"So it's an investment."

He swallows, or struggles to. "Fuck," he rasps. "I don't know."

"So…" I draw a big breath in. "Are you still sniping?"

"No, but—"

"Any of the other things I mentioned?"

He looks frustrated; tight-jawed.

"Okay." I shrug. "So what about your life is so terrible that it might hurt *me*?"

"You want that answered?"

I nod. "Yes."

chapter ten

Gwenna

"I see things sometimes," he whispers hoarsely. "When I started..." He laughs, just a hoarse rasp. "There used to be this stereotype about the old Nam vets. That they were all so head-fucked. Seeing things and hearing shit and ending up on street corners because they couldn't keep their shit together." He shuts his eyes and rubs his head.

"Is that what you're afraid of? That you'll end up on a street corner?" I'm surprised to find my eyes burn as I say it. My throat stings. I have to inhale slowly, to be sure no tears spill over.

He shakes his head. "I don't know." I step over to him, wrap an arm around his waist. When he doesn't tense and doesn't pull away, I wrap my other arm around his back. I stroke his hair and pull him closer to me. And I hug him—long and hard, the way I think his mother would have hugged him. Because regardless of his sins, right now, I can feel his pain, and I want to ease it.

When I loosen my grip on him, I look up and am relieved to see his eyes.

"You're secure here, though, yeah? You have a house. You have ideas about another job that you'd be great at. Barrett—you've been teaching your disabled neighbor new self-defense techniques. You leave your house, you hunt. I know you're having trouble sleeping, but from the outside, it looks like you're doing well. And without family close by, either. You don't see a therapist?"

He shakes his head.

"And still, you're getting by. It will get easier. If you can hold on—and I know you can—things will get better as more time goes by. That's the one thing I can tell you."

I press myself against his chest again and rest my cheek against his chest as his arm comes around me loosely. "I can help you with the seeing things, and the nightmares. Even for my measly case of PTSD, I pulled out all the stops and saw a really good therapist and did the right things. I can teach you all the things I know."

"You don't get it, Gwen." His voice cracks. I can feel his chest move as he swallows. "I don't deserve it."

"Why?" I lean back a little, so I can see his face.

He shakes his head.

"Try to explain it. You don't have to tell me word for word. But tell me something."

"Do you understand how Army convoys work?" he whispers.

I shake my head. I know what a convoy is, but I'm pretty sure I don't have whatever knowledge he's referencing.

"All the vehicles—tanks, Hummers or Bradleys—move in a line. It's usually when a large number of troops are traveling. Maybe moving camp. So you go through villages. They know." He blinks. "The people know to stay away. You know about IEDs, I guess?"

I nod.

"Well, they're always in our path. You don't stop unless... something specific happens. There's a chain of command."

I nod again, trying to keep my face soothing or neutral.

"Kids *don't* know." He takes a deep breath. "Sometimes—" his voice cracks a little—"All those fucking kids. You'd have to leave them. If someone gets hurt—a villager—you help them." He swallows. "We're all medics. Most of the older Operators, we're field medics. They were all ages. Sometimes…little, little kids. There could be no swerving. Sometimes drivers would—" He shakes his head. "But it wasn't allowed. The enemy would use children. Sometimes they'd come right at you with grenades."

I lean my cheek against his chest, where I can hear the fast boom of his heartbeat.

"So you can die, or you can kill a kid. The worst times, one of your guys already got hit. Maybe you're in front of them. So you can kill the kid or they can…" He swallows. I look up at him. "Would you let the kid blow up your buddy?" I can feel his chest start pumping faster. I wrap my arms around him again, hoping the sensation will center him.

"I dream about them on the ground," he murmur into my hair. "The way someone looks on the ground. I didn't see it very often through my scope…from far away. You'd make the kill and go. But in Ramadi. Syria…In other places. All the places with close quarters fighting. You would just walk away…and they wouldn't. Everyone I know, I see them lying on the ground." His voice cracks. "You know…cause you're human. You kind of—some part of you wants to pick them up. Not at that moment. They just tried to kill you. But you walk away and—sometimes you know them. Maybe it's a terp—interpreter—or…sometimes you can't get them out. Right then." He puts a hand over his eyes. "I always try to get them. And sometimes I'm taking fire. But usually I'm not. I see everybody I know and I'm just standing there. I walk up on them, don't know how they got there. I just stand there."

I can feel him shaking just a little now. I realize belatedly he's talking about his nightmares.

"Taking out a target, it's a fucked-up job. But that's not what I see when I'm asleep. I just see people on the floor."

I notice he said floor, not ground.

"People who weren't over there with you?"

He nods, his face still covered by his hand.

"Are you here in the U.S.?"

He swallows. Through the barrier of his fingers, I can see his blue eyes glimmer.

"Last night, I kept seeing this rug."

I look down. "Oh." *This* one.

He folds his arm over my back, pressing me to him. It doesn't calm the shaking.

I lock my arms around his waist and swallow against the aching lump in my throat. "Was someone on it—in your dream?" I whisper.

"You are." His arms around me loosen, and he leans away, so he can lock his hard eyes onto mine. "You're on the floor, Gwenna. It's you. So you see now? Why I think you should go?"

Despite the firmness of his voice, he bows his head and shuts his eyes again, as if he can't stand to see my reaction.

I chew on my lip. "I have an idea," I say slowly. "You can say no."

His eyes blink open. They're red around the rims, making his blue-gray irises look bright green.

"We want to change what you see, right?" I swallow, steadying my voice. "Just make it slightly different. This is one of the tenants of getting rid of PTSD nightmares. You want to control the way it goes. So you've dreamed of me, dead on your floor."

He doesn't move, but I can feel the weight of all his awful grief.

"What if I lay down now—and maybe you can lay down after that. With me. We could steer your dream this way."

His eyes squeeze shut.

"We don't have to."

He lifts a hand to his face, then he speaks through his fingers. "Do."

With one last glance at him, I get onto the floor and stretch out on my side. My side, because when he lays down, I want to wrap my arms around him.

This is also how I landed, though. How I was found. I lie there and my heart pounds thinking of myself alone, and all the blood and all the snow. I try to remember. I try to remember the smell of gardenias, the scent of road salt. Creaks and beeps and tires crunching on snow.

Funny how our nightmares are the inverse of each other's.

You're okay, I tell myself. I've been dreaming, too, but I know I'm okay.

Barrett grabs me so fast it startles me. I don't even feel him kneel down by me before his arms go around me and he locks me up against his chest. He squeezes so hard I can barely breathe. His face presses into my neck. I feel his hard back shaking. I wrap my leg over his.

He shakes so hard he makes a little noise, a whimpered sort of grunt.

"I'm sorry, Gwenna. I'm so sorry." His hand tangles in my hair.

I cup his nape and hold his head against me. "I forgive you." I hold him close and tight and try to give him all my love. My poor friend. Before I know it, my mouth is on his temple. The one with the scar. I kiss him there, gently.

I feel his lips brush up against my throat. He inhales; then his forehead nuzzles underneath my chin. He rolls away from me, but pulls me with him, so he's on his back and I'm above him.

He looks dazed.

I cup his face, stroking the light beard on his cheeks.

My mouth twists up on one side. "Hi, Bear."

"Can you call me Barrett?"

"Sure." I lay against his chest and wiggle a hand under his back.

"They called me Bear. Sometimes I miss it, but…"

He shifts his hips a little, and I look down and see a telltale tenting of his pants.

"I'm sorry."

I draw away from him. I didn't think about that, about how my rubbing up against him would make him react. Stupid Gwenna.

His eyes flip open, and he grabs my hair. His hand cups his thick erection.

"It would be…a terrible mistake—" He groans—"For me to keep this up."

"Why would it be?"

His eyes squeeze shut; he grits his teeth. Watching his palm press against his lovely bulge, I touch his leg.

He moans. His hand closes around mine. "Gwenna, please."

"Want me to move?" I can't tell where he is, or what he needs. I scoot back.

He sits up. Stands up.

I take hold of his hand. "Everything's okay."

"It's not." He turns partially away from me; we're still holding hands, but I can only see his profile now.

I whisper, "Why?"

"I want to touch you again. I've been wanting you. It's a *problem*." The word is whispered. "I fucked this up. I don't know how to stop. I don't know how to keep from telling you." He rubs the base of his palm over his face.

"Telling me what?" I ask him gently.

He pulls me to him, rests his chin on my hair.

"I would never, never hurt you. Please believe me." He pulls back; our eyes meet for a moment, then he pulls me back against him.

I reach my arm around his waist and run my fingers down the firm plank of his lower back. "I do."

"I wish I could leave it there. I wanted to leave it there. But it came with me. It's in here and I can't get away." He reaches in between us, tapping his chest. "It's a one-time thing." He moves his hand and rests his face on my head. "People should...fight and then die."

"No," I murmur.

"Every one of us—" His diaphragm expands, pressing against me. "Sometimes I think it would be better. I'm not the same."

"No. I know. No one would be."

He strokes my hair. He cups my body to his and hugs me tight. "You make things better. Too much better." I feel his deep breaths under me. I touch his stomach: hard and firm. I stroke his ribs.

"Gwenna—"

"Shhh."

chapter eleven

Barrett

"I can't do this."

Her fingers flatten over my lower abs, and I hold back a groan. My cock is so hard, it fucking *hurts.* Then her hand is cupping it, sending streaks of pleasure through my balls and down my legs. I swear, I can feel precum ooze against my boxer-briefs.

"I think you can." Her voice is whispered. "I think you want to. Why can't you? If you won't give it to me, I want to know why I'm missing out."

I blink and look at her through bleary eyes, trying to pull my thoughts together. My gaze wanders down to where she's stroking me. I drag an unsteady breath in and speak in a rough voice.

"It's been a long time...since I fucked. And you..." Her hand, warm and heavy even through my pants, drags up and down the length of my erection. "You shouldn't..." I groan. "You'd regret it."

Now I'm panting. Somewhere far away, I know I should do more to stop this, but she's soft and warm and...touching me with tenderness. It feels so goddamned good.

Gwenna shakes her head, looking up into my eyes as she reaches into my sweats, revealing the thick hose of my cock covered in charcoal boxer-briefs. The sight of her hand closing over the head of me is enough to make my balls draw up.

"I like touching you." She demonstrates by tracing the rim of my head with the pad of her thumb.

Her other hand wanders down my cotton-covered shaft and spreads out, pushing against the thin fabric until she's stroking my balls.

"God, Barrett…"

She smooths the fabric of my boxers over the fullness, gives me a Cheshire Cat smile, then pulls the boxer-briefs elastic to the side, and I groan loudly as my cock springs up. She drags the fabric over me, peeling downward, then hooking the elastic underneath my balls, creating gentle pressure in a sensitive spot behind them. Then she cups my sac, tugging it slightly away from my body so she can torture my poor, swollen balls by gently stroking each of them.

I bark a loud groan as her other hand glides up my shaft and cups my cum-slick head. My hips buck at the pleasure and my right hand wraps around her upper arm as I sway on my feet.

I hear her whispering to me but blood is rushing in my ears. My breaths are hard. My limbs buzz as if I'm being stimulated by low-level electricity.

Gwenna pushes lightly up against my balls, rolling them inside my sac. She's focused her stroking on the top half of my shaft, each upward pull tickling the sensitive rim of my cockhead. I can feel my eyes roll back as she keeps working me at both ends.

"Fuck…" I have the thought that I should sit down before I fall down, but then her jack-off hand glides down to grip my base, and as it strokes back up toward my head, one finger presses gently on the tender underside of my shaft.

I swear, I can feel the cum surge from my balls upward. I'm panting. Dizzy.

"*Ohhh* Gwen…I need to come. I need to fucking—" With a tortured groan, I pull my hips slightly away from her. I'm overwhelmed by what she's doing, rendered mindless and about to fall the fuck over. But she is unrelenting, and my half step backward only makes her grip me tighter.

"Gwenna…"

My hand glides down to her elbow, lending me a feeling of control even as my body shakes. My cock throbs underneath her firm, fast strokes and my balls feel taut and swollen.

"Fuckkk. I'm gonna…blow."

"Not yet." Her husky voice makes goosebumps spread over my skin. I think I hear her naughty little giggle, then she's tugging my sweats down.

I grab her shoulders, squeezing as I lose track of the world, except her warm hands, making my head spin.

"So big and hard." She wraps a hand around my shaft, grabbing hold just underneath my head and giving it a gentle squeeze before she glides the fingers of her other hand over my tip.

"Look at this…" She spreads a line of precum down around the rim of my head, tracing around it while my knees threaten to buckle.

"Jesus Gwen…" I grab her wrist. Her other hand—the one that's still wrapped partway around my cock—strokes down toward my throbbing balls. I suck a deep breath into my lungs, and the hand that's holding my dick lets it go—so she can tug my boxer-briefs down my thighs. Even there, I'm sensitive. The fabric tickles, making my cock ache. I shut my eyes and focus on not coming. Even the slight movement of lifting my feet out of the briefs makes my balls tauten, has my dick stretched up toward my navel.

She strokes a finger over the sensitive notch on the underside of my head, and my clenching fist catches a strand of her hair.

"Ow."

"Fuck."

I start to let her go, but she says, "No—I like it."

She leans down and licks me all around the rim of my head. I have to flex my toes to keep from pushing my cock into her mouth.

She strokes my balls, and I groan loudly. "Pull..." But she won't. She just fucking tickles them, and I hear myself panting.

"Gwen..." I run my hand over her shoulder, down toward her chest, where I cup one of her breasts and grope in the direction of her nipple. I rock myself against mouth.

"Please..."

I think about her pussy, slick and pink; I can feel the silky tightness...Fuck, I'd hold her hips and shove my cock so deep—

Her hands leave me. My eyes fly open. When I blink, I don't see her, but I hear her saying, "Come here..."

My imagination conjures Gwen on the couch with her legs spread, fingers dragging through her dripping pussy. So when I see her standing by it, fully clothed and nowhere near my tortured cock, I frown and feel my pulse throb in my temples.

"Come here." When I don't move, she comes to me and takes my hand. I catch her give my dick an indulgent little smile.

She leads me to the couch, and when I'm ready to fall to my knees and beg for her hands again—her mouth; her cunt— she rests her fingers lightly on my head and whispers, "Look at me."

And as I watch, she takes off all her clothes.

Her body is a temple—unmatched in its beauty. Her nipples are dark pink and sweetly pebbled. Her pale, full breasts were made to press around my cock: just big enough to make me think I'd need both hands to cup one. My starving gaze roves down her stomach—tiny at the waist; soft and curvy below. I see the scars

I remember from the other night and my heart skips a beat, but then she's whispering, "I want this."

With a wink and a wavering smile, she turns around, giving me my first view of her ass—and holy fucking ass it is. She has the kind of ass that could command its own Instagram account. The kind of ass I could get lost in.

My cock thumps against my abs. And that's before she lays face-down on the couch and draws her knees up, presenting that big, round ass to me with fingers peeking in between her thighs.

She strokes herself, and my whole body pulses.

"What—"

I step back, feeling faint.

Gwenna peeks over her shoulder. Her brown eyes are glazed with want. Her hair tumbles around her shoulders. She says my name, and I blink, realizing I'm stroking my own dick.

I swallow hard. "You want—"

Her legs spread slightly as she whispers, "Yes. I want you in me."

Her fingers part her pussy, and my cock throbs so hard I feel it in my thighs.

"Fuck." I step over to her, pressing hard against my dick so I don't come right where I stand. Gwenna watches with her lip between her teeth.

"It's been a long time for me," she whispers, "and you're big... so just go slow."

She means, *It's been a long time and I'm tight.* My throat constricts as I move up behind her on the couch and stare down at her ass cheeks and her pussy. I can't help myself. I have to touch her.

A wave of heat moves through me as I reach out. My fingers hover over her pussy for a few heartbeats, so close I can feel the heat of her. I squeeze one of her ass cheeks. With my right hand, I find her soft, wet folds and spread her gently.

"Fuck—you're gorgeous." My heart pounds as I shift a little closer on my knees and rub my tip against her wetness.

"Christ…"

It's been so long…

Gwenna wags her ass.

"That's right, babe." My voice is rough and barely audible.

She wiggles back against my dick. That first brush of hot velvet around my head makes me jolt, and groan. I push against her just a little more, shaking from the effort not to shove my cock inside her heat and fuck her like a beast.

"Oh God…" My knees tremble. I wrap a hand around my dick and give a slow, steady push, until she moans; I feel her tightness give, and then her cunt is squeezed around my head. "Aghh, you feel so good…"

She moans.

"You're beautiful," I breathe.

I rock forward on my knees, gritting my teeth as I ease another inch or two inside her. Gwenna groans and starts to pant.

"Oh God…you're big."

"You're tight." I reach over her slim back and grab a strand of auburn hair. With the end wound around my fingers, I squeeze her waist and take a few slow breaths.

"You okay?" I rasp.

"Oh shit…Barrett…"

"You…feel…so good." I shut my eyes so I can't see her perfect ass, and grit my teeth as I guide more of my dick into her almost painful tightness. I feel Gwenna's legs shaking.

"'S okay," she murmurs. She rocks her hips back against me, groaning as she takes another inch. Jesus Christ, she feels like a fucking virgin. When sweat is dripping down my throat and my cock is throbbing so hard I'm worried I'll come here and now, I slide my hand from her waist down to her hip, squeeze gently, and push myself in, balls deep.

She moans loudly, then starts panting. I grit my teeth to keep from shouting at how fucking good it feels—to look down on her back and ass and know that I'm inside her. She's so perfect. "You're so hot...and tight." My voice cracks.

I feel Gwenna clench around me and I grip her hip, pushing further still, till I can feel her dripping on my balls and my cock is enslaved by her plump pussy.

"God..." I draw myself out slowly, inch by inch. She whimpers, and I want to slap her ass for being so damn hot, so fucking tempting. Instead I slam back in, and Gwenna shouts, and once I start, I can't stop fucking her—the way I need it: rough.

With every thrust, I sink balls-deep, and Gwenna moans and shakes and falls down to her elbows on the couch.

"Barrett!"

I grasp her hips and fuck her harder than I've ever fucked before, angling myself so I can rub her G-spot with every thrust. When she starts to slide out of my grasp, up toward the couch's arm, I lock an arm around her hips and press her back against me while I'm buried in her.

"Fuck!" I pant.

I feel her shaking, hear her gasping.

"Oh God!"

I brace my right knee and thigh against the couch and balance with my right hand on her hip, and then I reach around her narrow waist and find her wet slit with my index finger. I stroke between her lips. It makes me throb, finding she's dripping everywhere.

"Who's full of my cock?" My voice trembles.

"I- I am."

"That's right." I pump in and out a few times, then I stop again and stroke her little swollen clit.

"You've been wanting it, haven't you?"

"Yes!"

"You think I didn't see you watching me? I watched you too," I grunt, and push inside her, holding while I stroke her dripping pussy. "I saw you wanting this. I tried—" I drag out back—"tried to let you be. But you wouldn't let me, would you?"

"No," she rasps.

I punch back in, and she lets out a low sound like a sob.

"You needed me inside you. You're so tight, I can barely fit, but you like that, don't you?"

She pants and bears down on my dick so I can bury myself deeper—and I'm not surprised: the way she grips me when I pull it out and how she shoves her tight cunt back against me as I slam inside.

I hear myself, from somewhere far off, moaning, "Babe...ahh, Gwen—" until I feel the tension tightening my balls and thickening my cock.

"I'm gonna come..." I reach around and stroke her clit once more as she rocks back toward me. I slam in...draw out...slam in...and as she starts to quiver around me, she rasps, "On the pill."

My cock thumps deep inside her as her pussy clenches, her muscles squeezing, milking, as my balls throb and I fill her up, and then I hold there deep inside her body: warm and spent; my hot balls pressed against her taint and throbbing with their own heartbeat. I find my body feeling light and empty. I can't think at all, can only feel and smell and stroke her ribs as chills race over her smooth skin.

"Holy fuck...you feel so fucking good." A shudder rips through me. I let my head hang over her for just a second as I try to get my breath.

Then I pull out slowly; cum spills as I leave her empty...dripping...such a perfect fucking sight.

I'm still half hard. Just looking at her, freshly fucked, makes my shaft twitch.

"Gwen?"

She looks back at me. Fuck, she's sweaty and her lower lip looks raw, like she's been biting it.

"Are you okay?" I whisper. Fear flares somewhere distant in me.

"Holy hell." She laughs. "Amazing." She squeezes her thighs together and grins. "Are you? You look like you just ran a marathon."

It's probably true. My eyelids are heavy and I feel sleep blurring my edges even as I stroke her hip one final time and make myself get up.

"Wait here a minute."

I walk into the kitchen and get a warm cloth for her. I come back to find her curled up on her side.

When I kneel beside the couch, she yawns, then smiles.

I can't help smiling too.

"You're fucking beautiful," I murmur as she takes the towel from me. I grab a blanket from the other end of the couch and toss it to her, then I disappear into the kitchen for a minute. When I return, she's got the blanket wrapped around her shoulders. She looks half asleep.

I remember last time she was here, she did the same thing: crashed right after. I only hesitate a second before I bend down and scoop her up.

She giggles as I climb the stairs with her, and rests her cheek against my chest as I open the door to my room. I'm glad the lights are off so she can't see how messy this place is.

I peel the covers down—at least the bed is clean—and lay her on the king-sized mattress. I tuck the covers up around her shoulders and walk over to the armchair where my .338 is.

She doesn't need to see it...or the pile of Red Bull cans. I lay a throw pillow over them.

"Barrett?"

I step over to the bed and find Gwenna's eyelids drooping. Fuck, she looks like heaven naked in this bed. I blink as she leans up on her elbow.

"You okay?" she whispers, reaching for me.

Warmth spreads through me.

"Yeah." I let her grab my hand. My eyes hold hers and for the first time, I hope she can see the way she makes me feel. I rasp, "Are you?" I squeeze her hand and then lift mine to stroke her hair out of her face.

Her smile is soft and bright. "I'm really good." As my fingers sift through her coppery locks, she grabs my wrist, her thumb stroking. "Get into the bed with me. I'm tired, and I want to snuggle up to you."

chapter twelve

Gwenna

The first thing I notice is the weight around me. Close second: the stinging ache between my thighs—a sensation that throws me back in time so powerfully I almost smell the vanilla condoms Elvie and I used to use.

I blink in the darkness as my stomach churns, remembering. I inhale to quell the nausea, and that's when I notice something else: a salty masculine scent…The kind of sweat smell that's illogically yummy because of pheromones. That and…something clean. Like deodorant or aftershave.

Barrett.

I'm in Barrett's room.

In Barrett's bed.

Barrett and I…

Holy hell.

I suck another breath in, and my stomach twists with glee and nerves. I have to take another measured breath to keep myself from jumping up and doing cartwheels—or turning over so I can look at him. Instead, I blink and scan the room. It's still nighttime. This place is pitch black except an "L"-shaped slit of light in front of me. I'm going to bet that's the light from the en suite bathroom.

Why don't I *know*? I don't remember even seeing this room.

Because I was sleepy when he carried me up here…

I shut my eyes and try to relish the feeling of his body behind mine. He's totally spooning me, with his left arm hugging me tightly to his chest. God, it feels so freaking good. He's warm, his body hard and almost twice as wide as mine. The weight of his arm…It makes me feel secure and loved and wanted.

Loved.

Hold your horses, Gwenna. It's just sex.

My heart pounds, and I turn my head just slightly, wondering why I don't feel his face against my hair. I get my answer in the form of Barrett's watchful eyes and gentle smirk.

My mouth drops open. "You…" I turn over onto my back so I can see him, and he moves his arm off me.

"You were watching me. When I was sleeping!" He's lying on his side, still shirtless, with his cheek propped on his palm. He looks smug and beautiful.

I slap his chest.

He rolls his body forward, so he's almost but not quite on top of me. His hand strokes my hair back while his mouth comes down to cover mine.

The kiss is deep and tender. Firm…His mouth is hot and smooth. His tongue strokes mine, surging a few times in a motion that makes me think of sex. Then his lips take charge, gently tasting mine, and his tongue is licking along the seam of my lips, teasing. I can't seem to think. I just…react. The kiss deepens, his beard prickling my hot cheeks. His mouth roves up my jaw and to my temple, kissing lightly, till I feel a throb low in my belly and I grab his shoulder. I try to pull him down on me.

And then he sucks the tender skin below my ear, making me writhe with need, and pulls away.

I pull him back to me. I'm surprised when he lays his heavy body over mine, presses his cheek against mine.

"Gwenna…" I can feel his chest pump with his heavy breaths.

"Barrett." I turn my head to kiss his mouth, and miss—because he's lifting his head and shifting back onto his side. He trails a finger down my forearm.

"How do you feel?" His eyes have that hawkish quality, as if he's watching me closely to make sure he misses nothing. But there's gentleness in his features, too. For someone so acquainted with violence, he really is a nice guy.

"I'm good." I flush, then laugh. "I can't believe I did that." I can't stop the grin that spreads over my face.

"Did what?" He smirks.

I shove him. "You know what, you jerk."

His smirk takes its usual route to smile.

"I've never done what I did with you." I bring my hand to my burning cheek. "Put my ass up in the air like that." I shake my head.

He grins. "I've never seen anything that fucking hot."

I look down at the sheets, not sure if I should beam with pride or die of embarrassment.

He smiles and strokes my jaw. "You look naughty, Gwenna."

"Apparently I am." I lean up so I can kiss his neck. I expect him to pull away, but he doesn't. His eyes are warm on mine, his arm around me steady as he holds me to him.

This time, I'm the one who pulls away.

"What time is it?" I whisper.

I see him swallow. "Almost three."

"Have you slept?" I whisper breathlessly.

"A little."

"Liar." I cup his prickly cheek. "Maybe it would help if I wrap you up and be your human blanket."

His eyes shut. I kiss his jaw. I feel the goosebumps on his arm, which is pressed against my chest. His tired eyes open.

"You're not holding out for me, are you? Trying to keep from having a nightmare with me here? I don't want to make things worse for you."

"Never," he says quietly.

I stroke a finger down his abs. He leans his head back.

"You make me feel good," I say, stroking his happy trail. "I want to make you feel good too."

I duck under the covers and, after a second with my heart in my throat, work up the nerve to grab his dick and wrap my tongue around the tip of it. I hear him groan and suck him into my mouth. I can feel him lengthen...harden...thicken. I'm not very experienced with blow jobs. I can't even suck my left cheek in as tightly as my right one. But I try...and at the same time, I try to run my tongue under his head and all around the rim of him. I'm rewarded by a muttered curse, and then his hands cupping my head.

I wonder how deep I can take him. I open wider and suck him into the back of my throat...so I can feel the pressure of his head there. I realize in a heartbeat that it's either gag or swallow—so I swallow.

"Oh fuck..." I hear and feel him take a heavy breath. His thick erection twitches in my throat. I inhale slowly, relaxing more so I can breathe around him. Then I swallow just a little more.

His hips jerk so hard, I cough a little and my eyes water.

"Oh God," he moans. "Gwen."

His hands clench my shoulders and I feel his legs shake slightly. Another slow swallow, and he's gritting out my name. His hips twitch, then his legs get very tense and still, as if he's forcibly keeping himself from thrusting deeper. I realize as I swallow again that I forgot about the balls. And what a shame, because his are seriously stunning: big and beautiful, the very definition of well-hung. Who knew balls could be so hot?

I drag my curved palm underneath them, tickling with the pads of my fingers, then gently cupping.

I'm rewarded with his frenzied breathing, and the feeling of his heavy sac tightening in my hand.

He's so big, I don't think I can take all of him into my throat, so with my other hand, I clutch the base of his dick. He seems to like it when I drag my thumb along the underside of his shaft, so I focus on doing that, swallowing and sucking, and rolling his balls.

"Oh...oh. Oh God...*Gwen!*"

I feel every noise he makes between my legs—and I imagine that the thickness in my throat is driving deep inside me.

My jaw aches and my eyes water, but it's worth it. When I think I might taste something salty down my throat, when his abs and thighs tighten, I feel a swell of heat between my legs and draw him slowly out of my mouth.

As his body tenses and he makes a low sound off loss in his throat, I crawl up his body, rubbing up against him until my pussy glides over his dick.

I get a flash of his dark eyes. Then Barrett flips me over on my back, positions his head at my wet entrance, and, with his eyes shut tightly, surges into me.

I hold onto his forearms as he pounds me fast and hard and we both pant and moan, and he says, "You're so...fucking perfect."

That's it for me.

He follows me a second later.

Barrett cleans us up, then disappears into the bathroom. I watch his tall shadow move through the room, and feel him crawl back into bed. He lies on his back and folds his arms behind his head.

"Thanks," I whisper.

He laughs, a low, smoky sound. I wait for words, and when none find me, I scoot over closer to him. I snuggle up against his chest and Barrett wraps his arm around me.

I watch him until his eyes shut and his body twitches. At that cue, his eyes shoot open, wide and alarmed.

I stroke his hair and hold him tighter. "It's okay..."

After a few minutes, his breathing has gone steady.

Barrett
December 29, 2011

Being back stateside is always fucking strange. The smell of soil and moisture in the air. The way every surface—floors, counters, walls—looks like it's just been spit-shined. The roads are smooth and wide and quiet. The cars look pristine. Everyone wears pants, carries an iPhone, wears sunglasses.

I catch a hop to Stewart, arriving at the base at 7:35 a.m. New York time. I grab the keys to a Chevy Suburban at the Enterprise desk and have to sit in it a minute before revving up. It smells new. Odometer says 10,000 miles. The car feels large and quiet with only me inside.

My first stop is a gas station. The number of food options inside overwhelms me. I don't recognize half the brands. Caramel apple bubble gum, blackberry-flavored water. The price of cigarettes is high. I buy some Marlboros, just to have them in my pocket.

Stewart is a little west of Newburgh, only 19 miles north of the family cabin at Iona Island. The drive is lined with trees and packed with big cars filled with unassuming Americans fiddling with earbuds, reapplying lipstick, talking on their smart phones at red lights.

I try to assess myself. And try to plan.

I'm told Kelly has his phone, but the two times I've called, he hasn't answered. I don't even bother to call my father. Haven't in years. The few times I did, after shipping out, he didn't answer. I wouldn't know where Kellan was were it not for my aunt. She told me Kellan bolted right after Lyon died. Ly was playing chess in Kellan's room. He'd been discharged. They thought he was doing better than Kellan. Anyway, Kelly took New York public transport from Sloan-Kettering Memorial to some hotel and passed the fuck out. Poor kid. When I think about him by himself—just one blond, blue-eyed, dimpled kid—my stomach feels like it's full of Jell-O.

I try to steel myself, but as the river weaves between the dense trees on my left and the roads narrow toward Iona, I feel sick. I have this bizarrely clear memory, which thereafter runs like a film reel in my mind. I'm in my parents' room, in that awful pale peach wing-backed chair. It must be sometime in the afternoon because the curtains are half-shut the way I did them when the sun got very bright. I can see Mom's hair in that braid over her left shoulder. The nurse, Odessa, showed me how to do it one day. I'm sitting there by Mom carving a squirrel. Just turned sixteen or about to. Regardless, spending all my days driving Mom to appointments. Except in this memory she's not going anywhere. The bandages are still around her upper torso, and her skin is angel pale. I sit the squirrel and my knife down and lay my head there on her mattress, just beside her hip. I remember a sharp ache in my chest when her hand didn't come to rest in my hair. Then Lyon and Kellan are coming through the doorway. A nurse—Charlene—is smiling when I lift my head. My stomach flips because they've never seen

Mom this way. Until a day or two ago, she hadn't been unconscious like this. Charlene shrugs and smiles. Lyon pulls a plastic dinosaur from his pocket.

"Look Barrett! I got a dinosaur for you!"

"Cool. Where'd you get that, buddy?"

He comes over to me. Kellan too. "Lisa took us to Target!"

Kellan looks from me to Mom as Ly hands me the dinosaur. Lyon blinks his blue eyes. "I have one too." He pulls his own brown dinosaur from another pocket. "Mine is triceratops." His little eyes peer up at me. "Barrett, are you sad?"

My heart misses a beat. "No. Why?" My jaw tightens and I want to look at Lisa, though I don't. What has she told them?

"Mommy told me if you're sad that we should cheer you up."

"When did she say that?"

Kellan tilts his face up to me. "A couple days ago."

As I drive, I hear their voices. Nine, ten, and eleven. The year Mom died. The two that followed, when I watched them half as much as Lisa did. I used to make them breakfast. Dinner. I could never drive them places. After I nearly failed tenth grade for missing class with Mom, I was on Dad's shit list. I don't think he wanted me around the boys. Of course, he worked all day and night, so what could he do?

I remember that big, leather couch. We would all three sit up there and play Playstation and I'd wrestle them and tousle their blond hair and help them with division.

I know I shouldn't, but I think about them then and can't believe Lyon is dead. My little brother only lived to be eighteen years old. I didn't even see him buried. Tears blur the road ahead of me. I pull over on the shoulder, find a napkin in the glove box.

"I'm sorry, buddy. I'm so sorry."

My hands feel hot and shaky on the wheel as I hurry to Forward Street. I've got five days. It's a long fucking time. Instead of going out to Breck's with Dove and Blue and him, I can spend all of it here at the cabin with my brother. I remember how they used to cry after she died. It will feel so good to hug him. My throat thickens just thinking about it.

The shoulders that run along the back roads leading to Forward Street are caked with the last snow. It's hard and slightly brown. I drive slowly, looking for our family's cabin. When I spot it, I park in front of the garage and step out onto the cold ground. My throat burns and tightens. I swallow and look around. This is the last lot on the road. If I recall, it's got about a dozen acres.

I walk slowly up the steps onto the small porch and knock. Three times. Then, a minute later, four. I hear footfall right behind the door. My stomach flips, my throat knots up. My whole head feels infused with heat.

I think frantically about what I'll say, but all I have is *I'm sorry.* That I wasn't here. That I didn't come while they were sick and missed Lyon's funeral. That instead of coming after the funeral, I went to Syria, and then Iraq. When did I get so fucking selfish, I wonder as I press my finger to the doorbell.

We spent the last six weeks orbiting Maliki: an important mission but non-urgent. I waited until after Christmas to fly home.

I hear more footsteps, then nothing.

"Kelly?" I shout at the door. "It's Barrett."

It feels strange to say my name when I'm so used to being Bear. I knock some more. And then I hear it. Faintly. "Go away!"

"K?"

I press myself against the screen door, wrap my hand around the locked door handle. I could break through it with ease—but I won't. "Kell, it's me! It's Barrett."

"No shit! Go away!"

The tightness in my chest loosens, and I can feel the blood rush through my heart. So he's pissed. Of course he is.

I swallow. "Please? I want to talk."

The thick, wood door behind the screened one opens slightly and I smell old house and...some sort of food.

"Kellan—hey..." I press my forehead against the screen door. "Please." My voice cracks there. "I need to see you."

He laughs richly. "Oh—I bet."

The door opens so slowly I don't notice until I can see him standing maybe a foot back, in shadows.

I blink twice, quickly, and my eyes adjust. I blink again. I just... don't believe that's him. I don't believe that's Kellan. He looks...tall. So tall and pale and thin. Goddamn, he's thin under that shirt that's hanging off him. I've seen better-looking POWs. The pants he's wearing lead to socked feet. He's got on a beanie. A few more blinks and I can see his face. His fragile, bony, unfamiliar face. And hollow eyes.

I feel a tremble move through my shoulders. "Let me in. Please let me in, man. I'm your brother. I just want to hug you."

I grip the screen door's handle, feeling like the world is tilting under me.

"I don't want to see you."

My throat swells, until I feel like I can't breathe. "Please?"

Kellan looks down at his feet.

I could break the door down. Easily.

Then his pale blue eyes bore into mine. In a low voice—in a man's voice—he says, "I don't want to see you, asshole. I don't even know you. You're just some military robot. You're *not* my brother."

I swallow—try to. "I'm sorry." I want to tell him what happened that day—about the liver shot. How badly I wanted to be here. But there are no excuses. I inhale and exhale, filled with icy-cold regret.

His face twists. "Lyon wondered why you didn't come. I didn't, but he did. Chew on that."

The door slams in my face, shaking snow loose from the roof.

chapter thirteen

Gwenna
November 6, 2015

"Don't be a quitter, *motherfucker!*"

I push my face into my pillow, distantly troubled, eager to sink back into dreamland. Something claws at the door of my mind. I should know…or do something important. Too tired…

Later.

For now, I curl into a ball and pull the blankets up, and as I shut my eyes, I feel the bed shake slightly. Hmm? Somewhere nearby, I hear panting, and that pulls me upward into consciousness. I blink a few times, feeling…*off*. There's something cold and heavy in my belly: dread. Alarm nips at its heels.

What's wrong? I roll from my side onto my back, and as my senses come online, I hear the panting clearly. Male. The sound is low and raspy, unmistakably a man…For half a second, I feel frozen in the center of the sound. Struggling. Winded. Someone running.

…In my room?

I roll onto my side and—*Barrett*.

I blink, but I don't see him. The only thing that stands out in the darkness is the gray light seeping around the blockade of the curtains on the other side of his bed.

Then his weight rocks the mattress. I realize the shape blotting the bottom of the curtain is the wide plane of his back; the triangle at the top of the blob: one of his elbows. He's lying on his side, facing away from me. He's got his arm over his head.

I hear a moan, the kind that people make when something's hurting them. Then his breath catches.

"Fuck you, Breck! FUCK YOU!" His voice breaks. Then he's breathing hard again, like he's been running for a long time.

I scoot toward him, agonized by empathy. My hand freezes as his back shakes, and I hear a soft sob.

Oh my God.

I can't move, can't even seem to breathe as I watch one of his hands clutch the back of his head, and another low, strangled cry breaks from his throat.

His big back jerks once more, and then he's sobbing: low bellows that punch out of him like drum beats. Then his throat tightens, his body coils, and the dam breaks on his grief. It's loud and unhinged, frantic in the way that anguish always is. He holds his head and tugs his hair and sobs so hard and uncontrollably, the headboard bumps the wall. He sobs like a child, overwhelmed and helpless, desperate in his pain.

And I just lie beside him, frozen though my every atom urges me to go to him, to hold him. *This is Barrett.* I think for a moment, I just can't believe it.

Slowly—maybe seconds, though it feels like years—my mind regroups; my pulse steadies; the empathetic horror that's gripping me lessens just enough to let me feel a heady swell of need—to comfort him.

Cold sweat sweeps me as I reach for him again. My hand touches his shoulder, and his body stills for just a second. Then he's sobbing brokenly again. He holds his head and shudders—I hear "Breck"—and something changes; I guess he starts shaking harder, less like crying, more like shivering. His sobs soften and run longer: wracking sobs that fade off into low whimpers. And every few seconds, I hear his breath catch on an inhalation, quivering a few times as if he's almost hyperventilating.

I rub his damp back. "Barrett?"

I think he feels me, and I feel him try to get control—his shoulders clench, his body stills—but I know how it is: he's on auto-pilot, somewhere else, someplace where a part of him remains. Still wracked with soft, pained sobs, he reaches out and fumbles with a pillow, pulls it to his face, wrapping both arms around it like he's trying to anchor himself.

"Barrett...Bear." My voice sounds small and hesitant amidst his solid sounds. I get him by his shoulders, try to turn him on his back so I can wrap myself around him. Fail. His skin is soaked, his body coiled and rigid. Shudders start to wrack him, and every few seconds, I hear a ghost sound seep around the muffler of the pillow.

I crawl over his bent legs and come around in front of him. I look at his long fingers, dug into the pillow, pressing it against his face.

After a breath of hesitation, I reach out and stroke a light hand down his forearm.

"Hey, Barrett..."

His chest and shoulders move more rhythmically, and when I try to gently pull the pillow down, I hear his hollow-sounding breaths, realize he's right there on the edge of hyperventilating.

Fuck. *What do I do?*

I stretch out on the bed beside him, scoot in close, and wrap my arm around his upper back. He's so much wider than I am, my arm can't reach too far; I clutch his shoulder and hold on.

I curl my body close to his and rub his cool, damp skin. Chills spread underneath my hand. He gives no other clue he knows I'm here.

I remember something from my own dark time. When I dissociated once at Helga's office...

I tap him on the arm—a steady tap, tap, tap—and with my right hand, the arm I'm lying on, I reach out and touch his chest. I tap both places.

"Barrett—it's Gwenna."

I scoot closer still, and stop my left hand's tapping, wrapping my arm a little more tightly around him, trying to hold him to me. He's still coiled in pain, still shaking.

"Barrett...baby." I press my lips against his throat and run my hand up from his back into his hair. The curls are sweaty. Everywhere our skin touches, I feel his chills. I spread my fingers through his damp curls, stroking softly.

"Hey...you're safe. I've got you." To my own ears, I sound scared and stupid.

He drags in a deep breath, and his shoulders twitch. I shift positions just a little, so the pillow in front of his face is right under my neck. Then I wrap my hand around his head and pull him up against my chest.

"I've got you. I'm not letting go." I hold him and I whisper and I stroke him and it hurts. To see someone so strong and capable—To see *anyone* in so much pain...

I feel the pillow pulled away and feel him bow his head. I want to look down at him, check on him. Instead I kiss his hair, offering him privacy. A second later, his face presses against my chest. His face is hot and wet, his breaths warm and still fast. My heart aches as I smooth his curls.

Jesus, if he does this every night…

Breath quivers through his chest and throat, ragged breaths like aftershocks.

When I finally glance down, I see his eyelids cracked, but can't tell where he's looking.

"You awake?" I whisper.

"I don't know." The words are raspy, almost whimpered.

I hold him tighter.

"Sorry," he says roughly.

"No, sweetheart."

He starts to shake a little harder.

I lift my arm from his back. "Just a second. Let me get…"

I pull the duvet up over his shoulders, leaning up so I can tuck it around his back and underneath his side. I pull it over him, and over me, and then behind my own back, where I tuck it so it's tight around us both.

Then I wrap an arm around his waist. He bows his head a little, his hair tickling my throat and chin. I feel him swallow.

"You're okay…"

I snuggle closer to him.

God, he's warm. And still. I can feel him breathing, but that's all. Then I feel him raise his arm. His hand touches my shoulder: just a brief caress.

Then he lifts the duvet off him, turns away from me, and gets down off the bed. I see his gorgeous body glisten in the dim light as he walks into the bathroom. He doesn't shut the door, just cracks it, so I hear the faucet running, followed by a slurping sound that makes me think he's drinking.

A minute later, he comes out and walks over to the bed. He stops beside it, looking at me for a long moment. His blue eyes are tired but clear.

"That's why," he whispers.

"Why what?"

He shakes his head. "I fell asleep with you but..." He shakes his head again, purses his lips, and lifts his fingers to his forehead.

"What?" I whisper, as he rasps, "I can't sleep."

I see his Adam's apple bob as his brows draw together. "I... can't."

When his stark eyes meet my own, I feel my throat tighten.

"Does that happen every time?" I whisper.

He looks down at the mattress, rests his fingers on its edge. Then his gaze sears mine. "No more sleepovers."

I look down at my hands, then back up at his vacant face. His beautiful face. "I think we *should* do sleep overs. For this reason. And others." My face burns.

He's looking at me, but I can't read his face.

"I can wake you up from square one next time, right when you first start dreaming."

He looks away, toward the fireplace. His jaw tightens.

"This is why I said I can't," he says flatly. Then, without looking back at me, he stalks across the room to a dresser by the fireplace and pulls a drawer open. He plucks a pair of boxer-briefs out, and as I watch him pull them up his long legs and over his flawless ass, I try to process what just happened.

He ignored me.

Insecurity wells within me, but I push it down. *Don't be an idiot.*

I scoot closer to the foot of the bed, closing a little distance between us.

"Are you embarrassed?" I ask, soft but clear.

His back stiffens, then he turns fully away from me and pulls another drawer open.

I feel a jolt of surprise, but then I realize: I shouldn't. He's a man—a man who had sex with me for the first time tonight—and he just lost his shit in front of me for not the first time. He might seem unaffected by a lot of things, but this isn't going to be one of them. Of course he's embarrassed. He shouldn't be. But I get it.

"I used to have nightmares too. Every night, for almost a year. I have a weighted blanket at my house. I took all kinds of pills. I saw three therapists. I cried every night. One time I woke up with my hand around this Diet Coke can. I had squeezed it...and it had cut my fingers." Remembering that makes me look down at my hand.

Silence blankets us. Then he turns to me, his face unreadable. "And now?"

"It's a lot better. I don't even take anything. Not that that matters. I just haven't needed to. I can tell you a few things you could try to maybe help. You have to write the dreams out—like, in detail. Then you go back and edit them and change things so it's more the way you would want it."

Skepticism flashes through his features: there, then gone.

"But I can be with you. I can show you how to start. There's sleeping together and there's *sleeping* together, you know?"

I sit up a little straighter, giving him my pleasant wide-eyed face, the one I use around people I'm scared to snarile for. Then I realize what I did and give Barrett a tiny smile. "We can do both if you wanted to."

"Why?" he asks tonelessly.

"Why do I want to?"

He blinks. *Yes, that's what he means.* Why do I care? My chest squeezes. "Because I mean it."

chapter fourteen

Gwenna

"Why?" This time, the word is thick with feeling. I feel a knot form in my throat as I look into his beautiful, sad eyes. "I would do anything to stop someone else from feeling like that. But you especially," I say softly.

"Especially." He blinks, then looks away.

"Especially."

His face softens as he looks back at me, but it's a sad kind of soft—a little vulnerable, a little shy. Before he can turn back to the drawers, I slide down off the bed. I don't even know what I'm going to do at first; I just know I want to see him smile.

His eyes follow me as I move, rolling up and down me once before he sets his gaze on my face. As soon as it's trained there, I want to pull it down again. I turn around, bringing my hand up to my mouth and tapping. As I do, I jut my hip out slightly.

"I had an idea, but I forgot it. Oh yeah—" I turn around to face him, wickedly satisfied when his gaze drops to my boobs for half a second. His eyes return to mine; more blue than normal, slightly widened in wait. I put my hand on my hip, casual, as if I'm wearing clothes, and give him what I know is a slightly silly look. "I was hoping you might get a bath with me."

He frowns like I'm a few cards shy of a full deck, but his lips twitch, and I know my mission is accomplished. "You want to get a bath right now?"

I bob my head. "A bath with you."

His eyes narrow in confusion. "Why?"

I grab his wrist, tugging him gently closer to me. "Because baths are relaxing. And they're fun."

He frowns, looking somber with his thick scruff and his wild, dark curls.

"C'mon." I stroke his wrist and look into his pretty eyes. "You know you want to. How long has it been?"

His eyebrows arch. "Since I took a bath?" His mouth twitches again, but this time, he can't hide a funny little smile.

I nod.

"A while."

"So it's a must."

He rubs his forehead, looking tired and unconvinced, and also like he thinks I may be crazy. "If you insist."

I feel a sharp sense of relief, like I've just pulled us five steps in the right direction. Like I've diffused things.

"I'm a great bath companion," I tell him as I lead him toward the door. "You have no way to vouch for this. In fact, no one does. I've never shared a bath with anyone since I was like, a toddler. But trust me, I have all the right qualities."

"What are those?" His voice, behind me, sounds a little lighter.

I sway my hips. "This." I barely manage to stifle a giggle.

Barrett smacks my ass, groaning as I gasp. I whirl and push against his chest. He thumbs my nipple.

"What else?" he asks. His eyes are heavy-lidded, and for a small moment, I think he may kiss me—but he holds himself back.

I can feel it. His mouth curves upward on one side, and it's enough for me to see that I'm amusing him.

I step into the bathroom, a palatial space done in rich earth tones. I step onto a fluffy rug and glimpse myself in the mirror. My stomach flip-flops; *no*, I tell myself.

I look over my shoulder at him and continue. "I can make bubbles from any…" My eyes land on his dick. Holy gorgeous boner.

Barrett blinks his hooded eyes. "What were you saying? Bubbles?" His hand wraps around the base of his cock. I force myself to look up at his face. I nod.

"Bubbles from any shampoo." My voice is raspy.

I turn around toward the tub and lean over the side to turn the faucet on. My backside tingles in anticipation of his hand.

"I give good backrubs too," I go on. Water pours out of the faucet. I grab a bottle of shampoo and squeeze it over the stream.

Then I turn back to him. I don't notice my nipples are sticking out until his eyes move over them. I cover them with my hands, blushing.

Barrett's dick is long and hard and pointed upward, toward his navel. My God, it's huge—and perfectly proportioned. Right in line with the rest of him, I guess.

He blinks down at himself, then locks his gaze on mine. "You sure you want a bath?" He lifts an eyebrow.

I smile sweetly. "Yep. I love a good, long bubble bath. You're going to love it too. If you're still horny when we get out, I'll blow you."

His eyes widen. He groans. "Goddamn, Gwenna."

I beam as I grab two towels off a shelf and set them on the side of the garden tub. "My Myers-Briggs shadow personality is decisive and authoritative. I tend to go shadow when it's sex time."

Barrett screws his face up like he thinks I'm nuts, but a smile blooms a second later, complete with dimples. He lets out a hoarse laugh. "What the fuck?"

I wiggle my brows. "You laugh now, but you'll respect it. I can guess your type, too—easy."

I really think a bath will do us good, so I climb into the garden tub and scoot back, giving him the front seat, where it's warmer and he can be ogled. Barrett leans over, slides his hands under my arms, and shifts me gently forward. I watch over my shoulder as he eases his big body behind mine. There's nowhere for his legs to go except around my hips and over mine. As he settles, I feel a warm throb in between my legs. I hope my momentary abstinence makes him feel cared for. In fact, I vow to make it happen.

I look down at his legs, warm and heavy around mine. They're bent slightly at the knee, his soles pressed up against the front wall of the tub. The garden tub is big, but Barrett's bigger. His legs are beautiful: muscular and thick, but also elegantly hewn. I take some soap and run it down his strong, hair-dusted calves. Barrett groans.

"I told you I was good at baths."

His toes curl as I massage his calves. He lifts one leg and makes a choking sound. "That tickles."

I can't see his face, but I can hear the smile in his voice. My chest loosens just a little more.

"Does it?" I look behind me, sporting a cat-that-ate-the-canary grin. I run the soap over his knee and up this thigh, and like a man, he lets me move on up as his eyes darken and the bubbles gather around his still-hard dick. When I can tell he thinks he knows my next move, I dig my hand into his thigh and tickle.

He moves so fast, the water sloshes, drawing his legs up hilariously around himself and wrapping his arms around him. I cackle at his crazy hair and wide eyes. I feint, going for his thighs although from this angle, I know I can't get him. I'm just teasing,

ELLA JAMES

waiting for him to come back at me with his ninja skills. Finally he grabs my arms, lowers his legs, and drags me onto his lap. There, with just the briefest hesitation while he looks into my eyes, he kisses me.

It's our first kiss since his nightmare, and it feels especially slow and sweet. He pulls gently away, a little smirk on his lips.

"You're a dirty fighter," he says in a low voice.

His eyes are warm enough to make my stomach clench.

"It's the only way to win." I laugh. "You're too advanced for me."

"I thought you had your shadow personality." He smirks again, and like so many times before, his mouth loses its self-control control and break into a gorgeous smile. His smile is beautiful. I want to ask him why he's so reserved with it. Instead I smile back, then splash him.

"Only sometimes. Your Myers-Briggs is INTJ, BTW. That's INTJ *by the way*, for those of you hiding under desert rocks." I wink.

"What does that mean? INTJ?"

"I'll show you when we get out, although I have to warn you, as an INTJ, I doubt it will mean much to you. I don't think your kind puts much stock in things like this."

I turn around to make the bath water hotter, and I hear him snort behind me. I take some shampoo and pool it in my palm and hold my palm under the water to make more bubbles. My eyes wander down to his feet—and of course, I can't resist touching them.

I run the back of my fingers over the top of his left one. "You have really pretty feet."

They're arched slightly, the balls of them pressed against the front wall of the tub. I squeeze one.

He makes a low purring sound. "Weakness."

"Foot rubs are?" I gather my hair over my shoulder and smile back at him.

"Yeah."

I rub his heel and he moans. He flexes his calf and ankle, and I squeeze the outside wall of his sole. He groans roughly. "Fuck... You're good."

"That's what I'm told." I squeeze his heel once more before I lower it back into the suds. "Remind me and I'll do that with some lotion later."

He chuckles, and I shoot him a look. "I know what you're thinking, mister."

"I don't think you do," he murmurs.

"That's what she said?"

He laughs again, all dimpled and fuck hot with that rough-looking beard.

"I know how you penis-havers are." I turn around and turn the water off, then hug myself, feeling nervous under the sparkly veneer of what is indeed my shadow personality: Regular Gwenna gone insane/hyper/confident. It happens when I'm stressed, even if the stress is good. Of course, if the stress is bad, it's more like insane, detail-obsessed drill sergeant.

My body freezes as I feel Barrett's hand stroke down my spine.

"Penis-havers." He chuckles. His arm wraps around my lower belly, and he pulls me back against his chest. I can feel his long erection pressed against my ass. I wait for him to rub against me, but he just strokes my shoulder and lifts his chin a little, so my head can rest in the softness between his throat and shoulder. I can feel his warm chest rise and fall below me.

Nestled between his powerful thighs, I can't help the throb between my own. His body calls to mine, and I can tell the inverse is true, too: After a minute, I can feel his dick twitch just above my ass.

ELLA JAMES

I unfold my lower body from the cross-legged position and draw my knees up toward my chest, pressing my thighs together in a futile attempt to satiate my lust. Barrett makes a soft sound: could be an exhalation, could be the ghost of a groan.

Heat tingles through me, starting at my chest and sweeping downward. I take a careful breath and slip into a strange state where I'm turned on, but I'm also strangely satisfied just lying back against him.

I wrap my hands around his forearm. His hand splays out over my abs. How intimate we are, for almost strangers.

My head is nestled against his pec. I snuggle in a little more and when his arms tighten around me, I whisper, "Do you like being here with me?"

He cups his hand around my hip, tracing a gentle circle with one fingertip. "It may be the only thing I like," he answers finally.

A flock of butterflies swoops through my stomach. He's been so reserved, so distant since we met, every little thing he says now makes me want to sing.

I run my hand over the back of his left thigh, smoothing over a deep scar I saw after we had sex downstairs.

His chest expands beneath me. He lets out a long, silent breath. "I've lost a ton of muscle mass since getting…home."

He raises his right knee, cradling my lower body with his own. I feel myself relax against him.

The word "home" seems laced with frustration—maybe even bitterness—and I want to ask. I even feel like he might want me to. But I'm not sure what to say. I don't want to say the wrong thing. Finally I relax more and look up at the ceiling, "Has it been like you thought it would be? Being discharged?"

His left thigh tightens underneath my stroking fingers.

"I didn't," he says roughly. "Think about it." I see his calf flex underneath the waning bubbles.

"How long were you in?" I ask softly.

"Eleven years." I glance back at him, finding his eyes shut.

"Does that mean you might be…twenty-nine?"

He lifts an eyelid and smiles, looking oddly miserable. "Old."

"No." I turn around toward him and drag my hand over his upper abs. His abs twitch, and he sits up slightly, looking at my face curiously, silently, as he piles my hair up on my head with his damp hands, and, with his hands spreading along my ribcage, leans me back against his chest. He folds an arm around me.

"I guess it probably feels like it," I say softly.

Like always, I wait for him to answer, and like usually, he doesn't—at least not with his voice. He trails his fingertips over my soft belly, tickling until I sigh.

It's been so long. "This feels so good."

I'm still needy for him. He's still hard. Maybe I should feel strange that he's not initiating sex, but this means more: lying against him with my body lit up. Knowing that he needs me, but he's holding me instead. This has been a gift.

With his right hand still playing with my belly, his left one comes down around my hip. I feel his face against the back of my hair. "You seem younger than twenty-six." His lips press behind my ear, and I have to struggle not to moan.

"That's funny," I manage. "I don't feel it." I realize who I'm talking to and feel self-conscious.

"I was at that meeting."

My muscles stiffen, and as much as I want to turn and see his face—I also don't. "The commission meeting?"

"Yeah."

I sit up straighter, pulling slightly away from him. I rub my face with my wet hand. "Mmm, let's maybe just pretend you weren't."

I feel his hand spread out against my back. "It made me want to know you."

"Really?"

"I didn't plan on it. But yeah." His finger traces an indention on my back where I think I have a draining tube scar. I let out a long breath.

"You were brave," he says softly.

I shake my head. "I looked pathetic."

"You were trying."

"Without you, I would have told those people all about myself for nothing." I draw a knee up to my chest and rest my forehead on it, hiding, I guess. I sink my arm into the water, watch it lap around my elbow. "I don't like to share my details."

He drags his fingers down my back, making me shiver. I feel cold and hot. Restless.

"We have that in common, I think," he says.

Then his mouth touches my spine. I flinch, then shiver. His lips drag up toward my neck.

"Barrett…"

I gasp as his mouth finds the curve between my neck and shoulder. I can feel his teeth, maybe. What he's doing hurts—and makes me moan.

"I tried," he breathes in puffs. His mouth moves down my collarbone. He grabs me by my arms and turns me toward him, licking at the side of my throat. "Please believe—" he trails under my chin—"I tried…" He bites my jaw. He's hungry, frenzied, reckless.

By the time his lips find mine, I'm crying out for him. I grab his head, his hair. Our tongues surge: gliding, reaching. We pull each other closer, kissing hard. Between the kisses, panting. I can feel his cock against my leg. I grab for it. His hands find my hips. He lifts me to him.

His eyes burn mine. "Tell me."

"Yes!"

He lifts his hips, groaning. I feel his head against me, thick and prodding.

"Oh God. Fuck." I spread myself. He pushes in. That's how we do it: rough, in water; splashing, moaning, screaming. My fingers dig into his neck and pull his hair. His hands hurt my hips and ribs. He slams into me, sending plumes of water through over my clit.

It doesn't take me long. It doesn't take me long enough. He moans as his cock thumps inside me. I can hear him panting as his muscles twitch and quiver. My eyes open and his eyes are shut tight. His face looks pained. I have never seen a thing more beautiful.

As his blue eyes open, I kiss his mouth softly. He's still in me, eyelids drifting shut.

Dear God, his tongue is soft, his lips are tender; careful now. When whoever pulls away, he brings my head down on his shoulder.

I can barely hear him say, "I needed you."

As he kisses my cheeks and picks me up, his face is bare; his face is tired or relaxed. I can't decide if he looks lost or found.

We get into the bed together, shivering and wet. He pulls the covers over us. The next thing I'm aware of is a sharp, gold light.

chapter fifteen

Barrett

I wait until she's breathing evenly, then I quietly dress, grab my .338, and go downstairs, where dawn is streaming sheets of amber through the windows by the door.

I put the gun in its case early last night, after I first put Gwenna in my bed. I set the case on the kitchen counter and pull it out. I take my time looking over it, and when I'm finished, I step away from the counter and just stand there for a minute. It feels important somehow, though I can't say why.

I leave the gun in the kitchen, but I can't stop myself from going through the motions of clearing the house. When I'm finished, I carry the gun case over to the coat rack, where I get my Lakers cap and fold it into my back pocket. I get my helmet from a nearby cabinet and realize I haven't left a note.

'*Going into town. Be back soon,*' I text Gwen. I'd like to add, '*Make yourself at home,*' but how would she do that? I don't even have real food here.

I look down at the gun case, waiting on the hardwood floor in front of the door. I could take it with me. Truthfully, I want to. Always. My McMillan .338 is the first gun I bought myself, way back before even the Rangers. Before it made sense for me to have a gun like this. It was my way of investing in myself, telling myself that I'd do it.

Looking at it now makes me feel strange. The plans I have for it...

I decide after a few minutes not to take it with me this morning. I stash it in the walk-in pantry, lying right along the baseboard, then arrange some empty cardboard boxes so they hide it from casual view.

I feel tense and restless as I pull my wrist brace on, then get on my bike and head toward town. As I drive down the winding, dew-damp road, through wooded foothills, underneath a fog blanket, I let my mind wander over last night. Most of it was surreal. Some of it makes me wish I never had to see her again. Makes me feel fucking terrible. I could go there...It would be easy.

But I also think about the moment I pushed into her. It felt so fucking good, like my whole body lit up. Everything went out of me, and light rushed in, and there was Gwenna, wiggling that ass against me, clamping that fat pussy down on my dick. I feel myself harden now and try to shift my thoughts away from her sweet body.

One thing I keep thinking about is her tucking that blanket around us. I'd woken up—sort of—and I was trying to breathe into that fucking pillow. Something about her pulling the blanket up...it just keeps replaying in my head.

I guess I thought she'd...

Most people wouldn't want to be around that. Someone losing it. Why doesn't she care?

I can feel her hand on my leg in the tub. The way her fingers brushed the back of my thigh. I couldn't stand it the first time her fingertips slide over the bumpy scar. I got that graze the day I hurt my head. I've always hated it. I've always thought it should have been more.

I still think it should have been more. I know I should have died with Breck. I couldn't shoot Maliha, even thought that was my goddamned job. That bomb blew up the square. She died, too. And then I end up over the edge of that building and I'm landing and so bright.

It was so bright and I heard Breck and everything was burning and...I look down at my left hand, strengthened by the fabric brace I have to wear to hold the handlebar.

You paid, I hear her voice say. I don't even think she ever said that, but I still hear those words in her soft voice.

I feel warm and...weird. Like I can breathe a big gulp of the air. It smells like dirt and water. Feels like heaven in my lungs. I look down at my hand and I think I may love it: this fucked up hand.

If I've already atoned, maybe things could be different.

It's a thought I don't allow to linger.

I'm getting into town now, navigating little roads lined with storefronts that are somehow quaint and tacky all at once. I like it, though: Gatlinburg with its rock-lined streams squiggling through the city, with its ragged sidewalks, with its silly mini golf and faux chateaus and strip malls. And then the mountains rising up around it. They're not really mountains. They don't seem like mountains to me. But they're still beautiful.

I stop at a gas station and fill my tank up. Not because I need it. Just because I like to have it. I go in to pay and look for breakfast. But...none of this looks good. I grab a bar of caffeinated chocolate, then I spend a minute looking at the Red Bull. I've got some at home. I could chug some now—in fact, I should—but...I don't know. I just don't want it. The taste. I'm fucking tired of drinking Red Bull.

I get a pack of white powder doughnuts, some beef jerky, and a bag of Cheese Its before wondering what Gwen would eat. I've seen a tube of Pringles in a grocery bag of hers before. I get some Pringles. While the short dude with a faux-hawk rings me up, I see these round rights by the register. Some are blue, others green, and one is brown.

"Mood rings," the guy explains.

"What do they do?"

He laughs. "It's based on temperature." He taps a stack of pamphlets in front of the rings. "They just change color. Want one?"

I can tell he's joking, so I deadpan nod and pull a blue one off the plastic display. I look right into his eyes and tell him, "It'll look good with this dress I have."

I get a kick out of watching his eyes bug out, then watching him compose his face, until it's so tight, he looks like some kind of doll.

I take the bag and nod. "Thanks, dude."

I can feel his eyes on me as I get back onto my bike and drive off toward this strip mall I see on the next corner. I can't help thinking of Breck. He's got this older brother, Casper, who was born female. Over the years, Breck would tell people at bars sometimes that he was born a woman. He was pretty big, not as big as me but ripped as shit, and more than once, I watched him throttle someone who had something negative to say.

"Just doing a little weeding," he would say.

He had this half-assed Southern accent, just a little bit like Gwen's, because his mom was from one of the Carolinas. South, I think.

I park in front of a bakery with a neon blue "OPEN" sign flashing in the window. I know, as I walk inside, that I'm walking into more than buying scones.

I know.

But I'm not sure how much I care.

Gwenna

His room is clean and quiet. The bed is empty. On the pillow beside me, I find a note.

HOPE YOU SLEPT WELL. I HAD SOME THINGS TO DO THIS MORNING. CHECK THE OVEN BEFORE GOING HOME. B.

I go downstairs and find the house empty. The stove clock says it's 10:43 a.m. Inside the oven, I find a tinfoil-covered dinner plate piled high with scones. Blueberry scones, apparently. In the garbage can, I find a box from Mona's Bakery in Gatlinburg.

My chest goes hot. He went to get these just for me—or us. I know he did it this morning, too, because Mona's only sells food baked the day of. I down two delicious scones and drink some orange juice, then I float into the den, where I find my clothes draped over the couch's arm.

I take my time upstairs, dressing and making the bed, and have to struggle not to check the drawers.

I wonder if he folds his clothes or they're just in a messy pile, shoved in. Somehow I doubt they're messy.

Before I go, I hug his pillow. Smells like him.

I wonder if he'll call.

chapter sixteen

I slide my Kindle into my carry-on bag, a little leather backpack propped against the arm of my black suede couch. Elvie stops messing with my new DVD player and walks over to me, wrapping an arm around my waist. "You and your imposter books," he drawls.

I wriggle free and swat his cheek. "They're not imposters. They're ebooks."

He snorts. "I don't know how you do that."

"You don't read, so I imagine not." I quirk an eyebrow at him.

"I read music. Isn't that enough for you, woman?"

"Of course it is." I reach instinctively for him, but remember he doesn't want me touching his hair. He's playing tonight.

He must have seen the intention on my face, because he cups my cheek and pulls me up against him. "You're looking good there in that little skirt, Gwennie." He rocks his hips against me, just to be sure I feel how turned on he is. "You want to fuck before Jamie gets here?"

I wince at the word—fucking is totally not how I'd like to describe sex—then shake my head and laugh. "She'll be here in five minutes, you lunatic."

"It could be a quickie."

"No one's that quick."

In fact—especially not Elvie. Especially not lately. When we first started having sex our sophomore year of college, sometimes he would come before he even got all the way inside. Now sometimes it takes him longer than me. I push that thought away. Models aren't allowed to feel insecure about their looks. I pat Elvie's itty-bitty beer pooch. "It's going to be a long five days without you. I hope New York is amazing."

"It won't be the same without you." He looks down at his big belt buckle, frowning as he rubs it. His green eyes lift to mine. "You could still come, you know. Back-up sing."

I push my hand at his face. "You arrogant asshole. I'm the star," I say in a dramatic Southern accent.

His eyebrows shoot up. "Too good to back-up sing for Elvie Wesson."

"Damn right I am."

He taps his fingertips against his mouth and frowns at me. "You know…" He shakes his head. "I feel like I've seen you somewhere." He slaps his jeans and twists his handsome face into a hillbilly *duh* look. "I know!" He snaps his fingers. "You're the lady on the billboard!"

I shove his shoulder. Elvie topples toward the couch, and just as I can see his face tighten with embarrassment, we hear a car horn in front of my house.

My house.

I glance around my beautiful space, and Elvie huffs. He doesn't say anything—he never does—but there are these times when he makes me feel like some kind of big, gross giant: when I wear heels, or when I can reach something he can't. As if it's my fault I'm tall for a girl, and he's short for a guy.

Jamie beeps again, and Elvie gets my suitcase while I shoulder my purse and carry on. He gets the front door for me, and we step outside without a word. Our breaths make pale clouds. I find myself smiling as I turn to lock the door. It's cold here in Nashville, but not as cold as it will be where I'm going. I can't freaking wait.

I take a small step back, admiring my little house. My dream. The little wreath on the door. I get chills as I think of going back to the studio. To work more on my album, which combined with my movie and modeling income, helped me buy this house.

My album!

Elvie frowns at me, and I flick him on the arm.

"Daydreaming all the time," he drawls.

"About the studio," I say.

"Aww, I gotcha."

But he doesn't. The only son of one of country music's most beloved duos, Elvie cut his first record when he was 9. He's had a CD in Wal-Mart since last year. A Christmas CD since the year before.

Next year, I'll have my own album too. My eyes tingle a little as we walk to Jamie's schmancy SUV, a Cadillac SRX. As Elvie opens the trunk, Jamie gets out of the driver's seat and throws her arms around me.

We both squeal, and Elvie covers his ears.

Jamie lets me go and jabs him in the arm.

"What is it with you women and the hitting?"

She shrugs and looks him over. "You look nice, cowboy."

"Singing at the Bluebell."

"Oh yeah, Gwenna told me about that."

"Gwennie." He settles my suitcase in the trunk and shuts it. Then he wraps his arms around me.

"You two. Get a room. Oh wait, I'm taking your girlfriend with me." Jamie sticks her tongue out.

Elvie flips her off.

She goes around to her side of the car while Elvie kisses me. He tastes like cigar and chicken. We had dinner at Miss Darcy's Grill. I wipe my lipstick off his mouth. He has the good sense not to complain this time.

He even kisses me again on the cheek. "Stay warm, Gwennie."

"Break a leg. Not both, though. Or I'll have to send you away on an ass's ass."

This is Elvie's and my private joke. One time I told him I would always love him, even with no arms and legs. It was meant to be funny. Romantic, dark funny—but funny. He said he would love me always, too. But when I got too old and ugly to be photographed with him, he'd send me away on a mule's ass.

"Such a comedian," he says now. He runs a hand along my hair. "Be safe, now."

"For sure. You too. Talk to you soon?"

"I'll call tomorrow."

I blow him a kiss and climb up into Jamie's silver Caddy, bound for my favorite place on earth.

chapter seventeen

Barrett
November 6, 2015

"Hey, man." I hold my phone against my ear and lean against the bathroom wall. "You probably won't remember me, but you did a tat for me about three years ago."

"Yeah, man. Sounds right. I've been here since '09."

"It was a snowflake."

"Yeah?"

"A little snowflake on my neck, kind of near my hairline in the back."

"I think I remember you. Real big guy? Dark hair?"

I nod, and blink into the mirror. "That was me." In my line of work, it's wise to assume you're going to stick out. When you're six-foot-three, you have to.

"So what can I help you with?" he asks.

"I was wondering if you drew it."

"That snowflake?"

"Yeah."

"I draw them all. So yeah. All my shit is custom."

"You give them out a lot?" I ask.

"You got a problem, man?"

"No. No problem." I inhale slowly, hoping to bring my voice up from where it goes down deep when I'm thinking hard about something. So I don't sound pissed off. "I saw a girl the other day—same tat. I was wondering if that means she got it up in Breckenridge."

"Exact same?"

"Yeah. You do the same snowflake on everybody?"

He hums, as if he's thinking. "For a while I did. Last year I started doing another one, seven pointed, kind of artsy. Gotta keep it fresh."

I exhale slowly. "Yeah. Well brother, thanks."

"No problem. Nothing I can help you with?"

I laugh, as if I'm embarrassed. "Just chasing a girl."

"Good luck, man."

"Yeah. Thanks, dude."

"Have a good one."

"You too. Catch ya later."

I hang up with Roy J. Bidd from High Altitudes Tattoo & Piercing and stare down at my phone.

So the tat we have is custom, sort of. He didn't get it out of some tattoo artists' stock art book. I couldn't tell if it was identical, because I can't see mine easily. But now I know it probably is. It doesn't matter. Gwen won't know.

I slide the phone into my pocket and walk back into my bedroom. Like I did a little while ago, I catch myself staring at the bed. Gwenna made it before she left. Piled the pillows up, straightened the duvet so there's no wrinkles. I don't think I've seen a bed this neat since boot camp.

I step over and look down at the note still lying where she left it right in front of the pillows.

How'd you know my favorite scones?

Don't be a stranger. Pretty please…

XOX

I tuck the note into my pocket and consider getting up there on the bed, but decide to leave it untouched for right now. I go over to the armchair, which I pulled away from the window when Gwenna was here. It feels strange, sitting in it near the middle of the room. I start to drag it to the window, but for some reason I stop halfway there.

I sink back into the chair and scroll through my phone. Sooner or later, someone's going to notice I still have it, or maybe they don't give a fuck. It is mine, after all. I did all the coding. They would need to gut it—software, hardware, all—so it's nothing more than just a case, and what would be the point of confiscating that? I could build the same thing inside any regular ass iPhone case. Easier just to let me keep the one I have already. That way they can still track me. We're told they won't do that once we leave the Unit, but when I called Alec Ludlum about tracking Blue, he asked me what I was doing down in Tennessee.

I look open my phone's screen and look briefly at the picture of Gwen's little snowflake tat, then nav over to track Blue. I find him sidelined in Kentucky, somewhere known as Berea, where he seems to be spending time at a local library.

Then I read Dove's latest text.

'All cool, Bear?'

'All cool,' I reply.

I shut the thing right down, then wash my face with ice cold water and pop a piece of MEG gum so I don't have to drink a coffee or a Red Bull. I make a mug of Keurig hot chocolate and take it to the back porch, where, for once, I don't do anything but sit there watching the trees.

Then, when the sun starts slipping behind the foothills, I grab the groceries I bought a couple hours ago, after I delivered

Gwenna's scones, and put them in my rucksack. I leave it at the bottom of the stairs and go back up to the bathroom, where I stare at the tub for a minute before brushing my teeth.

I rinse with mouthwash like a fucking teenager and can't resist a quick look in the mirror. Looking fucking weird with this long hair. I trimmed the beard down so it's kind of prickly. I rub my eyes and look down at my white shirt and black jeans.

I should maybe call first…but I don't. I go downstairs and get my pack and lock up. I put my hand against the swing, making a mental note to bolt it down or move it before I go down the stairs. As I step into the woods, I check my pants for my .38 and find I left without it.

That beats all. Unarmed and with a rucksack full of food. I smile a little as I trek toward her place.

Gwenna

It's too warm in Tennessee for hibernation—at least the kind you hear about. Black bears just curl up nice and cozy somewhere and don't move much. But they're still bears. Their bodies still know the cycle of things. So they still try to stock up on food before.

I have cameras set on two of their most common dining halls: a patch of wild grapes and a grove of oak trees, heavy with acorns. When I look, after I get home from Barrett's in the morning, both places look pretty picked over. So I make an unplanned trip into the enclosure a little after noon.

I throw out nine vitamin ball bombs and sink a wooden case of frozen rainbow trout in the pond. I don't see Papa, who I know from my pre-visit cam check is many acres away. I decide not to linger, even though it makes me sad. I consider going back in tomorrow to organize the stock shed. If Papa scents me and wanders over…Well, who am I to protest?

With a silly smile on my face, I walk back to my cabin, call the local Wal-Mart to ask about Christmas lights, and spend the next two hours catching up on work-related emails—with St. Jude's, with the stuffed bear supplier, with a few Beary Appreciated Donors, and with the fencing company, who last week was supposed to send someone to patch a weak spot on the east side of the fence, but didn't.

I realize as I wait on hold with the fencing place that I haven't even thought to check the cameras for my creeper. I skim through a few hours of footage, then Jamie calls and I keep on skimming as she tells me about Niccolo, and how his mom is depressed because she and his dad are having trouble, and Nic's brother—the poor, sweet, dead one, John—was honored recently with some kind of posthumous Army award, and did I know Jamie thinks she might have gotten her very first gray hair, and before I know it, I've skimmed 42 hours of cam footage and there hasn't been a single trace of anybody.

Sweet!

I hear Jamie stop her motor-mouthing and take a sip of something.

"Are you at Starbucks?"

"I'm meeting a client."

"When?" I giggle. "We've been on the phone almost an hour."

"Hmm, well then they're late. I should go find out what happened."

We hang up without me telling her about my night with Barrett, and to be honest, I'm kind of glad. It's nice to keep it to myself: my very own delicious secret.

I spend the next hour doing Bible study and then meditating, and by the time I'm finished, I'm feeling very zen about this thing with Barrett. Either it'll bloom into something or it won't. All I can do is open myself up to what God wants to give me and continue trying to be grateful for whatever comes my way.

I pass the rest of my afternoon fertilizing my gardenias, making a trip to Wal-Mart for a laundry list of household items, and then dragging a ladder around my bedroom, stringing lights from the ceiling.

I tell myself if nothing more happens with Barrett, I'll be glad to have the lights. It's getting colder, closer to the holidays, and usually when it gets near Christmas, I have a harder time with my own nightmares.

On that note, I decide to pull out my journal and get a hold of my feelings.

I spent the night at Barrett's last night. I went over there drunk, and he seemed really off from the first moment, now that I look back on it. I tried to leave after just a little bit, and he wanted me to stay. And then we were in his den and he started having a panic attack. I felt so bad for him.

Somehow he ended up telling me he's a killer. And of course, I had no idea what to make of that. I finally figured out he was saying he was a sniper, and somewhere in the night he said he was in ACE. I saw some random internet news story about Delta Force where they talked about the name change, so that's the only reason I even know what it is. (So, holy hell, Barrett came from Delta Force...I now understand the mad martial arts skillz).

Anyway—he talked so long about how he should keep his distance from me because of the things he'd been through, and at one point he even said something along the lines of 'people shouldn't come back from war,' or maybe just he shouldn't have. I know what PTSD is like but...I don't know. His stuff is so different than mine. He just seemed so lost. I can see that he's in so much pain, and I'm not even really sure what to do for him. It's hard, and it already really hurts, and we don't even know each other long term or anything. There have been so many moments that I've had my arms around him, just holding him. I can feel how much he needs it. I can tell he's trying to be strong. I asked once in bed last night if he was awake and he said he didn't know. And then he said he was sorry. For having this traumatic dream where he sobbed and sobbed. I can't even imagine him there by himself when that happens. Even last night with me there… he really didn't accept that much comfort from me.

Downstairs earlier in the night he laid on the floor with me after telling me about how he sees people he knows, dead. He let me hold him, and he held me back. But after his dream, the second he was collected enough to get up, he did. He had a really hard time accepting comfort from me at first. And I said we should sleep together more—like the close your eyes kind of sleep—and he didn't get why I would offer. I don't know. It makes me sad.

And then there's this entire other element because we had sex last night. THREE times. He took me from behind the first time downstairs, and oh my God—the way his dick rubbed my G-spot. He's…shall we say 'well hung' and he knew just when to reach around and rub. I still get all hot thinking of it. And then upstairs…We got this bath together after his nightmare, and I was in the bath with him and…Whoa. He's just so beautiful. I can't even. Even his feet are perfect.

I found out he's 29, and he says in special forces, that's old. He said he heard me talk at county commission, and you know what, I think I remember? I'm going to ask him next time I see him if he has a blue ball cap. Anyway—geez. He's said so many kind things to me. So many sweet things. Still, I didn't feel like I knew for sure what was going on until he jumped on me at the end of our bath last night. He said something like "I tried to stop myself." All his sounds, all his movements, they were frenzied. As soon as we finished, we went and got in bed, still wet. I've felt on guard for so long, and lonely, and then I'm with Barrett and I just feel like I can rest. I've got it bad. I know. The funny thing is, I'm scared but in a larger way I'm not. I feel like someone standing on a precipice with my arms *stretched wide. I'm not scared of falling. Especially if he falls with me, and I can hold onto him.*

I laugh when I realize I didn't write a thing about my own trauma or my own nightmares. But that's not bad, I tell myself.

I notice when I put my journal back on my bedside table that it's 4:30. I wonder what he's doing. Then I tell myself I can't wonder. I make a plan to take a bubble bath, in which I'll shave and groom…certain areas. Then I'll lotion myself up and re-paint my nails and maybe do a mask. After which I may have some Absinthe. I might cook the tenderloin I got the other day: an easy, crockpot thing. Then, if nothing else comes up, I'll read. I'm still a little tired from last night, so if nothing else happens, I'll hit the hay early and skip my workout today.

I do a good job sticking to my vows, and I do things in the order I planned. I'm lying on my bed, holding my phone up above my face so I can read *Kyland* by Mia Sheridan, one of my favorite authors, when I hear my doorbell ring.

I swear, my heart nearly explodes. I set my phone down, grab a deep breath, and look down at myself.

It's probably the mailman, I tell myself. Mom was going to send a package with some jeans she bought me at some special best-ass-ever jeans store. I tap my face—my cracking, blue-green face—and tip-toe to the door. I peer through the peephole and my stomach ties itself into a knot.

Not the mail man.

Barrett.

chapter eighteen

Gwenna
December 30, 2011

The Madisons always fly us out to Colorado first class—going back to when Jamie and I were geeky freshmen lugging dorm room pillows and dangling gemstone-colored earbuds from our iPods.

Jamie's dad is Larry Madison, the infamous economist, Machiavelli enthusiast, Republican talking head, and real estate magnate. It's true he loves a good debate, and I can't vouch for him in business dealings, but when it comes to family, the man is a big fluff ball.

Even though I just starred in a movie, and in October signed a really decent record deal, the Madisons would never dream of letting me pay for my own plane ticket. I imagine even if—no, *when*—I hit it supernova big, Larry and Jamie's mother, Fiona, will always book our New Year's flights.

Unless Elvie and I are married. Maybe then they'd let me pay for my own.

Jamie covers her ears. "Stop!"

I blink, and realize I'm slurping up the last drops of my screwdriver. I grin and give my red straw one final slurp. A gray-haired man across the aisle, wearing a pair of square-ish reading glasses and hunching over *The Wall Street Journal*, looks up at me. I wink, and he smirks.

Charm has always been a big gun in my repertoire of talents, but since about this time last year, when all the *End of Day* billboards went up, I've noticed almost everyone returns my smiles. Even more so since the movie premiered July 2 to really strong reviews.

I lean my seat back, shut my eyes, and start to run the song I'm composing through my head. Naturally, this is the moment Jamie picks to tap my arm. I glare up at her. Jamie's gaze darts to the stewardess standing in front of the first class section.

"Argh." I sit my seat up just as the woman starts her yada yada yada, preparing to land speech.

I'm eager to land, mostly so I can turn my phone on. Elvie should be setting up at the Bluebird about now, and I want to be sure I'm the only woman on his mind. I'm sure that hussy Heather is working tonight. She always works the nights he plays. I know he'd never leave me for an apple-shaped, 4'10 brunette with yellow teeth and body odor, but even I'll admit the girl has a nice voice, and she knows just how to stroke Elvie's XL ego.

As the wheels come down and the plane begins to tilt, offering a stunning, white-capped mountain view, I try to tell myself that I'm good at that, too.

With the famous duo The Wessons as parents, there was never any chance Elvie wouldn't be both a born showman and also completely full of himself.

I sometimes jokingly call him my sea lion, because I really think he could perform all day and night for the next sixty years and die happy. And unmarried. And childless. Probably with gonorrhea from the groupies.

Jamie bats at my hands. "Put that phone up, girl. You don't need to be his babysitter."

I give her a long blink. "I was looking at the weather, bitch."

She snaps her fingers in my face. "That's easy. Snow."

"And snow."

"And more and more snow." She rubs her skinny hands together. "I can't wait to ski!"

Five hours later, we're doing just that. I've got a hunter green snowsuit Elvie gave me for Christmas, "for when the paparazzi stalk you," and by all accounts, it seems to be doing its job. It's too dark on the artificially-lit slopes for anyone to recognize my face, but I've gotten three offers to head down to the bars, and two unsolicited phone numbers. This all in the last hour.

The night ski crowd is young and horny.

Jamie and I ski down behind a group of high schoolers, and afterward she says, "I'm going to the women's room."

"Okay. Meet you back down here in 10 or 15."

"You should give me your phone."

I stick my tongue out at her, then ski over to the lifts. I wait a few minutes for an unoccupied pod, and when the crowd around me only grows, I get into one of the little pods with two guys.

I try to ignore them, looking down at my phone. Somewhere along the ascent, I get two bars of service. I want to see if Elvie's texted me a compliment on the ski suit ass shot I sent earlier.

Just as I confirm there's no text waiting in my inbox, I feel a pair of eyes on me. A second later, one of the guys says, "Hey… are you that girl?"

Despite my lousy mood, I'm prepared, and flash a quick smile his way. "Yes. I'm *definitely* that girl."

I hear a cough, followed by rich laughter, and look up into a handsome face.

The guy who first spoke rolls his eyes at his companion, the dark-haired, dark-eyed guy who's giving me a lets-fuck look.

"I'm Dove," the first guy—a blue-eyed ginger—says. He jerks his thumb at brown eyes, beside him. "This is my buddy, Breck."

The dark one pulls a glove off. Holds his hand out. "John is the name." He cuts his eyes at Dove, who shrugs.

"I think I know you, too. Weren't you in a movie?" Breck-or-John asks.

I smile. "Was I?"

"She was," Dove says.

I flirt with them until the lift lets us off at the top of one of the easier black diamonds—the only one that's open at this moment for night skiing.

Even in my Elvie-distracted state, I've learned these two are in "the service," probably the Service-My-Cock-Tonight arm of the military, because they claim the last time they were here, they were skiing alongside President Obama and his family.

"You think I believe that?" I ask, cocking a thin, shaded brow at them.

When we all get off the lift, the one called Dove hands me a small pair of binoculars and says, "Watch and you decide."

I watch them until the course turns so sharply, they move out of sight. I have to admit, they're really fucking good. They ski like pros, and I would know. My younger cousin is one.

I find them beaming at me at the bottom of the slope. Jamie is standing by them, chatting animatedly, as if they all are friends.

When I stop, they ski over. I give her a confused look, and she smirks. "I see you've met our neighbor and his friend."

"We have a neighbor?"

John holds his hand out. I hand him the binoculars, giving him a skeptical look.

"That's cold." But he's grinning.

I shrug. "*That girl* is cold."

We end up in The Slopes Bar with them, sipping some weird, organic, spring water something or other vodka called Snow Queen.

"Not bad," I admit, although honestly, I'm not paying attention. I've got my phone in my lap and am texting with one of Elvie's tech girls, Louise, a pretty native New Yorker who dates mostly girls and sometimes drives E home when he's too drunk and I'm not there.

I'm hoping if I follow the conversation here with half an ear, the guys won't notice my rudeness.

"See, I knew she'd like it," one says.

"It's the spring water."

Jamie elbows me. "I'm going to take that thing," she hisses.

When we go to the ladies' room an hour later, she says, "C'mon, girl. They're nice, and they just moved into that house. Before then, they lived somewhere smaller, but the dad is Mayor Ferrara." She blinks, dragging her eyes wide open after.

"What does that mean?"

"Mayor Ferrara. He's the *mayor* of Breckenridge. You don't pay much attention to politics, do you?"

I roll my eyes. "Absolutely none."

She snatches the phone away. "He's not a texter. You know that. I'm keeping this."

I sigh dramatically and refresh my lipstick.

"Do you even want to stay out?" she asks.

I shrug. "I'm cool either way."

"Okay, well we're staying. I don't know John very well—or any of that family, really—but it sure beats watching you mope around at home."

I let out a melodramatic groan, and Jamie tugs me out the door.

When we get back to the table, the "military" guys are standing up, waving us toward the door.

"C'mon ladies. We're going down the way to Carlyle's Blues Bar. Our obnoxious friend is there, and he wants to meet you."

chapter nineteen

Gwenna
November 6, 2015

I watch his hand come to his mouth, his fingertips touching his lips as he blinks at the door, then shifts his gaze down to his feet.

He's wearing a white shirt and what looks, through the distortion of the peep hole, like dark pants. His curls are blowing slightly the breeze. It looks like he's trimmed his facial hair, so it's less beardlike and more scruffy again.

I wonder what's in the pack he's wearing on his back. I wonder what he'd do if I pulled the door open right now.

He blinks right at me through the peep hole, and I can't resist the urge to pull the door open.

"Come on in." I laugh.

His eyes widen on my blue face, then he's grinning. I forgot how beautiful he is when he lets loose a big, wide, dimpled grin: his clean, white teeth, his luscious lips, the way his sharp eyes squint and his cheeks curve.

He lifts a hand to touch my mask-caked cheek, and chuckles softly. "Who are you, and where's my Gwenna?"

I blink, then cover my shock—*his* Gwenna!—with an awkward little laugh. "She'll be back in oh...about three minutes." I remember belatedly that my hair is in a towel on my head, so I guess I look doubly weird.

I step back into my living room and motion Barrett through the door.

"If you dare..." I waggle my eyebrows.

With one long stride, he steps inside and closes the distance between us, wrapping me against his big body and pressing his face against the towel on my hair. The motion is quick and casual—like he's been hugging me forever. By the time my stomach nosedives like a roller coaster, he's already drawn away and is standing there in front of my door, giving me a charmed smile.

"I like the Smurf look."

I flip him off. "Fuck you," I giggle.

His eyes glaze over, pupils dilating slightly, as if he's thinking of that in literal terms. I watch him swallow, throat working as his eyes stay locked on mine. His hands are hooked around the straps of his pack and he's standing still, but I can feel what I would see if I let my gaze wander south. I can't help myself: my eyes are drawn like magnets down his long, lean body, lapping hungrily, until they come to the big, delicious bulge between his legs.

My heart pounds. Warmth throbs through me.

"I've got groceries. Kitchen?" he asks. His voice is an octave lower than usual, causing hairs to stand up on my arms.

I nod once and watch his back as he disappears around the half-wall. *Move, Gwen. Go wash your face!*

I can't, though. Move—that is. I feel hot and breathless. I try to get a handle on my raging hormones as I listen to him open my refrigerator. I hear his bag unzip, hear the sounds of him unloading items onto shelves. The rubbery *shhhnik* of the refrigerator door closing. A heartbeat later, Barrett reappears in the doorway between den and kitchen. He rests his shoulder on the partial wall and watches me with the stillness of a predator.

"You should wash your face." His gaze laps me up and down. With his eyes on me like this, his intentions screaming in the silence, I'm too nervous to glance between his legs again. Abstaining makes my cheeks feel even hotter.

I nod, reaching up to push a strand of hair out of my face. "Make yourself at home, okay? I'll be right back."

I wash my face, brush my hair, and change into some charcoal leggings, an olive-colored CareBears t-shirt, and a pair of thick, wool socks—as if thick socks will keep me insulated from the lust between us.

I find Barrett in the den, his massive shoulders hunched as he leans down to look at the photos on my bookshelf.

I come to stand beside him, tapping my socked foot against the back of his knee. Barrett has me on the floor in half a second. He's straddling me, wrapping his big hands around my head as if he's going to assault me at the Dokko pressure points.

Instead, his fingers drag along my scalp. His lips come down on mine, kissing me slow and deep and hard—until I'm breathless. His hands thread into my hair, pulling slightly. The weight of his big body between my legs makes me lift my hips and groan.

I wrap my leg around the back of his and grip the sensitive spot on the inside of his elbow. I'm trying to distract myself by feinting an attack move, because right now I'm throbbing so hard, I'm worried I might come with just him lying on me, kissing me.

His hand peels mine from the vulnerable spot. "Traitor," he whispers teasingly against my jaw. His eyes are hot on mine. "What am I going to do with you?"

He strokes my hair at my temple. I bring my knee up, trying to make contact with his bulge. He holds himself out of my reach, but then I see his blue eyes haze, and he shifts his hips so my knee is pressed against him.

God.

His eyes shut. "Mm."

I tug at his curls. His hooded eyes lift open. "Oh, so it's like that," he rasps.

I smile deviously, rubbing him with my knee. "Just like that."

He scoops me up so fast I'm dizzy, sits me on the couch, and kneels in front of me. He pulls my thick socks off, then slowly peels my leggings down my thighs. My heart pounds as the cold air touches my warm skin.

I look down, waiting for him to pull my leggings the rest of the way off, but he just works them to my knees, then sinks a finger into me. With his finger thick inside me, he lifts me up and carries me carefully to the partial wall between the den and kitchen. He backs me up against it, balancing me there as I moan softly from his ministrations and he works to take his jeans down with his free hand.

I groan as he drags his finger out of me. With one knee propped under my ass, he wraps both hands around my waist and lifts me up. My back is pressed against the wall. My legs, needing something to grasp onto so I don't teeter off his knee, lock around his hips—and here we are: like in a sexy movie.

I hold onto his waist with my legs, press my back against the wall, and Barrett shifts his hips until I feel his smooth head prod my folds. I let out a moan, and his head drags between my pussy and my ass.

"I can't wait to be inside you," he rasps.

His mouth nips at my jaw, and then he lowers me slowly, so I'm pressed against his thick head. The feeling of settling atop him—my slick lips pinching as he pushes up against me, then parting wetly around him, so he pops inside—makes me gasp like someone in a porno.

He shifts his hips a little, and gravity impales me, inch by slow, thick inch. He's really big...but I'm so slick. I bear down against the almost painful pressure of him, try to rock my hips and shove him, deep and thick, inside me.

Barrett holds my hips, though.

"Slow," he whispers.

I moan, rocking. "Please..."

I reach down and try to spread myself around him. I feel Barrett's muscles flinch—and then, with one hard thrust, he buries himself in me.

"Oh my God..." I grunt, my senses overwhelmed. He's *so damn deep.* I can't move, can only clutch his upper arms as he swells in me.

"God." I try to spread my legs as my clit throbs. His dick is so big...Fuck, I wish he'd touch my clit. I try to touch it with my own finger, but Barrett moves his hips. I stretch around him, groaning as he seems to fill me deeper still.

"Hold on with your legs, Gwennie."

I hadn't notice I had let go. Jesus. I can barely get my legs to cooperate. My body feels weak and shaky, molten. I can barely do more than just pant here, spread and stretched around him. I feel my clit swell as I clench around his thickness, shifting as if I can adjust to what's inside me.

Barrett thrusts, clutching my hips. I grunt as his head brushes my G-spot.

"Shit..." His lips brush mine, his soft tongue stroking into my mouth—and the two at once: his hot tongue surging in my mouth, his thick cock buried deeper than I've ever taken anything—they make me moan and shiver.

I think I hear him murmur, "Beautiful."

He lifts me by the hips and slides his thick erection partway out. I groan at the loss. He pushes me against the wall, rocks the tip of himself in me till I'm panting, then he surges back in.

I cry out at the incredible invasion.

"That's right," he purrs. His rough cheek brushes mine, and I can feel his mouth move over my ear. He licks around the rim of it and breathes against my throat. The sensations make my legs fall open wider, and I try to thrust against him.

He grunts as he pulls slowly back out. His breath catches, and I open my eyes in time to see the rapture on his face as he shoves back inside.

"God!" I'm getting fucked...

I grip his arms.

His hands have moved; he's got me by the ass now. Every time I sink down on him, he groans roughly. His chest pumps with his deep breaths as he draws out, then punches inside... losing his grip on my ass as he pulls back out, squeezing my hips as he ruts back in.

When he's buried deep inside me and I'm panting, dizzy and impaled, he lets go of my hip to rub a finger over my clit.

"God!" My legs around his waist go weak as pleasure swells between them. Barrett's mouth is biting me. He strokes my swollen clit once more. I wobble, grip his shoulders.

Barrett gives a tight laugh, then sinks to the floor with me still on him.

"Jesus Christ." The words are grunts.

I feel his dick throb in me as he lays me on my back and pushes in. He hunches over me, cupping my neck, kissing my mouth, his hips bucking against mine, driving him a little deeper. He draws out. I push against him as he sinks back in.

"Ahh," he grits. "You...feel...so goddamned...fucking... *good.*"

He lifts one leg and then my other over his tall shoulders. I feel myself tremble—or maybe him.

"Okay?" he rasps. His heavy-lidded eyes meet mine, inquiring through the haze.

I nod. I groan. It kind of hurts…and yet….the pain is good. I've never felt so full.

At this angle, every movement has me seeing stars. I grunt and groan and Barrett whispers words I'm too lust-drunk to understand. His finger finds my clit, my throbbing clit, and skates slickly around it till I'm screaming.

"That's right, Gwennie…" Distantly, I hear our flesh slapping together. The world seems to melt around his cock, his massive cock, his thrusting cock. I'm stretched around it, clenched around it…Fury starts to build around it. My shaking hands grasp at his thighs, spread around me. I clamp my legs down on his shoulders, so lit up with pleasure I can barely breathe.

I feel him shaking, hear him panting.

At a moment when he's buried deep as ever, he strokes around where we're joined, teasing my stretched lips, and then, with one more rock against me, he strokes my clit. I gasp as heaven swells between my legs and spills like lava through me. I can feel him twitch, feel warmth burst in me.

Barrett's groan is rough and long. I feel his hand squeeze my thigh and realize my legs are still over his shoulders. His hands come warm and gentle around my ankles, lowering my legs then drawing slowly out of me.

His eyes are sagging. He looks drugged. I laugh because I feel so good. He chuckles too.

"I'm sorry I…" He shakes his head and murmurs, "Hang on."

He disappears into my kitchen, coming back with warm, wet paper towels. As he presses one between my legs, he meets my eyes. "I'm clean. I should have mentioned yesterday. I'm—"

"No," I whisper, touching his wrist. "That was perfect."

I stroke his knee as Barrett cleans me up, and when he's finished, I grasp his damp forearm and tug him down beside me.

"I like this," I sigh.

Silence passes. Finally, I hear him rumble, "So do I."

Barrett

My dick has never felt this good. Yeah, it's been a while since I was with someone, but I don't think that's it. I think it's her. When I slide into her, I feel everything go still, and in that sweet void, the pleasure burns through me like a bushfire.

I look down at Gwenna, leaning back on her elbows, head tipped back, her body bare, her mouth curved.

Fuck, she's beautiful. So much more so than I realized before I spoke to her. And now I've been inside her. I think about the groceries waiting in her kitchen, how once I realized we would fuck first, I had planned to make her dinner afterward. Suddenly I can't abide that plan.

I ask her, "Are you hungry?"

"Not that hungry, but I could go for something."

I need to feel her skin against mine for a little longer first. I scoop her up and toss her carefully over my shoulder, then I stride off toward her room.

"What are we doing?" she laughs, gripping my waist with her arms.

"You'll see."

I carry her into the bathroom, where I set her on her feet and start the tub.

I realize she just showered—she had a towel on her head when I got here—but I can't seem to help myself. I want to hold her. There's no other way to do it without telling her I need it. And I don't want to show her that yet. I'm not sure I can.

"Do you like tacos?" I ask as I adjust the water temp.

"Is that what you brought in the giant backpack?"

I glance over my shoulder, giving her an exaggerated poker face that's meant to make her laugh. "Is that what you want to be in the giant backpack?"

"I'd like that." She smiles.

"Well you're in luck." I get the water hot, the way I think she likes it, and sit back on my heels while Gwenna pulls her shirt and bra off. She crosses her arms over her chest as she steps into the tub and dips her feet into the rising water.

"Mmm. That's nice and hot." I watch as chills spread over her smooth skin. She pulls her shoulders up around her ears and tucks her arms around her hips. Her brown eyes find mine. "Get in with me. You know you want to."

She curls herself into a little ball right in front of the faucet, and I pull my shirt over my head. I turn slightly as I get out of my boxer-briefs, so she can't see how hard I am just from watching her sit in a bathtub. I take a second to catch my breath and then I fold myself into the tiny space behind her.

This tub is so small, I wouldn't think I could fit into it alone, but with Gwenna curled up in the front, it's almost comical.

Right on cue, she looks over her shoulder and laughs. "Stretch your legs out, silly." She reaches back and grabs my shins. "Wrap around me. Better yet—switch places! I can squeeze right in behind you." Her eyes widen in excitement. "I want to wash your hair!"

I try to think of why she'd want to, and all I can come up with is maybe she thinks it looks unruly or dirty. I run my hand through it.

"Are you picky about when you wash it or how you style it?" she asks.

I feel my brows scrunch as I shake my head.

"Okay, good." She sits up straighter, reminding me hilariously of an energetic little meerkat. "I'm a sucker for guys with pretty hair, yours especially. If you let me wash it I'll...bake something after we have dinner. Something you really like. Or—something else. I'll owe you one."

I shake my head in confusion, even though the eager look on her face has me laughing. "Okay...You don't owe me," I add.

She's out of the tub with a giant slosh of water, dripping on the rug as I scoot up, bending my legs so she'll have space to sit behind me.

I'm not prepared for the feeling of her smooth, warm body settling behind mine. As she spreads her legs, her little feet scooting around my thighs and tucking over them, I'm painfully hard.

She wraps her arms around my shoulders and pulls me back against her. I grit my teeth and try to think of something grim—like IEDs. I don't put my full weight on her, but I'm pretty sure she doesn't notice. I see her grab a green thermos from one ledge of the tub.

"I keep this in here for when I make my own bath scrub out of coffee grounds and coconut oil." She fills it up from the tub, then tilts my chin up and smooths my hair off my forehead.

With one hand shielding my forehead from the warm deluge, she pours water over my hair. Chills dart all across my shoulders. My dick gets even stiffer.

She repeats the process, soaking my hair in the soapy-scented water. Then she rests her right elbow on the tub's side. "Lean back in the corner of my arm."

I do, even though I feel a little like a doll or some shit.

"This is good." I see her smiling at an angle that puts her upside down for me. "It's like the beauty parlor. Just relax." She sifts her fingers through my hair, and I can't help chuckling. The beauty parlor. This girl.

"These are the curls I always wanted, but my hair was only wavy," she says, poking out her lip. "I wanted Shirley Temple curls."

She starts to work soap into my hair, her fingertips massaging my scalp in a way that makes me shiver. When she's finished, she smooths her hand back over my forehead, keeping the bubbles out of my face, and I feel this weird, hot feeling in my chest. It's hard to breathe around the strange sensation, but I try not to focus on it. I smile up and back at her. "Your hair is pretty, Gwennie."

"Don't you call me that." She gently slaps my cheek. "It's Gwenna or Gwen. Gwennie is someone's pet piglet."

"You are a little piglet." I grin, leaning up a bit and turning so I can see her. Which I quickly realize isn't going to be enough. I turn more fully toward her, reaching out and trailing a finger down the inside of her forearm. "Pretty and pink."

She tugs my ear. "Lay back, you infidel." Her jaw drops open. "Shit. That's not PC."

Her blanched face tells me she's concerned about more than just being politically correct. Shame moves through me as I settle my head back in the crook of her arm.

"Doesn't bother me. It's not PC," I tell her with a smirk, "but I've heard it before. Some people used it to mean real insurgents, so we didn't joke about it. But it doesn't remind me of anyone or anything like that."

She's quiet as she massages what feels like an excess of conditioner into my hair. It smells like coconut sunscreen, which happens to remind me of training down at Benning.

"Did you have short hair when you were working?" she asks.

"Shorter than this, but not too short. Operators are supposed to blend in with civilians."

She pauses in her massage to trace the tats on my left shoulder. "Do these not identify you?"

I nod slightly and pull my sagging eyes open. "One time we got caught by the Taliban for a couple days. We tried to tell the villagers we were journalists so their leader would force the Taliban fighters to let us go. But they didn't believe us. Their village leader was afraid of my tats."

Gwen's hand shelters my forehead from another cupful of hot water. It sloshes hotly over my soapy hair, running down the back of my neck.

I can't help a rumble in my throat.

"That sounded like a purr," she teases. She pours another cupful over my head. "When's the last time you had your hair washed?"

"Never."

"Ever?" She pauses.

"Maybe when I was a little kid."

Another cup of water, another heavenly pass of her fingertips through my hair.

"Well that's a shame," she murmurs.

I try to stay still and keep the full weight of my head off her arm as she pours a few half-cups over the back and sides of my hair.

Then, just when I think she's finished, she parts the hair around my scars and feathers a light kiss over my head. It's fast, a no-big-deal thing, over almost before I notice. But it brings that feeling back into my chest. The heavy, hot one.

I turn around, because I want to see her, and as I trace her collarbone, I see a scar I've never noticed at the base of her throat.

Looking at it makes my own throat feel tight. I reach for her, but I can't seem to touch her.

Her eyes roll. "Yeah, yeah. Don't give me that look. You've got that wicked-looking shrapnel scar on your neck and shoulder back here—" she points toward it—"and I see a bullet scar on your back, no exit hole in the front, I noticed, BTW. What about the one on your thigh? Bullet, too?" She arches her brows. "Who knows what else I *can't* see. You're a pincushion, just like I am."

I finally manage to swallow and trace my fingers over the little scar at the base of her throat. I want to ask her if it's from a breathing tube—one of the ones they push in during a real emergency. I've seen one done in the field before.

Instead I ask, "Is that from the wreck?"

"Yes."

She soaps her chest up and I wait for her to say more, but she just blinks at me and looks down at her bubble-covered breasts. My gaze follows hers. My dick throbs as I notice her nipples poking out of the suds.

I'm about to reach for one when I see another scar on her right arm—long, straight, and about five inches long. I feel an almost painful wave of protectiveness for her.

"Do you still…have any pain?" Goddamn, my voice is raspy.

Gwenna smiles gently. "For the most part, no. It's sweet of you to ask."

"I'm not sweet."

"I think you are."

A moment later, she washes the soap off her chest and rises from the tub. She wraps a towel around herself, then holds one out for me. I tuck it around my waist, and she says, "Lean your head down."

I hesitate only a moment before I do as she asks, and Gwenna covers my dripping head with another towel.

She rubs it all around, kind of violently. I'm trying to decide if it feels good or bad when she stops. "Barrett—oh my God! Your *tattoo*. Is this—I have the same one, this exact tat, just like yours!"

My heart starts pounding as I straighten up. My eyes go to the inside of her forearm. "I saw that the other day."

I try to keep a neutral face as she looks from her arm up at me. "That is *so* insane! I wish I could put them beside each other and show you." She holds her arm up by my neck. "Yours looks exactly like mine. Identical. Where'd you get it?"

"Miami." My throat tightens around the word.

"I got mine in Breckenridge, the year before the wreck. Why'd you get yours? It doesn't exactly fit your badass special ops theme."

I blow my breath out, looking at the floor for just a second while I get my shit together. Then I look into her beautiful brown eyes. "I got it to jerk around with my friend Breck. He always wanted it to be colder out there in the middle of the desert. We called him our special snowflake." I smile a little at the memory, even though the tattoo angle on the story is bullshit.

"Breck...like Breckenridge?"

I only hesitate a moment before I answer. "Yeah. He was from there."

I see her eyes widen when she hears the word *was*—and for once, I'm glad she's scared to pry.

chapter twenty

Gwenna

"Can you step into the laundry room and get that giant salad bowl from the shelf over the washer?" I would grab it myself, but I'm grating cheese.

Barrett tilts the skillet against the sink's ledge, dripping the last streaks of venison grease from the pan into the Tupperware bowl where the browned meat is.

"Sure," he says quietly.

He sets the skillet in the sink and washes his hands. I watch the way he soaps his arms up to the elbows. I can't decide what it reminds me of—but something. A moment later I realize: He does it like a doctor. God knows I saw enough of them scrub into and out of my room after the wreck. I think of teasing him about it, but I don't think he's close to his doctor father, so he may not appreciate me mentioning him.

He catches my eyes on him as he turns. He smirks.

I grin unabashedly. As he walks into the laundry room, I want to laugh. I'm not sure why. It's just like...there's pressure in my chest—old pressure, stuck there for these last few years—and suddenly I need to let it out, so I can breathe and just...be happy again.

I smile as he turns toward the shelves over the washer and dryer. I feel so much lighter when I'm with him.

I let my gaze linger on him, drinking in his masculine beauty. Which is why I notice when he stumbles back, bumping the back of his head into the doorframe. He whirls around and, with wide eyes and a flushed face, staggers back into the kitchen. He stops by the dinner table. His face blanches. His eyes widen, and he just looks...like he's in trouble.

Shit.

His chest is pumping in and out and he's still got that look of frozen terror on his face when I get close enough to wrap my arms around him.

The second I lock onto him, a shudder ripples through his body and I feel his chest inflate and hold there as he struggles to breathe deeply. I tug the sides of his shirt.

"Barrett—look at me." His eyes open and close in that exaggerated way that makes him look like he might pass out. It's a blink in my direction, then he's struggling for air again, his big chest heaving as his eyes slip out of focus.

"It's okay." I hug him. My heart pounds. "I've got you."

I pull him with me to the counter and fumble for a lunch-size paper bag while he leans over, palms braced on his knees. The gasping sounds he's making hurt my heart and make me sweat with fear for him, even though the rational part of me knows he's just having a panic attack.

I grab his forearms—"Let's sit down, okay?"—and together we sink to the floor. He leans back against my cabinets, his hands grasping weakly for his thighs. I pull the bag open and look into his eyes as I lower it over his mouth.

"It's okay. You're here with me, with Gwen."

His dazed eyes cling to mine, even as his chest pumps and his muscles tremble. With my cheek against his chest and my hand straining to keep the bag over his mouth, I look up at him.

"Barrett, you're with Gwenna. We're in my kitchen. Feel my arm around you? You're okay."

I squeeze him tightly and a second later, he raises a hand to hold the bag. With my free hand, I stroke his neck.

"You're here with me, baby. We're making tacos. After we eat, I want to show you your Myers-Briggs profile, and you can laugh at what a dork I am. I thought maybe you would end up staying over...so I did something for you. Do you want to see?"

He blinks at me, and he seems to realize at the same moment I do that he's not sucking air out of the bag anymore. His shoulders are still tense, but his frenzied breaths are calmer now. His eyes are still far off, but they're holding mine.

I have this image of myself bursting out the front door when I used to have a flashback. Anything to move, outrun the moment.

"Come here..." I hold my hand out for him but he moves the bag off his mouth and stands without grabbing onto me. I clasp the hand that isn't holding the bag and lead him slowly through the den and my office.

We step into my bedroom and I turn out the overhead light. Then I lead him over to the bed, where I flip a button on the extension cord draped over my night stand and my ceiling lights up. It's striped with lines of Christmas twinkle lights.

"When I used to have nightmares, I would wake up to these and it would pull me back here faster."

I watch him blink up at the rainbow of lights.

"Come here..."

We lay down. He's slow and careful, like a fast movement might somehow startle him. I don't let go of his hand.

When he's lying on his back, I snuggle up against him, resting my head on his hard arm, gently re-lacing my fingers through his. "I think I know what happened."

Unless he's scared of laundry rooms, the overbearing scent of gardenias is the only thing that makes sense. Smell is tied tightly to memory.

"If it's the plants," I whisper, "I can throw them out."

"Why?" It's so soft I can hardly hear it.

I stroke his cheek. "Because I don't need them."

I wrap my arms around him. His shoulders jerk with leftover tension. Then he shifts onto his side and buries his face in my neck.

I'm surprised…but it feels good. So *right*. I wrap my arm around him, inhaling the scent of him: so new and yet so soothing. I feel the width and hardness of his back and think of where it's been. I wish he'd never been to those places.

I curve my hand around the back of his head. I barely know him—but it doesn't feel that way.

"I went into her brother's flower shop. In Syria." He doesn't lift his head, just rasps the words against my collarbone. "She said…I didn't look like other Westerners. She said my eyes looked different."

He stops, breathing deeply. I rub circles on his back while silence rolls around us.

"She put this aloe on my neck, and there was a freezer room. But to get to it, you had to go through this other room." I feel his forehead press against my throat as he breathes.

"She called it her gardenia room. They were piled in there… like yours."

My heart squeezes as I try to picture him standing in this tiny room filled with gardenias, sunburned, maybe shirtless as this woman rubs his back.

"She told me one day they meant secret love—gardenias. She was younger. I—the…ISIS was there…everywhere. The delivery drivers, everyone was in their pocket. Like the mafia." I run my fingers through his hair and hold my breath while he breathes slowly to catch his.

"I would go sometimes…around delivery time…and wait in that room. In case something happened. I was always hot. Summer. We weren't really over there yet—at least not officially. According to the head shed." Another few seconds slide by, and I can feel him draw another long, slow breath. "I had on the local dress," he goes on. "Clothes."

Despite the benign nature of his words, his body jerks with a hard shudder. I pull him a little closer. "It's okay."

I feel him breathing: measured breaths. "She wore a burka and—" His voice breaks. "She did want to take it off." He laughs roughly. "She'd come into that room and…I would never let her."

I trace the curve of one of his curls, and he lets his breath out slowly. "She would let me do overwatch from up above the store." He lifts his head, looks out across my room, toward the window, beyond which the world is indigo with dusk.

His eyes glide to mine. He frowns vacantly before moving his gaze back to the window.

"One day someone else—another operator," he rasps, "got some intel. Something was happening with IS in the area. I went. I thought maybe…" He swallows. "I thought I could get something, you know? She might know something. She gave me some tea and she was telling me her sister-in-law was pregnant, like it was so important. But I didn't think about it." His face blanks out, and his voice drops lower, like he's remembering this day so vividly, he's more there than here.

"I went up there on the roof and saw these women. Two with babies. One of them looked pregnant," he says slowly.

He puts his hand against my throat and curls his fingers. I can feel them shaking. I close my hand over his.

"After a little bit," he rasps, "they scattered—those three women. One of them blew up. I tracked the other ones. The babies…looked so *real*. But you can't—There were other people down there. Shopping. So I didn't hesitate. I took out a second woman, quick. And then I moved to the third one. Took her down. She blew up after a minute, so she had a bomb on her…"

He shakes his head and inhales deeply.

"That third lady," he whispers, "she was clearly…But the second one…"

I see him shut his eyes, and for a moment he is silent in the watercolor of the Christmas lights above us.

"Maliha ran out there," he chokes. It takes me half a second to realize Maliha must be the young florist. "I saw her drop down by this second lady…" His body jerks a little, and I press my hand over his. "I thought it was her sister-in-law…"

His eyes hold mine for just a moment, and they're stark with pain and—Maybe that's confusion on his face.

He shakes his head.

"It wasn't."

I watch his hand clutch at his temple.

"The tea she gave me…it had opium tincture in it. I can see her reaching for that woman's stomach. I can see her eyes…and they were wide. It was like a dream. Not just the tea. I saw her, but I couldn't…" His eyes find mine. "Anyway," his gaze flicks down, and then back to mine—"there was a backup detonator. She grabbed it. I saw her going for it, should have known, but…" He shakes his head. He drops his head down in a bow.

"They told me that," he rasps. "When I joined the Unit, someone warned me…" He shakes his head, like whatever he's trying to convey is just too much, too much effort. "She was young, Gwen. She used to listen to this band…*Icona Pop* and…*Taylor Swift*. She had this iPod." I see a tear drip down his cheek as he looks into my eyes. "Sometimes I think…I wonder why she said my eyes were different. If you notice…look. Sometimes in pictures. Older guys, the people just like me." He swallows. "Those old guys' eyes look hard and cold. Almost…dead. To people who don't know, but… they aren't. They're just sad," he whispers.

He lies down on his side, his head on a pillow. I lie in front of him and pull my knees up toward my chest. My shins touch Barrett's thighs. I reach out and stroke his hair.

"She liked my eyes. I guess…they weren't sad yet."

I see something twinkle: another little tear that falls under the lights. His leaking eyes lock onto mine again.

"You know…they told me that. In training. You can go… bad…one of two ways, a sniper can go bad," he murmurs. "Either you can't shoot or you go nuts and shoot up the block. I just… couldn't shoot her." His voice cracks as his eyes shut. "She detonated the bomb. I found out later IS made her do it. They had her sister-in-law." He stops to swallow, takes his time before he goes on, in a lower voice.

"She had blocked the roof off. Stacked a bunch of shit in the stairwell. But they knew I was up there. They'd given her the tincture for me, hoping they could fuck my aim up. I had to get away, I ended up jumping…off the roof. And when I landed—When I landed," he sighs deeply, "there was this IED. I don't know…my head hit something. Or…" he shakes his head, "maybe just the blast. I was fucking out of it. That's how I got the brain bleed, the shrapnel. Breck came. We could track each other. He had to get me out. We made it to the Bradley before he got…hit with this bomb," his voice cracks, "…it had *acid* in it."

My stomach clenches, and I wrap my hand around his. His hand squeezes tightly.

"They had pushed me in…so I was safe." His fingers squeeze more tightly, so tight I almost cry out. I feel his body start to shake again, and I scoot over closer to him. When I wrap my arm around his shoulders and his head, he curls into me. "It got him...kind of in the back," he rasps. "They got him in and...his skin was... *hissing*."

When he speaks again, his voice has dropped down to a whisper. "The phosphorous was eating...through his skin...and he was trying...to smile. He was a tough son of a bitch, my buddy Breck."

I feel him swallow, and I wait a long time without moving, but he doesn't speak again. He just lies there breathing on his side, his body stiff, his shoulders shaking, and there's nothing I can do.

I stroke his hair. "Oh, Barrett. I'm so sorry."

"I just...can't ever stop thinking about it." His body shakes against mine.

"No. Of course not." I cradle his head against my chest. "Of course you can't." I hold him closer to me, speaking quietly near his ear. "It makes so much sense—and no one could. You know that, right?" I cup his jaw. "*No one* could forget that. It gets deep inside you...because you're human. Even though you were a warrior, you're a human being. And you're strong, but you have a heart. It's not supposed to be strong, you know? It has to be vulnerable to work."

"I know." The words are soft and tiny. His hand grips my side.

"But you're tired." I smooth his hair back, press my lips against his temple. "It's so tiring. I know." My mind spins with dead ends; nothing I can say will help him, and the hopeless feeling makes me feel sick to my stomach.

Finally I think of something. Something small. "You know what? Nightmares don't happen in the first hour of sleep. You've never woken up then, right?"

After a second, he shakes his head.

"Do you want to take a nap? One hour on the nose?"

I can feel him hesitate, his body pausing.

"I'll stay with you. I'll hold you," I whisper.

Barrett turns over on his stomach, wraps an arm behind his head. He takes a few deep breaths. Then he rolls onto his side. His eyes are on my face. I can feel them burn into me, even though he doesn't touch me.

Finally he reaches out with his left hand, closing it over both of mine. His thumb strokes me. With every stroke, I watch his eyes grow heavier.

chapter twenty-one

Gwenna
December 31, 2011

"That is seriously what you did while I was showering."
Jamie blushes. "It was totally impromptu. I was getting back from the general store, and he had just dropped off this giant tin of roasted nuts for Mom and Dad. We started talking and I threw a snowball at him. Then we somehow ended up building this adorable little snowman. He's so cute and so funny. Niccolo, not the snowman." Jamie brushes at her snow-damp shirt sleeve, and then looks back up at me. "I don't know John since we don't live here full-time, but I've never even heard of Niccolo. Apparently he's thirty."

I arch my brows. "So what does he like...*do* or whatnot? Does he have a job?"

She scoffs. "Of course he has a job. I asked Mom after he left, and she said he works in Hollywood." Jamie beams.

I can't help rolling my eyes. "He probably works in a bar."

She shakes her head. "Nope. He does something with movie production. Something on the business side, with money. That's what Mom said. She said Mayor Ferrara was really bummed he wasn't interested in politics, but Niccolo and Casper have a different mom than John, the younger one, so they haven't lived in Colorado with the mayor since they were children." She lowers her voice. "Word is Mayor Ferrara cheated on Niccolo's mom with John's mom."

"Well *that's* original." I pull the towel off my head and frown into the mirror at my eyebrows. They really need a wax, but all I've got time to do right now is pluck them.

"Anyway…" Jamie pulls her fleece sweater over her head, then wiggles out of her insulated snow pants and, in just underwear and her hoodie, starts to rummage through her suitcase. "The point I'm making here is you know how we were going to maybe meet up with the guys from last night if we got bored? Now we're meeting up with them for sure…at 9:30." She smiles her pretty, lipsticked smile and holds her head up high.

I flop back against the bathroom door. "Boooooo."

Jamie has been single since our sophomore year of college, since her honey was caught making out with Duke's all-star history professor in a campus bathroom. I can't even remember the last time she took a shine to someone, so two hours later, we're bumping along the isolated mountain road toward downtown Breck in her mother's white Range Rover.

Jamie looks hot in black leggings and a red designer parka, with silver-gray fur-lined boots. She's wearing fun earrings and her signature red lipstick, which always seems to make her teeth look radiantly white. I've got on a thigh-length, gold-brown sweater hoodie over dark brown leggings, and my own pair of fur-lined boots, which are caramel suede.

I intentionally skipped the lipstick and allowed myself to wear my ridiculous peacock feather earrings, hoping the two choices will lead to decreased male attention.

After almost twenty minutes struggling to find a parking spot on Breckenridge's snowy-as-hell Main Street, I tug on my beanie,

Jamie hides beneath her jacket hood, and we trudge toward Gemütlichkeit, a German "beer bar."

The place is small and probably what a more people-friendly person would consider "cozy," with lots of dark wood and mounted animal heads, plus a giant fireplace that makes me sweat within the first five seconds.

I see a hand shoot up in a dark corner of the place, followed by the friendly, bearded face of a man with dark eyes and a receding hairline.

"Come on! That's Nic!"

Jamie grins as we move toward their table.

The guys seem drunk already, like they've been here for at least an hour or two, which in Niccolo's case isn't even possible. The table is littered with beer bottles, and almost as soon as we sit down, the arrogant guy we met last night—Michael—starts trying to convince me to share a beer bowl with him.

"It's like a fish bowl, but with beer, and it's craft beer. Really good shit."

I decline his offer twice in the first ten minutes. After that, I walk toward the bathroom, getting distracted as I pass a wooden door on the side of the building that's painted with the word SMOKE and bears a pitifully rendered, hand-painted cigarette.

I haven't smoked for years—it's terrible for the voice—but I'm just bored and desperate enough to slip outside despite that.

It's snowing hard, and the building only has a small awning on this side. I stand with my back against the wall and wonder why I'm so unhappy. Two girls burst out, laughing.

"He looked grumpy!"

"But that hair…"

They're paying so little attention to where they're going, one of them crashes into me.

"Oh my God!"

The other girl looks me up and down. "Do I know you? Is she—Sheri, she looks like—"

They both shriek, "Jessica!"

Half an hour—and two cigarettes, and six swigs from a rhinestone flask later—I teeter back inside, feeling pleasantly buzzed.

Before returning to our table, I call Elvie from the women's bathroom. He's in New York. Times Square, where his parents are part of the celebrity countdown. The first time I call, someone hits the "fuck you" button. I call right back and someone answers wordlessly. I can hear the roar of guitar amps and laughing. I hear some girl's voice coo "Elvie."

I hang up the phone and run my hands under the cold sink water till my heart stops racing.

chapter twenty-two

Barrett
November 7, 2015

A bright, twinkling rainbow. Something tickling along my jaw. I smell a hint of fruit and feel…a face. Her hair tickles my neck. Warmth floods through me. I crack my eyes and see the Christmas lights. And I realize *she* is *Gwenna.*

"Wake up, you…" I feel her soft brow against my beard, her warm lips pressed against my chin. "I brought you dinner in bed," she whispers in a husky voice.

Even in my groggy state, her voice makes me hard. I reach out, wrapping an arm around her neck and pulling her down beside me on the mattress.

I let out a soft sigh and turn from my back onto my side, where I can wrap myself around her.

Gwenna laughs. I like her laugh. It's rough and unrepentant: nothing veiled, nothing held back.

"You woke up snuggly," she murmurs as I wrap an arm around her.

I woke up wanting to be inside her.

"You cooked?" I ask her in a sleep-graveled voice.

Before she can answer, I hook my leg over one of hers and move closer to her, close enough to wrap my arm around her.

"This feels good," she whispers.

Gwenna pulls my head against her chest and starts to stroke my nape and shoulders. I fix my attention on the sweet sensation. Gentle fingers…Her other hand is wrapped around my shoulder, holding me against her.

My eyes feel hot. I don't know why…she keeps on doing this. *Why* does she keep doing this?

The way she touches me…I inhale slowly, carefully, around the lump in my throat. I clench my jaw before I try to swallow. Gwenna's fingers cut a slow path through my hair.

I mean to whisper "thank you," but I groan instead.

"I love it that you like this so much," she whispers.

All I hear is "so much." Do I like her soft touch more than someone else would?

I feel her lips against my forehead. She keeps on stroking me. She kisses my right eyelid, then the left.

"Doesn't work," I whisper.

"What?" I feel her pull away from me, see her frown down on me. "What doesn't work?"

I inhale slowly, my eyes on her waist. "Left eye. There was a clot there. A stroke. Just the eye." My voice sounds rough, and I wonder in a distant way why right now is the time I chose to tell her this.

My gaze returns to her face, finding it troubled. I look into her eyes and feel my insides go cold.

"You can't see at all from it?"

I blink down at the bedding, shake my head.

The moment spreads out around us, rippling like a stone's punch through the surface of the water, slowly fading back to clear and calm. It doesn't even last that long, although it feels as if it does.

Gwen's palm brushes my cheek. She strokes my hair off my forehead, letting her nails tickle along my hairline.

"I didn't know," she murmurs.

I shut my eyes and focus on the way my ribs expand as I inhale. I've laid alone so many times and tried to pay attention to my body. To tell myself I'm still alive. I'm *here*, not there. The one thing that I always wanted most was to feel someone else's arms around me. Thinking of it now, with her beside me, brings a feeling of contentment, followed quickly by a bite of shame.

"I think this is probably the wrong response," she whispers in the dark, "but after 'I'm so sorry you lost some of your sight,' I'm kind of tempted to say how amazing it is. I mean…I couldn't even tell. When we were sparring…How'd you do it?"

"It would be harder with someone else," I say after a minute. "I couldn't fight another Operator. Not most of them."

She laughs lightly. "So I'm an easy target, is that what I'm hearing?"

I reach a finger out to trace her cheekbone, smiling softly at her. "Still harder than most," I tell her, aiming to appease.

Gwen leans over, smooths my left eyelid shut, then feathers a kiss over it.

"I'm not sure when I'll stop being impressed with you. I hope you don't think I'm being patronizing. It's just like…you always hear about these badass vets, like Michael Stokes guys, and I've never actually known one." Her eyes shine with kind sincerity.

I smirk. "Michael Stokes."

"You should pose for him. People would go crazy."

I chuckle, shaking my head. I want to tell her that I'm at my fucking worst. That I'm embarrassed by myself. By how I've changed. I can't even get a bullet through a target. I can't shoot a gun or bow, although I'm trying to relearn. But I look at Gwenna in the darkness, and I know that shit holds no weight with her.

I take her hand and bring it to my cheek, and then I press a kiss into her palm. I search her eyes for…something.

She's not afraid to hold my gaze. Her mouth is soft and thoughtful. After a long moment, her free hand tucks a curl behind my ear.

"Who are you?" I rasp.

She smiles, and there is something bared in it. It's like the absence of pretense. It's like she's smiling all for me.

I cradle her hand, bringing it back to my cheek. "You make me feel almost good," I whisper.

"Only almost?" She strokes under my chin, and like a fucking tiger, I have to struggle not to purr.

I don't know what to say to that, so I don't even try.

"That's a sad smile you've got there, B."

I'm smiling? I move her hand off my face, but don't let go of it. Her fingers curl around my wrist, around my hand, until she's squeezing gently.

Fuck me.

"I'm 'B' now?"

She nods, smiling. "I need to shorten Barrett. I'm too lazy to use it all the time."

"No Bear?" I give her a teasing smile.

Her own smile falters. "I didn't know if…you'd want that." She looks worried. I think back to why. Maybe I said something about it? That it reminded me of my time in ACE? Of Breck?

I shrug. "It works."

She swings my hand, still wrapped in hers. "So I can call you Bear? I have my very own Bear?" I swear, she fucking giggles.

Fuck. I think I get all red like she does sometimes. I can't help giving her a lopsided smile.

"And on that note…" She reaches behind her and holds a plate out to me, grinning like she knows she's crazy but she doesn't care. The plate is stacked with tacos, made in a variety of ways.

"Which ones are yours?" I can't help laughing at the big, unruly pile.

"The ones that aren't yours. I like literally any kind of taco. So good choice, by the way."

We eat right there in her bed, under the twinkle of the lights. Gwen avoids the tacos with the jalapenos. I have a couple different ones, after I ask which she prefers and she answers with a poker face.

The room is filled with crunching, with the sounds of chewing. By the time we're finished, Gwen's area is littered with lettuce, tomato, and little bits of taco shell. Mine is spotless.

She gapes at me.

I smirk.

"Aloof and reserved! I just looked up your Myers-Briggs while I was finishing the food. Want me to read it to you?"

I watch her navigate to a web site, and when the letters INTJ appear at the top, I grab the iPad from the bottom, sliding it right out of her hands before she even knows what happened.

She shoves me. "Sneaky ass."

I turn away from her and skim the description, shooting incredulous looks over my shoulder at her as I start reading them aloud: "'Values intelligence, knowledge, and competence. Lives in a world of ideas.'" I widen my eyes, shaking my head. "Aloof and reserved. That's what you think of me?" I ask with mock fury.

She giggles.

"'INTJs spend a lot of time in their own minds, and may have little interest in other people's thoughts or feelings.'" I turn toward her. "Little interest? Self-centered? Difficulty expressing themselves?" I arch an eyebrow. "Gwenna, this is very telling. What you think of me..."

She swats my arm. "It doesn't say self-centered. I don't think it says that other stuff either."

I'm only teasing, but her cheeks are red.

I give her a pointed look. "What's yours, mmm?"

I can't help it: I enjoy watching her squirm. She doesn't want to tell me her type, which I find fucking hilarious.

"Let me see if I can put my finger on it...Hmmm." I look at her with arched brows, then glance through the site index as I tap my chin. "I'm going to go with...The INFJ Advocate."

Her eyes widen, and I grin because I know I'm right. I skim the first few paragraphs of this personality's description, then fix my eyes on hers and recite what I just read.

"The INFJ is very rare, making up less than one percent of the population. INFJs see helping others as their life's work, but while people with this personality type can be found involved in rescue and charity work—" I arch a brow—"their real passion is to get to the heart of the issue so people need not be rescued at all."

I blink back down at the iPad screen, stricken for a moment by a feeling of unease.

"INFJs need time alone to decompress and recharge, and at times may suddenly withdraw. They take great care of others' feelings, and they expect the favor to be returned."

I reach out and ruffle her hair, and Gwen snatches the tablet from me. "You're making fun of me. I can *so* tell."

I grin so wide, my cheeks hurt. I pull her close so I can kiss her, and I look into her brown eyes. "I wasn't, but I am now. Kind of fun. You get all flustered." I press my forehead against hers, and she tugs at my hair.

"Maybe you just don't care about my feelings," she teases.

"What are they?" I narrow my eyes in mock scrutiny. "Are you trying to save me, Gwenna?"

I watch her throat move as she swallows, watch her face and eyes—because despite my joking tone, her answer to the question feels important.

She stares at me without expression for a few long seconds, and then speaks slowly, thoughtfully. "I don't think you need to be saved. Maybe just fed and occasionally cuddled." She finds her smile again, and she looks confident and beautiful. "I don't expect you to confess to that, of course. Not Mr. Secret Agent GI Joe."

I arch my brows and give her a damning stare—100 percent jest, not that she can likely tell. "*Now* whose feelings are being stomped on?"

"Fine." She laughs. "I guess GI Joe does seem a little…tacky and stereotypical when you really think about the name. We'll shorten that to Mr. Secret Agent."

"Not so secret."

"True," she murmurs, smiling her cute, lopsided smile.

"You haven't asked me more about it."

She winks. "All in good time, soldier boy."

I can't help wondering if she's avoiding all talk of my past because she knows I'm so fucked in the head.

That gnaws on me as she gets our plate and slides down off the bed. "You want to make something, or watch me? Or maybe skip the baking and watch TV?" I bring my eyes up to meet hers. "I bet you're behind on a lot of shows."

I nod. "I've seen some from start to finish and others not at all. Like *Game of Thrones*. Never seen, but I've read the books."

"We have to fix that, then. *If* I'm up to reliving the soul-crushing angst."

I slide down off the bed behind her, wrapping an arm around her shoulders as we shuffle toward the kitchen. "You pick the show. I'll watch anything but the Kardashians." I give her a sideways smile.

"No reality TV for you?"

I shake my head.

"It's not my thing so much either. Would you eat cake if I wanted to make one?"

"I guess if I *had* to," I sigh, and Gwenna bumps my shoulder. More my arm, really, given our height difference.

"I was thinking you could get another hour of sleep before we really go to sleep. For me, if I'm less tired, I snap out of it quicker." *It* meaning nightmares, I assume.

"Been thinking on it?"

"Yeah." Her cheeks flush as we walk behind the couch. "You can tell me to shut up. You heard the Myers-Briggs. I'm the… advocating type." She winces, and I chuckle.

"What does this have to do with cake?"

She slides me a guilty look. "I thought the sugar might make you sleepy."

I can't help a low hoot. "Gwenna…" I laugh as she hangs her head.

"Go on," she says, looking rueful. "Tell me to bug off."

I wrap my hands around her waist and pull her back against me, kissing her neck. I groan as my cock swells against her lower back. "Please don't."

I shut my eyes as I hold her to me. The sweet scent of her shampoo seems to fuzz my senses. Somewhere very far away, I hear my conscience urging me to get away from her, but it's too late now. Those stern words are whispered. Her body is so soft and warm. Her hands are careful, gentle, reaching back around to stroke from my hips down my thighs. Illogically, they seem to know me. What I need and what I like.

"Gwen…" Her fingers reach for my dick.

"Yes?" The word soft and sinuous.

I blink at her coppery hair as words rise up within me. They float to the bottom of my throat, and I can't seem to let them out.

My mind is racing. Pulse is racing. Gwenna's hands are smooth on my pants. My cock is squeezed between our bodies. How do I tell her? And I realize that I can't. I can tell her nothing, so I whisper, "That feels good."

chapter twenty-three

Barrett

On the kitchen floor, with the lights on and the TV droning in the background, I come faster than I ever have, and she is right behind me, laughing. I laugh too. I don't know why. It doesn't matter.

Afterward, I wash our dinner plate as Gwen lines up bowls and utensils for making something she calls Guinness cake.

I arch my brows, skeptical, and she tells me all about the beer-based layered cake and how to make it, pulling ingredients from the pantry and the refrigerator and assembling them on the counter like a little army.

I can't help admiring her from every angle. The way her hair shines like a penny when she turns her head. The awkward way she lifts her shoulder to try to scratch her cheek while her hands are flour-covered. I watch her hands bend as she cracks eggs into a bowl. I think about her fingers on my face.

I think about us in her bed. *Me* in her bed.

I think about my bedroom at my last spec ops base. Maybe because it was about the same size as her little kitchen. I used to always wonder why the ceilings and the walls in that place were so fucking ugly, this gray-brown color that made you feel like you were in a file cabinet drawer. My bed there was too small. I remember turning on my side and covering my head and curling up and wanting to feel…real. No one knew how dead I was.

I look at Gwenna, and I try to remember how her hands feel on me. Did she really ever touch me, though? I'm just a watcher; almost never touched. I look at my left hand and it's shaking. All the fingers. They can't move, but they can all still shake.

Gwenna pours the batter into a pan. As soon as she's finished, she turns and takes my hands. She squeezes them and looks into my eyes. Hers are dark and knowing. A small notch forms between her eyebrows as she tilts her head, her face impassive in her quiet assessment, her hands still holding mine firmly.

"Can you finish this for me?" Her eyes gesture to the cake over her shoulder. "One of the egg shells cut my hand."

Gwenna

His moods remind me of an ocean. It's a pattern I remember from my own PTSD and I still know sometimes: crest then trough, crest then trough…

I'm good at feeling his. Maybe only good at troughs. His crests are smooth and sometimes small: like when he wrapped his arms around me from behind, before we ended up tangled on the floor.

I can feel the trough over my shoulder as I pour the cake batter. It's like a disappearance, even though he's still right here. I can tell for sure I'm right—he's gone away somewhere—because when I cut my eyes at him, his don't meet mine. His face is vacant and his body seems too still.

It's like our traumas are swirled together, because every time I sense this happening to him, I start sweating and my heart pounds. As soon as I can sit the batter bowl down, I turn around and take his hands and squeeze them tightly, tight enough so his gaze lifts to mine.

"Can you finish this for me? One of the egg shells cut my hand." It's true. I turn my hand so he can see the small cut on the outside.

He blinks slowly at me. "Yeah."

God, I love his voice—that low, sweet voice.

I wash my hands and lean against the counter as I tell him how to pour the batter for the other layers of the cake. It makes me glad to see his eyes on his hands, his body moving steady in the present.

I pre-heat the oven and we slide the round pans in.

"Now for the icing." I turn a slow circle, trying to think of where I put my big bag of sugar. "Sugar, sugar…Laundry room." I hold a finger up, but Barrett moves past me.

"I've got it," he says quietly.

I'm holding my breath as he opens the door.

I watch as he stops in the doorway. He turns to me.

"Gwenna." His voice is very soft. He turns back to the laundry room.

"I moved them into the garage. No biggie."

He looks back at me, and he reminds me of these horses from the stables where I rode when I was younger. His eyes are kind of wide and leery, like he might buck and run. I move slowly over to him.

I take his wrists in my hands. Turn his palms over. I trace his fingers and his palms and look into his pretty eyes.

"Have you ever had your palm read?"

He smiles, small and slightly pained. "In Hindi."

"Sit down."

He does, and I sit in the chair beside his. I take one of his hands and trace my fingers gently over his palm. "You have big hands."

I look up to find him smirking.

I smile and roll my eyes. "Pervert."

His brows arch. He chuckles. "I'm the pervert?"

My face flushes. "Yes. You were thinking something like that."

"Something like what?" His hand squeezes mine as he gives me a small, dimpled smile.

"I'm not going to spell it out."

"I don't even know what you would spell." He makes this little "o" with his mouth and arches his brows, looking like a surprised owl.

"Shut up." I smack his hand gently. "You let me do my thing now." I trace a fingertip over his warm palm. "Glad to say, your lines look pretty good. Your life line is nice and long. Looks like your health's not perfect, but it doesn't suck. Maybe kind of what I'd think. Couple bumps in the road. Probably most of the stuff already happened. And this one…" I trace the children lines and give him what I hope is not a sad smile. "Two kids."

His brows draw downward. "Not sure about that."

He turns my hand over. "What do your lines say?"

"Mine suck."

His sharp brows scrunch as he strokes my palm. "Why's that?"

"Short life, no kids, meh health."

His eyes widen. I note the way he draws my hand a faction closer to his chest as he murmurs, "That's not true."

I smile and shrug. He doesn't know how true it is—and I don't want him to.

"Gwenna…" He gives me a funny little smirk, which morphs into a Cheshire Cat grin. "I wanted you to give a reading for me, but now I have to let you know, you're doing it all wrong. Trust me—I learned palmistry in India."

He taps the long, vertical line that starts at the side of my palm, above my thumb, and arcs down toward my wrist. "You're right that this is the life line, but I don't see an early death. Just a lot of chaos and disruption." He raises his brows. "And a lot of what they call vigor." His face lights up with silly humor.

I can't help laughing.

He touches the line that starts just under my index finger and stretches across my palm. "This is the head line." He grins. "This—" he taps—"is a little off. And this—" he touches a line that starts under my pinkie and flows toward my thumb—"this is your heart line. Black as soot."

His face is so grave, my stomach dips before he breaks into a dimpled grin. "Your heart line is what they call chained." He leans in and kisses my lips. He squeezes my hand. "Passionate."

I smile and feel my cheeks sting with self-conscious heat.

"Says you wear your heart on your sleeve."

I nod slowly. His hand smooths my hair back.

"You read your marriage and children lines wrong, I think."

"Did I?" I give him a poker face.

He nods. He traces my palm underneath my pinkie finger, along the outer edge. "Your marriage line right here is long and straight. That's good. And these vertical streaks right above it— they're some of the hardest ones to read—but they're definitely there. I see at least two."

I sit back, grinning. "You're making this up. You said you had yours read in Hindi."

Barrett winks. "I'm fluent in Hindi."

ELLA JAMES

Barrett

I watch her perfect mouth form a little oval. On anyone else, it would be an "o," but I think her oval is fucking adorable.

"I thought…" She shakes her head and laughs. "My friend Jamie and I went to a palm reader one time in New Orleans. It was before the wreck. She gave both of us terrible predictions, and she wanted us to come back to find out more. Then the accident happened and…"

She shakes her head again, biting her lower lip, and my chest aches for her.

"I thought maybe she was a real medium, you know?" She lets out a sexy chuckle, her tits bouncing slightly. "Since my shitty fortune seemed sort of true, Jamie has been waiting to lose all her beauty and her intellect."

I don't know anything about her friend except that she's Niccolo's girlfriend and I need to stay away from her. But still, I laugh with Gwen.

She rubs her mouth, still smiling. "You have to read hers, too. Like, ASAP. Put Jamie at ease."

I reach into my pocket, looking up at her as my hand finds the mood ring. "Close your eyes and hold your hand out one more time. I want to check one other thing."

Her lips curve as she looks at me. "Do I trust you?"

"Yes." I can't help the way my voice cracks on the word. I clear my throat so she'll think that's all it was. When she shuts her eyes, I take her hand and slide the ring on her index finger.

She blinks down at the smooth, oval-shaped blue stone, then up at me.

"Oh my God, is this a mood ring?"

I smile. "That's what I'm told."

She holds her hand up as it turns deeper blue. "I haven't seen one of these in years. I freaking love it!" Gwenna throws

334

herself at me, and I close my eyes as she hugs my neck. "Thank you!"

Her hand plays in my hair. I swallow back a moan. Her lips brush my cheek. "I love it." With her arm still around me, she leans back and looks down at the ring. "It brings back all the memories." She beams at me. "Seriously—you're the best."

Seeing her so happy chases away the remnants of my dark feeling from earlier.

We laugh and talk and make the icing, and then we put the cake together. While it's chilling in the refrigerator, I carry Gwenna to the couch. I lay her on her stomach, straddle her while keeping one foot on the floor, and rub her shoulders.

"The ring is purple now. What does that mean?" I ask, looking at her hand.

"It means…feeling really good," she murmurs.

I rub her for a few minutes, focusing on the pressure points I learned while I was rehabbing my shoulder. Then, while one hand rubs, the other pulls her leggings down, parts her asscheeks, and sinks a finger into her wet pussy. Gwenna moans and rocks herself against me.

"God, Bear…" My name is fucking *whimpered*. My cock juts against my pants.

I slide my finger out and press my thumb into her from behind. I know I hit her sweet spot when she bucks against my hand.

"*Ohhh.*"

I reach around in front of her and spread her lips with careful fingers. I drag one through her soft, slick folds; I drag up and down, and up and down, until my fingertip is coated in her sweetness. Then I find her clit. I brush it, and she groans. I encircle it, teasing. She moans again and shimmies back against my thumb. I ease another finger inside, stretching gently.

"Please," she gasps, writhing.

"Please what?" I stroke her G-spot and she rocks her hips, wiggling on my thumb and finger, then pushing her pussy forward, seeking out the fingertip that's near her clit.

"Please...touch me," she gasps.

"I am touching you." I chuckle softly.

She thrusts her hips sharply again, trying to find my fingertip with her clit. "Bear..."

I stroke up and down her slit, loving the way her body rocks and writhes, seeking more pleasure.

Every time I brush her G-spot, Gwenna groans. Once, she even shivers.

"That feels...*so* good!"

I stroke her clit.

"More..." She wiggles back against me.

I shift my thumb, bearing down a little harder, so she feels fuller. Then with two fingers, I make a V around her clit and drag down gently.

"Bear..." Hearing her say it like that makes my balls tighten.

I swallow back my own groan, toying with her swollen lips, and then reward her with a brush of my slick finger against her clit.

"Rub...me there..." She's panting.

"Here?" I stroke the swollen little nub, and she rubs it against me. "Yes!"

I start to stroke her firmly with my thumb, making her feel full and pressured on the inside while I paint circles around her bud and she grinds herself into me with sexy-as-fuck fervor.

"Yes..."

Her soft thighs clamp around my wrist. Her legs urge me deeper, press against my fingers, then she's spasming around me, clamping down around my thumb, moaning loudly one last time.

I see her eyes shut and her face slacken as she slumps down on the couch—and on my hand. I chuckle, even though my dick is throbbing painfully against my fly.

I carefully withdraw my hand and stroke her back and hair. She looks over her shoulder at me, smiling a cute, lazy smile.

"Turn me over. I want you inside me…"

And fuck, I fucking want to be. I've realized she likes to have her neck rubbed, right there at the base of her skull. So instead of getting into her, I focus my attention there and I ignore my aching boner. As predicted, it doesn't take Gwen long to fall asleep. I keep stroking her until she's really out, then I lift her easily and carry her into her room.

Her eyes flutter as I tuck her into bed.

"I fell asleep?" Her voice is raspy.

I grin. "Not your fault, Piglet."

"Oh, God…"

I tuck the covers to her shoulders, and she looks up at me one more time before her eyes drift shut.

Barrett

Being near her—I'm still fucking hard. I move silently into her office, where I sink down in her desk chair, lean my head against the back of it, and think of Gwen's sweet pussy as I jerk myself off under her desk.

I come into my hand when there's a box of tissues right in front of me because I'm so damn fixated on Gwenna. Even with her asleep on the other side of a wall, my mind and body feel as if they're anchored to her.

As I wrap a wad of Kleenex around my dick, my knee bumps the underside of her desk. The monitor lights up, displaying her desktop.

…She has no password?

I blink at the background: a luscious summer shot of the Rocky Mountains in what looks like June or July. Hmm. It's just a nature shot, no Gwen anywhere in sight, so I turn my attention to the folders on her desktop. Dammit. For all Gwen's teasing, I never did like the tradecraft, secret agent shit. I feel like I'm violating her. Which is ludicrous, considering.

I push past that and quickly find the place she keeps her camera footage: *Cam Archives*, the folder says. I luck out and find she's got a folder inside labeled *The Ghost!*

She's got the spook part right, anyway.

It doesn't take me long to sift through what footage she has of me and modify it some—just enough so no agency would recognize my Operator tells. Within Spec Ops, there are little things each group does differently. The way I'm walking in the footage, the way I scan the woods, is very Ranger. Despite some changes in the organization over the last ten or fifteen years, the Unit still recruits more from the Rangers than any other group. Even *I* can't see much of myself—I make a mental note to burn the very, very good camo I was wearing here—but I would still think 'Ranger' from the little bit I can see. And the way I took that glove off, stretching my numb fingers, is a major fucking clue, unique to me.

I take care to doctor the images slightly enough that if Gwen takes another look at them, she won't feel crazy; the edits are too subtle for her to notice. Then I take the dates on the shots and use them to lead me back to the longer reels from those days I was captured on her cams.

I spend an hour searching for myself in spots she might have missed me. Sure enough, I see myself a handful more times when Gwen didn't. From that footage, I erase myself completely.

Twenty minutes later, I've erased my tech tracks, modified the computer's sleep/wake log—fucking hard on a damn Mac—and stood up from her desk, a wad of cum rags in my hand and the weight of guilt on my chest.

I can hear the echo of her voice and feel the ghost of her touch as I move quietly into the kitchen. Channeling Gwenna, I tell myself not to worry too much about things, not when I'm about to fix it all. I dispose of the tissues, wash my hands, and stare down at our cake. It looks damn good, but I'm not cutting it without her. I look around for a cake cover, and when I don't see one, I know where to look.

I step slowly into the laundry room. On the floor beside the washer, there's a single, milk-white petal. I can't resist picking it up, even though I know my hands will stain it brown. I press it to my cheek and inhale deeply, slowly, until my heart starts pounding like I knew it would.

It's just a fucking flower.

I tell myself to grow a pair. Cold sweat sweeps me, and I sit down at Gwenna's kitchen table.

I tell myself to focus on the softness of the petal. Soft like satin…Soft like Gwenna's skin.

I peek down at the blue of her table.

She moved the flowers into the garage for me.

Anguish stirs inside me…

I don't know why. Why did she do it?

It doesn't matter, I tell myself.

I bring the flower petal closer to my nose and inhale. Heat prickles my skin, and I can feel my throat tighten, but I keep breathing: slow and steady. I fucking hate the smell…the feeling of that day…It's all twisted up, mashed into one long, awful reel of horrors, from seeing Maliha dash into the square, to the moment I had to jump off the roof, to the awful, awful moments looking down at Breck. The fucking shock of it. And waking up so fucked up at Landstuhl.

I can almost hear her whisper, "It makes so much sense."

Does it?

I inhale the fucking gardenia again and squeeze my eyes shut. "Fuck."

I bring the petal down and narrow my eyes at it. It's all brown now, a little torn. I stuff it in my pocket anyway. Maybe I could get my own gardenia plant and make myself smell the damn thing every day. Until I'm okay with it. Then Gwenna could bring hers back inside.

I drag myself to my feet, find the cake cover, and spend a few minutes engineering a transport so I can move the cake without ripping it apart.

Then I check on Gwen again. She's sleeping peacefully. Which means she'll never know what I'm about to do.

chapter twenty-four

Barrett

I look down on her for a moment. Watching her ribs expand with breath. Running my gaze along her soft form, cushioned by the blankets. Smelling the sweet, fruity scent of the air in her bedroom.

As I look at her, I try to look inward at myself. All I really see is the fury of desire I feel for her. It's consuming, dangerous. I know this. From the first day I watched her, I felt things for her I'd never felt for any other person living on the other side of my crosshairs. Things I've never felt for anyone at all.

I told myself that there were reasons for that: all our parallels; her strength; her undeniable beauty, so much of which remains untouched, despite her worry to the contrary. I told myself that maybe right then, anyone would do. I'd been lonely before, and fucked up. But never like this…

I try not to think right now about those details.

Gwenna wants me. I want her—so much, my eyes are wet. My throat aches as I blink down at her.

I ask myself: if she knew…

If.

And the awful thing is, I trust in her goodness so damn much…

If Gwenna knew. I'm able to tell myself that maybe…

It's possible she wouldn't care.

She's just so good. And kind. Forgiving.

There's a voice that says I don't deserve it, but there's a louder one and it screams *need*.

I need her now, like air and water. More.

I think about it—not a whole thought, even, just a frame of memory, the sensation of my jaw clenching around the barrel of my 9mm. How cold it was. And how I couldn't do it. Not there in the Ft. Bragg place I shared with Breck, with all his shit boxed up around me.

So I thought I could do this instead.

I turn away from her and hold my head. I walk through her office and lean against the doorframe, facing the living room. I don't belong here, and I know I don't. But…I can't help myself. I'm *bad*, and maybe I can fight that by being *good to her*.

The whole thing—what I know—it would be a fucked up kind of self-flagellation on my end. Which I like. Which seems fitting.

I can make this up to her. *Not really*. But I can spend as much time as she'll let me trying to.

With that thought pasted to the forefront of my mind, I touch my pocket, feeling the hardness of my phone. I look over my shoulder, as if I'll find Gwenna waiting there, and when I don't, I quietly go outside. Down her steps, into the woods between our properties. So I'm too far from her cams to ever be picked up, even the echo of my voice.

I call Dove.

It rings twice before he answers.

"Well, look who's calling me. I must be special."

"Fuck off." I smile, even though my eyes are burning.

"To what do I owe this honor?"

"I've been tracking Blue."

The line goes so quiet, I can hear the tinkling of the dry leaves blowing over the forest floor.

"I don't know if you have, too—"

"Nah," Dove says. "You know none of them like me too much." *None* being the Unit's support staff with the capability of tracing Blue's phone. Dove pissed off their head girl years back, and they've all blackballed him since.

I nod. "Well, Blue seems headed my way. I want you to tell him something for me."

"Yeah?" Dove is quiet, waiting, probably with bated breath, for what I say next.

I inhale slowly. "Tell him I'm not doing it."

"You're—What are you saying?"

"You heard me." I blink and grit my teeth as a slash of wind sends moisture tracking down my cheek. Then I swallow, because fuck if I want Dove to know this shit. "I'm not doing it."

"Really?"

"Really."

"I think I must be missing something," Dove says. Silence fuzzes on the line. I shake my head.

"Changed my mind."

He waits a beat, probably stunned. "After all that. Changed your mind."

"That's what I said."

"Well, hell. So are you leaving town?"

"Not yet."

I can see the wheels in his head turning. "What are you doing down there if you're not...?"

I think quickly, carefully before I give my answer. "Plotting my next move."

"Which is what?"

"I don't know. That's what 'plotting'—"

"I fucking knew it!"

"Knew what?"

"You have a boner for her. You have a hard-on for the fucking girl who—"

"Shut up," I snarl.

"This is bad, Bear. Really bad. Bear...Fuck, man, this shit won't go away. It's never going to go away. Can you even fucking *do* that?"

"I can do what I need to." My voice is thick. I lean against a tree trunk. "I could protect her. I don't have a choice," I rasp. "I love her."

"Goddamnit, Bear. You went and got yourself fucked *up*."

"I know." The words are whispered.

"Do you?"

"Tell Blue I don't want to see his fucking face. Nowhere near here. Make him understand. I mean it, Dove."

I hang the phone up. I stand there in the moonlight for a long time, just breathing.

Gwenna
December 31, 2011

I march straight to the bar, order two Jäger Bombs, down them in quick succession, and on a whim, decide to get Mr. Friendly at my table a fish bowl. The bartender hands it over, gentle as if he was handling a baby, and I clutch the cold bowl to my chest. As I whirl around, I bump into something solid.

"Oops!"

A guy. My heavy-lidded eyes peruse him, processing, after a second, a striking face, with kind eyes, princely lips, and model-gorgeous features. "You're like...a wall. A nice wall."

He chuckles softly.

He's got sad eyes, my drunk mind thinks, but the thought is lost as my gaze reaches his hair. Curly hair...Mmm. My sluggish pulse surges.

"Are you a model?" I ask, blinking as I do, because I'm slightly dizzy.

He gives me the funniest little smile that starts out kind of smirky and turns into a gorgeous grin—with *dimples*!

"No—I'm not a model. Are *you*?"

"Yes."

His face gentles, looking curious and, I think, charmed. "Yeah?"

"A model and a singer," I say proudly.

He gives me a thoughtful-looking smile, as if he thinks I'm cute and is pondering the model-singer part of the equation. Heat roars through me, and I realize I can feel my heartbeat in between my legs.

Because he's beautiful. And he seems nice. Someone I should stay away from on a night like this.

I turn slightly to head back to my table, forgetting, in my drunken state, that he's still right in front of me. Beer sloshes over my arms.

"Shit!"

His big hands steady the fish bowl. "You need a hand?"

I groan and push my right sleeve up, baring the tiny snowflake tat I got on the inside of my forearm last Christmas, with some of my modeling money.

"Sigh."

"Did you just say 'sigh'?"

I look up into his nice, sad blue eyes, which just now seem to be dancing with amusement. He tilts his head back as he chuckles.

"I text too much," I say.

I have no idea if he understands what I'm trying to say—too many times typing "sigh" has got me saying that aloud rather than sighing—and I find I'm too drunk to guess.

I hold out my hands. "I can get it."

He passes my bowl back to me and I allow myself another look at his beautiful face. "I should be able to hold a fish bowl, even though I am drunk."

He pushes a curl out of his eyes. "Where ya headed?"

I nod in the direction of our table.

"Over there with John and Nic?" he asks.

"How'd you know?"

He smiles again, this time smaller and more fleeting. "They're good guys."

"I'm too drunk to tell," I confess.

Tears fill my eyes as I remember the voice on the other end of Elvie's phone. I try to tell myself it's nothing. Just some stupid fangirl. He'll call me later tonight, after the ball drops.

"Trust me, then," the guy says.

I blink, surprised anew by the gorgeous mug in front of me. I smile absently, imagining his lips on mine when the ball drops. My drunk self thinks, *He's much cuter than Elvie.*

The guy's hand is on my forehead. He presses a fingertip against my hairline. "Snowflake," he says softly, looking at his finger, then at me.

"What's your name, snowflake?" he murmurs.

"Gwenna."

part three

"How much can you change and get away with it, before you turn into someone else, before it's some kind of murder?"

—Richard Siken,
from "Portrait of Fryderyk in Shifting Light," *War of the Foxes*

chapter one

Gwenna
November 8, 2015

I awaken to a troubling noise: one that's loud enough to rouse me but forgotten when I crack my eyelids open. A smeary mess of colors winks above me…Twinkle lights. I blink up at them, wondering for a heartbeat if I've fallen back in time. But I remember: I hung new lights for Barrett.

Barrett!

As if on cue, the sounds of retching reach my ears. I sit up, feeling dizzy. He's not in my room. The harsh, strained sounds are coming from the bathroom.

"Shit."

The horrible sound fills my ears as I cover the ground between my bed and the bathroom door. The toilet flushes as I pull it open.

I find Barrett's big, nude body curled around the toilet bowl. He's got one of his arms around the seat, his face resting in the triangle between his bicep and his forearm.

His hair and skin are damp, his shoulders pumping as he pants. A long look shows me that his skin is pocked with goosebumps, and he's shaking slightly.

"Bear?" I drop down beside him.

His back rises with a deep breath, but he doesn't lift his head. His shoulders still, then resume a slower, gentler rise and fall. My hand reaches for him, but I stop before I meet his skin.

"I'll get a towel for you," I whisper.

Does he like his washcloths cold or warm? Maybe I should go and not invade his space. I war with myself as I hold the rag under warm water. Then I see his shoulders twitch, a sad little aftershock, and I'm not sure I can go. Not unless he asks me to.

I crouch back down beside him, and after a moment's debate, decide to drape the warm towel over his bicep. As I rock there on my heels a few feet from him, Barrett takes the towel. He lifts his head, but before I can see his face, his towel-covered hand covers it.

I can hear the air whoosh from his lungs into the terrycloth, see his shoulders rise and fall a few more times. He's struggling to get himself together, and I want so much to soothe him—but I'm scared to do the wrong thing.

"You okay?" My words are soft and quiet. Useless.

Barrett pulls the towel down his face, cupping his throat with it. His blue eyes are strangely luminous, his handsome features fragile in a way I can't explain or understand. He blinks at me, his thick brows scrunching in what looks like confusion.

"Gwen?" The word sounds caught in his throat.

"Hey…" I scoot closer to him, putting my arm awkwardly around his shoulders. He freezes for a moment. Then I tug him closer, and he wraps his heavy arms around me.

"You're okay…" His voice cracks as he leans back, looking into my eyes.

"Yeah, I'm okay. Are you?"

He leans his face against my shoulder. I remember what he said—about the dreams. Did he have a dream about me? One so bad it made him sick?

I stroke his neck. "You must have had a nightmare."

"I'm sorry." His words are warm and quiet.

"Why are you sorry?"

He shakes his head. I feel him take a heavy breath.

"Do you still feel bad?" I whisper.

"No."

The word itself belies him: soft and pained.

I stroke his hair. "You want a shower?" I hug him more tightly. "I'm not leaving. Not unless you want me to."

His grip on me loosens, then he lifts his head and blinks. "Gwenna?" He squints, as if the lamp beside the sink is too bright.

"Yeah, it's me."

He frowns and looks around, confused. Then looks down at himself. His eyes widen. His gaze flies to the toilet.

"Did I get sick?" His voice is hoarse.

I nod. I stroke a curl that's pasted to his temple.

Barrett cringes. He brings a hand up to his forehead, shuts his eyes. I notice it's his left hand, and my heart squeezes as the thumb and index finger curve around his head.

"I'm so sorry I didn't hear your dream. I was really out, I guess."

He moves his hand, so I can see his anguished eyes. "Don't be sorry. I'm sorry I touched you. Go back to bed, Gwen. I'm just going to get a shower." His eyes drop to his knees, his face expressionless as his gaze lifts back to mine. "Maybe I should go," he says more firmly. "I'll come back in a little while. I'll bring you breakfast. Anything you want." He gives me a small smile.

"Did you dream about me?"

I see his throat move as he struggles to swallow, and I wish I hadn't asked. I put my hands on his knees.

"It's okay." I try to hold his gaze, as if I have that power—to keep him focused on just me. "You see me right here. I'm okay."

His eyes shut. I lift one of his hands, enfolding it in my own. "Let me start your shower. Then I'll go if you want some space." I squeeze his hand lightly before I let it go and step over to the shower.

Maybe I said the wrong thing, I think, as I point the shower head away from me and turn it on. If he doesn't want space, he might be too embarrassed to ask me to stay, and now I've mentioned leaving.

By the time I lean out of the tub space, he's standing over by the wall. He's got his arms folded across his chest, a towel wrapped around his waist. His body is so big, so chiseled and strong, and yet...he looks vulnerable. I can see it on him, now that I know his face.

I wave him over. He keeps his eyes on the floor as he steps to me.

I can't help reaching out and touching him again, my palm against his lower back. "I could get in with you. If you didn't mind company." I hold my breath as I look up at him.

His eyes still have that dazed look. My stomach clenches, seeing it. Without further debate, I pull the shower curtain back a little more and step in. I turn around to him and hold my hand out.

With his jaw tight and his eyes hard now—or just blank—he throws his towel over the rod and steps into the shower without touching me.

The surge of pleasure I feel watching him move is dampened by how serious he looks, how unhappy. I can feel it radiating from him.

Once again, like many times before, with him, my heart pounds and my head feels light; I want to freeze up, step away, but instead I close the gap between us, praying when I wrap my arms around him—

Yes.

You're never wrong about this, I tell myself as the tension leaves his muscles and his forehead lowers to my shoulder.

He's never going to ask; I make a mental note of this as we stand here together, his cheek warm against me. One of his hands cups my hip, and I lean my cheek against the top of his head.

As the water warms fully, I bring him into the spray and rub soap over his steel-hard arms and shoulders.

I notice his curls are plastered to his face, and push them gently off his forehead.

He lifts his head and looks down at me with a grave expression on his face. With his lashes and his hair wet, his eyes look round and blue and earnest.

I run the soap bar from his triceps to the soft crease inside his elbow, then along the inside of his forearm. Despite how thick and muscled he is, his soapy skin is soft as silk. His wrist is lean and square. I thread my fingers through his, squeezing gently in the spaces in between digits, then moving up toward his knuckles, massaging his hand the way a physical therapist once did mine before I left rehab.

His face slackens and his eyes slip shut.

I rub all the pressure points on his hand, hoping to draw his attention here and out of his head. Maybe I do, because a moment later, his free hand takes the soap from mine. He pulls his other hand out of my grasp, lifts his forearm up to push his hair out of his eyes, and holds my gaze with his raw, bare one as he runs his soapy hands down my arms, then down my lower belly.

He shuts his eyes and groans, but he continues stroking me, from collarbone to ribs, from ribs to hips; he soaps my lower back, the curve of my backside, and then his hands rove up my ribs and find my breasts. He cups them.

His head is down, so I can't see his face, but I can hear him breathing as his fingers catch my nipple. I let out a soft squeak.

His length presses against my belly. I reach down and catch him with both hands. With one I cup his soapy head; the other glides down his thick shaft.

"I never got the chance to do this earlier," I whisper.

His eyes shut, and his hips jerk.

"Gwenna, you're too good…"

He pushes himself closer to me, causing my hand to glide down to the base of him. Bear grips one of my shoulders, breathing loudly as I thumb his head and drag the hand that was gripping his shaft under his heavy, soapy balls.

I see his eyes roll slightly. His jaw locked, his features tense, he moans low in his throat as I pump up and down his shaft, lingering at the rim of his head and tugging gently on his sac.

"Oh fuck…" He pushes his hips toward me, and his mouth takes mine the way he does so often: gently at first, and then hard, desperate, as if he can't stop, like he's dying and my mouth is life.

He strokes my breast with gentle fingers, though his mouth is more and more demanding; needy: rough and almost hurting. He moans; I breathe it in. I stroke up and down his long cock, loving his small shiver.

"Gwen…"

I look up at his face, so starkly beautiful, so dazed with lust. I squeeze the base of his cock. "I want you inside me, Barrett."

He makes a low, hoarse sound. Then he pulls me close and guides me as we get down in the bottom of the tub: him lying on his back, me straddling his hips. He lifts his knees. I feel the plump head of him pressed against my crack.

I reach around behind myself and grab him just under his head. I move so that I'm crouching over him instead of kneeling. My legs shake as I rub his head against myself, loving the warm, slick pressure of him gliding against my lips, then pushing at my core.

When he's thrusting into my hand, grunting and grabbing at my hips, I lift my ass, position him so he can drive straight home, and sink down on him, moaning as I'm filled beyond the point of pleasure, my ass kissing his balls. Having him so deep inside me makes my legs feel weak. Makes me moan and sigh and cry out.

Barrett moans, too.

Without lifting my hips, I thrust against him, pushing him into me and holding. Then I wiggle up and off him, reaching down to hold his shaft with only his head penetrating me for a minute. I sink down slowly.

"Fuck…"

When he's so deep, and I'm so tightly spread it's almost painful, I draw a shaky breath and grind against him, rolling my hips as if I'm doing a hula hoop. Barrett's hips lift under me.

"Oh, God…" he moans. "Fuck."

His big hands grab my hips and hold me to him. He rolls his hips, too, so I can feel his head probe deep inside me, kissing my G-spot. I gasp as my core constricts around him. Or maybe he swells. All I know is *it gets tighter.* I'm seeing stars and panting like some kind of animal.

"You feel so fucking good," he groans.

I clench around him, rise slowly up, then center him and sink back down again. It feels so good—God, every time! My back arches. I make this grunting sound that would embarrass me…but I'm so full of him, there's nothing I can do. He's breathing harder now, faster. I shut my eyes and feel him lift me slightly off him. I grip his thighs as he lets go of me, so I'm impaled with his dick.

"Aghhh!"

"God—that sounds so fucking sexy. You're so beautiful."

My greedy hands stroke his lower belly, my fingers skating down his happy trail and toward where we're joined.

"Touch yourself," he rasps.

I slide my hand toward myself, feeling my swollen lips, my dripping pussy, and the steel girth of him, hard and thick, spreading me open.

I've never felt anything so hot in all my life.

"Oh, Lord…" I lean back on instinct, exposing the base of him so I can grind my clit against it. As if he can hear my thoughts, his fingers part my swollen pussy lips. He finds my clit and rubs.

It's just the barest touch—but his finger is calloused. As he touches me, he thrusts, bouncing me atop him so I feel every inch of his stiff, thick, swollen dick, even down to when it pulses slightly.

I reach back and find his balls and watch his face come undone: lips parted, his eyes rolling. I see him moan. He strokes my clit. I cup his balls. I manage to rise off him one more time before his finger makes me burst.

I've never felt my pussy go so crazy on a dick. I clench and pulse around him. Barrett groans as he explodes inside me. I can feel the warmth, the blissful fullness of him as he comes.

Barrett groans again and pulls me down atop his chest.

"This feels perfect…"

His hand cups my cheek against his chest.

"You're perfect." I can feel his lips against my hair. "I didn't hurt you?" he asks.

"No." I give a giddy laugh. "Hell, no."

His legs hug my lower body. I stroke his forehead.

"Let's get out. This tub is so hard…"

His eyes are tired. His smile is soft. He sits up and scoots us back, so he's leaning against the back of the tub. Then, with gentle care, he slides out of me.

"Water's going cold." He blinks and smiles this funny little smile.

Even as his hand smooths over his thick halfie and I quickly clean myself, I'm dizzied by the most delicious throb.

"That felt amazing," I murmur.

He leans forward, grabbing my hand and drawing it to his lips. He kisses my fingers, then he stands up, lifting me with him.

He climbs out of the tub ahead of me, thrusting a towel behind the curtain.

"Thanks."

"You're welcome."

Damn—his voice is sexy. I tuck my towel around my chest and step out. Barrett wraps a towel around my hair and kisses my lips.

"You're so fucking good." He looks into my eyes.

I smile. "You are." I can't resist reaching out to touch one of his curls.

He strokes my jaw. "I like it when you touch me." His voice sounds lower, rougher than his norm. I realize it's thick with emotion.

I step closer to him, wrap my arms around his hard back.

"You know you're supposed to talk or write about your dreams," I smile up at him, "but maybe I can sex them out of you instead."

"You volunteering?"

"I think I may be."

He chuckles. "Sex them."

"I don't often say the F-word. Nothing wrong with it, just doesn't feel right to me."

He grins. "You're blushing just from saying 'the F-word.'"

"You're dimpling, so there."

I smack his pec and step to the sink. "I fell asleep last night before I could show you where I keep things." I open a drawer and get my toothbrush and toothpaste out.

ELLA JAMES

Barrett smiles, crooked and dimpled. "Is that a Nemo toothbrush?"

"Yes. And look, don't laugh at it, because it's the only one I have. You can borrow it if you want—*have* it. And tomorrow I'll buy both of us new ones."

His face shutters. My stomach flip-flops. I thought things were going well with us, but—

"You don't have to use mine. I would totally—"

"I will."

God—he looks serious. Like he just found out…something awful. I chew my lip.

"Barrett?"

He blinks, still solemn. I step slightly closer to him, and am stunned to see his eyes look glossy.

"Oh…" I reach for him. "Are you—"

He blinks and leans away from me. He smiles, but it's a half smile—and it's sad. "I'll use your toothbrush, Gwenna. I'll get you another one."

I realize how he worded that, and I think maybe I understand. "It was the thing I said about getting us both a toothbrush. Too much?" My head throbs. My throat aches. "I get that," I manage in a steady voice.

He pulls me to his chest so quickly I don't know what hit me. I feel his big arms lock around me, his cheek press against the top of my head. I feel him take a breath, and then another one, before he whispers, "Not too much."

I don't know whose heartbeat I hear: his or my own—but it's racing.

"Not too much."

I feel frozen as I press my cheek against his chest. He strokes his big hand up and down my back.

This.

This is what was missing.

This is what I've waited for.

I hold him, and he holds me, and warmth seeps into my heart. Words crawl through my mind, but they're so flimsy, so inadequate. My eyes are closed, and all I feel is his big body around mine. Protecting me—and wanting me.

"Go wait for me in bed, Piglet. When I get in, I'll rub your back."

"You figured out my weakness." I smile against his chest.

"It was easy."

I run a finger down his abs.

"Another weakness?" He smirks down at me.

"Oh, yes."

With one more long smile shared between us, I go wait for him in bed. A few minutes later, Bear climbs in behind me, tucking me against him for a long moment before he eases me onto my stomach.

I awaken the next morning to an eyeful of Barrett's beautiful back, bathed in sunlight. He's lying on his stomach and he's reading—

"What is that?"

He gives me sexy side eyes, followed by a hot-as-hell smirk. I lunge at him. He bounces me off his broad back with so much precision, I land right where I was lying to begin with. Then he stretches above me, holding the book above my head.

Finding Calder.

"Don't be grabbing at my book," he says in a gravelly voice. "They're at the springs and Eden's clothes are off." He wiggles his eyebrows, and I reach out and grab the one thing I think might make him drop the book.

The expression on his face—that pained shock morphing quickly into pleasure—

Good Lord, it's hot as Hades.

He falls onto his ass, leaning back on his strong arms. I bend down to lick the head of him, loving the moan that comes from deep inside his chest, the tremble of his thighs as my tongue winds its way down toward his balls and then back up.

I love how inarticulate he gets, just moaning as he leans his head back. A few long licks later, he falls fully back onto the bed, lifting his hips and grasping at the covers as I suck him.

At one point his eyes slit open and I catch the groaned words "on your back"—an order for me?—but I take pride in keeping him right where he is. He thrusts at me again and tugs at my hair. I cry out at the unexpected pain, but the vibration of my mouth around his cock just makes his fingers twist my hair more tightly.

I can tell he's out of it: the way his body jerks, the loud, unsteady breathing…I can taste his precum when I swallow.

"Gwen…"

A second later, his dick swells, his legs tense, and he barks my name as he comes. I swallow, and his big hands cup my head against his thighs. I'm still finishing the job as he says, "Fuck."

He jerks away from me, drawing out of my mouth. I look up into his wide eyes as his hand touches my hair. "Did I hurt you?" he asks in a low, regretful voice.

I grin, wiping my mouth and shaking my head. "Did you like it?"

Rising to his knees on the mattress, he wraps his arms around my head and pulls me to his chest.

His fingers massage my scalp, but I can hardly even feel it. All I feel is warmth and need. I'm so turned on, I find my tongue flicking his abs.

He reaches down into the panties I pulled on before I got into the bed last night and parts my pussy lips with agonizing care. He drags a finger down my slit and sinks into me. "So *wet*, Gwenna."

Then I'm on my back and his tongue is writhing up and down my slit, teasing my core, where his finger is still buried, then rolling like melted butter over my poor, throbbing clit. I grip the fingers of his hand that's holding my hip.

Barrett groans, and by the time I'm panting, *needing* to get off, I look down between our bodies and I see how hard he is. I have to have him.

"Please...*inside*."

His gaze flicks up to mine as if to make sure that I'm sure. I nod.

There is nothing sexier than Barrett with one hand around his dick, rolling his head around in my wetness, teasing my clit until I'm whimpering.

When he finally pushes into me, I actually scream. I laugh. He laughs, but his eyes are closed. His face is tense and reverent. His cheek rests against my breast; he sucks me as he surges deep inside me. I clench around him and feel him swell. I come the next breath. Barrett grunts and spills into me right after.

Then I'm lying in his arms. His eyes look tired and his lips are quirked up in a gentle smile.

"I'll go get something..."

He drops a kiss on my temple and pushes up, to leave the bed and get a towel. I pull him back down.

I can't say it out loud—too naughty—but I like the way it feels...Just us, and no cleanup. I'm sleepy, too, and I just want him curled behind me for a minute.

chapter two

Barrett
November 12, 2015

"**F**ucking hell, man." *Bluebell's hand comes under my right arm,
holding me against him as the car swerves. "Dove, take the road
right there. That one!"*

"*Is that a road?*"

"*Yes. Take it!*"

"*Fuck, we're gonna track.*"

"*They'll be gone in half an hour.*"

*I feel Blue shift back against his seat and hear his voice closer to me.
"Shit, Bear. Is it just the liquor?"*

Between hurling, I rasp, "Yes."

*I wrap my hand around one of the metal rods that lock the headrest
of the front passenger's seat into the chair and try to aim toward the floor.
Far away, I feel the chaos of anxiety as my teammates buzz and the world
riots around me.*

"*All right,*" *Blue says roughly.* "*We'll get where we're going and
there'll be a shower.*"

Between gasping, I groan, "I don't care."

I open my wet eyes, see the toilet, feel the towel pressed against my mouth. Thank fuck.

Another spasm jacks my stomach, and I hold the cloth over my mouth and nose as bile stings my throat. I can't help groaning—but I *can* leave a wash cloth on the bathroom rug. I can tell myself before I fall asleep that if I wake up from *that* dream, I'll run in here and grab the towel, even if I'm stuck in flashback land.

So far, it's been working. I feel a bolt of pride, even as my shoulders shake, my eyes stream, and I struggle to get air through the towel between retching.

Nothing comes up. I've found if I cut out food and water in the two hours before I go to sleep, I just get bile, which burns my nose and throat but isn't as bad as vomit. So far, Gwenna hasn't heard me, so when I finish, I've got time to kneel here, half lost in my memories: *penance*. I pay it gladly.

Sometimes in the last few days, I'm even thankful for it. In a fucked up way, the demons driving me led me to her. The circularity of fate—the putrid whiff of nihilism I've never been able to outrun—seems to have some meaning now.

Would I change this? Yes. I would go back, of course. I would change our course to spare Gwen, and I would likely lose her. Still, I would. Even as I thirst for her, I know I would do anything to change things. Anything.

In the absence of that option, I press my fingers into my dripping eyes and try to pull the blanket of self-hatred over me—for just a minute. I try to see the awful things I see—try to see Gwenna, as she fits into the dream—and I'm finding that I *can't*.

I try to feel that pain, the abject pain that used to leave me gasping in my bed, as I wash up. But all I see and feel is Gwen.

The first few nights, I tried to make myself stay in the bathroom paying homage to the memory, to the truth of who and what I am. And I did stand here for a while. But no guilt, no pain can break through the warmth inside my chest, that addict's tunnel-focus on the woman sleeping in the room behind me.

I climb back into bed and Gwenna reaches for me in her sleep.

Gwenna

I press my cheek against his pec and listen to his heartbeat. His chest expands with a deep breath, and his pulse slows down a little.

That's right, baby…

I feel his arm come gently down around my back. He never puts the full weight of it on me. When he gets sleepy, he moves his arm down to my hip, and that's the way he drifts off. He must think I'm much more fragile than I am.

I tell myself that's why he's lying to me. Because he wants to shield me, not because the thought of getting truly close to me repels him. For someone as kind and conscientious as Barrett—a guy who won't even rest the full weight of his arm on my chest— to be unable to share themselves with another person—That would be so freaking sad…

When we wake up in the morning, he'll tell me he slept fine. He doesn't know I hear him whimpering my name every night before he stumbles to my bathroom and gets sick. I see the washcloth he leaves on the rug beside the tub, or on the tile near the toilet, so he can grab it and press it over his mouth. And in the mornings, when I wake up after he does, I notice it—and everything else we'd both put in my hamper the previous day—fully laundered, still warm in the dryer.

The night after the one where I showered with him, I woke up when he bolted from the bed. When I peeked into the bathroom and found him over the toilet with a towel pressed against his mouth, I went icy cold—and then I crept back to bed.

He slid under the covers a little while later smelling like soap and toothpaste, quiet, with measured breaths, even though when I snuggled against him, I could hear his heart racing.

The weird thing is, I think he suspected I was awake that time. He didn't seem to relax until I slowed my own breathing and made my body go limp against his. I wonder where he learned to be so observant…but I guess it's not a mystery.

Everything else about him feels as though it is.

I wonder what he's dreaming when he writhes and whimpers my name. I wish I knew what's haunting him.

But I feel like my hands are tied. He's trying so hard to hide the nightmares from me, and I don't know why. I don't want to pry and send him running. Not yet, anyway.

For now, I just accept that the only thing I can give him is the warmth of my body, pressed against his, when he gets back into bed. I love his breath on my neck, the way his chest expands as he inhales against my hair. I love the way his lips tickle my jaw, and most of all, I love the way, when he succumbs to sleep, his big frame softens subtly behind mine.

I feel his muscles twitch as he sinks into sleep. For the next half-hour or so, I keep my mind alert by saying prayers and making mental lists. I wait until his body coils behind mine and he groans.

He doesn't wake when I turn around and wrap my arm around his neck and kiss his cheek. I can tell he never feels the first kiss—because he starts to pant, his muscles tighten, and he often groans again. I take that as my cue to kiss his neck.

And it's magical, the way my mouth and hands, just kissing his neck and stroking his hair, can pull him from that place and back to me. His hands grip me. He'll murmur "Gwen"—another good sign; during nightmares, I'm "Gwenna"—and then, after a rub of his erection against my thigh, he'll drift into untroubled sleep.

It all goes off without a hitch tonight. Except instead of rubbing himself against me and nodding off, his hand sinks into my panties, his finger strokes into my pussy, and he presses himself against my ass.

He makes a low rumble in the back of his throat and whispers, "Gwen."

I push back and rub against him.

"You awake?" he asks me in a raspy voice.

I reach around behind me, touching his hard chest. Barrett rocks against me, curls his finger in my pussy. "I love this pussy…"

He sounds half asleep. I can't help giggling, even as I push myself back against him. I feel his long, thick cock between my ass cheeks.

He moans. "Gwen…"

Another finger finds my clit. He skates over it with slick precision.

"God!"

"I need to be inside here…"

What he's doing to me feels so good, I thrust against his hand and groan and hope he will take care of things somehow so I don't have to move, so this doesn't have to stop.

I feel him wrap his hand around his dick. Then he repositions his body behind mine. For a moment, my heart thrums as his hand parts my ass cheeks. Then the finger in my pussy slides out. My eyes roll back as his hand spreads me gently open and I feel the firm, delicious pressure of his dick notched against my center. With one firm thrust, he pushes inside.

"Bear!"

Coming from behind like that...The angle...

"Ohhhhhh."

I press my legs together and shimmy back, taking more of him.

"That's...oh yeah..." He moves his hips, rubbing his head against my G-spot, and I start shaking.

He pulls himself out, moaning, too, as his cock rubs between my upper thighs. He sinks back in. Oh God...

"Barrett."

I feel his arm around my waist, and then he's fingering me from the front, his finger teasing my clit until I'm bouncing back against him in a fit of lust.

"Ahh...you're tight...so wet, baby..."

His hand plays around my clit and strokes between my pussy lips as he continues fucking me: the plunging in...and easing out....and shoving in. Fuck! I feel his muscles quake with effort... or arousal.

"Goddamn...you're so *tight*."

I can feel him throb and swell inside me. I pant, my shoulder blades kissing his thick chest. I love how his body feels behind mine, big and bulky. Every time he fills me, pleasure spills through me; I push against him. Two of his fingertips skate from my creaming core—as he pulls out—up through my slit and linger sweetly on each side of my clit.

My head and neck burn as I flex my legs, my thighs stinging. Barrett buries himself deep. His thrusts speed up. Our legs tangle, both strained and shaking, his hips pumping...I can feel his torso curled around mine, his chest bumping my back with his deep breaths.

He grunts and pants a little louder. I sigh sharply. *Almost...*

"Fuck—oh, Gwenna, you're so fucking...good." He comes inside me with a hard, deep thrust, and I groan as my body milks him.

I feel his sweat-damp face against my back, nuzzling me. His breath against my skin makes chills race down my arms and shoulders.

"So good, Piglet."

I reach around behind me, wanting to touch him. The first thing I feel is his arm. I wrap it tightly around my chest and close my eyes.

"That was amazing. That position," I whisper.

He plants a kiss on my shoulder, then puts a gentle hand on my hip as he pulls out.

"Thank you." His voice is hoarse and sweet. I turn around and snuggle up against him.

"Thank *you.*" I kiss his chest.

We just stay there like that for a minute, me inhaling his yummy, sweaty, man smell, him stroking my shoulder blade.

I look up at him. "You like this?" I ask softly.

"What?" His mouth curves slightly in one of his small, sweet smiles.

"Being at my house."

The smile widens. "Maybe a little."

I nip at his chest. His big hand smooths over my hair. "Gwennie..."

"Don't call me that."

"Piglet..." His eyes briefly close. When they open, he looks more content than I've ever seen him. The knowledge brings a flutter to my stomach.

We get up and start grabbing for clothes. We've been holed up in my house for four days now, reveling in the newness of... whatever this is.

"I have to go to the enclosure later. Want to come?" I ask him.

"Sure." He smiles. "I want to see Papa in action."

I snort.

"What? I mean it."

"You better mean it," I tease.

"Go with me on a hike?" he asks, pulling his shirt on.

"Now?"

He nods. "You want to go to that rock way up there on my side of the line?"

The property line. I realize after a second what he means. "That little cave place? I always loved that place, but once I saw a coyote there and I haven't gone back since."

"Bear keeper can't handle a coyote?" he teases.

"Unlike you, I'm not some crazy, badass gunman." As soon as the words flow from my lips, I flinch.

Barrett steps to me and frames my face with his hands. "Gwen?"

"Yes." My eyes on him are wide.

He whispers, "I'm not going to break."

I nod slowly. "I know."

He pulls me against him. I have the sense he's going to say something, but he never does. We both finish dressing, and while we're eating protein bars—two for him and one for me—we talk about my bear babies.

I can't help admiring Barrett's body as we stretch outside. I get a cramp and he kneels, propping my foot on his shoulder as his fingers...I groan. "God—you're good."

"Important skill."

"For...?"

"Staying alive."

My eyes widen.

He winks, then ruffles my hair. "Race you to the rock, Piglet."

chapter three

Barrett

I hold her hand, and we walk up the hill. It's strange—to be here *with* her and not just watching her. I caress her hand. She smiles up at me. Emotion moves through my chest: gratitude, shock, guilt. Warmth.

"I like having you around," she murmurs.

"I like being around," I say, hoping she can't hear how hoarse my voice sounds.

"Did you think I was crazy when I kicked you that day?" She laughs.

"No. Just scared. Pretty badass, honestly."

"Did it trigger you, having your head get hurt and stuff?"

"Nah."

"I don't believe you," she says.

I chuckle. Then I think of something sobering.

"That night I left you—you went in, and I went home?"

Her brown gaze searches mine; it makes my chest hurt somewhere deep I can't touch.

"I let you paint it as you reading too much into things."

She nods.

I press my lips together. "I'm sorry."

"So...I wasn't?"

I squeeze her hand and try to find the words I need. "I was going out of my mind...trying to protect you."

"I know why you want to meet Papa. The two of you have a lot in common. Both very—beary?—" she gives me a silly smirk— "protective. I can see you doing your old job. Or teaching martial arts. Were you always that way?"

"How?" I frown.

"Protective."

I think about my Mom. I'm tempted to give her a generic "don't know," but I owe Gwen all the honesty that I can give her. So I confess, "Yeah."

"I want to know about the young cub Barrett." She smiles up at me, and I swear to God, her eyes seem to radiate happiness.

I laugh, because it's wonderful to see. When she keeps looking at me expectantly, I let a long breath out. Her hand squeezes mine, which makes it easier to go on. "My mom was a painter. My father is a surgeon. They had me first, and then had my brothers five years later." I shrug, as if I'm not sure what more to say—and that is true, I guess. I hate to drop the sordid story of my younger years on unassuming Gwenna.

"Were you close to your mom?" she asks carefully.

I swallow. Out of nowhere, my eyes feel kind of hot and tight. Fuck.

"You don't have to talk about it. I lost my dad last year. I don't know what it was like for you, but I know for me sometimes I don't want to talk about it, and I think I'll always have some days like that."

I look down at her tender face. All the understanding she throws my way...It makes me want to tell her.

"She got...cancer. Breast cancer." I swallow, locking my gaze on the leafy slope in front of us, focusing on the movement of my feet. "Some of the smart drugs…" I chew my lip and rub my brows, where pressure seems to be building. "They had started coming out…" I inhale, "but…" I shake my head. Gwen's arm bumps mine; the small touch spurs me onward. I look down and find her eyes are clear and understanding.

Despite the pressure behind my eyes, the tightness in my throat, I find my voice. I keep it low and steady. "I think my father thought they should have taken lymph nodes that they didn't. I don't know." I struggle to swallow as again my head pounds. My hand, around Gwen's, clenches. Hers grips mine tightly.

"She was barely healed up when they found it in her brain."

I clench my jaw and bite my cheek. Finally, I get a deep breath.

"My dad…" I stroke her fingers as I think of how to explain Robert. "So he's a surgeon, right?" I feel more than see her nod. "He fixes baby hearts," I add on, my eye still fixed on the sloping ground. I blow a breath out, wondering how much to tell her. What she even wants to know.

"I guess he was…he's kind of hard." My gaze drops to hers, and hers is steady; of course it is. Like other times, her blend of warmth and distance makes me feel more forthcoming.

"Robert had to work to get where he was. He joined the Navy to pay for school. Medical school. He told me once she almost died…my mom. When she was giving birth to me."

Gwen's hand squeezes mine. I steal another glance down at her, but her eyes are out in front of us.

"She told me one time, there…near when—" I swallow hard to get my voice clearer. "She said he was a good person…Robert. That he had trouble showing it. He always worked a lot. I don't think Kelly and Ly saw him, really. I mean—I know they didn't. Never home," I say of Robert.

I take a measured breath. My head aches to tell her—the need to recount what happened to another living person is almost physical—but the ache behind my sternum makes me cautious.

"He wasn't home…when she was sick," I rasp. "I never understood the way he worked the whole fucking time. He hired staff, home care. I didn't leave, though. He wanted me to." I shake my head, remembering how fucking stupid Robert was. Fucking asshole. I inhale. Exhale. "I used to drive her to appointments. I was only 15, but she was there, you know. She would mostly sleep and stuff, and I would get us fries with ranch from fast food places. She liked greasy fries."

Gwen's thumb rubs my hand.

"So I…I, um, missed too many days of school." I laugh, the sound harsh and dry. "I dropped out. Just for a day or two. He found me at home…Robert. I used to carve things. You know… animals. Chisel. I was carving something. A squirrel." I smile at her, even though my chest is aching. "He came in…I left." I take another shallow breath.

"Slow down." Her hand comes to my chest. Her arms wrap around me. "You're okay." It's true; she feels so warm and fucking soft against me.

"He made me leave the house…and I drove to a gun range. I had a teacher there. From school. A 'Nam vet. That's how I started," I say hoarsely. "I went there and…it was something I could do. I liked knowing I had something in my hand that could end a life." My voice goes hollow on the last word. When I get the nerve to look down at her, I'm stunned to find her eyes are pools of compassion.

"That makes sense," she says softly.

I wanted to die. I never really realized until now, but that's why I joined up, I think. Not because I was a good shot. Because I had to go somewhere, and there was nowhere else, and it made sense. "I left, like he wanted."

"Yeah?"

"I liked the risks." I chuckle dryly. I take a deep pull from my water bottle. "I'm glad I didn't carry you up here like I thought about doing."

"I wish I could carry *you*." Her hand squeezes mine as the mossy boulder comes into view.

I feel raw inside. Like someone peeled a scab off.

"So your dad wanted you to leave?" she asks, and I can hear her hesitation. She's probably nervous about keeping the conversation going, but I want to. For some reason, I need to tell her.

"I didn't do well after…Mom. All I wanted to do was watch the twins or go to the range—the gun range. Robert wanted them to have a nanny. He made me move out into my own place while I finished school."

"High school?"

I nod, looking into her wide eyes.

"I'm sorry." Her fingers stroke mine. "I just…"

"What?" The leaves crunch as we near the boulder.

"I don't think I like your dad. Making you move out…" She shakes her head. "If I ever find a time machine, I'm coming, okay?"

I smirk. "Okay." I kiss the top of her head, and we close the distance to the rock. It's dappled with sunlight, covered with a smattering of leaves. From side to side, it's about the size of a sedan, a giant, dark gray, volcanic-looking rock with greenish splotches.

"I bet you didn't go home very much on leave," she says as I climb up onto the rock and hold a hand out for her.

I shake my head. I can't quite swallow. There's this memory I have of the boys when I moved out…The way they cried. And then I never really came back…

Fuck.

Gwen sits cross-legged on the rock and pats her lap.

I frown, smiling a little in confusion even though my chest and throat feel like they're on fire.

"Lay down for a minute. I'll play with your hair."

I'm not surprised that Gwenna knows exactly what I need. I lay my head in her lap and wrap my arms around her waist.

His body feels so limp and heavy, I think he must have nodded off. I keep up the rhythm of my fingers in his hair. I have to use my fingertips to say how very sorry I am—because I don't know the right words.

Even now, so many years later, I can see the raw pain in his eyes as he talks about his mom. The way he looked eviscerated when I made my dumb comment about how I figured he must not have ever gone back home. I think back to the way he said he liked shooting a gun, because it could end a life. His mother's life? His life?

God, baby…

I drag my fingernails gently along the nape of his neck and I wonder how long it's been since he had a girlfriend. Someone to do things like this for him. I'm having a rough time leaving him to struggle on his own at night, so I just want to love on him as much as I can during the day.

I hope he is asleep and he can't feel the tension in my body. How much I want to find his dad and kick him in the balls for making younger Barrett live alone when all he wanted was to huddle with his little brothers and try to heal.

What's wrong with people? Why are they so bad? I'm so lost in my own thoughts, when Barrett's voice cuts through the quiet morning, I jump.

"Tell me about you, Piglet."

I blink down into his blue eyes, calm and solemn. I can't help smiling at what seems to be my new nickname. "The piglet and the bear. Are we Winnie the Pooh?"

He smirks. "That was a favorite."

"Was it?"

His hand strokes my side as he nods. God, he's handsome. That little smirk. Even a sad smirk…

I sift through his silky curls. "What do you want to know, Bear?"

"Everything." He smiles gently.

"There's not much to tell really. When I was little, we lived in Birmingham. In Alabama. My dad was the head of his own company—that had to do with the technology that makes cell phones work. I have a slightly older brother, Rett—Everett—who has Asperger's Syndrome. My mom had a high school friend who lived in Memphis, who also had a child with Asperger's, and she said the services in Tennessee were better, so when I was 7 and Rett was 9, we moved to Memphis. Dad just moved the company with him."

I peek down at him and find his eyes are focused on me.

"Mmm, so from day one, I really liked to sing. We would go to Nashville sometimes, like for plays and social events and things like that, and I got obsessed with country music. One of Rett's obsessions is country music trivia—he knows all the trivia," I smile, "so maybe that's why I got turned on to it. But anyway, I went through phases where I was into all the major country singers, from Reba to tween Taylor Swift.

"It wasn't a big deal or anything, though. I played on the tennis team, sang in school plays and stuff. And did Taekwondo. When I had a little extra time, I'd write songs and sing them and pretend to be famous."

That word still stings a little, not because I crave it now, but because I lost it so cruelly.

Barrett's eyes are looking up at me, urging me to go on, even though this feels like ancient history. "Mmm," he prods, his lips curving.

"Mmm, sooo. I would sing, at church and things like that. I even recorded a few of my songs, but I didn't understand how—or what, even, to do next. I tried reaching out to small record companies, but you know how that goes. Or if you don't—" I stroke his hair—"it's basically impossible. I had this idea that I could be a doctor and I'd sing on the side or something. Weddings. I don't know." I laugh at that idea now.

Barrett takes the hand stroking his hair and brings it to his mouth, brushing his lips over my palm.

"Go on, Pig."

I feign pressing my palm against his face, and Barrett nips at my pinkie.

"Anyway. I got into Duke for pre-med—" His brows arch, and I smile, just because he's so handsome, and looking at him makes me feel a little lighter. "So Duke is where I met Elvie. Elvie Wesson."

Bear nods slowly, his gorgeous face expressionless.

"He was pre-med too. We met in the registration line the very first day." I pause, remembering that moment. The way Elvie stepped behind me and wrapped his hands over my eyes, as if we knew each other. "His parents, you know, are pretty famous, so Elvie never had trouble breaking into music. I kinda put my singing stuff on hold and just did school and sports and stuff. I got discovered during a tournament. Taekwondo tournament."

"Discovered?" He smiles, but it's more sweet and sad than teasing.

"As they say." I arch my brows.

"Did you like it? Modeling?" he asks.

I bite my lip and shrug. "I was in a different place then. Honestly?" I blink down at him. "It made me feel good. Important. This is weird to say, but I was hanging out with Elvie's family a lot, and compared to them, I felt like a nobody. Almost like a groupie. So the modeling made me feel like I fit in more. And then I got the part of Jessica in *End of Day*, this indie film, and that was even better. That whole time period, when I remember it…" I shake my head. "It was like one long Christmas morning. And then I got a record deal." I can hear the wistfulness in my own words. As if he can feel the way my heart squeezes, Barrett's gentle fingers stroke my side.

"I thought I had it *all*. I mean, I kind of did. Elvie and I were serious, or I thought we were. I bought a little house. I could tell myself…you know, in retrospect, that I had always been going there. I put myself up on this stage in my head, and even before I had an album…" I swallow. "I never had an album." I laugh, and even to my own ears, it sounds a little bitter. "I was living the dream in my own mind. I'm kind of glad it was so good. Probably even better than reality would have been. So there's that."

Barrett's lips meet the inside of my wrist. He looks up at me with this wondrous expression on his face. Wondrous, yet serious. Sincere. "Have I told you I think you're fucking incredible?"

My cheeks sting. My lips curve, all on their own. "I'm not," I tell him honestly. "At all. In my position, being positive and moving forward was the only option that made sense."

I cup my hand around his face. "I think you're the same way. That's the feeling that I'm getting, anyway."

He pushes up on one elbow, resting his cheek in his palm. "What do you mean, Piglet?"

I smile at the name, then sober some and look into his eyes, so he can see the sincerity in mine. "It's just this feeling that I get from you. That you're really trying." I smile down at him. "That, and one of my gardenia trees is shedding petals that end up in your pockets when I do laundry."

He cuts his eyes away from mine and makes a funny kind of embarrassed duck face, which I have to struggle not to laugh at.

His eyes boomerang to mine. He's smirking, but it really looks more like he's struggling not to laugh. "You found those, huh? I need to get my own tree."

"Just to pull its petals off?" I ruffle his hair.

"You make it sound bad." He gives me a mock sad look.

"Mine can spare some petals. Only for you."

He chuckles, looking a little embarrassed. "I've been…smelling them."

"Exposure therapy."

"Something like that."

"And? How's it going?"

"It's working, I think."

I beam. "That makes me really happy. Don't be doing it for me, though. I can give those plants away."

"Nah."

"Have you ever thought of talking to someone? Like a PTSD type person? Tell me if you feel like I'm being pushy. Because I don't want to be. I'm not."

He takes a long breath and blows it out. "Those people help?"

"I think so. You're doing amazing on your own," I add. "Unless there's something I'm missing, you're not doing half the things a lot of other people do in your position."

"Like what?" he asks, looking skeptical.

"Drinking. Drugs." I shrug. I don't want to sound like some kind of lame after school special, but it's true: it is impressive that he's held himself together so well.

I watch Barrett's face, but there is nothing to be found on it. Maybe a vague haunted expression, which I could easily be imagining.

"No," he finally says.

A grave look passes over his face: there and quickly gone.

He takes my right hand in his and turns it over, and I see his eyes fix on a scar that runs from the middle of my forearm up to my elbow. It's more white than pink now, not easy to see.

"The accident?" he murmurs, looking into my eyes.

I nod. "They thought maybe it was from…the windshield."

His jaw tightens. "You remember anything?"

I shake my head. He lowers our hands, his fingers stroking mine. I shut my eyes for half a second, just to focus on that feeling—and not getting anxious. This is not something I usually talk about except with Helga. "Nothing from the night at all," I confess.

He swallows, eyes fixed on me. I can feel his words—unsaid. So long unsaid, I have to ask: "What are you thinking?"

He swallows again, and shakes his head.

"You were alone," he says in a soft monotone. His eyes are on the rock below us.

"How'd you know about it?"

"Internet." His eyes on mine are hard. They soften—almost sad—as I touch his shoulder.

"I could barely stand it," he says thickly.

"That's…" I shake my head. It makes my throat tighten and my eyes sting, just seeing the look on his face.

He sits up and covers my knees with his big hands, stroking softly as he speaks. "You'll never be alone like that again. I swear." He looks emphatic—almost angry.

Barrett wraps his arms around me, pulling me onto his lap and hugging me so tightly I nearly can't breathe.

"How long were you out there?" he asks hoarsely.

It takes me a minute to put together what he's asking. *How long was I on the ground...*

"Around three hours." His grip on me loosens, so I'm able to pull back a little and look up into his eyes. "I was kind of...like, my head was kind of down...A little off the road and on the shoulder. I was so cold," I say, hoarse despite trying to sound impassive. "That's part of why they were able to save me."

He rubs my back briskly, as if he's trying to warm me. His lips meet my forehead and my cheeks.

I grin. "You're sweet."

"I would do anything to keep you safe."

"And warm." I nuzzle his chest. "Sometimes I have nightmares about being cold."

"I'll keep you warm, Pig."

"You want to keep me warm on the way to the enclosure?"

"Sure." He pets my hair and gently sets me down. Then he hops down off the rock and turns his back toward me. "Get on."

I giggle.

I wrap my legs around his waist, my arms around his shoulders. "I won't hurt you?"

"Are you serious?"

I giggle. "No?" I hold onto him, and he wraps an arm behind himself, holding me against him as he picks his way down the hill.

chapter four

Gwenna

For dinner, we hit up Lola Lombardi's, a family-owned Italian place with a gorgeous, blue-tiled wishing well, ivy crawling up the tall brick walls, and an extensive wine menu.

We park a block or so away in downtown Gatlinburg, and Barrett buys me a rose from a street vendor as we walk toward our destination. We end up each holding part of the rose's stem, holding hands with the rose between us, which makes me giggle.

The place isn't too crowded, so we get a giant corner booth—too wide, Barrett claims, for us to sit across from each other, so he slides in beside me. He tells me it's been years since he had Italian food, which launches us into a conversation about all the countries he's visited. I brace myself at first, but he enjoys regaling me with stories.

The more we talk, the more we drink, until Barrett kisses my neck and, as he does, he grabs our bottle and moves it across the table.

I shove his chest. "You thief."

"Non più per te, donna."

I poke my lip out. "Why'd you take the wine?"

His lips brush the bridge of my nose, trailing up my forehead, and his hand smooths over the hair at the back of my head.

"Why do you think, Piglet?"

"Because you're a mean ole Bear?"

He shakes his head, smiling sweetly. He takes my hand and brings it up to his head, to the spot where—

"Ohhh. The TBIs. Righhhht."

He chuckles.

"Did you ever have a seizure?" I ask, wrapping an arm around him.

"Two. One before surgery, one right after."

I lean against his shoulder. We lace our hands together.

I look at his face, trying to determine if he'll mind questions.

He smirks. "Thinking?"

"Yessss."

Our waiter brings a basket of ciabatta and lights the little candle on our table, and when he goes, Barrett looks down at me. "And?"

"And what?" I bring a piece of bread up to my mouth.

"What were you thinking?"

"Oh, just if you had to take anti-seizure medicine, what your recovery was like, that kind of thing."

"Did you have any seizures?" he asks, poker-faced.

"Some. Right after. I was in a coma for a few weeks, so it was after that."

His face pales.

I look down at the table. "Sorry. This is kind of weird date talk."

"Not weird." His arm comes around me, folding me to his chest. His scruff brushes my hair. "I'm sorry if I made you feel that way."

I steal a wary glance at him. "You just looked…"

"I know." His voice is rough.

I feel him take a deep breath, his chest pressing against me. His eyes are everywhere but on my face, and then they come back to mine, and they're so intense it startles me.

"I have to know—" His voice roughens on the *have to*— "But…" His mouth flattens. He shakes his head.

It upsets him. Heat sweeps through me as I realize that's what this is. It bothers him, hearing about the accident.

I wrap my arms around him, and that's the way our waiter finds us when he returns for our food order. He gives us a funny little wink, and Bear and I place our orders.

When he leaves, Barrett takes a long swig of his water and turns to me. "In the Unit," he says slowly, "there are short gunners and long gunners. The short gunners, some people call them assaulters…they burst into places, clear buildings. Do hand to hand. They're on the ground. Task-oriented. And the long gunners, the snipers, cover them. We're watchers. But nineteen times out of twenty, you know the person that you're covering." He shuts his eyes for a small moment. When they open, they glow in the candlelight like gemstones. "You asked earlier…I am protective."

I hug him tight and wrap my legs around his underneath the table. "Barrett Drake…" His neck and chest flex slightly under my tight grasp. I grip him more tightly, brushing tickling kisses along his collar bone.

The little groan that rasps from his throat gets into my own chest, spreading through me in a lazy tendril that seems to center in between my legs. I feel Barrett shift his hips, and slide my hand down his flat abs until I feel his hardness.

"Gwen." It's practically a sigh.

"So hot." I rub him.

"Stop." The word is hung between a moan and chuckle. "Damn, Piglet. I'm gonna need another pair of pants."

I giggle evilly. It's a good thing that our food comes moments later. We chat as we eat, the conversation never dipping as deep as it did a little earlier. We're almost finished eating and have just realized we're both NFL fans when my phone rings.

"Oops, forgot to cut it off." I fish it out of my purse. "Jamie. Hey, I bet she wants to—"

Talk to him. But Barrett's standing. "Bathroom," he mouths with his signature small, dimpled smile. It's such a peaceful smile. A happy smile. *Mine.*

The word streaks through my brain as I answer Jamie, so it's forgotten as she asks to Facetime Bear and me, and I give her a rain check from us.

"He's kind of the quiet type, remember?"

"So? I'm your bestie. Tell homeboy to pony up."

I laugh. We're off the phone by the time Barrett comes back. As we wait for the check, he and I debate whether this should be Peyton Manning's last season, and before I realize what's the what, our waiter comes, and Barrett sends him off with his card.

I catch his hand in mine. "You don't need to do that."

He brings my hand up to his mouth, kissing my knuckles. "It makes me happy to take care of you."

We leave the restaurant holding hands, me with the rose in my free hand. We pass a Native American craft store as we head toward my car.

"Do you mind if we go in?" he asks.

"Let's do it." I have a thing for pottery and handmade jewelry, not surprising when I think about the kinds of crafts that adorned my childhood home.

"I've got a Native friend. Native American. He used to have a dream catcher, when we'd be at different outposts."

"You want one? That's a nice idea."

"His broke. He mentioned it a while back, so..." He shrugs.

ELLA JAMES

My God, this man is sweet. And gorgeous. I admire him in the soft, purpleish light emanating from a stone-looking lamp just inside the shop. I'm checking out Bear's amazing bicep when something behind him catches my eye. Is that—Oh, yes! That's a dude mood ring.

I keep myself from glancing over at it while we pick out a beautiful dream catcher for Bear's friend, and then one for my room. As we move toward the register, I grab his hand and point toward the door we came through. There's a soda machine across the courtyard.

"Could I convince you to grab me a drink?" I ask him, pointing. "Just something carbonated, while I pay for this? My stomach kind of hurts."

His thick brows draw together. "Of course." He brushes a kiss over my hair and looks around the shop, taking in the short, gray-haired woman behind the counter before he walks back outside. Swaggers, really. Lord, that ass.

I jump slightly as someone moves behind me, turning on my heel to see a tallish, red-haired guy standing in the doorway punched into the pottery wall. Judging by the landscape behind his wide shoulders, I guess it's an adjoining door that leads into a moccasin store. His eye catches mine for half a second before he turns and walks slowly back into moccasin land. I figure he must work there.

With a quick glance out the window, I race to the ring display, grabbing one I pray is his size and paying for it and the two dream catchers before he comes through the door. We leave a few minutes later, clasping hands while Barrett carries the bag with the dream catchers and I harbor his ring in my pocket.

"So, Dove," I say as we stroll along the sidewalk. "That's his real name?"

He gives me a strange look. "Seth. Dove is his tribal name, I guess you'd call it."

"That's cool. Is he nice?"

"He is." Bear's hand catches mine, his gaze warm on my gaze as our fingers intertwine. "Lives out in bumfuck nowhere with his wife, a writer."

"Ah, so, married. He's retired like you?"

Bear nods. I sense a story there, and also catch a vibe that makes me feel as if he doesn't want to tell it.

When I see, between two sandwich shops, a little white fence with a sign bearing an image of a stream, I stop in my tracks. "Ohhh, we can go down right here and see one of the streams. Want to?"

Gatlinburg's downtown is striped with tiny streams that rush between motels and behind strip malls. You can hear the water rushing over rocks from where we stand on the street.

"Sure." We pause and as we turn toward the gate, he rubs his cheek against my head again. He pulls away and smiles down at me, his eyes squinting sweetly. "You're pretty," he says in a low voice.

I've got my hair in a long side pony tail, and I have to say, I feel pretty.

I stroke his chest through his shirt, smiling up at him. "So're you, mister."

We make our way down a narrow set of stairs to a little stream that rushes between two balcony-dotted motels. As we veer off the little walkway and onto some boulders near the stream's edge, I trip and shout, "Bear!"

He catches me around my waist, and when I latch onto his arms, I see he's smiling.

"What?" I tease.

He shakes his head. His lips curl.

I arch my eyebrows.

"I like it when you call me Bear."

"My favorite Bear."

He puts an arm behind my back to keep me steady on the rocks and kisses me, cupping my jaw as his tongue strokes mine. I cling to his shoulders, and I want more.

"Take me home…"

The second we're out of my car in the garage, I go for his pants. I have aspirations to make it into the laundry room, where the floor is softer, but we wind up on our hands and knees on the cold cement.

Barrett pulls my shoes and pants off, taking his time pulling my panties down before he runs a finger down my asscheek, parts my pussy lips, and fucks me hard and fast from behind. I love every dirty second of it.

It's not until I lift myself up off the floor and notice all the leaves around me that I realize: we're right by the gardenias. I turn to Barrett with wide eyes.

He winks and shifts back on his heels, giving me a gorgeous view of what's rocking between his legs before he tugs his boxer-briefs and pants back up.

I hurry to dress myself as he watches with a small, smug smile that's somehow also sweet and indulging.

When I've got my clothes on, he takes my hand, brushing his lips over my knuckles as I work the key into the laundry room door.

"You want a bath?" he murmurs in the dim light of the kitchen.

"How'd you know?"

I'm still hot and bothered from what just transpired, so just the graze of his big body against mine as we move through the den makes me feel sparkly and warm.

He runs the water really hot the way I like it, then motions me in. I settle in the back so I can wrap myself around him and try not to gawk as he folds his breathtaking body into the small space in front of me. He looks so ridiculous, though, and I can't help laughing. Barrett chuckles too, a rich, warm sound I love more every time I hear it.

I rub my damp hand over his shoulder tats, looking more closely at a small pile of spent bullets on his right shoulder blade. Out of one of the shells, a flower sprouts; it's a gardenia. My fingers are wandering down his spine, over a few long coordinates etched vertically between his shoulder blades, when he leans back against me.

"You're heavy," I whisper into his curls.

He starts to sit up, but I grab his shoulders. "I like it."

"I don't want to hurt you," he says, but he lets me press him back against me. It's strangely pleasant to be under him like this. Makes me feel protected.

I drape my arm along his collarbone. "I know you don't."

I want to see his snowflake tat again, but with him leaning back, I can't, so I decide to kiss it. I drag my lips along his hairline at the nape of his neck, sucking lightly, nibbling. With him lying on top of me, I feel every quiver of his muscles; I can hear and feel him let his breath out. I suck on him, and he moans, wrapping his right hand around my slightly raised knee.

When I reach the spot where I think his tattoo is, I bite. He chuckles as he arches his back. "Piglet…"

His voice cracks, and my body throbs.

"Mmmmm?"

I feel his left arm move and…God, he's got his fist around his dick.

I kiss down his nape and nibble on the upper ridge of his shoulder. The muscle there is thick, and he tastes salty. I suck his skin into my mouth and find his nipple with my fingers.

I'm rewarded with a moan. "You better quit that, Piggy." His voice is a delicious rasp I feel between my own legs.

"Or what, Bear?" I breathe my words against his skin.

He whirls around so fast I have no chance of escaping his snare. With his arms around my shoulders and his mouth on mine, he rasps, "Or I'll huff...and I'll puff...and I'll blow your house down."

I laugh into his blue eyes, and Barrett gives a wolfish grin.

I'm the one who blows him, as it were. Before I finish, he lifts me up onto the tub's side, spreads my legs, and huffs and puffs until my hands are running through his hair and my legs are locked around his shoulders.

"You think that's all?" I rasp, lowering my feet back into the warm water.

He gives me a handsome, almost shy smile, and shakes his head.

"Lay down."

He does, and I ride him.

We come clutching each other and as Barrett sits up with me still on his lap, I'm struggling to keep my eyes open.

He nuzzles my cheek with his scratchy one.

"C'mon," he murmurs, and grabs a towel from beside the tub, scooping me up in his arms before he gets out of the tub, wrapping me up first and balancing me against his wide chest as he tucks a towel around his waist. With a small half-smile— the shy, sweet one that seems to wreck my heart a little more each time I see it—he takes me to my bed and we lie down together.

I push my fingers through his wet hair and Barrett, curled around me, kisses my forehead. He's rubbing my shoulder with his warm palm when I feel his body twitch. For once, he's out before

I am. I pull him closer to me, joyous at the miracle of our two bodies folded so sweetly together.

When, after a little while, my heart's still soaring too high to sink into sleep, I gently disentangle from him and slip off the bed.

chapter five

Barrett

I'm going for my toothbrush when I see—
Is that a ring?

I lift it off the toothbrush handle, set it in my palm, and hold it up near my face. My eyes are still blurry, but it looks like...I chuckle, despite my raw throat. That's a fucking mood ring: just like hers, but a thick band.

I grin down at it. All the tightness in my chest: the cold, tight, empty feeling—That shit dissolves as I look at the ring in my palm. I set it down and wash my hands and try it on before I brush my teeth.

It's too tight on my middle finger, but it fits the one beside my pinky, on my right hand. I watch amused as it turns from brownish green, before I brush my teeth, to sea green when I'm finished. I take it off so I can clean the sink up, put away the cloth I stuffed into my mouth, and use a spare hand towel to soap off my neck and chest. I don't think they're really dirty, but I want to be sure before I get back into bed with her.

I put the ring back on and smirk at myself in the mirror. *Pretty princess.* Breck used to call me that when I called him our special snowflake. Breck would like her, I think, as I run a hand back through my hair. He was so outgoing. He always liked the quiet, sweet ones. Gwen's not quiet—she's more talkative, which is a good foil to me—but she's sweet as hell.

I give the ring one more glance—dark blue now—before I turn out the bathroom light and step quietly into her room. It smells so fucking good in here. Like fruit and sex and…vanilla. I look up at the ceiling, at the twinkle lights, then I let my gaze find Gwen. Her narrow shoulders, her small body curled into a little "c." She isn't skinny, but compared to me, she's tiny. So small and soft—and warm.

I climb into bed. She's facing me, so I position myself around her, arranging things so her pretty face is tucked against my throat. I wrap an arm around her back and bring my knees up below hers. It takes all my self control to resist kissing her, but based on her breathing, I don't think she seems soundly asleep, and I don't want to wake her up.

It feels so good to be here with her, but I don't want her knowing how fucked up my head is. It would be best if she could think it's better when I'm near her. One, because it really is. But also because I don't want to be trouble to her. She said she could tell me what to do for the nightmares, but that's not what I want. She doesn't deserve to have to deal with that. It's mine. *I* deserve it.

I inhale right by her hair, trying to find a label for the sweet, unique scent.

I wonder how I'll ever be away from her again.

Maybe I really don't have to be. Now that I know her and care for her, I feel more sure than ever that I can keep my secret. I can take it to my grave.

I'm so damn glad I didn't tell Kellan or Cleo. No one knows but Dove and Blue. I can handle Dove and Blue.

I shut my eyes and with her silky hair against my face, I think about my mom. I have the weirdest, hot feeling right under my throat. My chest feels like it loosens up, so I can breathe. I take a deep, slow breath, and it feels good.

Gwen's lips tickle my throat.

"Hey…" Her voice is raspy.

I kiss her temple. "Thank you," I whisper.

"You like it?" She smiles sleepily.

"Blue—for happy." I kiss her nose. "Yes. I like it."

I end up inside her, breathing hard in time with her soft breaths…Groaning as my pleasure takes me over. We fall asleep entangled in each other.

Knocking wakes us.

Gwenna

The mattress bounces as Barrett gets down off the bed. I hear the swish of fabric over flesh as he pulls pants on.

"Stay there."

Before I can clear the sleep from my eyes, he's disappeared. A minute later, I hear the echo of his laughter.

"What the fuck?" He sounds happy as he chuckles; very male, as if he's greeting a guy friend. At my house?

"Come on in—well, wait a second. Gwen's—How are you here?"

I can't hear the answer, but my stomach does a slow flip. Does he have Delta Force friends? My pulse pounds in my head as I hop out of bed and race into my closet, throwing on the first things I touch: Lularoe leggings in magenta and black, and an oversized heather gray sweatshirt with a hood and a big hand pocket on the front. Thank Jesus for the tiny mirror on the back of my closet door. Looking into it, I smooth my hair and do the universe's quickest braid, then bind the end with a small rubber band I find around the door knob.

"Piglet?"

I suck in a deep breath and poke my head out of the closet. "Yeah?"

Barrett's face is radiant: his eyes alive, his smile bright. He's shirtless, too. He steps into my closet and throws a big, bare arm around my shoulders. "Kellan's here. And Cleo."

"What?"

He gives a low laugh. "My brother and his fiancé." He rocks back on his heels a little, soft affection shining in his eyes. "I want them to meet you. They're only passing through—Not really," he corrects himself. "They were down in Georgia seeing Cleo's family and the bank called. House is closing. I put Kelly as a reference. They didn't know I was even here, so they're surprised."

"So they just…drove up here?"

"He said they called last night."

I blink a few times.

Barrett laughs and cups my chin. "C'mon, Piglet…You look pretty. Come meet them. Cleo wants to see the bears."

I groan. "So one of those."

"One of what?" He swats my ass, shooing me out into my room.

"People either think the bears are fun, or they think bears eat people all the time."

"So…one of the ones who thinks they're fun." He arches his brows and makes a faux *for-shame* face, then gives me a warm, teasing smile. "You don't think bears are fun?" He puts a hand to his chest.

"I think bears are really fun." I twine my arms around his neck. "I just…need a shower." I press my cheek against his chest and try to calm my racing heart. "How'd they find out you were here at my place anyway," I ask, peering up at him.

"I sent K. a picture of my bike a few weeks back. They tried the doorbell at my place. When I didn't answer, they walked around the property to check it out and saw my bike beside your porch."

"Why *is* it there?" Last time he returned home on the bike, he parked in the grass to the right of my porch, near the edge of the enclosure fence rather than in the driveway.

"Long story," he says, arching his brows.

I give him a skeptical look.

He leans down to kiss my lips. "Mine," he murmurs.

I can't help it. He's so freaking sweet and handsome. I lace my fingers through his curls and sigh, then groan and nip at his chin. "Okay. I guess…"

He grins.

"But only because you do bad things to me."

That makes him throw his head back and chuckle. "Gwen…"

He takes my hand and kisses it, then lets it go and turns a circle, eyes scanning the floor.

"Footboard." I nod at a shirt of his that's draped there.

"Ah. Thank you." His voice is soft and kind of polite. I smile, thinking how adorable he is. He grabs the hunter green shirt and pulls it over his head, and I drink in his glorious body.

I guess he can tell I was lusting after him after he surfaces, because he grins. "You're a dirty little Piglet."

"Told you I needed a shower," I shrug.

He laughs. "You're not nervous…?"

"Yes! Of course I am, you goose."

"Don't be nervous. They'll love you." His voice is soft and low as he grabs my hand. "You want to grab breakfast somewhere? I know you didn't expect anyone."

"Yeah, sure." I smile for him, for once. "And mi casa, su casa. Is that right?"

"Su casa es mi casa, sus osos son mis osos. Soy tu oso. Que me ama, te amare."

"Was that for real?" I gape.

He laughs again, a soft punch of sound.

"I don't know much Spanish. I took French in school."

He kisses my head. "Piglet." His hand comes to my shoulder. "Let's go."

I grab some boots and socks, and also my phone. Barrett squeezes my hand as we walk through the living room.

"Don't worry," he says gently.

He wraps an arm around my shoulders, making me feel safe and sheltered. Then he pulls the door open and I behold our guests.

I'm not sure which face is more surprising to behold. My eyes go from the blond, tanned version of Barrett to the stunning brunette and back to the guy as everyone smiles, talks, and grabs for each other all at once.

The girl reaches for Barrett, leaving me face-to-face with his brother. Ever awkward, I murmur, "You look like Barrett. Sort of."

The guy smiles, and I feel slightly warm. Magnetic: that's the way his face is. His smile is beautiful, like Barrett's, and his face, like Bear's, is chiseled, classically handsome. He's got Barrett's gorgeous man lips and, like Barrett, sports something between stubble and a light beard. Which only enhances his great looks.

But where Barrett's skin is creamy, Kellan's is tan. Where Bear's hair is curly and dark, Kellan's is slightly wavy, golden blond. This guy's eyes are blue like Bear's, but they're more ocean blue than gray-sky blue. His eyes are kind, his smile is white. His eyes are brighter, I think, as he reaches for my hand. He looks more peaceful than Barrett.

I feel a streak of hurt at that thought, and shift my gaze down to our clasped hands. After just another millisecond of me taking in brother's wide shoulders and tall, slim build, I turn my gaze to his girl—Cleo.

And two things happen really fast. The first: my heart squeezes in an aching, awful way—because she's seriously breathtaking: wavy, shoulder-length dark hair and wide, green eyes. Her brows are flawless; her cheekbones are high and delicate; her lips, less full than mine but perfectly shaped, now pulled into a pretty smile.

For half a second, I'm swamped by raw inadequacy. Then she lunges for me, pulling me into a hug—or trying to. Barrett's arm is still around me, though, so when she pulls me toward her, I don't move. Cleo stumbles forward, and seconds later, we're all laughing.

Her laughter is ridiculous: almost a howl.

I grab Cleo by the shoulders just as Barrett's heavy arm releases me, so she and I end up wobbling comically into each other.

Her face is right in mine; her light, fragrant perfume fills my nose as my stomach rolls. *My face is right by hers.* A kind of shame-based terror fills me, chilling me down to my toes. But Cleo's eyes are bright and kind. She clings to me as if we're friends.

Still laughing, she says, "I'm Cleo."

"I'm Gwen. Nice to meet you." I don't notice until I pull away from her and shift my eyes back to Kellan that I gave the shorter, more familiar version of my name. I hesitate only a breath before I smile at him again.

"Hey." I hold my hand out, forgetting we already shook. Kellan takes it anyway, squeezing slightly; smiling. Where Barrett looks like a gorgeous warrior, his brother, in his pale blue button-up, dark jeans, and Ray Bans, looks like a movie star.

"I'm Kellan, or as Barrett likes to say, Kelly." He shoots Bear a sulky look that barely masks a smile, and then he reaches out to slap Barrett's arm.

"How are ya, man?"

Barrett smiles; *oh God, those dimples.* "I'm good, K." His gaze shifts to Cleo, his eyebrows arching. "Does that work for him," he asks Cleo. "K.?"

She grins, with a glint in her eye. "I think you should stick with Kelly."

"Only if we call you Fi," Kellan says to Cleo. He waggles his eyebrows.

Barrett frowns, and Cleo puts a hand to her forehead. "Y'all's dad heard Kellan call me Cle."

"He called her Fi, and then Fiona." Kellan shakes his head. "Dad says to have you call him, *Bear.*"

"You talking to that jackass?"

Kellan quirks an eyebrow. "He's talking to me."

Kellan sticks his hands into his pockets, looking cold—or awkward. Cleo gives me a *'hi, other outsider'* kind of look, then looks at her boots and mumbles, "He is a jackass, though."

I nod, my eyebrows arched in what I hope is neutral-curious fashion. Until I notice her brown boots. Then my mouth falls open just a little. "Nice boots. I like the little fringey things."

"Marc Fisher."

"Oh yeah, right."

"Yours are awesome, too," she says. "Kors?"

"Yep."

She smiles brightly. "I like you. I think we could do some damage in a shoe shop."

Kellan puts an arm around Cleo's shoulders, fixing Barrett with an exaggerated, brain numb kind of look, which is actually hilarious. I giggle, and Kellan raises a brow. Damn, he's charming. He's got this sort of…rakish vibe about him. Where Barrett is so quiet and mysterious, Kellan has this swagger…

"So," he blinks at Bear. "You guys want to go get breakfast?"

"Sure." Barrett looks at me, and I nod. He steps out of the doorway and I move past him to lock the door.

"Cleo wants a breakfast burrito," I hear Kellan say from behind me. Barrett's hand strokes up my neck, sifting in my hair and making me shiver. The touch is brief and soft, a kind of touching base, I think.

I turn around, door locked behind me, and he folds his big hand around mine.

"I said I'd do waffles, too. Like Waffle House," Cleo is saying. "Mmm, I've been missing me some Waffle House."

And this is how it happens that, two hours later, the four of us are talking over napkin-covered plates and half-drained sodas at the nearest grease palace. Cleo and I are seated across from one another by the window, talking about Lularoe leggings and being from the South, and whispering about her and Kellan's covert business—which is insane. And incredible.

"So you're like the king and queen of...?" I mouth the "M" and "J" silently because I'm too nervous to say it aloud in public even though Cleo just told me the story herself in murmurs.

Long story short: the two of them get medical marijuana to cancer patients in states where it isn't legal yet. At one point, they financed the venture by dealing to college students, but now, since Kellan got his bone marrow transplant, some of their friends are overseeing that part of their operation, while Kelly and Cleo live in California, by the ocean.

Cleo smiles at my question. "Maybe more like Robin Hood and Little John."

I laugh, and Barrett's arm settles around my shoulders.

"So wait up...how'd you guys meet?" Kellan cuts in, looking from Bear to me. I see his eyebrows quirk as his gaze settles on his brother.

Barrett squeezes my shoulder and smirks down at me. "Gwenna laid me out."

Kellan and Cleo look from him to me, smiling expectantly. When Barrett doesn't supply deets, Kellan lays his big palm on the table, leaning forward.

"All right Bear, what did you do?" At the same time Cleo tells me, "I'm impressed." She shoots me a look of wonder. "Barrett is a badass."

"It wasn't my fault." I give Bear a guilting look, earning a smirk. "I was working out in the woods early one morning and he scared me. I attacked."

Barrett shakes his head, mock shaming. "Split my scar open." He taps his head.

"His head is so hard, I bet she hardly even dented it." Kellan grins at Barrett, who commandeers Kelly's coffee cup and gives Kellan a funny, mock-threat look as he steals a long swallow.

"Ah, shit," Barrett says as soon as he lowers the cup.

I frown, confused, as Kellan holds his palm out. "I was finished." He smiles, and his eyes glide to me. He smiles at me, but it looks…strange. Not self-conscious? He seems too confident for that, but…

Cleo leans her head against his shoulder and changes the subject. "We went to the beach. I wish you guys had come, too. It was so amazing."

Kellan kisses her temple. It reminds me so much of something Barrett would do, my stomach flips a little. "Not like we live on a beach or anything," he teases.

"The Gulf is different," Cleo argues. "White sand versus cliffs; hot, hot, gloriously hot sun versus the breeze. They're all good, but man…"

"I get it," I nod. "If you're from the South, the Gulf is everything."

"We live overlooking the beach," Cleo tells me. "And it's amazing. So beautiful and breezy. But we don't get out that much.

I'm finishing my degree online—" she jerks her thumb toward Kellan—"and he's working on his MBA online, too. We are not about the party these days."

Minutes glide past like an easy breeze. By the time we get up, almost an hour later, I feel like I've known Cleo for years. Kellan, too. He's not quite as open as Cleo, but he's really nice. Charming, too. I can see why Cleo likes him so much.

I ponder the difference in their backgrounds, even their childhoods, I'm sure, as we wait for the check. Kellan's so much easier to read than Barrett. His manner with Cleo is more relaxed than Barrett's is with me. More natural, or maybe just easier.

Of course, all that is changing...

The whole time we were eating, Barrett kept his left hand on my leg underneath the table, or his arm around me. As we walk back out to Kellan's ride, a sleek, charcoal Porsche Cayenne Hybrid Kellan claims Cleo made him get—something about *The Lorax*—Barrett wraps his arm around my waist and pulls me up against him, so close we almost can't walk without tripping. When I stop to laugh and look up at him, his lips feather over my cheek.

I hear laughing and turn to find Cleo and Kellan smirking at us as Kelly heads around to her side of the car, to get her door, I guess.

Barrett gets my door—he's been schooled by Cleo; this is what a Southern girl expects, she told him—and he and I sit holding hands, my right leg and his left one intertwined, as we ride back toward home.

"So how'd you end up buying a house here, B.?" Kellan asks. "That seems random as hell."

chapter six

Gwenna

I look at Barrett. I can't remember what he told me about this, or if I even asked.

He shrugs. "Knew an Operator friend from here. Said it was a good place. Noticed that it didn't have a mixed martial arts place."

Cleo turns around in her seat, looking excited. "So are you going to open one?"

Barrett lifts a shoulder. "Thought I'd look at space."

"That's awesome, man." In the rear view mirror, Kellan's eyes look warm and caring.

Barrett's fingers squeeze mine slightly as he gives his brother a small smile. I'm starting to learn his smiles, and this one is the sad one. Or maybe I should think of it as the forced one. Like, he's trying to be nice, lighthearted, but he feels unsure or unhappy, so it looks a little strained.

I squeeze his hand back, wondering what's up with that.

"He taught me some new moves," I tell Cleo and Kelly. "That's kind of how we got to know each other."

Barrett's brows arch, and he smirks, his handsome face showing his dimples.

"It's true." I look from Kellan's blue eyes, in the rear-view, to Cleo's green ones; she's mostly turned around in the passenger's seat. "The kick was a bad first impression," I say, smiling at Barrett. "I'll admit that. But afterwards, I helped him clean his head up and I got a crush on him. Which of course, he didn't know about." I grin at him. My cheeks are so hot they almost hurt, but Barrett's grin is real now, so it's worth it. "He offered to show me some hand to hand moves since I have a weak ankle and am limited with kicks, and I told him if he did, I'd bake him cakes."

"Gwenna has an advanced black belt in Taekwondo." Barrett's eyes slide from Cleo to me. His smile is soft and indulgent, and also proud.

"I love it." Cleo nods, turning a little more in her seat. "So you guys could run the martial arts place together. Not that anyone is marrying you two off or anything…Pinning you together indefinitely, because you are *such* a cute couple. Definitely not me."

"Never." Kellan smiles at Cleo, and they latch hands.

"She is." He winks into the rear view mirror.

"You should be glad my sense of romanticism is strong," she teases.

"Oh, I am. I really am." I can hear a cord of sincerity in his low voice, and I wonder what it means. Then I remember his history, and I realize it's probably that. I don't think I got quite the whole story at breakfast, but I gathered the two of them met through Kellan's marijuana business, and he was admitted to the hospital for a long time with a relapse when he and Cleo hadn't know each other very long.

"Ah, shit." Barrett tilts his head back, gritting his teeth. He lets my hand go, heaves a breath out, and fishes into his pocket. "I had a meeting with Mallorie, to see a place. Right now. Damn," he murmurs as he texts.

"She's so nice." I bump his arm lightly. "Don't worry."

Sure enough, Mallorie Pryce tells him he can see the space later today, or any day.

"Just a minute, Mallorie." He covers the mouthpiece and looks to me. "One thirty?"

"Sure."

"We should go too," I hear Cleo telling Kellan as Barrett gets off the phone with the realtor.

Kellan laughs. "Maybe—if Barrett wants us to. Whatcha say, B.?"

Barrett leans back against the seat and finds my hand again with his. "You guys want to stay around that long?"

"Are you trying to get rid of us?" Kellan smiles at his brother in the rearview mirror, and I can feel a warmth between the two of them.

"No way." Barrett surprises me, loosening his grip on my hand so he can lean up and ruffle Kellan's blond hair. He drapes his arm loosely around Kellan's neck and says, "I missed my little bro."

Kellan's hand closes around Barrett's thick forearm. I can't see Barrett's face, but I can see Kellan's. For just a second, I can see the relaxation in his features: a kind of peacefulness. It's one of the most beautiful things I've ever witnessed.

A millisecond later, Barrett's back beside me, smiling like he, too, feels good. It's no wonder, if you think about it. He probably felt like all the guys he served with were his brothers, and it seems he lost the closest one. So he needs Kellan. Having lost his twin, I'm going to guess that Kellan needs Bear, too.

With that in mind, the next few hours spent with Kellan and Cleo—touring Barrett's house; going into the enclosure, where I sneak Cleo over to see Brooksie, curled up in a hollow tree; then drinking wine on Barrett's back porch while Kellan and Barrett shoot a bow—feel blissfully satisfying.

It's been ages since I hung out in a group like this, and maybe even longer since I spent a long day with a non-Jamie friend with whom I felt as comfortable as I do around Cleo.

By the time we load back up into Kellan's ride to see the studio space, Kellan and Barrett are chumming it up like the bros they (literally) are, and Cleo and I are giggling about things that possibly aren't even funny unless you've got a midday wine buzz.

As it turns out, the studio space is almost perfect: 1,600 square feet of former yoga center space along **a main thoroughfare**, priced under market because the owner's husband has some rare disease they need to move to Germany to treat.

I catch myself watching Kellan's face as Mallorie explains how the only real treatment the guy can get is experimental, and not legal in America. I swear, I think he loses a little color in his cheeks. When, as we move down the little hall between two rooms, Cleo catches Kellan's hand and squeezes, I feel almost sure that I was right.

He probably has PTSD from having cancer. Damn, that sucks. As we walk back toward the front door, Barrett warms an arm around me. He strokes my arm and gives me a quizzical look.

I smile. "I love this place," I murmur.

His brows arch, and he nods. The walls already have mirrors and the floors are covered with those foamy mats whose vinyl scent takes me back to the Taekwondo studio where Rett and I learned. They only major thing we—Barrett, really—might want to do is busting out two walls to make the two rooms in the front of the space into one giant room.

Barrett drives us home: to his home, and as Kellan opens the front passenger side Bear leans into the back seat where Cleo and I are sitting. "Be right back," he tells me quietly. "Just going to let them in."

The three of them go up the stairs, and I wait, feeling slightly awkward and admiring Kellan's car, which smells phenomenally new car-ish.

Cleo and Kellan disappear through Barrett's front door, and I watch Barrett descend the stairs. I can see him smiling toward me even though I know he can't see me through the windows' heavy tinting. Still, I smile back.

I'm still smiling when he opens my door. "Over the river and through the woods?" he asks, nodding back toward my house. He gives me a little smile that makes a flock of birds swoop through my stomach.

"Sure." We fall into step beside each other, weaving between pines and through the crackling leaves. "So are they leaving?"

"I invited them for dinner. At my house if that's better."

I shove him. "Psshh. My house. You and me, Bear. We'll make something good for them. Are they just taking some alone time at the moment?"

He nods. "Kelly's tired."

"So what's it like with him? Is he like…done with everything or…?"

"He takes some maintenance medicines, I think. Most of it for his heart."

"His heart?"

Barrett holds a branch back for me, nodding.

"He has some damage from the chemo."

"Really? He seems…so healthy." I shake my head and laugh unhappily. "That's a stupid thing to say, I guess."

"No." His hand brushes my lower back as the wind blows a strand of hair into my face. "He's doing pretty well. And his heart is healing up, they think."

"Still." I exhale slowly. "That's just…I hate that."

"Because *you* have a soft heart."

"INFJ Advocate here," I say, in an exaggerated, Valley Girl voice.

Instead of chuckling like I think he will, Barrett leans over and brushes his lips across my forehead, then surprises me by wrapping an arm around me, pulling me back against him so I'm stopped there in the woods. His mouth finds my neck. He kisses up behind my ear, making me shiver as I latch onto his arm, around my waist.

He kisses my throat until my knees are shaking and I feel all warm and needy. Then he comes around in front of me and takes my face in his hands.

"They liked you, like I told you they would."

His lips meet mine for a soft kiss.

His big hands stroke my hair out of my face. His gaze holds mine. I can feel him wanting to say something...but he doesn't. Barrett just keeps kissing me until I'm clinging to him, and he picks me up and carries me to my door, to my room, and to the bed. There, he pulls my leggings down, spreads me gently, and feasts like I'm a succulent dessert and he's starving.

When I come around again and open my eyes, I find Barrett's are dark with lust, his long cock tenting his jeans.

Holy hell, I want him.

I lower my legs, so they're hugging his sides, and stroke my hands up his triceps. "Come here," I murmur. He crawls up my thighs, straddling me...stroking my hips and looking down on me with lust-dazed eyes.

"You're so beautiful," he rasps.

"You are..." I sit up a little, going for his fly. Barrett watches, hooking his thumbs at the waist of his pants; then, as I unzip the jeans, he shuts his eyes and drags his hand down, cupping his bulge.

"That's so hot," I whisper, working his jeans down his hips, so I can see the outline of him through his navy boxer briefs. I stroke him through the cotton. Barrett groans. I slide my palm up the inside of his thigh, stroking his warm skin, then delving into the leg of the briefs so I can cup his balls.

His hips jerk. "Gwen..."

His big hand covers my head. The sounds he makes as I peel the boxer-briefs down and catch his head in my mouth are raw enough to make me throb.

I lick him a few times, all around the rim of him and underneath his head. I run a hand along his shaft, and his eyes open.

"I need you."

I rise up and kiss his mouth hard. "Me too," I murmur.

I spread my legs and Barrett lowers himself over me. "God... the way that looks," I murmur as he lines up at my center. He runs his fingers up and down my slit, then brings them to his mouth, shutting his eyes as he sucks.

With his head pressed against my slickness, he rolls his hips. I lift my own to meet him. With his eyes on mine, he thrusts in. I grunt, and then moan as he fills me. He strokes my arm as he pulls out, then exhales, pushes in.

"So good...Oh, Gwen..."

I feel him swell as he picks up the pace. I love watching his gorgeous features grow so tight and strained. He swells some more inside me, and I widen my legs. Barrett reaches down and strokes my pussy, holds himself still. I look into his heavy-lidded eyes.

"You feel so fucking good. So tight." His eyelids sag shut as his fingers work my clit. I pant, lifting my hips.

I look up to see him watching my face.

"Gwen."

"I love this."

That's the last thing he says before I clench around him and he comes undone. He sinks down on me; we roll onto our sides, facing one another, kissing until I laugh, and he groans.

"I don't want to leave." It takes me a moment to realize the tip of him is still inside me. He slides out, leaving me swollen and sore.

"I could go all day like that." My voice is husky, and I'm smiling slightly. I can't help myself.

Barrett pulls me to him. The way his arms settle around me... I feel closer to him than I ever have. Maybe closer than I ever have to anyone.

I stroke his hair and cheek, and I can feel his body relax. I wrap my arm under his and nuzzle closer. "Sleepy?"

"Yeah." His voice is gravelly. His eyelids sag as he gives me a rueful smile. "You're wearing me out."

I smile. "Good. That's been my secret plan." I stroke the smooth skin over his ribcage. "If you fall asleep, I'll lie here and read."

"Kelly might text."

"I'll check your phone if you want."

"'S okay." His lips brush my forehead as his eyes shut.

"Bear?"

His eyelids lift; his mouth curls. "Mmm." Even when he's half asleep, he looks at me with warmth.

"I'm glad I met you," I rasp.

Tears well in my eyes. I hope he won't notice, but I know he has when he pushes up on his elbow. I blink to see his features tight with worry.

"What's the matter?"

I think I love you. I shake my head, covering my face with my hand as I tell myself to stop. It doesn't really work.

"What's wrong?" His voice is low and soft as velvet. I feel his hands on my hair, stroking firmly, somewhat frantically. "Talk to me, Piglet."

But I can't. I don't even know what I feel. What to say...

He draws me closer, his big body drawing up around mine. He holds me tight in his strong arms and strokes my back—and

I cry. Because I'm happy now? Because I was sad before? Finally I get a handle on myself and look up at him. I'm surprised to find his heavy brows are pinched together; his whole face looks troubled: anguished, almost.

He just looks at me with hurt on his face—my hurt. His face is such a…mirror, my eyes fill with tears again. His lips, pressed together, soften just a little. His finger traces my jaw.

"I'm embarrassed." I wipe my eyes, laughing soundlessly.

"No." He kisses my wet cheek. "Never with me."

And God, it's like a freaking vow. I swear, I feel the kindness and sincerity like they're some white light pouring from his heart and over me.

His kind face and his tender hands…They're…so much more. Everything with him is so much more.

I think of Elvie. More tears drip. He didn't come to me. He never came after the accident. I wasn't enough. I wasn't good enough. I don't even know what—but I wasn't. Since then, I think I just concluded he was right.

I don't know I'm shaking until I see Barrett's eyes widen, and his hand squeezes my shoulder.

"Gwenna?" For a moment, he looks frightened.

I blink; more tears fall. "I'm okay. I'm sorry. I've—always been a shaker. I used to shiver during hide and seek in preschool."

"Oh, Piglet." He pulls me closer, so my breasts are mashed against his chest and his thick arms are locked around me. "That's adorable," he says softly. "And sad as fuck." He pulls the covers over me and holds me so close, I can hear his heartbeat, feel his body heat.

His hands run up and down my back, moving in circles. "What's got you shaken up, Gwennie?"

I swallow. My face is tucked against his neck, and I don't want to look at him. More tears drip down my cheeks.

"I read this quote somewhere," I rasp. His arm tightens around me. "It says something like, 'Tell me they were wrong for leaving.'"

"They were wrong," he says.

Which prompts another little shiver.

"Fuck, this rips me up, Pig."

"Sorry."

"Don't be." His lips find my forehead, brushing over my brow. "It's cute, too. Sad and fucking sweet. Just like Piglet from Pooh Bear."

I laugh for just a second, and I almost ask him if he watched a lot of Pooh. Instead I hear myself say, "Elvie never came to see me."

"What?"

"In rehab." My voice cracks.

"What do you mean?"

"In the hospital I said he couldn't, then he went to Spain. He didn't want me," I whisper. I swallow back more tears, and Barrett's hand cups my face. His eyes bore into mine, gentle and guiding.

"He's an idiot. He was wrong. I swear, Gwen."

"I think he was nervous or something. I don't know."

Barrett's body tenses. "That's bullshit." His arms tighten around me. "No. He was a coward. Not you. Him. A fucking crazy little coward."

He takes my face gently in his big hands and tilts it back, so he can see my leaking eyes.

"You hear what I'm saying? He. Was. Wrong. That's all there is to that. Trust me."

I bite my lip and try to nod, and cry as I do.

"I didn't know I was upset still."

His jaw tightens. "Of course you were. Who wouldn't be?" he asks in a rough whisper. "He's a fucking fool. Believe me there."

I nod, and find the nerve to wrap an arm around his lean waist. "Thanks."

I'm still crying. His arms tighten around me.

"No thanks needed, Piglet. Just speaking the truth."

I decide, sometime after we kiss, and Barrett strokes my back and arms and shoulders, and I lace one leg through both of his and he drifts off to sleep, that Barrett is my angel.

Where he came from—What he did before now—Doesn't matter. It will never, ever matter to me.

I love him. I love him, and he's mine, and I'll do anything for him. Be it rational or stupid, sensible or foolish…

I would fight for him. I think I'd help him hide a body.

As I lie beside with him, I feel stronger. Healthier. I feel like a superhero, my wounds healing just from being pressed against him, being near his magic. Just from breathing his soft breath and feeling his warm skin, I'm getting better.

This man is the other half of my heart. I didn't even know that I was missing it—but now I've found it. I feel like it's beating for the first time ever.

chapter seven

Gwenna

I could get up while he sleeps, but I stay beside him. His big body is warm and comforting against mine and I relish the smell of him. I like to listen to his breathing. When he's sleeping, I feel like his protector. The one time his brow rumples, I kiss his cheek, and he tightens his grip on me.

Holding him like this is pure joy, a sensation stronger than I've ever felt.

My mind swims with images of Kellan and Cleo. The sly, sweet way he looked sideways at her and took her hand when she said the bit about wanting to marry Barrett and I off to each other. I think about her reaching for his hand in the hallway of the studio. I think of Barrett reaching for my hand in the car. Mutual affection. Even as I feel Barrett's heart beat against mine, it's hard to believe this is real. After Elvie...I blink against the blurriness in my eyes.

I was a model, and even then I wasn't enough for Elvie. How is it that I'm enough for Barrett—the me that I am now?

Is it because he's desperate? My chest aches at the thought, but I can't deny how lost he was...how lonely. I know him more now, think I can see him clearly now. His head thrown back as he laughs at me. His radiant grin as he pulls me against him on the couch. The notch between his eyebrows as he watches football, one fist drawn up in support of his team's efforts. But because I watch, I also see the way he'll be standing somewhere, sometimes, and his face will bleach out. I notice when he reaches out and touches his fingertips to the nearest piece of furniture. The dizzy-looking blinks when he thinks I'm not watching. And of course, I know his haunting dreams. Who could blame him for latching onto the first person he finds?

I try to tell myself we like the same TV shows. We have amazing sex. We like cooking, the woods, the bears, and motorcycles. Martial arts.

More so than that, I feel it. I feel this between us, and it's good. I know it's good.

But…God. He's spent ten years in war zones. What if, after being home a while, he wakes up one day and feels differently? What if his needs change? That's part of what went wrong with Elvie. As his ego grew, he needed a girlfriend who could double as a fangirl. I was never that.

I hear Bear's hoarse "mmm" about the time I feel his finger stroke along my eyebrow. "Gwen?"

His voice is dry. His lids are heavy. "You okay?"

He's so, so handsome; I can't help the smile I give in answer.

"I'm okay." I kiss his cheek. "You woke up fast."

He gives me a crooked smile. "Missed you."

His big, rough hands smooth down my belly, stroking my waist, as we kiss until I have to pull away to breathe, and then his hand strokes down toward my pussy.

"So perfect," he rasps as he slides a finger in.

I clench around it.

"Fucking God…" He finds my breast and starts to suckle at it.

"Someone woke up horny." I giggle.

"The way you smell…" He inhales deeply, and I wrap an arm around his head.

"My Bear…"

We find ourselves in the classic "69" pose. Barrett tortures me with his soft, hot mouth and wicked fingers. In return, I take him deep into my throat and tease his balls until he's blowing hot breaths on my swollen pussy; he's got a finger hooked inside me, but his tongue can barely move. For my part, I'm shaking, collapsed on his face because my legs can't hold me. As his breaths pick up, I start to throb harder.

Our groans mingle in the soft, still air until my body draws up and I start to spasm hard around his fingers. At that moment, his cock throbs.

"Ahh…"

I love the way his hips shake and his hands squeeze my thighs. I suck until he's finished and let him rest inside my mouth for a moment before I draw off. I love the dazed look on his face as I look over my shoulder.

"Lie beside me." He holds his arm out, and I snuggle in.

Barrett and I get dressed and start on eggplant parmesan. We fill the kitchen with our smiles and laughter, and then Cleo and Kellan show up, and they help us. Someone opens two bottles of pinot noir, and we wind up eating around the counter. Finally I shoo them to the table, where we talk until we're all old friends, and then we move into the den and play *Cards Against Humanity*. Somehow it's midnight; Cleo and I are braiding Barrett's hair, and Kellan, in my armchair, looks half asleep. After Barrett extricates himself from us, I show Cleo my scar, and she "ohhh"s, and Barrett says he'll go next door to get the place ready for them to spend the night.

"You don't need to," Cleo tries to tell him, but he waves her off. "No prob," he murmurs, and I watch him get his jacket on and slip into his boots. He looks kind of drunk, and very handsome.

"Be back in a few," he says, and with one final glance at Kellan, zonked out in the chair, and one soft-eyed look at me, he goes.

I get my fleece blanket and lay it over Kellan's long body. Cleo steps over to the chair and drapes herself along its puffy arm, curling herself around Kellan's upper body without actually touching him.

"You guys are so phenomenal together."

She smiles, and I look at Kellan, then back to her. "Is he going to be okay?" I ask softly. I only ask because I've been drinking. Maybe that's why she answers.

"Yeah. I mean, I hope." Her eyes gleam, and she touches her forehead to his shoulder. "I love him. He's mine...and I could never..." She lifts her head off him and shakes it once. She inhales deeply, and I step over and hug her. It's a drunk sort of hug: an awkward head pat. But I mean it.

"I'm so sorry. Not because I don't think he'll be okay, you know? Just...I know it sucks to worry."

"Do you?" She looks over her shoulder at me. "Like—with Barrett?"

I think of mentioning the nightmares, but it feels like a betrayal of his privacy, so I only nod.

"I know he had a rough time after he got back."

I nod, although what I really want is to pounce on her and make her tell me everything she knows about him.

"Preaching to the choir," she says.

"Well, kind of, but there's always more. I missed almost all of—everything with him so far. I want to know everything abut him."

"Do you love him?"

I blink. My face feels hot. My stomach twists. "We just met." The words are raspy, like my heart knows they are false.

She laughs. "If that matters, it's news to me. Girl..." She grins. "I can tell. I'm happy for him. You too! When we met him at the airport..." She shakes her head and sighs. "I don't know who was worse, him or Kellan. He was...so sad." She shakes her head again, her eyes filling with tears. She laughs and wipes under her eyes. "I'm a weepy drunk. But really, everything about him was like...so *sad*. He looked so tired. You just wanted to hug him, you know?" She giggles. "You do. Anyway, they had him on a thousand types of medicine and he looked like a zombie." My heart clenches, but she doesn't seem to notice. "He was like..." She bites her lip, as if she's thinking hard. "His eyes were kind of flat...You know that look?"

I nod, trying as hard as I can to keep a poker face, so she'll tell me more.

"Anyway, I just worried about him. It was Kell who noticed all the meds and he got off them. I wanted Barrett to come back home with us, but he ended up in Breckenridge."

"Barrett?"

She nods. "He spent the summer up there somewhere in the mountains, in this cabin."

"In Breckenridge?" My throat tightens.

"Mmm-hmm. Some isolated cabin. I might be wrong about that part. Maybe it wasn't isolated, I just *see* it as it was." She shrugs, her eyelids drooping. "We were worried, though." She yawns. "He just had that kind of look." Another comical yawn, during which a strand of dark hair falls into her face. Cleo pushes it away. "A look like he needed some hugs." She sighs dramatically. "I tried to give him some."

"Thank you," I whisper past my aching throat.

She gives me a tired, kind smile. "You look all sad now. Gwenna, it's like night and day now." She shifts so her butt is balanced on the chair's arm, but she's facing me, her back to Kellan's sleeping form. "Let me tell you, Gwen…this Barrett here is like, the best Barrett."

I giggle. I don't even know why. After a minute, we both start laughing and can't stop. Cleo leans forward, tossing an arm around me. That's how Barrett finds us, slumped against the back of Kellan's chair.

Cleo wakes up Kellan, and he gives Bear and me a sleepy smile. I can't help noticing his arm's around Cleo's shoulders. Looking at the two of them, at Kellan and how good he looks, you'd never guess, but since I know, I think I notice all the small things. God, it must be so scary for Cleo. And Kellan, obviously. I say a prayer that his cancer stays away forever, and they have a long, wonderful life.

Then we're closing the door behind them. Barrett kisses me. He rocks his boner up against me, driving me gently against the wall. We hump there before winding up on the floor, having frantic sex.

"I'm half drunk," he says as we lie there, satiated, afterward. His husky words are filled with comical wonder, like he doesn't quite know how it happened.

I laugh and kiss his scratchy cheek. "I am, too. Stay with me," I murmur. "Don't go next door."

"I wasn't going to."

He gets to his feet, and I look up at him.

"You're mine." I giggle.

He scoops me up, trying to hold me carefully against his chest without throwing me over his shoulder or carrying me lamb style. I can tell by the way he moves that he's trying to be careful with me, but he *is* drunk.

I giggle some more. His steps are slightly unsteady.

"My mule," I cackle.

My mind whirls. Isn't that what Elvie used to say? If I got ugly, he'd send me away on a mule?

"You're my mule," I whisper again. Goodness fills me, soft and warm and right as rain.

chapter eight

Barrett

"Barrett?"

The clear, sharp voice is out of place. It doesn't go with what I'm seeing: Gwen's small body, crumpled, her hair spread around her head, her blood leaking on the roadside. I hear my name a few more times, but it's just background noise. I'm consumed with what is wrong with Gwen. I've got this feeling I should know, but my brain's sluggish. I don't understand. How did she get here? Her face is white and slack. Her lips are stained with dark liquid that drips out of the corner of her mouth and down her throat, into the snow.

I drop down beside her, but my knees sink into the warm puddle of blood, and I have to turn away. My stomach lurches. I cup my hand over my mouth. After a second struggling to shut my stomach down, I remind myself that I'm an Operator—and this is Gwen; *I love her!* Then I put my hands under her hips and shoulders and lift her.

As I pull her onto my lap, warmth spills over my lap. My throat constricts.

"Oh God..." My hands loosen their grip on her. I almost drop her; then I hold her to my chest and sob.

"*Gwen*...oh God...Oh God, oh please..."

"Barrett—I'm okay." The voice is distant: background noise.

Our bodies shake together. "Oh my God...Breck. Gwen..."

"Bear...Baby. It's me—it's *Gwenna*. Open your eyes, baby... Look at me."

I'm looking up at Gwen. Relief transforms her features as she clasps my cheeks and pulls my face toward her.

I wrap my arms around her.

"Bear...that's right." I feel her hand stroke my cheek, feel her rocking me. I blink around. The lights...

"That's right." Her voice is a thick whisper. "You see the lights?"

I hear her, see them, but...the snow. I smell the salt and I can feel the blood and Ly and Mom and Breck...all dead. I feel myself shaking, am aware some distant somewhere that Gwen's arms are around me. I'm shaking...and trying not lose it.

"It's okay...."

I blink and realize I'm lying in Gwen's lap with my arms around myself. One hand is clutching my face. Shaking...

I try to think of something I can tell her, but my mind feels stuck. Oh, fuck. Freaking out like this...

I told myself I wouldn't—

I frown up at her. She looks...fine.

A shiver moves through my shoulders. Her face blurs, so I can't tell if she is...

"Gwen?"

Her eyes are gentle. "Barrett?" Her arms pull me closer. I close my eyes and grit my teeth and try to breathe. It's all still there—the things that blow me open...and the blood...and...

"Come here...Let's lay down." She does, and I half fall on her.

I wince, trying to shift back on my arms so I'm not lying right on her.

"It's okay," she whispers, holding me against her.

I can't stop the flow of tears. Can't forget what I saw. I can see the blood on her mouth. I cut my eyes so I can see her face—she's lying on the pillow—searching for the damage that I fear will be there…

I find her brows are drawn together. Her hand cups my cheek as she searches my face.

"Hang on a minute, baby…" Gwenna sits up. I shift onto my side, feeling unsteady and weird. She's gone for a moment, and then she's moving in my field of vision with a big blanket. She spreads it over me. It's oddly heavy

"That's my weighted blanket." I watch her out of the corner of my eye as she pulls it up to my mid-back. My eyelids seem to grow heavy with it. Gwenna doesn't seem real.

"Okay, now…" She does her best to wrap her hands under my arms and tug me up against her, guiding my head to her soft belly. I can feel her body curl around mine. "Feel that blanket? It's keeping you here…with me. You're okay here. Nothing is the matter in this time and place, okay?" She holds me tightly as her whispered words flow through me. Things feel like they're swirling around me.

I smell the blood. Regret and horror swell like balloons in my chest, until I can barely breathe enough to whisper, "I'm sorry." I feel my body tremble, and I feel so fucking bad to burden her like this. I shut my eyes. "I love you."

My stomach plummets as my raspy words make their way to my brain.

I'm off the bed so fast, the room careens; into the bathroom where I lean against the wall and brace my hands on my knees.

Fuck!

My mind is racing, even as my throat feels like it's closing up. I think of crawling out the bathroom window.

Get a fucking grip. I stand up straighter, scrub the heels of my palms over my eyes. Even as I stop my leaking eyes and regulate my breathing, something hard and cold encases my chest.

It's not going to work; it's never going to work. I can't keep it together…

I hear Gwenna come into the room. Can see the shape of her, but I can't look at her. My eyes shut of their own accord, but I force them back open. Force them to meet her wide, brown ones.

"I'm sorry."

I make myself take in the look on her face: kind. I grit my jaw so hard it sends a bolt of pain up my temple.

"Barrett…" Her voice is so soft, I can hardly hear it…but I see her mouth move. I feel her step closer to me.

"I'm wrong for you," I manage. My voice sounds raspy; weak.

I watch her eyes absorb the words: the way their dark pools seem to deepen.

"Bear…" She steps so close our bodies touch and runs her fingers up my cheek. She strokes my temple. Her eyes flare, demanding things before she even says, "You love me. You said so. And you know what? I love you too." Her fingers curl against my cheek. Her eyes flash. "I love you too." Her voice cracks. "It's scary to say, even though you just said it. Barrett…" She wraps an arm around me, pressing her softness against me, looking up into my face as she speaks softly. "I think I knew I loved you when I brought the wine over that night. I felt scared and kind of…helpless. Like what I was doing was out of control and maybe stupid. And I couldn't stop." Her voice goes raspy. "You know why?" She blinks.

I shake my head.

"Because I love you. I love everything about you." Her hands grasp my wrists. "I like your arms and legs…your hands." She brings one up to her face, turning my hand so her lips can brush over my palm. "There's this callous right here—" Her mouth tickles the spot between my left hand thumb and forefinger that used to mark me as an Operator. "I like it," she murmurs, her eyes burning mine. "I like your long fingers. I even like your little fingernails." She smiles gently, and squeezes all the fingers with her own.

"You know what I like the most, though?" She sounds breathless.

I swallow.

"The thing you know best, you can't do it anymore, Barrett. You lost your vision in one eye, you lost basically a *life*, and what are you doing? Taking time for some random girl next door. Teaching her hand-to-hand. Making her care about you." She shakes her head as sorrow fills her eyes. "You keep running from me...I knew you were getting up at night." Her lips press into a thin line as she shakes her head again. "Don't you think I care?"

"You don't know me." The words are hoarse. My jaw aches, referring pain up to my ear. She doesn't know me. If she did, she'd never love me. She wouldn't be able to, and in my honest moments, I can see this with terrible clarity.

I feel a clawing sensation deep inside my chest.

"I don't know you well enough to take care of you?" Her eyes glimmer. She frowns, and I watch her throat move as she swallows. "Barrett—*this* is when we met. This is how things are right now. I love you because...I do. I want to be here with you. What bothers you about all that?"

I look down at my feet as my eyes throb with building pressure.

"Talk to me, baby." Her voice is so soft; it makes my chest feel like it's ripping open.

I look up at her, even open my mouth, but all I see is warm love in her eyes and I just...can't. I shudder. Gwenna holds me to her, and it's horrible. It's wonderful. I want it so much. More than the sum of all the good parts of me.

"All I want is to make you feel better," she says in her sweet, soft voice, "but I feel like I can't get to you, if that makes any sense."

I inhale deeply and let the words inside my head croak out. "I don't see why you want to."

The world is still while she looks into my eyes, seeing through my soul. "Bear, because you're mine. I feel it. You are *mine* to hold and take care of and check on...and fuck. I want to hold your hand. I want to know about you. Why? Who cares why? *I'm* not asking. I don't have an answer, either. Who does? Why'd you say you love me?" Her throat moves as she swallows; her eyes twinkle as she hoarsely asks me, "Did you mean it?"

"Of course."

"Why do you love me, Barrett? Is it the color of my hair? The baked goods?"

I lick my lips. "I like your smile," I rasp.

Her face slackens, and I can feel her gaze grow a little more serious under the weight of what I think must be self-consciousness. I run my fingers over her jaw.

"I think it's sexy... *You*." How do I convey to her that there is only one Gwen, only one sweet, kind, sexy, crooked smile. "Your eyes," I manage. My throat feels full, but she looks somber, so I push past it and give her some of me, whatever I can muster. "Your eyes make me feel...better. About life. The way you look in leggings." I stroke her ass. "So fucking hot. The lights on the ceiling." I kiss her temple. "You're good, Gwen. You're so good, I can't help but love you even though I know I shouldn't."

"Trust me, baby..." She trails her lips over my cheekbone. "You're good, too."

Her breath is warm and sweet. I shut my eyes. "Don't say that."

"I'm going to keep saying it," she warns me in a murmur.

A strange panic burbles in me. I look at her and I feel my heartbeat in my shoulders and my throat. "I gave pain, and I deserve it. That's the way it works. There's nothing good about me."

If she's going to be with me, she should be warned.

The ache—in my head, my jaw, my chest—fuzzes into numbness as I try to breathe. She melds her soft body around mine.

My hands, on her shoulders, shake. The two of us are locked together, her tethered to me and it's so wrong. So wrong.

"You seem like a dream…to me." The words swim in my head; unsteady words. "Rewrite the story…" I clear my throat so my voice isn't as cracked and get the nerve to look down at her. "You said I have to rewrite what happens…But I *can't*. Because I don't deserve it."

Gwenna

"Does Kellan think that?"

He frowns.

"Does he agree with what you said? That you deserve pain?"

He shakes his head, looking troubled. "I don't—"

"You *are* in pain." I stroke his wrists; I look into his desperate eyes. "You're here, you've been back for a while, but you're still hurt. I know." He looks down as his face hardens. I can feel his body still: embarrassment or shame. I stroke his strong arm. "You're doing the best you can, baby, trying to hold yourself together…I know. And you've done really well. You're so strong. But you know what? I think you can't trust yourself on some things. Not right now. A part of you—" I swallow. His eyes flick to mine; our gazes hold and it feels tender, then bright like the sun, almost painful. I push forward in a breathless whisper.

"I think you want to hurt yourself. You don't know what to do; you can't see your way out. And you can't trust yourself right now to know what you deserve. Kellan loves you." I swallow, clearing my throat. "I love you. Cleo loves you, too. So I think you have to at least take into consideration what we think." I take his hands in mine and squeeze. "We don't think you should be hurt, or that you deserve to be in pain. We want you to feel better. I just want you to feel good."

I hold him to me. His body is shaking. I can feel his pain seep into my own bones.

"Whatever happened over there?" I lean away so I can look into his tortured eyes. "That is in the past. That Barrett? He's gone. Maybe you can think of him as dead. He's gone, just like Breck. You can't reach him anymore, because he's gone. Maybe things were so bad, you wanted the pain. To have control over yourself or…I don't know. But you can be a different person now, I swear, I know you can. Not can—*are*. You're here now. You won't go back there. You couldn't if you wanted to. So I think maybe you should let that person go. Because he *is* gone.

"You're not a sniper anymore…" I wrap both arms around his back, and Barrett leans against me, quiet and still. "You're not a killer, Bear. You're my neighbor…You live in the woods. With bears, and a weird girl who makes cakes with beer. You still look like the other Barrett…You have scars of his. But *you*—I know *this* Barrett. You're sweet and brave and strong." I stroke his soft hair. "What was left from all that stuff, what you came back with—the day you met up with Kellan and Cleo and they drove you to rehab your arm—that guy: the one who moved here and saw me at the meeting…You are *him*. And he does *not* deserve to hurt."

I take his face in my hands; he lifts his head off my shoulder and I stare deep into his eyes.

"If it doesn't ring true to you, you have to believe *me*. Because in this way, I can see more clearly what's right…your brother can…Cleo can…You are someone new now. The other Barrett, that one…" I shake my head, struggling for words. "Maybe you feel so bad because you're holding onto someone who is gone. And maybe you should mourn him. He isn't coming back. And who you were before then?" My voice cracks. "I have one of those too. This ghost version. She isn't coming back either. You know what I mean?"

His wet eyes blink at mine. His sweet, still face…I cup his jaw, stroking gently over his soft skin.

"That Bear is gone. And you can miss him. Miss him. I miss the old Gwen. She was different, but you might have liked her."

Tears slide down his cheeks.

"The Barrett who enlisted? Dead. The Barrett who was over there? He's gone, too. He probably died with Breck."

His features tighten. He pulls me close and buries his face in my shoulder.

"I wish he had," he chokes.

"I know." I hug him tightly, wrap my hand around the back of his head. "I know. Now you're someone else, and even though they feel so strong, all that, your memories—are only memories now. We can't reach back in time, you know? So you have to think of yourself as someone new now. You're what's left. And all the misery? That stuff belongs with the dead."

"You can't see it?"

"See what?"

He shoulders shiver. "I feel…like everyone can see it," he says in a broken voice.

"What can we see?"

"I'm not just a guy."

"You are." I stroke his strong back. "You're my guy next door."
His eyes flicker to mine. They're dark. "Let me ask you this, Barrett:
Have you killed anybody here?"

His face pales. I feel bad about asking such a harsh question,
but I press on. "Have you?"

"No."

"Have you lost any friends in that house next door? In real
time?"

He shakes his head.

"Heard a bomb?"

He shakes his head again.

"Have you been wounded there?" I smirk slightly, remembering our meeting. "In a serious way?"

He shakes his head.

"You're not going to see another IED, Barrett. One time
when you were dreaming, you were talking about a tourniquet.
You don't have one of those here. You don't need one here. The
Barrett who needed one is gone. You have to leave him there. I
think you did already. Maybe part of you feels like you have to
get him back. To sort through all that and atone…" I gnaw my lip,
shaking my head. "I don't know what's in your mind, but I know
you can't. The only thing you have is from this point forward, and
from here on out, you are not an Operator. You're just my neighbor. Someone I love. You can't be anybody else, unless you want to.
Choose to. And that person would be new, too."

I stroke the back of his head. "You—the one here now—are
who I want. And I love you, Barrett. I want you to be fed well and
feel good. You are beautiful to me…and valuable. I want to keep
you."

He holds me tightly. "I love you…Gwen. I don't know how
to…not be scared."

Of what, I almost ask, but I think I can fill in the blank. Scared I'll leave. Scared everything will fall apart. Scared that his past will reach into the future and get him. I squeeze him to me.

"If you start to worry, just tell me. I'm scared too. Nervous. I think the more you've lost in life, the harder it is to invest yourself in the future. I get that."

"Yeah." The soft word fades into silence. Barrett just keeps holding me, and my heart aches, and breaks, and swells again with love for him.

chapter nine

Barrett

Finally, I lift my head. My face is hot. My throat still feels kind of tight and thick. But the second our eyes meet, I feel all the tension melt away.

She smiles, and it's a smile that says *she really does love me*. I think of what she said—about how the other versions of me are dead and gone. It sounds weird, but…I think I like it. Gone is where I want them. It's the only thing that feels right.

How strange that she knew. She knew what to say. But then… of course she did. From the first day I watched her, I had a feeling she and I were linked.

I smile back at her. I have the impulse to pull my dick out, just to show her I still have it after all the waterworks. The thought makes me smile a little more, and her smile widens, too.

"I love your smile," she says.

I rub my thumb over her lip. "I love yours more."

She wraps her arms around my waist and speaks against my chest. "You want to get a bath? I have a dumb, funny idea…"

"Dumb and funny?" I swallow against my scratchy throat. "Sold," I tease.

I carry her over to the tub and set her on its ledge while I start the water. She undresses. I watch every move she makes until I'm hard, and then I take off my clothes, too.

Her little "mmmmm" as my dick springs free of my boxer-briefs is enough to make me throb. We get into the tub together, but this time I set her down by the faucet. We face each other, and she strokes my shaft as the water laps at my balls and I play with her clit.

"Ahh." The noise is breathy and delicious. Fuck, her nipples are all hard and tight. I can see the goosebumps on her creamy breasts. She grips me tighter, strokes me faster.

"I love that look on your face," she says with a smirk. Her lids are heavy, cheeks are pink.

"What look?" I smile, and I can feel that same sedation on my own face. Everything inside me builds and tenses, but somehow on the outside I feel slower.

"The turned-on look," she whispers. "Your face gets kind of red up here…" She reaches out and strokes under my eyes. "Your eyes look like they're trying not to close…" Her fingers trail around the rim of my head, and I can't help panting as the pleasure spins out through my thighs. Then she strokes the tender notch there at the underside of my head, and I do close my eyes as I shift my hips.

"Fuck…" She's still pumping my shaft.

"Your voice gets low…and your nipples get tight." She strokes me with a firmer hand, and with her other hand, she pinches one.

My dick throbs, and I groan.

I try to up my game on her clit, and I feel her shimmy closer to me.

"Christ…" She's doing something to my fucking balls. "I want—*ohh, Gwen.*" A burst of heat spreads from my thighs up to my belly, where it pools and pulses as my dick pounds to the rhythm of my heart.

I stroke her clit and run a finger through her lips, and in the water I can feel her slickness, the lack of friction as I spread her open.

"Oh, fucking…hell," I breathe. I need inside. Which way? I can barely visualize positions as she rolls my balls and strokes my dick. The way her wrist twists, her hand cupping my head…

It's all I can do to wrap my hands around her waist, pulling her atop my lap. I rub myself against her soft curls.

Gwenna spreads herself for me. I hear her gasp as my head rubs against her where she's slick and swollen. Her hands grab my shoulders. With her legs around my hips, she tries to push herself against me, push me into her.

"You need a dick inside that pussy, don't you Piglet?" I can't help enjoying her frenzy, even though I feel the same way. I find her core and linger there, applying gentle pressure so I spread her, but not pushing in. Gwenna's body trembles.

"Please!"

"My pretty, pink Piglet…"

"Barrett!"

I chuckle as I thrust, burying the tip inside her.

Gwenna moans. That sound is music to my ears. "Sweet Gwen…"

I bury myself balls deep, and now it's my turn to moan—more of a grunt, really. "Aghh…so fucking *tight.*" I lift her by her hips, pulling her off my dick and slamming her back down on it. She gasps and grabs a handful of my hair. Her cunt squeezes my cock. I feel my balls draw up and throb; my cock swells inside her. Gwenna feels it too. She squirms and grabs my neck, pushing her breasts against my chest as my hands grip her hips and she starts to bounce atop me. I can feel her coming as I start to lose control myself. My hands lose their grip as her pussy milks my dick and with a final grunt, I blow inside her.

As I carry her to bed, so clean and soft and sweet, life feels right for the first time in as long as I remember.

Gwenna

Barrett has his usual early morning dream, but this time, I pull his torso into my lap and rock him, patting his cheek until his eyes peek open. His brows draw down, and I watch him blink a few times as he tries to come fully awake. I kiss his throat and jaw and cheek and whisper sweet things to him. There's this moment when his face twists like he's eaten something bitter, and I think he might cry. I pull his cheek against my neck, and Barrett locks his arms around me. He squeezes me so tightly it hurts my shoulders.

"It's okay…"

"The liver shot," he rasps. He swallows, folding himself around me.

I don't press for details, just cuddle him and say a silent prayer. A few minutes later, I feel his body slacken against mine.

A few hours later, I wake up in Barrett's lap, with his mouth brushing over mine.

I smile. He smiles down at me.

"Wake up, buttercup."

I snuggle up against his chest. "It's too…sunny."

Barrett laughs. "You're cute, Piglet." I feel his lips press against my forehead. "I've gotta say bye to Kelly," he says softly. "Want to walk over with me?"

"For sure."

In front of Barrett's house, I hug Kellan and Cleo, then watch as Barrett hugs them both. He squeezes Kellan tightly and pats Cleo's back as he hugs her.

"Be safe. Let us know how the driving goes."

I'm giddy that he said *us*, so as they get into Kellan's car and we sit on the steps together, I'm hiding a big smile behind one hand.

I watch them load up as Barrett's fingers thread through mine. Kellan, like Barrett, is protective, his hand brushing Cleo's shoulder even as she hoists herself into the SUV. I see him smile at her before he closes the door, and it's like the smile I get from Barrett sometimes—pure sweetness.

I'm surprised when Barrett gets up one more time as Kellan walks around the car to get into the driver's side. The two clasp in a firm guy hug. I can't tell who hugs whom harder, but it's wonderful to see. They both look calm and bright-eyed when they pull away. Satisfied, I think.

Kellan grins and slaps his brother's arm one more time. "Take care, B."

"You too, little bro." Bear pulls his brother close and I think I hear him say, "I'll do it."

I find out later what he means he'll do is see a counselor. I'm pleasantly surprised that, at some point last night, Kellan mentioned the idea to Barrett. Bear tells me both Kelly and Cleo had "some issues" after what they went through with the bone marrow transplant, so they were both "seeing a shrink."

I flash him a knowing smile. "It's not a bad idea."

"What's yours' name?" he asks, a glint of skepticism in his eyes.

"Helga. And actually, I see her tomorrow. Would you like me to ask her for the name of someone who works with veterans?"

Barrett leans his head against the couch's back and blinks up at the ceiling. His eyes glide to mine. "What would I do?" he asks in a quiet, low voice. "If I went?"

I deadpan, "Well, the first thing is the physical. You'll just undress, and he or she will check for—"

His eyes get so wide, so fast, I can't help laughing, which morphs into howling. Barrett wraps his arm around my neck, scoots so close he's almost sitting on my thigh, and gives me a gentle noogie.

"Liar, liar…" He chuckles, pulling me into his lap.

"Pants on fire?" I offer.

His gaze darkens. "You want that?"

"I always do," I whisper shyly.

Barrett sprawls me over his lap, like a naughty student with a very dirty-minded schoolmaster, and fingers me until I'm desperate, almost miserable. Then he throws my fleece over the rug, urges me down onto my hands and knees, and enters me from behind.

Bliss of the highest order…

God, I think I'll die before I come.

And afterward, a shower. And after that, we make omelets, and then I spend hours showing him how to make bread, and making the bread into bread pudding.

When we go to bed that night, Barrett nods off wrapped in my arms while I read something on my phone, over his shoulders. When he's solidly asleep, I turn the twinkle lights on, pull the weighted blanket to the bottom of the bed, go into the kitchen, and pour lemonade. Kellan told me Bear hates lemonade, so if he wakes up dissociating, I plan to offer him a sip and watch his face scrunch back into the present.

I don't get the chance. When he wakes up this time, he sits up for only a second before staggering toward the bathroom. I find him crouching in front of the toilet. He doesn't seem sick—his arm is draped over the front of the seat, and his eyes are closed—so I wonder if he came here automatically, triggered by other nights when he *was* sick. I rub circles on his back and wrap an arm lightly around his waist when I notice his calves are trembling.

A few heartbeats later, he turns and curls against me. His head is down, so I can't see his face, but I can feel him breathing—fast.

"It's okay." I cup his jaw and try to hold his body against mine. "We're okay…"

I feel chills sweep his skin. He nods once, just a quick jerk of his head, like he's trying to believe me. My heart aches as I whisper, "I love you. Can you come back to bed with me?"

He nods. Our eyes meet in a brief spark as we stand up together. His hand grips mine as we walk back to bed. He follows me closely, his face tired in the shadows. When our eyes catch this time, Bear gives me a tiny smile that makes my chest feel warm and tight.

When we're tangled together on the bed, his body damp, his muscles tense, he tucks his chin against the top of my head—and I decide to gamble.

"Do you want to tell me…what it's about?" I whisper haltingly.

I feel him take a deep, slow breath. He's still so long after, I think he fell asleep, until he murmurs, "You."

"The dream where you get sick…" My heart pounds hard. "It's about me?"

His arms around me tighten. I can feel his sorrow, an invisible ribbon winding around both of us. *Oh, Barrett…*

I work to breathe around the lump in my throat, to make my voice normal when I ask, "What happens?"

His head shakes slowly. I feel like an ass for asking.

"It's all right." I pull the weighted blanket over us and smooth his damp curls off his forehead.

"We're together, okay? That's real life. It feels good to be in bed with you."

"I know." He shudders once more, just the barest little tic across his shoulders. I rub in between his shoulder blades, and pretty soon, he's breathing evenly again.

The next morning, Barrett meets an inspector down at the studio. I spend my morning taking samples from the pond in the enclosure, then packaging them up and sending them off via UPS to a lab where they'll be tested to ensure the water's safe and healthy for the bears.

The nearest UPS place is downtown near Helga's office, which is good because I have an appointment with her in two hours. I shower, and as I leave, I spot the paper bag from the Native American store on the counter. On the outside of it, Barrett had scrawled his friend's address. I fold the bag closed, setting it on the passenger seat beside the little box of water samples. Before I open the garage, I peek inside, my intention to make sure it seems ready to mail. Barrett told me it was, but since he's not around, I want to be sure.

When I look inside, I see a square of my thick, papyrus "GW" stationary and find myself reaching for it. I want to see Barrett's handwriting again, but that's not the only reason I unfold the note. I still want to know him more. Want to know what he's thinking, what he's feeling. Want to know his friends. I tell myself there's nothing personal in such a short note, and open it before my conscience can kick in. I feel a pleasant jolt at the sight of his familiar handwriting.

THANKS FOR WATCHING MY BACK, BROTHER. -BEAR

I bring the note to my chest for a second, then slide it back in.

Half an hour later, I'm paying the woman at the UPS store, and she's telling me about how her pet parrot has gotten into the habit of telling all her houseguests "Go clean those feathers, honey!" when I realize…I'm laughing. Really laughing, right here in the store. I'm laughing, and on my right side, someone tall is maybe laughing, too.

I turn my head as I get my receipt and change, and my gaze catches on a pair of pale blue eyes. Heat sweeps through me as I realize he's familiar: his hair is red like mine; he's tall and built, kind of like Barrett…

The guy from the moccasin shop.

I give him a small smile, more to push out of my comfort zone than anything else. He gives me a wink, and when I turn to go, I think I feel him right behind me. Then I push the door open and I see Barrett's smiling face, and the guy is forgotten in the warmth of Bear's arms as he pulls me to him and I melt against his body, my arms twined around my neck, until an older couple smiles at us from down the sidewalk, and we laugh and they laugh, like we're a spectacle, and I think maybe we are.

"Let's get lunch," he says. We hold hands and walk to a little sandwich shop with old-fashioned, burnt-orange, plastic booths, Coke clocks with swinging hands all along one wall, and a green glass vase with a carnation poking out the top beside the napkin holder.

Barrett smiles with mustard on his lip and tells me about the inspection.

"The place is perfect."

He's glowing, which makes me smile, too.

His leg rubs mine under the table as he talks. We brush each other's fingertips as we sip soda and Barrett eats his sandwich, then the rest of mine.

"How about your morning, Piglet?"

We talk through a drink refill, top our lunch off with peppermints from this adorable little glass jar by the door, and latch hands as we step into the sunlight. It's a balmy, humid day, springtime-warm.

"How'd you find me at the UPS place?" I ask.

Barrett smiles. "I was watching for you. Want a walk to Helga's office?"

"Yes." I lean my cheek against his arm as we walk slowly toward her little, white brick building. "You'll go home after?"

He nods. "Unless you want me to stay. I could kill some time down here. You need anything done?"

I smile, and Barrett smirks. "That's some Cheshire Cat stuff there."

"I know." I laugh. "That line is every woman's wet dream."

We nuzzle each other outside Helga's office, and Barrett agrees to meet me here in fifty minutes.

"I'll pick up a helmet for you. Pink?" His brow quirks up.

I nod, smiling.

"Second choice neon green?"

I grin and blow him a kiss.

Fifty minutes later, I emerge, feeling lighter and holding the business card of a local therapist who works with vets.

I see Barrett's yummy, thick back leaned against the glass window at the front of Helga's office, and my heart does a little tap dance of excitement.

I launch myself into his arms as soon as my feet hit the sidewalk. He pushes a hot pink helmet on my head. I lean my head back. "Do I look sexy?"

"Very sexy. So damn sexy," he murmurs, kissing me lightly, "it's a shame you have to drive yourself back."

"Race you there?"

He smirks. "C'mon…"

I punch his arm and dart off toward my car. When I pull into my driveway, Barrett's standing on the porch with his arms crossed, an adorable smirk on his face and his dark hair blowing in the perpetual mountain breeze. When I get out of the car, the first thing I notice is his dick tenting his pants, a dark glaze on his eyes.

I unlock the laundry room door, but before I step inside, I unbutton my pants so as I walk, they'll fall down.

"Fucking hell, Gwenna. I hope that pussy wants a dick inside."

I lean over slightly and wiggle my ass at him. Barrett tackles me. We fuck on the rug beside the couch like dogs, my pussy stretched around his steel-hard length, his body heaving as he pants and pounds me.

It's not until after our bath that I manage to get the card in his hand. I'm making chicken salad at the counter when he strokes his hand over my hair.

"Be back, Pig," he murmurs.

My walls are thin enough that I can hear him calling from my office.

Sean Eddins, PhD. His card says he does *PTSD Recovery, Cognitive Behavioral Therapy, Brainspotting, and Exposure Therapy.*

My stomach twists a little at the thought of Barrett going somewhere. Talking to someone.

So when his appointment rolls around, two days later, I can't help offering to drive him. I sort of expect him to say "yes," so when he shakes his head, picks up his helmet, and says, "I've got it, Pig," I slap his arm, pretending I'm offended by my silly, new nickname. In truth, I kind of love it.

"Okay, Bear." I plant a kiss on his scruffy jaw. "Be careful for me."

"Will do." He wraps an arm around my shoulders, drawing me in close against his chest. His lips brush the crown of my head. "He said this time will be an hour and a half. I'm going to do something right before, so it might be more like two hours."

I squeeze his hard waist, kiss his chest. "I hope it goes well."

"Me too."

I frame his face with my hands, thumbing his cheeks. "You know I think you're brave for trying it."

His eyes cut down before he raises them for mine. They burn a little. "Thanks." I get the small half-smile, the one that lets me know he's nervous.

"Love you."

"I love you more." He wraps me tight against his chest and shuts his eyes. I feel his heartbeat for an awesome moment. Love fills me. I hope he feels it, too.

chapter ten

Barrett

"How much you want for it?"

"Won't take less than nine hundred."

The guy behind the counter peers down at my .380, shaking his head. "It's real nice," he drawls. "I'll give you that. I can do nine hundred—if you tell me where it came from." His eyes meet mine.

"I had it over in Iraq," I tell him, shifting my weight. And a lot of other places, but it's easier to stick to places troops were stationed for long stretches.

The guy nods slowly, knowingly. His Braves cap casts a shadow over his face, but I can see his chapped lips tighten. He touches something I can't see behind the counter, and I hear a jingle. His hand lifts up dog tags on a chain that seems to be hanging from a nail in the back of the counter.

"I get that," he says, nodding more. His hazel eyes meet mine. "I might keep this one for myself." He looks down at the gun. "If you change your mind and not much time's gone by, you let me know."

I smile, because that's kind, but I won't need it.

"No worries," I tell him.

We share a hard handshake—it still feels odd with my right hand—and the guy reaches over the counter to clasp me on the shoulder.

"Take care," he tells me. As I head toward the door, he says, "Hang on."

I turn to find him holding out a business card.

Gatlinburg Veteran's Association is embossed in black across the front.

"It's mostly younger guys," he says. I look at the lines on his face, putting him at maybe mid-30s. "Me and a couple Marines. One Ranger. Just got started up."

I look from the card to his eyes. "You work out around here?"

He steps out from behind the counter, lifts his pants leg. I see metal. "Not much working out these days."

"I'm opening a martial arts place. Free for vets," I hear myself say. "How long have you had the prosthetic?"

"Not long, man. About four months. Just got done rehabbing it around the end of summer."

I look down at the prosthetic, trying to figure out if it's transfemoral or transtibial without lifting the leg of his pants. I settle for asking him, "Knee, too?"

He nods. "Lost the whole thing from the thigh down."

I nod. That does make it harder. "Ever ran on it?"

He laughs. "Hell no. Barely even walk on it."

"You got another card?"

He grunts, not meeting my eyes as he moves back behind the pawn shop counter.

"I'm gonna give you my number, man. Let me know if you want to work out sometime. I could help you with it. Used to train a bunch of guys."

He jots my number down and slides the card into his pocket. "Thanks, man. Means a lot." He holds his hand out. "Patrick Rice."

"Barrett. Drake," I tack on. No reason to be evasive. Not anymore.

Sean Eddins is an old Ranger. He's short and round around the middle, with a brown comb-over and delicate, silver wire-rimmed reading glasses. His office is on the second floor of a downtown office building where he's the only mental health professional in the unit. To get to it, I have to walk by the offices of two CPAs, a masseuse, a pediatric dentist, and a cosmetic salesperson. There's a small, gold nameplate on his door.

"Doc" it says. That's all.

The door opens before I close my hand around the handle. I can't help laughing.

"Good ears."

He gives a deep, belly laugh, slaps me hard between the shoulder blades, and waves to a lumpy, corduroy couch in the small, dimly-lit office.

When he asks about my background, I say spec ops, and after a minute cop to Delta Force, newly known as ACE.

"I could kind of guess that way," he tells me. Like most other people around here, the guy has a drawl. His voice is low and always kind of soft, I find. We spend the first half-hour talking like two new acquaintances, which he tells me in the second half-hour he did for my benefit, because he knew I'd want to know a lot about him.

"Just makin' it easier for yeh."

I find out he's 53, an Army brat who graduated high school in Daytona Beach and went to boot camp as soon as he could to escape his dad, a Vietnam vet who had a drug problem.

When he says, "My mom had died when I was younger," I feel chills race over my arms.

"Yours too?"

I manage to nod. He gives me just a second to say more, and when I don't, he doesn't miss a beat. I find it easy to tell him I'm here to get help with nightmares.

"Can you tell me more about them?" he asks.

My throat seizes up, and I'm stunned to find I can't.

"Not the fun kind," he says, jotting something down on a notepad.

I shake my head. My jaw is clenched. I haveto unlock it and take a slow, careful breath so I can say, "About my friend. He…" I swallow hard, fisting one hand on my knee. I shake my head.

"It's okay. I'm not timing you."

I feel my eyes get hot. My face feels hot too.

"I got myself into a bad situation. Stupid," I choke out. "He got hit after he put me in the Bradley."

I can tell by Sean's face that I like him. He doesn't look falsely upset, like he knew Breck, but he's not wearing a poker face, either. I can tell he cares. I feel like maybe he gets it. I don't know. I can't seem to say anything more. There's an awkward few seconds where I try to think of what else I could say, and can't.

"What's his name?" he asks evenly.

"Breck. John," I add. "We called him Breck."

"Breck from Breckenridge?"

I nod, impressed he knows. Most people wouldn't think of Breck as a shorthand for Breckenridge. Most people probably haven't been there.

"Great slopes," he says quietly.

I grit my teeth. What is it about this place that makes me want to fucking cry? I decide as I tell him superficially about how I knew Breck that being here makes me feel like a fuck up. I knew it anyway, but this makes it seem official. I can't control myself. I can't stop the dreams. Not even with Gwen beside me.

"How long has this been bothering you? The nightmares?"

I take a deep breath. Let it slowly out. "A while." I rub my head, remembering. "Breck used to wake me up."

"Bunkmates?"

I nod.

"Long gun?" he asks, arching a brow at me. I'm impressed he knows the Operator term for sniper, though I guess I shouldn't be surprised.

"Yeah. Both of us." I tell him about Dove and Blue as well. How I met Breck and Blue—"his real name's Michael"—at basic. They joined together. Families knew each other. They both went to boarding school at Carson Long."

"John Ferrara?"

My throat locks up. I can't even nod.

Doc nods, his features soft. "Good guy, I heard."

I don't even plan it. I just stand up and walk out of his office, right down the hall, jog down the stairs, and outside where I stand with my back against the wall and wonder what would stop the pain inside my chest, what sort of damage I could do outside that might ease the hurricane of pain inside.

Good guy...

He was. He was.

Breck was a good guy. Breck should be alive.

"Aw now, I thought I had lost you." Sean's right there, his hand on my back, tapping. I blink, turning to him.

"Sorry." I look down at my feet. He must think I'm such a fucking loose cannon. Not much of an Operator if I can't even—

"Want to come back up? Tell me what set you off?"

I swallow back the urge to snap at him—or turn around and run the other fucking way.

"I don't," I say stiffly.

"You don't have to."

"You said he's a good guy. How'd you know that?" I look him in the face because I want to see his eyes.

"Read the obit," he says.

"And the obit told you he was a good guy?"

I can see the hesitation on his face. "Just heard in certain circles. People talk, you know."

"When an Operator dies. Yeah, they talk."

"What do you mean by that?"

"People talk. Opinions, assholes…"

He chuckles. "Opinions are like assholes, and most of them stink. Come back upstairs with me, and tell me what the talk was about Breck's death."

I look him up and down. "How long were you a Ranger?"

"Thirteen years," he says. He lifts his shirt up, revealing a long, jagged scar along his ribs.

"Blown up around the time that Baghdad fell. IED our bomb guy couldn't get."

I nod, forcing myself to look at the ruined skin. Because I know how much it sucks when someone looks away. If they can't see it, how can you live with it?

I nod.

"It blows." He chuckles. He heads inside, and I follow him up. Not because I have to, but because I know I need to try. For Gwen, and maybe me as well.

I feel like shit the whole walk up, and when I sit back on his couch, I feel that detached cold come over me.

I see him roll his chair over and feel him tap my forearm.

"Hey, guy. Look up here at me, will yeh?"

It takes some effort, but I do it.

"I've got white eyelashes. Blond, really. Since birth. Can you see them, or does it just look like I don't have any?"

I look down at my hand, where his finger is tapping, then back up at his eyes. I can see eyelashes. I nod.

"See them?"

"Yeah." Embarrassment moves through me, followed by a wash of prickly heat. Somewhere distant, I know I should say something to explain my weird behavior, but I can't think of anything. My brain feels like it's wrapped in cotton.

Sean moves away. "Can you tell me how many blue things you see in this room?"

I frown. Did he say *blue* things?

"Just look around the room and point if you see something blue?"

"The clock," I manage. Then it's just too hard to shake it off. I feel too numb.

I see him reach into his pocket. That makes me flinch.

"Oh, okay. No reaching into the pockets. I think I can handle that." He hands me something small. "Can you open this?"

I feel a pinch of panic through the cool blanket that's over me. I hold up my left hand, shake my head.

"That's right. Let's see…" He opens it and holds it out to me. "Smell that?"

It smells like peppermints.

My head starts to hurt. I'm startled when I look around, at where I am. At—Who is—Oh. Sean.

"Doc," I murmur.

"How do ya feel? I think you took a little trip. Dissociated. People do that often here. Must be the décor."

I give a shaky laugh. Is this guy serious?

"I'm going to guess you didn't start doing that yesterday," he says. "Keep that peppermint oil up by your nose. Smells can help. I want to ask you a few questions about your body, how it feels right now. They're easy ones. Then we can talk about football."

"Cold and…foggy. Like I'm under a blanket. Or a cloud." I rub my forehead.

"Hard to talk?"

My chest feels heavy and numb, even now, but I manage, "Yeah."

Doc's face is kind without pity, blunt but not exaggerated. "Look," he blinks and leans forward, "it's not unusual. It's a learned response to trauma. Anyone who's been to war, they've got some trauma." He lifts a shoulder, like we're talking about sports. "It's something I see all the time. Something we can work on."

Fuck, that's kind of good to hear.

"Hard to move around and think straight when it happens?" he asks.

I nod.

He points to a tall, blue mug on the table out in front of me. "I've got some crayons in there," he says. "Next time we really talk, I'm going to have you color me a picture. That should make it easier to stay. We'll go slower. Fast or slow as you want. I'll know you better after a while. Then we can really work on things."

We spend the rest of the session discussing the basics, like where I live and how I came to Gatlinburg. I have to be evasive about why I came here. I hope that doesn't fuck things up, but I don't feel like I have much of a choice. He asks if I know people here, and I tell him I've gotten to know my neighbor. It's discreet, but not enough. I can't downplay it that much.

Making an effort not to tap my leg or otherwise fidget, I keep my tone flat and tell him, "We're seeing each other."

His brows raise.

"What?" It's sharper intended.

"How is that going?" he asks.

I rub my aching eyes. "Fucking good." I let a breath out. "It's the only thing that's easy right now."

I can tell by the twist of his lips that he is skeptical.

"You think I'm…what? I shouldn't be with her? Because of all this shit?"

His eyes widen slightly.

I shake my head, my heart pounding. "C'mon, I saw your little mouth thing there. Why don't you share your thoughts, Doc?"

His lips press together, like he's thinking. Fury builds within me, sharp like fear but tight and hot like anger.

"Do you?" he asks. Both of his bushy brows lift. "Do you think you shouldn't? Because my 'look'?" He shrugs. "Sympathy."

I blow my breath out.

Doc's lips press together in a little smile. "Next time, maybe you can tell me what about this new relationship is worrying you. In the meantime," he shuts his notepad and slides it into a pocket on his chair. "Write your nightmares out, after you have them. Every detail you can think of. Bring the notebook here. If you have problems with it, if it's too much, let me know tomorrow." He smiles. "Tomorrow? Do you have time and desire to come see me again?"

A tired feeling moves through me, painting me from my forehead down to my knees. I find myself nodding. My mouth opens, but no words come.

Doc puts a hand on my shoulder. "This was good."

I move in to shake his other hand. He's not a squeezer. Guess he doesn't have to prove himself when he's got that little notepad. "Sorry for…" I shake my head.

"No apology required. You good to drive?"

I snort, as if it's funny, even though we both know that it's not. "I'm good."

Before I get on the bike, I pull a knife out of my seat bag and make a little cut inside my ankle. Shit like that helps me keep from drifting, and I want to make it home to Gwen.

As soon as I get through the side door, I see soup and bread on the table. My stomach growls. Gwen is at the sink. She puts a towel down and strides toward me.

"Hey…" She grabs my hands and looks up into my face. "How did it go?"

I find I'm waiting for her to come closer. When she doesn't, I step closer and pull her up against me.

I can't think of anything to say.

Her arms squeeze me. "I'm glad to have you back. It's kind of lonely here without you."

"Thanks."

I'm surprised to find I want to talk to her. I want to tell her that he said Breck was a nice guy.

Oh fuck. My stomach seizes up. I let go of Gwen and lunge toward the sink. I shut my eyes and try to fight the sick feeling back down.

I feel Gwen beside me. "It's okay. I have bleach spray underneath the counter."

I can't help laughing. Gwen's trying to get me to barf in her sink. Somehow that pulls me out of it. I turn slowly to face her, smiling even though I still feel like someone scrambled all my insides.

"It was hard, huh?"

My jaw clenches, aching. I set my gaze down on my shoes. I don't want this. I don't want to keep being this way in front of her. Why can't I just be normal?

Gwen's hand catches mine, her pinky finger hooking through mine in this gentle, flirty way that makes me smile.

"Want me to tell you a funny story about my first time in therapy after my wreck?"

My stomach bottoms out again. I force myself to nod through it.

"Come sit down—if you want, that is." We move toward the table together. Gwen guides me into a chair and takes the one beside me. "Beer cheese soup."

"Smells amazing."

"So," she says, spreading a napkin in her lap, "I was taking anti-seizure meds, and something else too. Who even knows what. I was having bad headaches then, after the craniotomy I had those for a while, so could have been some kind of painkiller. They tried the low-dose thing, but that doesn't really work for me, so I was out of it." She laughs and shakes her head. "But I freaked out anyway and tried to run away. Of course, I was still using a wheel chair, so that didn't work out well. I ended up rolling uncontrollably down this long ramp outside the building." She cackles, covering her mouth. "And I crashed into this old man on crutches. He called me inconsiderate and asked what happened to my face. I was too doped up to think of something good to say so I said, 'Your mom.'"

Gwenna's silly face makes me laugh even though the picture she paints doesn't. She howls and has to wipe her eyes.

"I wish you could have seen it. He was small and skinny, like this mean little old bird. Had to grab the rail to keep from face-planting." Her eyes shut as she shakes her head. She's smiling softly when she opens them, her eyes glowing as she looks at me. "So, did you mow anybody down?"

"Can't say I did."

"Well, I'm calling a win."

Somehow, Gwen pulls me through dinner. I polish off a bowl of soup and a bunch of that good bread she makes, her leg hooked through mine under the table. Then we settle on the couch. I lay across it and Gwen stretches out between my legs. She rests her cheek on my chest, with her back to the couch's spine.

We watch an episode of *30 Rock* that's old to Gwen and new to me, but I can't focus. I can't think of anything but Breck. My chest and shoulders ache, as if they're trying to cave in on themselves. My stomach feels weird and unsteady, like a hole is growing there.

I wrap my arm around her shoulders, and I think of talking to her. But I can't. I shouldn't. If it's going to last with her, I can't take more than I already do. It's one of the only vows I've made regarding her. That all the time I'm with her, I'll try to do good. Be good. She doesn't need my darkness.

When she snuggles against my chest and turns her big brown eyes on me, I tell her I'm okay. When she turns to me and unbuttons my pants, I welcome her hands on my hungry cock. Before I lose control, I find my way inside her, fucking her slowly at first, then faster, harder, until she's almost crying. Then she comes and she does cry.

"Too good," she giggles, wiping her eyes.

I savor the word, trying to hold it in my mind, let it expand to fill my whole head.

"You're good," I whisper.

"We are."

But she's wrong. Gwenna's everything that's good. I just have to change until I'm someone better.

chapter eleven

Gwenna

The next few weeks are something like magic. Barrett sees his therapist, Sean, two days in a row, then every other day for four more days. His nightmares go unchecked until he comes home with a prescription for Prazosin from Sean's partner, a psychiatrist.

"I don't know if I'll take it. I told Sean that."

"I tried it for a while."

"And?"

I rub his leg with mine under the dinner table. "I thought it kind of helped. It made me dizzy. But I got some sleep before I went off it."

He passes me the folded paper. I open it. "So just one pill right before bed? That's a pretty low dose. I have that in a drawer here. You don't have to fill this if you want to try mine."

He nods, chewing tenderloin. The subject drops while we make ice cream: Bear's idea—something he and his brothers used to do with their mom on their back porch. We have sex on the armchair in the den, and while I slip off to the bathroom, Bear slips into the garage to pluck a petal from one of my gardenias. I find him cupping it in his big hand, looking embarrassed.

I grin. "How's all that going? Blossoming?" I tease.

He smiles. "You can probably bring them in soon. Even now."

"I'll let you do that."

He does the dishes while I package some stuffed bears and watch Papa on the tracking software. He's not staying in one spot, which is strange, so I've been monitoring him. No sign of anything odd, and definitely no humans, so that's good.

When I go back into the kitchen half an hour later, one of my gardenias is in the center of the table.

The dishwasher is going, and Barrett's leaning against the counter going at a block of wood with—

"What is that?"

He stops carving and smirks. He holds a knife up. "This?"

"What is that?"

He turns the block of wood around. I laugh. "A pig!"

"For you, my dear." He grins.

I throw my head back laughing. "That's—adorable. So I'm Piglet now forever, am I?"

"Pig and Bear. Next thing I do, I'll do us both."

"That sounds dirty."

He arches one brow. "Dirty Piglets need baths."

We find ourselves lying underneath the shower water, fucking more like rabbits than a pig and bear. After that, we watch *The Princess Bride* while Barrett whittles the pig's flank, and after that, I brush my teeth. When I come out, he asks for one of my Prazosin.

We go to bed wrapped in each other's arms and Barrett wakes me up some time later, his hand locked around my upper arm.

"Gwen?"

I frown up at him. Is he…standing by the bed? His face is troubled. "What's wrong?"

"I'm sorry…I can't stand up straight."

"Ohhh...I see." I sit up, take his shoulders. "It's okay. Can you get on the bed?"

"I don't know. Fuck." There's a cord of desperation in his voice that makes my heart twist.

"It's okay..." I slide down with him, and we sit together on the floor.

"What woke you up?" I murmur.

"Thirsty I think."

I stroke his hair. "Do you feel sick, or just dizzy?"

"I don't like being dizzy."

"I'm sorry."

He draws his knees up, rests his temple against one of them, and I take his hand.

"I should have thought about it," he says roughly.

"Thought about what?"

His hand squeezes mine. I see his shoulders rise. "Reminds me of Landstuhl."

Oh. The U.S. Army hospital in Germany, where he went after the awful day on which his friend was killed and he was so hurt.

"I'm so sorry," I whisper.

I scoot close to him and wrap an arm around his back... another one around his front, until I've pulled him into my arms. I wrap my legs around him, too, and lean against my bed. Barrett's weight is heavy on me.

I take a tiny trigger risk, stroking his hair over his scar. I try to think of what it must have been like for him: waking up at Landstuhl. The first time he was fully aware of what had happened to him. I've looked up epidural hematoma since he mentioned it, and if I'm correct, he would have had a period of normal consciousness after he first got hurt, maybe when he and his friend Breck were making their way to the armored car. During the time his friend died, too. And after that, he would have not really been conscious for a while. They probably drilled some holes to relieve pressure at the nearby hospital, and if I was betting, I would put money on the fact that they did the full-scale craniotomy in Germany to get him really stable.

"Was anybody with you there?"

He shakes his head.

I struggle to swallow.

"I had the shrapnel wound. The craniotomy."

So he probably woke up sedated, having no idea what had happened, with tubes everywhere, a piece of his skull removed and then screwed back together with titanium plates, a drain going into the site of the surgery…

"I remember waking up," I murmur. "I was scared. I had a lot of people there…and it was terrible, still."

I kiss his temple.

Barrett pulls away from me, or rather sits up straighter. His hand squeezes mine. His eyes on mine look depthless.

"I wish I had been there with you."

His lips find my forehead…then my mouth. We kiss sweetly, then harder, then he pulls away, his shoulders heaving.

His eyes shut.

"Some of the nurses there were German. Some were American. When I first woke up…I had trouble talking. Not for long. Just for a few days while my brain was still swollen. The doctors were busy. Lots of bad shit happening, a lot of wounded coming in. They would be in and out, the nurses would. They'd have to turn me over to get to my back. I couldn't move my body. Too doped up and…I don't know." His hand goes to his head. "Maybe the swelling. I don't remember it that well. I just remember, they would turn me on my side and…touch me. Just my head…and back. I had a tube in my nose…"

"G-tube. I had one of those too."

He nods. His hand covers my cheek.

"They would talk about me like I wasn't there. Like they would say, 'You've got those pretty eyes,' and, to each other, 'It's sad that he's blind in that eye. Wonder how much he'll recover' and 'why is no one here.' One of them said once, 'Maybe he's an asshole.'" He shakes his head. "They were the only people touching me. The IVs." I see him struggle to swallow. "They had to change the catheter. All this shit that made me think about…my mom dying. I was always dizzy."

"When I came to more, and thought about Breck…" Tears fill his eyes. My heart feels shredded. "I could talk, but I didn't care enough. They kept testing my hand." He draws into to himself, shaking his head.

"You were by yourself. You probably needed someone with you. Kellan couldn't come, I guess?"

"He'd had his relapse. But he wasn't talking to me. Just a little bit. Because…of Lyon," he says with difficulty.

"What about your dad?"

He laughs, a small, dry kind of sound. "Tight OR schedule." The words are bitter. I don't even think he tries to hide it.

I think of lying in my own bed, wishing to be held. Crying underneath my covers for Elvie, who'd left me.

"I think I might write the dreams down." He hugs me, and in a quiet voice, says, "Tell me it was different for you, Piglet."

"I had parents there. My brother. Jamie. I talked right away, even though I cried all day too. But my boyfriend never came. He went on a study abroad program. Just couldn't handle it I guess."

Barrett's eyes are hard. "I'm glad you're not with that asshole, but him leaving like that? It makes me want to kill him."

"It was for the best. He was all about himself, Elvie was. With parents like his, he'd been raised to think he was the second coming, there to rapture country music fans. I can tell he still thinks that. I've watched an interview or two."

"I don't care. I still want to hurt that bastard."

"It was hard, him leaving me like that. I think his parents were embarrassed. Felt bad."

"I hope they did."

"Want to lay down here on the floor and go to sleep?"

"I'll try getting up."

We go to sleep with my head on Bear's chest, his arms around me.

"I won't leave you." That sweet promise is the last thing I hear before I drift off.

The next night, I find Barrett in the bathroom rug with a little yellow reporter's notepad on his lap.

He looks beautiful in the dim lamplight. His eyes are heavy and his face is drawn, but something about the way he's sprawled out, legs out, one knee raised, his bare, broad back against my wall, makes him look fierce.

I step partially in the small room. "Hey, you."

His face is tight.

"Just checking on you. I can go now."

"No."

He holds his hand out, and I go sit by him. I lean my head against his bicep...take his hand when he offers it. With no prompting, he passes me the notebook.

I arch a brow, and he nods once, and then looks down at his lap.

I'M DRIVING AND THERE'S MOONLIGHT, EVERYTHING IS COATED IN A WHITE SHEEN. I'M CRYING AND AN ANGEL FALLS. THE BLOOD IS EVERYWHERE. I CALL FOR BRECK. HE COMES AND HELPS ME. HE TAKES ME AWAY IN ANOTHER CAR. I GET SICK.

There's a few blank lines and then:

EDIT—

I'M DRIVING. I HIT A SNOW BANK. EXCEPT IT ISN'T SNOW. IT'S SAND. THE SAND SCATTERS EVERYWHERE. I KEEP DRIVING. BRECK AND I LISTEN TO THE RADIO.

I hand it back to him and lean my head against his arm again.

"That looks good. That's how I did it, too."

He moves so that his arm is behind me.

"Sean wants me to bring it every time."

"When you talk about it over and over, it will become boring."

He smirks, but it's a sad smirk, like he can't believe that's true.

"I've never understood time," he says in a low voice. His eyes hold mine. "I saw a quote once—Einstein, maybe?—that said time exists so everything doesn't happen all at once. I wish I was there for you like you are for me."

"What do you mean?"

He squeezes me against him. I feel him inhale, but he just shakes his head. He stands up. "Back to bed?"

He helps me up. I go with him.

As we get back into bed, I see his phone light up. He grabs it. "Dove."

"Did you say Dove?"

He frowns down at the phone, then puts it back on his nightstand.

"Seth," he says.

I nod. I've heard him mention his friend before.

I wonder why the name Dove made me feel so weird just now. Maybe I'm just tired and delirious.

We go to sleep together. The next morning, we go into town on his Harley—me wearing the helmet he grabbed me the other day—and look at the studio again.

"What do you think?" he asks me with his big hands in his pockets.

"I like it. It's in a good location."

I go use the restroom and when I come back, he's hanging up with Mallorie.

"I'm making an offer."

I squeal and he swings me around the empty space.

"You want to ride bikes home?"

"Um...huh?"

"You told me you used to love to ride your bike. When's the last time you had a bike?"

"I don't even know."

"Let's get some. On me."

I laugh. "That's crazy?"

"And?" He grins and kisses my nose. "C'mon. Any color you want. There's a bike shop half a block away."

"You and your GPS."

"You think it's hot," he teases.

I giggle. "I totally do."

Holding hands, we walk down the block and exit the bike shop with matching royal blue Giant bikes. Barrett's got a charcoal helmet; mine is lime green.

"You think we should ride these home?"

He laughs. "Gwen. How else will we get them there?"

"We could stash them in the studio?"

"The one we don't own yet?" My heart leaps a little. "We."

His fingers grip my chin loosely. "I know you're not scared of a little bike ride."

"It's on a big road. What if someone hits us?"

"There's a wide bike lane. I looked. I'll ride on the outside."

"No way." I grab his hand and squeeze and end up kissing his knuckles. "Gotta protect my prince charming."

I get the small, sweet smile. "Are you my princess?"

"Yes."

The ride home takes about an hour, and by the time we reach the top of my driveway, all the endorphins swimming through my brain have made me giddy.

"I feel great!"

Barrett takes his helmet off and leans his head back. His chest swells with a deep, half-panted breath. "Me, too."

Damn...His curls are dark and pasted to his perfectly-shaped head. His temple and throat are damp with sweat. His beard, which he trimmed to just scruff last night, looks so freaking sexy; I just want to lick him.

I take my helmet off, and his eyes roll up and down me. He takes my bike's handle. "Why don't you go inside? Wait for me on the coffee table?"

My neck flushes.

"No?" His eyebrows lift.

"How do you always know?"

"Know what?" He smirks.

"When I want it."

"Because," he says darkly. His hand slaps my backside. "I do, too."

I scamper in and wait for him, bent over the coffee table, even though I feel insane. He uses a secret agent trick to come inside without making a sound, so the first thing I know of him is his hands pulling my pants down, his fingers delving into my slick pussy.

He's rougher than usual; he seems hungrier. Like he needs it bad. It's so, so hot, I come before he has his dick inside me. Barrett flips me over on my back, my legs hanging off the table, bent at the knees. He spreads me with his fingers, rubs his tip around my slickness, and then pushes in.

The table is just the right height so he's neither standing nor fully crouching, more like leaning over and driving into me. He holds my arms and nibbles at my breasts. After we're finished, we get in the bath and Barrett rubs my shoulders till I think I might just slip into the soapy water.

The next few days are much the same. We bike downtown and get coffee or hot chocolate, grab some lunch, drop by the studio, to which Mallorie gave Bear a key, and make plans for what we'll do with the interior if the owner accepts Bear's offer.

Finally, a few nights before Thanksgiving, Mallorie calls Bear and tells him she heard from the owner, who accepted his offer.

We celebrate with a long walk through the dark woods, making a pit stop to have sex in the stock shed before winding up in the attic library looking at the stars. I fall asleep on Barrett's chest, and when he wakes us both up sometime later murmuring curse words, he just blinks at me a few times and says he's okay.

Most of our stuff is still at my house, so we walk there hand in hand. When we get inside, he sits down on the couch, his legs slightly spread, his head leaned back against the couch's spine.

His hands are lightly fisted on his thighs.

"You want some water…or hot chocolate?"

When he doesn't answer me—I see him swallow—I sit down beside him. I take his hand and trail my fingertip over his knuckles. They're marked with lots of little scars that make me wonder what his life was like before he retired.

"I love your hands."

I bring the left one up and kiss the thick callous on his palm between his thumb and index finger.

"Why'd you do that?" he rasps, his eyes cracking open.

I shut my eyes, letting my lips trail over the spot. "It's from shooting, isn't it?"

He tries to pull his hand away. I press it over my mouth, look at him over his fingertips.

"I thought it could use some TLC, that's all. I didn't mean to upset you."

I loosen my grip on his hand, waiting for him to pull away. Instead, I feel his arm relax, even as his eyes shut and his face tenses.

"Why?"

"Why what?"

"Why did you think that?" he rasps.

I kiss the callous again. "This is where I think most of your memories come from. The dreams." I press his palm against my mouth, drag his hand up so it's curved around my brow. I kiss his wrist.

"Maybe it's a mark from another Barrett...one I'm never going to know. But it's on your hand, and I love your hand."

He sits up, hugs me close, and presses my cheek to his neck. "Why are you so good?"

"Why are you?"

"I'm not." His body goes tense and still. I bite his neck.

"You are so. Come to Thanksgiving at my mom's with me?"

He frowns down at me. "When's Thanksgiving?"

"Two days from now." I giggle.

"Damn."

"So that's a yes?"

"Who all's coming?"

I shove his chest. "You, me, and some other people. Jerk."

He shuts his eyes and shakes his head. "I'll go." A faint smile touches his lips. "You know I'll go, Piglet."

chapter twelve

Gwenna

Thanksgiving starts off freaking amazing. Like, *amazing*. Mom opens her front door wearing an apron and sporting an oven mitt, the smell of macaroni wafting out around her. Barrett smiles roguishly and holds his hand out, but the second my mom's eyes hit his face, she freezes up—completely obvious—and just stands there gawking, finally blurting out, "So you're my daughter's *hero!*"

Mom knows just the basics about Bear, so she can't know how perfect those words are. How they're exactly what he needs to feel welcome and wanted at my family's Thanksgiving.

Mom hugs him with warm, maternal affection, and I watch Bear's face from the side. He looks surprisingly relaxed, maybe even peaceful.

"It's so nice to meet you, Barrett." Mom reaches for his hair, her fingertips not quite touching it. "Look at those beautiful curls. Gwenna didn't tell me you're a model, too."

Barrett's face blanches. My mom falters. "I'm just teasing you. Come on inside, you two." We step into the foyer, and Mom hugs me to her flower-speckled apron. "You look beautiful, sweetheart."

"So do you, Mom."

When she pulls away, I note the red "Hers" on the black apron, and I try not to let it throw me.

Holidays without my dad feel strange, wrong even. But this is the new normal. Just like old Barrett is gone, life before my dad died is not the life I have now. And I can be sad about it, and miss him, but I can't let it ruin what I have in this moment.

"Come into the kitchen. Rett and Laura beat you here, and Mee-Maw will be pulling up any time now."

I watch Barrett look around my mother's glossy, high-end home. It's not as casual as my cabin. Mom has good taste, and she loves to decorate. I don't think someone who didn't know him would be able to tell that he is checking out the details, but I can tell because his eyes aren't on me, and as we walk down the hallway toward the kitchen, he's not focused on my mom either.

I make a mental note to ask him later if he's mapping an escape route, and then we're in the kitchen. Rett and Laura are both coming off the bar stools, ready to hug us.

Laura is Rett's newish girlfriend. She's only twenty-four, a fellow teacher at his school, and I think she's adorable. Pink hair, wire-rimmed glasses, and a little pixie face. She's sweet and energetic, and she seems to adore Rett.

Turns out, Barrett is a decently ardent baseball fan, so when Rett starts chattering about obscure baseball stuff, Bear can bat the ball right back. They hit it off better than I could have dreamed, and Laura, Mom, and I work on the food until my Mee-Maw shows up from the assisted living complex she's been in since she broke her hip last year.

We have a peaceful afternoon, and I feel so thankful. Barrett holds my hand under the table, and instead of being awkward about his combat the way I had worried he might be, he seems to enjoy regaling the table with tales of his exploits. He tells a story about feeding an injured owl food from his MRE, and then another one about him and some people from his "unit" going skiing with the president.

"Oh my goodness! Which one?" my grandma asks.

"President Obama," Barrett says between chewing his turkey.

"That man…I'm a big fan," my Mee-Maw says. "I've got the bumper sticker."

Barrett and I haven't really gotten too much into politics. I say a silent prayer he's not a Tea Party conservative, and if he is, he won't mention it to Mee-Maw. She's got a pacemaker, after all.

As it turns out, he and Mee-Maw get drawn into a long political discussion. Mom and I exchange nervous glances at first, but Barrett takes things issue by issue and point by point, so careful even I can't tell exactly what his politics are. By the time that portion of our discussion ends, everyone is still happy. I stroke his leg under the table, veering up to brush between his legs. He hooks his foot behind my ankle and rubs his leg against mine.

"Who wants dessert?" my mom asks.

Things roll on at such a cosmically wonderful pace, the conversation good, the spirits bright, I can't help thinking that Dad is watching over us today. After the food, Mom shows us her newest sculpture. At this stage, it's just a woman hunched over. Mom tells us her plans for it, and Barrett watches her with what looks like awe.

He asks several insightful questions before I remember, belatedly, his own mother was an artist. And Barrett carves, or whittles. So of course he would care.

I take his hand as we go back inside, and he and I drift upstairs to the study.

We kiss and touch each other gently.

"Doing okay?" I murmur.

"More than okay. This has been…nice."

"Mom likes you. I think they all do."

"I like you," he says. "And them."

I relish the warmth of his skin under my hands as I trail up and down his sides under his shirt.

"You better not try that here."

I giggle. "Not game at my mom's house?"

"Fuck, no." He chuckles and stands up. He casts his eyes downward and sighs, and I laugh.

"Down boy."

He rubs his big hand over it, and I groan.

"I've got something that will help." I pull him over to a portrait of my dad, and we spend the next half-hour talking all about him. Barrett stands close to me the whole time and takes my hand when we move from the library into the guest room that I use as mine.

After a while we go back downstairs, say bye to Mee-Maw, who's trying to get back home early to spend some time with her new boyfriend, Herbert.

I find home videos in the DVD player, and so begins an hour of personal torture, with Mom and Rett exposing all my most embarrassing moments. At the end of the video, there's static, followed by a view of a pink room—wait, a white room. Just looks pink to me. *A hospital room.*

My stomach nosedives.

"Mom," I whisper.

The room goes silent as the TV beeps the sound of monitors and puffs the awful ventilator noise and Barrett's eyes cling to the screen, where I lie swollen, bruised, and stained. Even as he holds the camera, Dad's breathing is heavy and emotional.

I watch the blood drain out of Barrett's cheeks and feel my own head spin.

"I'm sorry, I didn't realize..." Mom jumps up.

I stalk out of the room, fly out the back door, and dash around to the side of my mom's sculpting shed. I wrap my arms around myself and lean my head against the wall. A few seconds later, I hear Barrett coming through the grass and feel his hands on my back.

"Gwen." He clasps my shoulders and turns me toward him, enfolding me against his hard chest.

One arm wraps around my head as if he's trying to protect my mind from its own lousy memories. I feel his body stiffen, then he lets a long breath out. He just breathes for a minute, and my eyes sting.

I can hear his heart pound through his chest. I think I feel a little twitch of his muscles, but—

"Bear?" I rub his shoulder. I don't know if it's his rigid posture or some other nonverbal SOS he's sending out, but I can feel his distress. I realize: *his nightmares*. If he dreams of me being hurt, I wonder if the video was triggering. God, it must have been.

"Baby. Hey…" I wrap my arms around him, stroke his sides and arms, and still he doesn't move.

"Bear." I touch his neck. "Are you okay?"

He lifts his head. His face is pale. His eyes are red.

"What's wrong?"

He stares at the wall behind me. "Nothing," he rasps.

"C'mon now…We can't go with that: *nothing*." I smile a little, trying to tease.

His face grows even more anguished. His mouth goes soft and fluid. "Seeing you like that…" He shakes his head. He rubs his forehead. He lets go of me and turns away, facing the fence-line at the back of my mom's yard. I can see one hand is raised to his face.

I stand there frozen, not sure what to do or say. Thank goodness, he turns back around a second later.

"Sorry." He shakes his head, rubbing his hand over his eyes. "You want to go back in?" He tries to smile, and it's a total smile fail.

"Sure." I step to him and wrap my arms around his waist. My sweet Bear. "You know I'm okay now, yeah? And so are you? And we're together?"

He hugs me tightly against him. "Yeah." The words are soft. "It's just…hard to see you like that." His hand strokes my hair.

"It wasn't easy for me to see that, either. And if I had seen you like that, I would feel the same way, too."

We stand there hugging for a few more breaths, and then, hands clasped, we head into the house.

My mom is pouring wine. She looks from me to Barrett, back to me. "I'm so sorry, both of you."

"It's okay, Mom. No big deal."

Bear and I both take a glass of pinot. Several hours and a bunch of card games later, we head home. I fall asleep with his big jacket tucked around me like a blanket, his scent sweet in my nose, and a vision of him skiing with the president in my dreams, which turn to nightmares as the snow falls.

Beep…beep….BEEEEPPPPPPPPP.

chapter thirteen

Barrett

I'm not the only one thrown off by that footage of Gwenna in the ICU. Right before we get home, she starts moving all around in her seat, making small, sad sounds. Her chest starts heaving and her eyes fly open, arms flailing to grab onto something. I have the Mini Cooper pulled onto the shoulder before she gets herself upright, my arms around her before she lets out the first whimper. As I rub her back and hair, she settles down.

"I dreamed about you skiing," she whispers.

"What?"

"You were skiing…" Her shoulders tremble. She shakes her head. "I dreamed about the wreck," she rasps.

I press my lips against her hairline and just wait. For her to tell me something. For all I've told her about my shitty past, Gwen hasn't told me much about her accident. I would never push her, but I'd be lying if I said I didn't feel a need to know about it. Seeing her in that bed…

I kiss her forehead and the bridge of her nose and squeeze her, praying to be better than I am. "I've got you, Pig. I won't let go."

"Thank you." Her voice is small and strained. It makes my own throat ache.

I smooth her hair against the back of her head. "I love you."

"I love you too." She squeezes me tightly, and then she pulls away. "Wow, you pulled over. Sorry."

"Don't be sorry. You okay now? Want to talk about it?"

She gives me a funny little smile.

I smirk. "Talking helps, that's what I'm told."

She smiles wanly.

I give her one last kiss before we start back home. We play music loud and Gwenna holds my hand, and I try not to think of what she said.

"You were skiing..."

The next morning, I've got a meeting with a vendor to measure for cubbies on one wall of the studio. Gwen's still sleeping when it's time to go. I kiss her head and leave a Reese's Peanut Butter Christmas tree thing on her nightstand. Her mom passed me a bag of them on our way out the door and told me that they're Gwen's favorite.

I intentionally make a little noise as I get dressed, because, pathetic as it is, I want her to go with me. But she's sleeping pretty hard, and her sleep doesn't seem troubled, so I can't justify waking her up. As I walk out the door, I get a call from Dove and hit the 'fuck you' button.

I'll find time to call him soon. I haven't been able to track Blue anymore. I think he ditched his car. But Dove will have told him I'm not planning to do it, so there's no reason for Bluebell to try to interfere.

I feel peaceful as I ride my motorcycle toward town. Tomorrow, I have an appointment with Sean. I'm supposed to go over my notebook. I had a nightmare last night—Gwen, of course—and wrote it down for him. I wrote it in Italian because I don't want Gwen herself to read it. But I can be open, or almost open, with Sean. So I guess I will be.

I think of what Gwen said about adding some more rocks to the enclosure. I've been thinking of buying a truck. Maybe if she's still sleeping when I leave the studio, I'll swing by a dealership. I'd love to drive her around in something safer than that little Mini Cooper...

Gwenna

I think there's something wrong with Papa. All my other bear babies are tucked into hollowed trees, thick underbrush, or little coves spread over the 300-plus acreage, and Papa was, too—for a while.

In the last week, though, he's been unusually restless. Bears have social things they do before they hibernate, and even bears that live in climates too warm for "true hibernation" do these things. I've narcissistically wondered once or twice if Papa wanted to see me again, and for this reason, I've avoided the enclosure, even postponing a scheduled trip inside the day before yesterday, hoping Papa will settle down and get some rest. Instead, I wake to find his little green dot on my phone's screen positioned right inside the gate of the enclosure.

Weird.

I move into my office, watching on the cams, but I can't see anything out of the ordinary. Just Papa, moved from the gate over to the pond, where he is walking by the water. I check the temperature outside. With all this El Nino stuff, I wonder if maybe the warm days are messing up his hibernation or something. But the weather app on my phone says it's 39 degrees. Cold.

I have a flash of memory of my dream from the car: Barrett, racing down the slopes. At the bottom, he falls, and he and I are wrapped up in the snow they way we were on the rug at his house that night I brought the wine over. The weirdest thing about the dream is, the snow was white. Usually when I see or think of snow post-accident, I see it slightly pink, in keeping with my new reality. Wonder why it was white. Maybe longing for my life before the accident? Wishing I'd met Bear before it happened?

I dress in thermal leggings, a pair of tall, gray Merrill snow boots, and a roomy, dark green fleece from Mountain Hardware. Then I braid my hair and toss it over my shoulder. Just to top it off, I pull on a cream-colored beanie. I can't find the bear spray, and after a few minutes looking, I decide it doesn't really matter. It's just Papa. I trust him.

I take my time walking along the fence line, enjoying the sunlight on my skin, getting lost in my own head as I watch my shadow drift over the planks. By the time I get to the enclosure gate, Papa's dot has receded deeper into the woods. I go inside anyway, figuring I'll wander a little ways past the pond to see if I encounter him.

To my slight disappointment, I don't. I daydream about Barrett, imagining unbuttoning his pants and rubbing my hand along his happy trail as I step out of the enclosure, into a burst of wind. With leaves swirling at my feet and golden sheets of sunlight slanting through the limbs, I think it's beautiful here.

Then the world goes dark.

I'm pulled against a hard chest. Someone's voice is in my ear—a voice I know but can't place. "Shhhh, I'm not going to hurt you. You don't fight and I won't. I just want to talk."

I blink and try to touch my face. He's got me by my wrists. They're pulled behind me, bound together by his large hands.

I hear a low keening noise. Somewhere far away, I know I need to curse and scream and fight and kick, but I'm just frozen. I stumble as he pushes me.

"No—please!" It's half scream, half sob. My pulse is racing so fast now, I can't think straight. I can't breathe. I feel my body fumbling through empty space. My feet land on the ground at odd angles. I'm moaning, my racing mind worried about hurting my ankle even as I know I'VE GOT TO DO SOMETHING, RIGHT NOW!

"*Help!*" I shriek.

His hand is on my face. I notice fabric flapping and realize it's dark because he's put something over my head.

"Good girl," I hear him say, and realize that the ground has slanted downward. The driveway!

SHIT! HE HAS A CAR HERE!

His hands find their way around my wrists again. My brain lights up. This is called a back arm lock, my brain regurgitates. All I have to do is stumble forward and throw one foot behind me, toward his crotch.

I wait until we're almost sprinting down the driveway. Then I feign tripping, and when he loosens his grip on me to keep from tripping, too, I kick behind me, toward his crotch, and feel my shoe connect.

He grunts. I jerk away and fumble forward as I grab the hood off my head. I see in that second that he's wearing one, too.

I can run downhill toward the road, or cut back up toward my house. House! There's a key in my shoe. My body jolts into motion, flying up the incline of the top part of my driveway, kicking rock and dirt behind me.

"Fuck fuck fuck fuck fuck!"

I stop before I reach my porch and reach down toward my foot. My fingers fumble between shoe and sock. I get the key but something hard slams into me, sending me flying, landing on my backside. Pain flares through my lower back and for a moment, I can't move.

He's right there over me, his hands on my shoulders, his black mask face not really black, I realize, but dark camouflage.

"I told you to stay calm!"

I bat at his face like a crazed cat until he grabs my arms. I try to knee him in the crotch but he's not at the right angle.

He laughs. "Feisty."

"What do you want?"

"Just to talk, like—"

I punch him in the face. When his hand flies to his nose, I wriggle out from under him and fly toward the enclosure. Papa, Papa, Papa...save me! I think I may be screaming as I punch the code in: wrong, again, then right. The gate clicks open. I rush in and slam it shut behind me.

"Fuck!" I start to sob. Run to the stock shed. I start running toward the stock shed and am almost there when I hear a loud smack. I whirl and shriek. He jumped the fence *oh God he jumped the fucking fence!*

I fly at the shed's front door, but it's too late. He's on me, hard and harsh; his elbow comes around my neck, I hear him say something but my brain's flying too fast to process. Then there's something sharp in my neck. I feel a blinding flare of heat sing through my body. Before I fall down, I pull his hood off.

I frown up at him and see a fish bowl...

Then the ragged pattern of the fallen leaves engulfs me.

Barrett

Doc is right. The more I write it down, the easier it's getting. I'm going to try the Prazosin again tonight, but half the dose. Or maybe not. Maybe I can just push through. With Gwenna by me, it seems possible.

I wish there was some way I could tell her how much I love her. Something I could do. I remember how much buying my house helped her, and that makes me feel good. As I drive, I see a green and white striped awning that I recognize from satellite view: a florist.

My throat feels tight as I park out in front and walk slowly inside. Behind the counter, there's a girl with shoulder-length black hair and big brown eyes. I feel her gaze roll up and down my body, see the slow curl of her red lips.

"Ziggy Stardust?"

I blink.

She pulls on her blouse. My eyes linger there before I look down at my own ragged-out, charcoal t-shirt.

"Oh." I found it in my bike's seat bag the other day and forgot I pulled it on today. I nod. "Big fan." A surge of prickling heat moves through my body, and I drag my gaze around the room, looking for blue. I latch onto the blue specs in the wallpaper, then tell myself that's all I need, I'm stronger than this.

I step over to the counter. I can feel the heat of the girl's gaze. I feel her eyes on my left hand, but know for sure she's not gawking at my sidelined fingers; I don't think she's even noticed they don't bend. She's checking for a ring.

I give her a smile I hope says *taken*. When my mouth opens, I hear myself say, "I need something for my fiancé."

I watch the girl's eyes comb my face and realize my eyes are wide. My fiancé. "Flowers, and..." I glance around the little gift shop. "I don't know what else you have, but something with a squirrel or pig?"

The girl smiles.

I smile back.

Fuck, it sounds right. *Fiancé.* My heart starts hammering again. I take a deep breath and watch as the girl goes over to a shelf.

"I've got these little coins…They're not real coins, of course. More like paper weights." She smiles over her shoulder. "One has a little squirrel on it. As for pigs, I've got a pig, but it's attached to a bird bath."

She walks across the room and points to a shallow bowl atop a two-feet-tall cement stem. In the middle, there's a pig with wings.

She shrugs. "Not sure if you want something that big."

The pig has the most adorable smile on its face, and a little curly tail. I grin. "I'll take both. And some flowers. Something with gardenias?"

"That's more of a bush. But our florist could maybe work them into something. What about white roses with them? Maybe some eucalyptus, too?" I squint, trying to picture it. "Yeah, sure."

Oh, shit. I laugh. "I've gotta go somewhere." To get that bird bath home, I'll need something bigger than a motorcycle. "I'll be back in an hour, maybe two?"

"Of course."

I pay, slip the little squirrel token into my pocket, and laugh as I walk to my bike.

I pull back up an hour and a half later in a dark charcoal Jeep Grand Cherokee. It's a 2015, with 12,000 miles. The dealer said it was used as a rental car, but it still smells new. I smile as I walk back in to get the flowers and the bird bath. I texted Gwen, but she hasn't replied, so I played a game of how fast can I buy a car. It helped having the full sticker price in my bank account, so all I had to do was call the bank and let them know the debit card was going to take a hit. I was out of there in less than an hour.

The arrangement looks really good. I take the bird bath, in two pieces, to the Jeep, and open the console between the two front seats and put the flower vase in there. Then I text Doc, who lives in an apartment across the street from his office, and ask him to keep an eye on my bike for the next few hours.

I drive to Gwen's house feeling victorious and…happy. Strange feeling, that. I smirk when I think of how few nights I've spent in my own house. Maybe we should move the party there. Or not…

I like her house. It's small, but in a good way. We fill up the space. After years of combat, any open space feels like a threat.

As I turn off the highway onto Blue Moon Road, I feel my phone buzz. Dove. I let it ring so he won't be offended by the fuck you button, but I don't answer. I just want to see Gwen. I'll call D. later. Sometime soon, we need to really talk. I think if I tell him all of it, I can make him understand. I need him to. I need Dove's blessing. Even Blue's—one day. They're my brothers. Without Breck…

I swallow, tossing my phone into the passenger's seat as the Jeep climbs Gwenna's driveway.

I smile as I park behind the garage, anticipating her reaction to the new wheels—and the gifts. She's going to be surprised.

I wonder what she's been doing. She must be really caught up in bear-keeping, because I haven't heard from her.

I slip my keys into my pocket, turning around for a second, walking backward as I smile at my new ride. The garage is shut, so I half-jog to the porch and try the front door. Locked. I feel a tug low in my stomach.

So she's with the bears. That's okay. I don't want to go in, though, so I should call her. I start back to the car and something glints in the grass. My heart clenches. I freeze in place, my diaphragm locked up, waiting for flames, a burst of sound, but whatever it is just shines in the sunlight.

You're here, not there…New person, Barrett.

I take a slow breath and reach down for what I now see is a key. It must have fallen off Pig's key ring. I turn it over. Looks like her house key. I slip it in my pocket, and for reasons I can't articulate, even in my own mind, I turn toward the enclosure. I can jump up on the damn thing and peek inside without disturbing Bearville. I just want to see her—now.

With every step I take toward the gate, my mind feels hazier, my chest feels tighter. I don't know what's getting to me...

God, the dread rolls through in waves. I have to stop before I reach the gate. I think of Breck and try to shut my mind down, but I realize that's what Doc says not to do. I inhale deeply and try to relax, just let what happens, happen. I can see Breck, just a blurry, second-long view of his contorted face; I can almost hear low voices shouting in the Bradley.

I can feel the abject shock, the fucking horror, as I look at him and see he's already half gone. My whole body screams out at the memory of holding Breck and looking down at him. Panic. Agony. Remorse. Shame. Blame. Rage. Desperation.

My throat locks up and I can't seem to get it working right. I step to the gate on weak legs, my hands cold, my head spinning. I just need to get to Gwen.

Gwen...

Gwen...

I watched her so much from up on the hill before I bought the house, I know her password. I pull the door open and for once, the turmoil in my body matches the vision out in front of me.

chapter fourteen

Barrett

The bolt of terror that rips through me is so bright, it whites me out. Awareness returns and I'm on the ground beside her, clutching her limp shoulders, fumbling for her jugular.

My fingers shake…I press down…

Heartbeat.

There's a heartbeat. Okay…

"Gwen?" My hand cups her cheek, fingertips feeling for thick, sticky liquid. "Gwennie, can you hear me?"

When she doesn't move, my hands fly up and down her spine, over her neck, the base of her skull. When I feel nothing wrong there, I wrap one hand around the back of her head and roll her onto her side, my gut clenched, anticipating…

"Ohh." My throat constricts and I'm worried that I'm going to be sick but, "It's okay." There's nothing. No blood or…

"Okay." Christ, I'm panting. I slide my arms beneath her, lift her up onto my lap. I can barely hold onto her, have to clench my hands around her.

"Gwen?"

Her lashes flutter and my stomach clenches hard. "Gwennie... Look at me. Open your eyes."

She does. They roll, so all I see is white. My gaze tears up and down her, seeing no wounds.

"I've got you. I've got you." I stand up with her, stumbling toward the enclosure gate. I'm still well trained enough to comb the ground for footprints—and I see some. Maybe one.

I swallow hard and look down at her. "Pig, it's Barrett. Look up at me. Let me see those pretty eyes I love so much."

My heart clenches, because again, she does. They roll a little, but she holds on. I can see her eyes, all iris, pinpoint pupils. Fuck—"What happened, Gwennie?"

Her face crumples as she starts to cry.

I hold her tighter as my heart pounds. "What's the matter? Are you hurt?"

She clutches my shirt, shaking her head. "I don't know." Her mouth twists, and her eyelids flutter. "I can't see."

My heart stops. My legs do, too. "What do you mean?" I rasp.

"Your face is blurry..."

"Did you hit your head?"

"He pushed me. That...man..." She presses her face against my chest, pulls on my shirt, and shudders, this full-body shiver that makes me hold her closer.

"What man?" Fuck, I need to use a lighter tone. I hold her close and drop my head down, nuzzling her forehead with my chin. I take a deep breath. "I've got you, Piglet. No one's going to hurt you. Who did this?"

I look down into her confused face as tears drip down her cheeks and she explains, in halting, half-slurred words, that someone with a mask showed up and said he wanted to talk to her. When she ran, he jumped the enclosure fence and tackled her.

"I think he cut my neck…" Her eyes roll slightly as she fumbles for her neck. "Bear…"

Her tears start to flow again, and I'm torn between rage and sorrow.

"Gwennie…I'm so fucking sorry. I'm so sorry." My words catch in my throat. I feel like I'm being strangled.

My fault!

"Let's go inside. I'm taking you inside. You're safe now. We'll call the police."

"I don't feel well," she whimpers.

I crouch in the dirt and hold her up while she gets sick: a side-effect of what he shot into her neck.

I clean her off with my shirt and take her to the bath. I have to get in, too. She can't stay upright. Not with those drugs in her system.

My chest aches as I hold her and wash her gently, as she cries and cries and cries and asks if we can leave.

"I'm scared."

I keep telling her, "I'm here. I won't let anybody hurt you."

Gwenna cries, "I'm scared for you, Bear!"

"Don't be scared for me, baby. I'm just fine."

"Someone's going…to take you…"

"No," I whisper, carrying her to bed.

"Don't go."

"Go where?"

"Overseas," she sniffles.

"No way. I'm not leaving. I would never leave you, baby." I climb into bed with her and count her breaths to try to get a read on her oxygen saturation. I check her pulse, which seems to be okay. He dosed her lightly, I think.

He must think that's good. That it will dim my rage.

Blue has no idea. That fucking prick has no fucking idea. When Gwenna drifts off, I call the police out to file a report and sit at Gwen's computer. There I find him on the footage, just as I knew I would.

Bluebell.

No. Not Blue.

Someone wearing ACE gear...but not Blue. Someone I'm pretty fucking sure he hired. Who else would be behind this, except his paranoid, self-important ass?

This is bad news. Such bad news.

Because this means I have to kill him.

Gwenna

The next morning, I wake up aglow in sunlight and have no idea where I am. Barrett's there beside me, stroking my hair, his strong arms around my back, his hard, warm chest against my cheek.

"It's okay..."

I squint and blink up at the rafters.

Ouch. "My head..."

"Open your mouth."

I do, and I feel three round, slick tablets pushed inside by Barrett's careful fingers.

"Let's sit up..." He helps me up and brings a straw to my mouth. "Just Advil." He's got one arm around my back. The other hand is at my shoulder, holding, stroking. "How ya doing?"

His face is a mask of sympathy and pain.

I squint at him and wonder why the hell I feel so...dread-filled. Then it hits me: the slam of one domino into the next until I remember.

"Oh my God…"

The hand around my back comes to my other shoulder. His fingers stroke my shoulders as his eyes bore into mine. "You're safe, Gwen. We're upstairs at my house. Do you remember coming over here?"

Tears fill my eyes. I shake my head. One falls.

"That's all right." He scoots closer and tucks me up against him. "The police came, and a paramedic came inside and checked you over. You didn't want to go to the hospital, so I told them 'no.'"

I nod slowly. I do have this hazy memory of a woman in a light blue shirt, saying something about the ER.

"I don't like the hospital." My voice sounds small.

Barrett's body tenses, even as his hand rubs my back. "I know, babe. We don't have to go."

I take a deep breath as a feeling—this black feeling rolls through me. It's like a dark cloud. Tears stream down my cheeks. I start to cry. I can't help it.

I feel Barrett shift until I'm in his lap, lying between his legs and on his chest. He pulls the covers over us and gently cups my head with his big hand.

"It's what was in the dart. Those sedatives will throw you off the next day."

I hold my breath, then sniff softly. "They will?" I look into his gorgeous eyes; hard eyes.

"They will."

He looks so…mad.

"Barrett—are you mad at me?" I whimper.

"Of course not." I feel his cool palm on my forehead. "Why would you think that?"

"I don't know."

"Never mad at you, Piglet. You're my heart," I think I hear him say. It has an echo, though.

I don't remember falling asleep. I wake up to dark windows and an eerie sense of stillness in the little attic room.

When I get down off the bed, my knees feel wobbly. A quick look at myself reveals I'm wearing a huge flannel shirt. It's rolled up nearly to my elbows—neat, square rolls by Barrett's deft hands. It's got navy blue, light blue, red, and white in the plaid pattern.

I stand there with one hand on the mattress, listening to the silence. It feels big and heavy. I can feel it in my chest, my hair. I look at my hand on the bed. Over the knuckles, there are red scrapes.

Tears tighten my throat. I can hardly even remember the man in the mask. That's why he gave me the shot in my neck. So I would forget. Who was it? Who was it, and what did they want to talk about?

I smell the snow. The road salt. I can feel the cruel, pervasive cold. I feel like I'm turning *real* to *ghost* and back again, as if I'm flickering as I stand here.

He already killed you.

I don't even know where the words come from, but they make my chest feel tight, my body even less substantial. Suddenly, I just want Barrett. I need him.

I'm worried about making it down the ladder, but I go anyway. I hurry from the second floor to the first and find Barrett sitting in an armchair in front of the fire. He's shirtless, in a pair of loose, black sweats.

As I near the bottom of the stairs, he springs up, lithe and gorgeous in the firelight, bounding over to me like…"a leopard," I giggle.

"What?" He tilts his head and smiles, taking my hands.

"You remind me of a leopard."

He gives me another handsome smile and squeezes my hands. "You seem to be feeling a little better."

I nod, even though a mere moment ago, it wasn't true. "I feel better when I'm with you."

He kisses my cheek and cups my shoulder with his hand. I look at his face and notice that the beard is longer. Even though he's smiling, his eyes look...tired? Or red? I can't tell in the dim light. I wrap myself around him and he holds me against him. We sit in the chair, and as happy as I felt a moment ago, now my eyes start leaking.

"What did I miss?" I ask in a raspy voice.

His hands rub circles on my back. "Not much."

I look around the room and notice a small glass on the table beside us, filled with amber liquid. I squint. Is that whiskey?

"Nothing happened? While I've been in zombie mode?"

"I missed you," he says softly.

I look up at him and find his face looks tight, despite a small smile. "Are you upset?"

He cups my cheek. "I should be asking you that, Pig."

I kiss his jaw, rubbing my lips over the little beard hairs. "That is not an answer," I whisper.

I cut my gaze upward in time to see him blink. The way his face is frozen—it looks like he's struggling to stay composed. He shuts his eyes and exhales.

So he's upset. Well, of course he would be. Given his past...He probably has a hard time knowing that he couldn't stop it.

"I love you." I burrow my hands behind his back and draw my knees up, so I'm tight and cozy in his lap.

"I love you too," he says a little roughly. The fire crackles. I watch his Adam's apple bob along his throat. "I'm sorry I wasn't there."

"You didn't know."

He laughs dryly. "I bought a car." He shakes his head.

"What?"

He blinks at me. "That's where I was."

"Can I see it?"

I'm out of his lap before he even answers. Barrett's up behind me, chuckling as I dance around to make him laugh. We bound down the front porch steps like puppies, him catching my hand as our feet hit the dirt.

He turns slightly to the left and there, along the house's side, I see a Jeep.

"Oh my God, I love it! Take me for a drive?" I dart over on my rubber legs and lean against the driver's side window. The glass is cool under my splayed fingers. A shiver ripples through me, making my mind hazy. But I shake it off.

Who was it? I push the question down.

"C'mon," I grab Bear's hand. "I want to smell the new car smell."

He obliges me, of course. Half an hour later, he runs off the road, onto a grassy shoulder, moaning as I make us both feel better with his dick stuffed in my mouth.

chapter fifteen

Gwenna

By the time we get back to Barrett's house, I'm ready to hear more about the attack. Did they see the man on camera? (No). Did they find footprints? (Just one. Shoe size 10). Have there been any other attacks or any suspicious people in the area? (No). Was it for sure a syringe or a dart that went into my neck? (A mini dart gun thing). What was the medicine? (A fast-acting sedative called Haloperidol). Who the hell was it? What if they come back?

I swallow both questions, and Barrett seems to read my mind.

"I think the police asked you. Do you remember what you told them?"

"About what?" I ask.

"Who it might be."

I shake my head.

"I don't know either. I wasn't in the room with you. Do you want to call the station and see if they recorded it?"

I shake my head again. "I can just think of it again. Who would it be? Someone relating to the bears maybe. Sometimes enviro people get weird about bear places." I swallow. That's not what I really think, but I'm not sure I want to talk about what I think.

Barrett squeezes my leg under the table. "Can you think of anything else?"

I swallow hard. Again. Finally, I force myself to look at him. "Maybe," I whisper.

"What?"

I shiver. "The person."

"What person?"

"Where am I, Daddy?"

"Oh my God." My mother's voice.

"The one who hit me."

"You mean the driver from the accident."

I nod. "They never found him."

"What do you mean, found?"

"He just…took off."

"He?" Barrett's eyes are wide.

"It could have been a female. I just think of it as a male." My eyes fill up with tears.

"What's wrong, Gwennie?"

"I just wonder if the person keeps track of me. If they know where I am. Is that crazy?"

"No. It's not crazy. But I doubt that's what happened."

"What did? How is it possible that once again, I don't know what happened to me? I got attacked a second time. It's like a ghost is after me."

Michael

'What the fuck?'

I cast my eyes in the direction of my father, my fingers texting under the table cloth even as the General drones on about my mother's campaign. *'What?'* I ask Dove.

'What did you do to Bear?'

'What do you mean?'

'Answer your phone.'

"So…we have options," Dad is saying. "What your mother needs to see is…"

'Dinner. Dearest dad.'

'He flew in?'

'Tracked me here. We're in Nashville—Capitol Grille.'

'Fuck.'

'That's the word. So—what's up?"

"Do you see my reasoning?" Dad's asking.

"I do. I think your theory makes good sense."

'Shit, let me slip off to the RR.'

"So—what?" I ask a few moments later.

Dove's voice is low. "Bear's fucking pissed off, man. He texted me and said to tell you to watch your back. He said to tell you that the 'brother operator' shit is over."

"What kind of cryptic shit is that?" I pull my dick out, aiming for the little round blue toilet freshener thing hanging along the back of the bowl.

"You know. Means you're not his brother anymore."

"So—what? He gonna take me out?" I hit the blue thing—score—but waver as I chuckle. Then I sigh and run a hand back through my hair. "He should appreciate this shit I'm doing for his ass. My whole fucking fam would like to see him—You know what they want. My dad is shitting gold bricks, man."

"You don't know why Bear's pissed off?" Dove asks.

I laugh, the sound as miserable as the pounding of my head. "I didn't do dick shit to Bear, except protect his ass. He been acting okay?"

He sighs. "I can't tell. Too far away. You'd know more than I would."

"I didn't see much, but do we need to? Maybe he's finally gone off the rails, D."

I prop the phone on my shoulder, tuck myself back into my pants, and zip.

"Maybe," Dove says. "Maybe so."

"Tell him I'm fucking *campaigning* for him." I laugh bitterly. "I've done nothing to get his panties in a fucking wad. Didn't even do much looking in on them when I was in their neck of the woods. Told my father's team to settle down, there's nothing dangerous going on." I lower my voice. "Is that true, Dove? When I saw them, they looked like more than friends. You told me—"

"So when you met up with your dad today, it wouldn't be all over your face, I didn't give you all the details, no."

"All over my face." I snort and push my sleeves up, pump some fancy coconut soap into my palm. "I'm better than that."

"You're not the best, Blue. C'mon."

"I'm a good liar."

Dove's silence is an indictment. I grit my teeth. "So he's what, fucking her now?"

"He says he loves her."

"Holy fuck. You kidding me?"

"I wish I was."

"Goddamnit, Dove."

I hang up, and wash my hands again. The water's cold. I close my eyes and feel how cold it is. I focus on that detail, and I wish to fuck that Dove was wrong. I *am* a shitty liar. Always have been. Guess the ole politico gene skipped me.

I dry my hands with the plush towel on the marble countertop and straighten up my tie. My dad will wonder where I've been all this time.

My dad, General Hubert R. Broomfield—Chairman of the Joint Chiefs of Staff.

My dad will want to know soon who he should take out: Barrett, Gwenna White, or both.

Barrett

At first, I think it's Bluebell. The guy walking a half a step behind Gwen's friend Jamie has his head covered with the hood of a gray sweatshirt. He's got the same large build as Blue, and something about the way he moves is familiar.

Pain streaks like a rocket mortar through my chest.

Not Blue. *Breck.*

He moves a little bit like Breck. Because—oh *God*—it's Breck's brother. That must be Nic.

I didn't know he would be here. I didn't know when Gwenna left to go to lunch with Jamie, she was seeing Niccolo as well. If I had…

I push my fist into my jeans pocket, gripping the fabric flap with my fingers.

Even if I'd known I would see Nic, I'd still have come. Because I have to protect Gwen. I have to be sure Blue can't get to her. Even though that means following her.

It feels wrong, given our history. Before, she was no one to me. Not beyond the circumstances of my knowing her. I didn't care about her. We'd never spoken. Most of the time I watched her through my scope, she was no one to me.

Now I feel as if I'm lying to her.

But I do it gladly. Just like after she returns to my house, says she's tired, and tucks in early, I push a silencer onto my handgun, break out some night goggles, and practice shooting with my right hand until my eyes are crossing. It scares the shit out of me that I can't protect her. Not the way I could in the past.

I try to ball my left hand into a fist and feel the same vague, numb discomfort that I always do, the nerves protesting. I hiss my irritation, go inside, put up the shooting stuff and pour myself some whiskey.

I down it in a few swallows and watch the flames blur in the fireplace.

Need to stop this. Hiding. But it feels good to hide. I need the numbness. When Gwen wakes me up some hours later, my head aches a little and my throat is dry and scratchy.

"You're having trouble sleeping," she murmurs, her hand pressed against my scratchy cheek. She leans in to kiss my cheek right by my nose. "I can tell, you know. Is it the nightmares?"

I shake my head. It's really not.

"Whiskey," I murmur, not looking at her face.

"You're drinking at night?"

I nod.

She sinks down onto the couch beside me, wrapping me in her arms...and her legs. We fall together softly on the cushions. Her cheek rubs my forehead.

"Bear."

And I love her for it, for just saying that. She doesn't ask me why, and so I want to tell her. I just need to have her sweet words whisper in my ear that it's okay. Because it's not. It's not okay, and it will never be. That's why I have to have Gwen tell me that it will be. It's why I need her so much in these moments.

"Did you know you've been dreaming, too?" I whisper. Around 3 a.m. every night.

I get her back to sleep. That's why I'm not sure she knows.

She whispers, "Yeah."

"You talk about how cold it is."

"I know." I feel her lashes tickle my cheek, stopping when her eyes shut. "I think what happened made me think about the wreck."

My heart aches. "Tell me."

I hear a sob catch in her throat and want to bleed, it hurts so fucking much. "I just…sometimes I dream I'm lying there. And it's so cold. I'm by myself. I think about how I was by myself in the hospital and Elvie left. It just makes me feel alone, I think." Her voice is soft and broken, but she doesn't outright cry, which makes me love her more.

I hug her tightly, kissing up her throat and all along her jaw. "I love you, Gwenna White. I'll always pick you up and carry you away."

I mean it so damn much.

I do it now. I lift her in my arms and spread a blanket in front of the fireplace, and I show her, in the warmth, how much I love her.

I'm going to find a way to fix this. When I do, we'll have our happily ever after. I'll do anything I have to. I lie awake beside her that whole night, seeing snow.

chapter sixteen

Barrett
December 31, 2012
11:07 p.m.

All the whiskey in this place won't be enough. I can drink myself into a blackout, and it still won't numb the raw throb in my chest. I know for sure now that the bar has got that heavy, amber glow and everything feels slow and surreal. Like an old home movie.

There's this girl on the movie. Snowflake girl. I watch her dancing with her friend, Red Lipstick. Snowflake never looks at me while she's in motion, but between songs, as she drags a palm over her silky copper hair or presses her lips together, her eyes drift to me. Once they touch down on me, they feel warm and patient. As if she's drinking in the corner table scene. She's just observing. I wish she'd come closer. To the table.

I polish off the rest of my scotch and feel my body shift. I blink, then turn my head. Oh. Cause Blue is elbowing me.

"Think we could put a sandwich on that redhead?"

I blink a few times, trying to focus on his words. "Sandwich?" I rub my numb face.

"More like bagel," Blue murmurs. "I could take her from the back and you could fuck her cunt. She would be the cream."

I chuckle. "Fuck." I moan, shaking my pounding head. "That's bad. Even for you."

"You've heard of that shit, Bear, c'mon. You're not a choir boy."

I watch the girl. She's shaking her ass like she's in some kind of contest. She's good enough to get me hard despite all that I've had to drink. I have to reach down to adjust myself under the table.

"She's too good for you," I tell him, slurring slightly.

Blue laughs. "You're fucked up, Bear."

"Not enough," I murmur, staring at my empty glass.

"I've got some molly. Pot, too. I would recommend the molly, though, and not a lot, just—"

I shake my head as he speaks, trying to mold my mushy thoughts into coherent words. "Tried that shit," I say. I shake my head again. "Tomorrow."

"Oh, the comedown. Ehh. That can be managed, bro. You'll be feeling good I tell ya."

I shake my head. Don't want good. I don't deserve to feel good.

"She's a good one. Gwenna, that's her name." He makes a low sound of approval. "Actress. Staying next door to Breck's fam. The other one, the friend, is getting hit up by ole Nic."

I nod, not really hearing. I drink water and wait for our server to bring more scotch. I could quit for the night, but I kind of want to fuck myself up. I need to sober up a little, then have a few more. Get just shitty enough to pass the fuck out in a bed at Breck's. I'll take a cab home. Get someone else to drive my rental.

I watch the girl some more, then look down at the table. I don't know how obvious I'm being. I don't want to leer at her, and I'm already fucking wasted, so I might be.

I feel a hand on my neck, see Breck lean around from behind my chair. "Hey, bro. Want to step out for a smoke?"

I get up. Follow Breck out some door, till we're outside underneath the roof's edge with our backs against the brick wall. Fuck, it's cold and snowy. Everything looks glittery and crystalized.

Breck hands me a smoke. I pull a lighter out of my pocket. Breck hands me one. I frown until I realize I've been flicking mine, and it's not lighting.

"Thanks," I mumble. My hands feel heavy and numb, but they remember how to light a Marlboro. I inhale.

"Hey, man."

Breck's arm comes over my shoulders—heavy. "I'm gonna go back home. Wanna come with?"

I frown, trying to understand. For a second, my muddled mind can't even place us on a map. The snow brings back a flash vision of Moscow.

Home, he said. "Like—your parents' place?" My voice sounds weak and raspy. I swallow.

"Yeah. I might go back out later." His hand slaps my shoulder. "Let me get ya home, brother."

So Breck thinks I'm a mess. He lifts his arm off me. I watch him light his cigarette. I should go with him. Just end this shitty fucking New Year's.

"Who's the girl?" I ask instead.

Breck frowns, and I realize I should clarify. "The gorgeous one."

He's still frowning. I watch him pull his phone out of his pocket. Oh. He got a call.

"Ma," he says affectionately. His face rises slightly in a smile that falls fast. Puzzlement twists his features. "Dammit. Okay—just sit down. Let me talk to Nic. I'll call you right back. Don't move."

He huffs as he hangs up, and turns to me. "My fucking father and his fucking dick."

"Damn," I manage.

"I'll be back in a few. Nic will go."

Go home, I guess. That sucks for Breck's mom. I've met her a time or two—not this trip, since I flew out by myself and got here later than everyone else. But she's a nice woman. Acts like a mom to me, too. Breck's dad is a dipshit.

I hear a creak and look over my shoulder. My stomach lurches and I have to blink my bleary eyes.

She smiles, looking so clean and sweet and shy. I watch her snap the buttons on her jacket. The fog of her warm breath surrounds her face, making her look ethereal. I watch her lips pinch as she digs into a pocket. Her mouth twists downward, then she laughs softly.

She holds something up: a broken cigarette.

"Could I bum one?" she asks, smiling sweetly.

"Sure." With some effort, I manage to extract an almost-empty pack from my pocket. I don't really smoke, but I got some after I left the cabin in New York and I held onto them.

I hold out one to her, and then the lighter.

"Thank you so much."

"You're welcome." I lean slightly against the wall. The glittering snow all around us makes me feel as if we're standing in a snow globe—that someone's shaking.

I feel something on my arm and blink down to find her bare hand. My gaze shifts to her lovely face. "You okay?" Her voice is quiet and soft, beautiful and delicate as snowfall.

She asked if I'm okay. Fuck, that feels kind of good.

I smile for her. "I'm fine."

She smiles, too. A melancholy, thoughtful smile that pierces through the numbness, prickling my heart. "You look sad," she says quietly.

I try to laugh, and nudge her with my arm. "Why do you care?"

It's a teasing tone I use and normally it works. Gets people off my back and makes it hard for them to see...the things I wouldn't want them to. Of everyone I know, Breck and maybe Dove: they are the only ones that see through it. This girl isn't fooled, either. Her face is still drawn up in what looks like pain. When her eyes lift to mine, I find them rounded with sincerity.

"I'm not having a very good night either," she tells me. "And," she blows some smoke out, arching her eyebrows self-consciously as she smiles slightly. "I care about everyone. It's just the way I am. For better and worse." She takes another drag. I watch her blow it out.

"There was this article one time. About Saddam Hussein. In some magazine. And these American soldiers who had taken care of him when he was in prison somewhere. It said he had a thing for Cheetos. Saddam." She laughs wryly, shaking her head. "I found myself feeling bad for him. Like, sympathetic. It's a curse."

I open my mouth, because I want to tell her she shouldn't feel bad for that POS, she should feel bad for all the innocent civilians he murdered.

But I look at her face, I see the sadness that's still there, and all I think to ask is, "Why are you sad?"

My voice is rough and raw, and even through the scotch, I feel...exposed. I'm not up front like this. I don't talk to anyone, about anything. It's how I am. I guess I'm this girl's opposite.

I definitely am, I decide as I watch her face twist up in pain. "I don't even know," she says, blinking at the snow-caked firs in front of us. "I just feel a bad vibe I guess. Also, boyfriend trouble." She blows a trail of smoke out. Fuck, she's gorgeous.

"Is it just me, or is smoking lonely? Inherently lonely. And bumming one off someone, what is that? Here, have some cancer." She grins. My chest throbs a little as her brown eyes thaw me.

"No, you're right," I offer her. "It's kind of lonely."

I exhale a cloud of smoke, and the girl blows her own stream toward mine. The gray smoke mixes. "There." She smiles.

My drunk brain makes a note: learn more about her. *Anything*, I scribble desperately on the dry board of my mind. My throat is tight. My lungs ache. *Want*.

I turn toward her, noticing her beautiful, bare throat. She draws her shoulders up toward her ears. I want to put my arm around her. I don't want to scare her, though. Invade her space.

She smiles at me, a little smile that's just for smiling's sake. For me. A fucking gift.

"I bet your boyfriend is an asshole," I hear myself say.

She laughs. "Why?"

"Assholes always get the good ones." I give her a sloppy smile as my head buzzes. "All the nice guys know."

"Are you a nice guy?"

"No, snowflake." I throw my cig down and cover it with my boot. Then I take my scarf off. I drape it around her neck, our eyes holding like magnets as I lean away. "Stay warm."

I press my lips together so I don't say more, and go inside.

Gwenna
December 11, 2015

I used to like December. Years ago, it was my favorite month. I loved Christmas. Reindeer. Crackling fires. Snow. I adored the evergreens, the way your breath in cold air makes that little cloudy puff. I thought the winter sky, a sheet of black with burning white pinholes, was simply magical.

I used to have almost an entire drawer of holiday socks. I'd start wearing them before Thanksgiving. I still try. I try to like the holidays. I put out Christmas early most years. Decorate a tree.

But in my dreams, I see that black sky, with its fever-black white stars, and I am haunted by the moaning coming from a place I can't see. I can sometimes feel the weight of the ambulance crunching snow beneath its tires, the way a large vehicle shifts and slips on fresh powder.

My last memory before the accident is of Jamie and me on the plane to Colorado. We shared a Rudolph fleece as the plane started landing. I remember how the round window was icy-cold. I remember getting in the car that came to pick us up: a black Tahoe with chilled wine in the backseat. I think maybe I remember the Madisons' sprawling wood chateau, with its wrap-around porch, sharp, high ceilings, and three levels of art, alcoves, faux fur rugs, and plush armchairs. The huge stone fence around the place. But my neurologist tells me that's from other visits. Previous years. Because of my brain injury, I don't remember anything beyond a snippet of our laughter and the wine in the SUV.

I think about the wine as Barrett and I take communion. This is our second week coming to church together. He suggested it last week, thinking maybe it would help with my nightmares.

"Are you a churchgoer?" I asked him.

"No. I always liked the chaplain with our unit, though."

"Perfect," I teased.

But—it really is. Now on Sunday mornings, I get to see Bear in a suit. He takes communion with me even though he knows I don't care if he does, and I think he honestly likes the priest. It's... funny. Funny strange. But nice.

Back in our pew, he leans his arm against my shoulder and plays with one of my pigtails as the priest clears away the chalice and paton and the Eucharistic ministers stack the kneeler cushions at the altar. I think about the wine again. Do I remember what kind it was? Probably Sauvignon Blanc, one of the only wines both Jamie and I like. Her mom would have known that. Would have stashed it in the car for us.

I try to think about the drive. What did the roads look like? I can't remember.

Soon we're standing up, singing the recessional hymn , then filing out with everyone else during the organist's vigorous post-lude. Barrett and Father Ryan exchange words as we leave the church. I'm glad they seem to get along.

By the time we get into his Jeep, I'm tired.

"You still want barbeque, Pig?"

I can't help giggling. "That sounds super weird."

"Is that a yes?"

I straighten my shoulders. "Yeah. I guess it is."

When we get into the booth at Ed's Barbeque Pit, he slides in beside me, wraps an arm around my back, and pulls my head against his arm.

"Gwennie."

"Mmm."

His lips find my head. "I love you," he murmurs.

"I love you too."

I can feel the question that he doesn't ask. Can feel him want to ask me. *What's wrong?* I know I've been more distracted lately, but I'm not sure how to explain it to him. I've talked about the accident a few times, but there's no way I'm telling him how scared I feel lately. Scared that whoever hit me has found me and came here to "talk." I don't want to make an issue of this, telling Bear all about what happened to me. I want my feelings to go away. Also, I'm not sure my fears are rational.

So I keep my mouth shut, silently thankful for the way he keeps an arm around me on the sidewalk, never leaves my side when we're in public, even for a moment; for the fact that he hasn't pushed us to move back into my place. I think Barrett knows my fears without me saying, and I love him for it.

I love everything about this man.

chapter seventeen

Gwenna
December 19, 2015

I wake up one morning with the knowledge that I have to go. Back into the enclosure. It's been more than a week. I've put off my usual hibernation-season walks through the land inside the fence, telling myself the bears are all doing well, staying in their little nooks, so clearly nothing's wrong. That's irresponsible. It's not okay.

When Barrett leaves to go see Doc, he tells me to keep the doors locked and the new alarm system turned on. I tell him I will. When his Jeep disappears down the sloping driveway, I go up to his room and dress in boots, jeans, and a brown fleece, then take my handgun from the nightstand drawer and strap it to the waist of my jeans.

Back downstairs, I scribble a quick note letting him know where I'm going and what time I left, so if something happens to me, he'll know where the clue trail starts. Then I check the cameras via my phone one more time. After what happened, I had four more cameras installed, and had the infrared capabilities for all the cameras turned on. It costs me an additional $400 per month, but for right now, it's worth it. No one's in the enclosure.

He could jump the fence again.

Who *does* that?

I've been wanting to ask Barrett—is jumping a tall fence some special secret agent skill, or might my attacker be a "normal" guy?—but I just hate to bring it up at all. Maybe I don't want to know.

Correction: I *don't* want to know. I never considered myself someone who would hide like this, but that's what I've been doing. Hiding at Barrett's house. Hiding like a child.

My mom and Rett have both offered to come and stay with me, as has Jamie. Even Nic offered to spend the night, or hire additional security if I needed it, which I thought was really sweet. I haven't wanted that, though. I just want to be with Bear, but even that is strained because I'm such a zombie: paralyzed by fear.

Barrett knows it. I can feel his tension, too.

I say a quick prayer before I step onto the porch, and then stuff my fists into my jacket pockets and start into the woods between our houses.

Who could it be?

Who?

I want to know. I want to know so badly. God, it's driving me insane. Who did that to me? What did they want to talk about?

The police have called a few times, letting us know they've been patrolling the area and also that they don't have any leads. They seem to think my attacker was someone interested in the bears. Maybe someone who wanted to take and sell one, or some enviro freak who thinks keeping even injured bears in captivity is somehow wrong.

Detective Anderson, the guy we've seen the most of, says the public meetings about the property zoning probably drew a lot of new eyes to my little operation here at Bear Hugs—and I know that's true, because I've seen an uptick in donations through the web site.

I sigh, and then cast my gaze around the woods. The wind is light today, meaning the leaves are fairly still except the crunching of my boots, so that's a positive. I tell myself that I would hear him coming.

As I move toward the enclosure gate, I sing hymns in my head: songs my grandma used to sing, and some I sang back in the day when I would play piano or guitar sometimes at bars. I always wondered if it was sacrilegious, but I would put a haunting sort of twist on one or two old hymns, and people used to love them.

By the time I've reached the gate, I feel a little calmer. As soon as I step inside, my pulse begins to race, but I breathe carefully and check my phone and no one is around. I see that. There's no hazy red splotches from a person's body heat.

I do an hour-long walk around, texting Barrett when I think he's almost back to his house, so he doesn't have to deal with the anxiety of finding the note and wondering if I'm okay.

I walk past Aimee and Papa and vow that tomorrow, I'll do walkbys on the others.

It's almost Christmas, I think, as I sit down on a stump near the gate. Barrett texted back and said he'll be here in a minute.

What should I get him for Christmas? Will he want to go somewhere? To Kellan? I'd love to be with him. Is that clingy?

I wrap my arms around myself as the breeze picks up. I talk to Helga tomorrow, and it's a good thing, I guess. All this cold is getting to me.

I look down at my boots and notice that I'm humming "Pumped Up Kicks" by Foster the People. Geez, that's random. Old song. Inappropriate, but catchy. I always feel wrong for liking it when I hear it. Not that I've heard it much in the last few years.

"It's like a fish bowl, but with beer, and it's craft beer. Really good shit."

My body freezes, muscles seizing, as I hear that same voice say, *"What do you think of your friend's new dude?"*

What the fuck does that mean?

Barrett's arms are wrapped around me, and I'm shaking. He's gentle and strong and sweet, but he can't shield me from this.

Craft beer.

Gemütlichkeit.

Beer bar.

I was at a beer bar New Year's Eve 2012.

The realization stops my shaking. I manage to pull myself together before Bear calls Helga.

I know now. I know now. I'm not crazy. I'm…*remembering.*

December 20, 2015

'Blue is in D.C. now. With the G. Have him tracked if you don't believe me. It wasn't him, Bear. Thank you for the dream catcher, by the way. I keep forgetting to say so.'

'That doesn't mean he didn't do it. You're welcome.'

I blow on my numb fingers, then slide my glove back on and take aim one more time. The .38 is steadier in my right hand than it used to be. I hit the target this time. My phone buzzes in my pocket.

'Why would he? We're brothers, man. Remember that. You and me, we're out now, but we're still bros. We protect each other.'

I see the little bubble indicating Dove is typing, then he sends another message.

'I'd think you would know that, Bear.'

Rage billows up inside me, followed quickly by remorse.

'You know how Blue is. He's scared of the fucking G.' We try not to say General in text transmission, no matter how encrypted these messages are supposed to be. General Broomfield of all people can probably take a peek whenever he wants.

'Blue's still batting for you, brother.'

'Bear...' another message says. *'His father's guys know what you're doing. He's working his ass off to keep yours safe.'*

I call right away, turning around toward my car, in the gun range parking lot, as if keeping my eyes on it will help me reach it faster. I start running. "What the fuck are you talking about?"

"They watch you, Bear, like common fucking sense would dictate. You knew they might. We all knew."

"What do you mean, smart ass? They watched me and what, Dove? Goddamn it!"

"They know that something's going on with you and her," he says quietly. "It's like we thought it would be."

"Meaning what?" I snarl as I throw my driver's side door open.

"Meaning they've been eyeing both of you for the last week or so. Blue wanted to learn a little more before we told you. No one's on you right now, Bear. They peeked in, botched that shit with Gwen that day, and left. Blue's on it."

"Blue is fucking on it. Like hell. FUCK!"

I hit the wheel so hard it groans and the airbag light starts flashing.

"Oh, fuck. Fuck, Dove. Do they think I told her?"

"They don't know. Your correspondence with both me and Blue is being watched by more than one set of eyes. Blue told me that today. You should answer his calls, you know."

"Is this why he was coming down this way?"

"He came and left, yes, a little while back. So he could tell anyone who asked that everything seems okay. I reassured him about it, too. So he could tell the G's team things are safe. Tell me I'm not wrong, Bear."

He's not wrong. We're all still safe.

"I *can't* tell her," I breathe. "I couldn't. It would—It would... wreck things." I laugh, desolate as fuck. "Dove." I yank at my hair.

"It's okay, dude. We've got you. Who would they send? Some contract fucker? Bart or Greene or Whissle from the SEALs?" He laughs. "Who would they send to take you out? That guy—the one who hurt your girl? It wasn't Blue. It was probably one of them, just trying to sniff shit out and do a little data mining. If you don't tell her, she'll be safe. I don't think the G would take a civvie out for no good reason. This is all just G keeping his asshole baby-fresh clean."

I snort, even as my tires spin out on the dirt road that leads away from the gun range.

"Think of this, too. They won't get your lady twice for data mining. That looks weird to the local oinkers."

"True," I breathe. "That's true."

We spec ops don't want to draw the eyes of local law folks if we don't have to. They tried to get information from Gwen once; they won't try again.

"Blue's ass is safe," I say. "I hope the G's guys know that. You guys fixed it up okay." My throat tightens. A wave of heat moves through my cheeks, making my eyes feel hot.

"You're really fucked, you know that?" Dove asks me a second later. He's using his gentle voice, which alone is scary.

"I know," I rasp.

"What you gonna do, Bear?"

My eyes blur. I exhale roughly. Inhale. "What can I do?" I manage in a steady-ish voice.

I can't be honest with her—ever.

"I can't leave her, Dove. I...*can't.*"

"You love her."

"She's everything." Tears drizzle down my cheeks. I don't bother to wipe them.

"Maybe you could...swear or something. Swear that to the G. Maybe all of us could meet with him or something. Get him settled down. I don't know. We could fly up for dinner. I'll be thinking on this, Bear. We've got you covered. You can never tell her. That's the only caveat. You give her everything else, man. Do what you have to do so you'll be fucking happy. Breck would want that."

Do what I have to do, but lie. And keep Gwenna in constant intermittent danger. Whenever G starts feeling nervous, or if Blue moves up the ranks and into politics just like his fucking family, I'd be putting her at risk. *I* would be at risk, and so if she loves me like I love her—and she does; my God, I don't know why, but she loves me—then I would put her heart at risk.

"Thanks, man." I get off the phone with Dove, and he says he'll keep me posted.

I can't do this. That's my conscience talking. My heart.

Leave her.

Keep her safe, dumb fuck. She'll find somebody else.

I pick her up from Helga's. No one's on my tail. No one's on her. Gwenna is quiet as we Christmas shop. She's soft and warm and quiet, her hand tight in mine. She tells me she loves me more than usual as we buy gifts for all her family. The plan is to spend Christmas at her Mom's, and then fly out to California to see Kellan and Cleo sometime after.

But I'm not surprised when we get to her house, and she starts on lasagna, and says, "Bear?"

"Yeah?" I kiss her forehead, smiling gently down on her.

"I need to tell you something."

My gut clenches. "Okay, Pig."

"I think I want to go to Colorado after Christmas. Maybe you can go to California without me and we could meet up after."

"Breckenridge?" I ask her.

Her face pales a little. "I do it every year," she tells me, setting the lid back on the pot.

"You don't want me with you?"

"Oh, no." She looks up, her eyes wide and round and...wanting. "That's not it. I just—"

"You think I'd leave you on your own?"

I wrap my arms around her from behind and press her up against me. "Pig. We'll go there first and California later. It doesn't matter. Kellan doesn't care."

She nods, turning to me. "Barrett—thank you."

She looks troubled, though. Through dinner, too, and after, when we take a bath together. She seems unhappy. Distracted.

On Christmas Eve, as we sleep underneath the glow nights in her bedroom with our gifts piled on the couch, the refrigerator stuffed full of food for tomorrow, I learn why.

She talks during a dream, and I hear names I know.

Michael's.

Niccolo's.

John's.

And mine.

chapter eighteen

Gwenna
December 31, 2011
11:39 p.m.

I step back inside and am greeted by the sound of "Pumped Up Kicks" coming through the ceiling speakers. It seems the band is taking a break and they're playing radio. As a musician, I like this song. As a person, I'm not sure. I haven't analyzed the lyrics or anything, but I'm pretty sure it's about kids running from a school shooter.

Should I hum along with it?

I'm not sure I can help myself.

I press my lips together as I walk past the bar. The taste of Marlboros in cold weather takes me back to K-ville at Duke. I can smell the mix of stale material—sleeping bags and tents, the whiff of body odor (even though everyone in our tent tried to shower when they weren't on shift), the lingering pall of smoke and tang of liquor. I can almost smell our textbooks, see our phones' lights as we lie there like sardines in sleeping bags, trying for weeks to stake our claim to UNC or one of the other tented games. That's Duke: basketball, and being there for years, that's what winter is to me.

The memory evaporates as I blink at a brunette who's planted in my path. She's tall; I have to look up to see her face, which is oval-shaped, with pretty lips, and framed by brown curls. As I look at her, her brows narrow.

"You're the model?"

"Huh?" I catch my cheek between my molars. I'm about to ask her if we know each other when she shakes her head and bursts out laughing.

"Sorry! I'm Marina. Where I'm from, in San Juan, there is this big, big billboard. You're wearing a beige dress?"

I smile, nodding. I remember that shoot.

"And the Alexander McQueen clogs."

I nod, half-sad because McQueen is dead now, half-impressed because this girl knows her shit.

"Are you a model, too?"

She shakes her head. "The bartender, he's my friend, he heard you telling someone you're a model. I want to be one too."

Ten minutes later, I'm sitting at the bar with Marina, jotting down phone numbers for her on the back of a bottle-cap-shaped coaster.

I'm still there when someone taps my shoulder. I turn, my stomach taking flight, hitting my throat, but it's just Jamie.

"Let's go! Do you want to? I spilled beer on myself and I want to go back home before it gets more cold and gross. Nic is coming too," she says in an excited whisper. "Problems at his house, so works out perfectly for me." She wiggles her eyebrows, and I glance around the bar.

I don't see my guy.

"I've got this scarf…"

"Stylish," Marina interjects.

I give her a smile. "It isn't mine. If I tell you what this guy looks like, will you give it back to him for me?"

"You got it from a guy?" Jamie's mouth is hanging open.

"Never mind," I tell Marina. I sigh. "If I don't see him as we walk to the door, I'll give it to Nic. Does Nic know the guy who was sitting at our table while we danced? Dark, curly hair?"

"The hot as sin one?"

I smirk. "Yep."

"It figures he'd have eyes for you." She pokes me with her finer and then turns to our new friend. "This girl is honey to the boys."

"They're bears or bees." I look from Jamie to Marina, finding that the girl is smiling.

"Are you a model, too?" she asks Jamie.

Jam is still gloating over that—in her teasing way, of course—as we walk toward the car. I didn't see the guy again. Barrett, Nic said his name is. I'm still wearing his warm, wool scarf as I get into the Range Rover.

Gwenna
December 25, 2015

"Ho, ho, ho," I murmur, nipping at Bear's earlobe as I reach into his boxer-briefs and wrap my hand around his sleepy cock.

He makes a hoarse sound, and I feel him swell in my grasp.

"Pig?" His eyelids flutter. His hips shift. I pull his underwear down with my free hand, hooking the fabric underneath his heavy balls.

Bear groans. "Jesus…"

"It's his birthday," I say, laughing.

I scoot up a little on his strong thighs, rubbing his head against my wetness, framed by holiday red crotchless panties.

His eyes open…They rove down me, dark and dazed…

I feel his cock twitch. It's so fucking hot. I rub my fingertip along the rim, then let the tip of him part my lips, skating through my slickness. He loves that—and I love his desperate moans. His eyes are half shut, but I smile down at him, causing my Santa hat to flop down by my cheek.

"Let me in," he rumbles.

"Soon." I giggle.

His hand wanders up my teddy-clad chest, his fingertips finding my nipple—which isn't difficult to do: it's peeking out through a circular hole in the teddy, lined with fluffy white.

I shift a little, and his thighs flex under me. I cup his balls and his face tightens.

"Oh God," he grits. "Gwen."

There's this little thing I do with my thumb…teasing his balls. I do it while I pump his shaft just underneath his head, and Barrett grunts, his ass coming up off the bed.

"Santa," he murmurs. Then he arches up and takes my breast in his mouth, sucking as I work his cock, until he's thrusting at me, looking wild-eyed.

"I've been good," he rumbles, and I guide him so he's right there where I need him. Then I sink down on his thick cock, gasping as his head fills me.

I can feel his legs tremble. Or is that my legs?

"You feel…so good." My voice shakes as I clench around him: thick enough to spread me open just right. I lock my thighs to keep from sinking all the way down. I need him deep inside, but first, I want to see him beg.

He twines his fingers through mine, squeezing. Then his lashes lift a little, and he gives me this sexy-as-fuck little smirk that says *I know you want all of this.*

He rocks a little; I take more, and then—*oh God*—he grabs my hips and lifts me off him.

"No!"

He chuckles as I try to work myself back down on him.

"What do you want, little Piggy?"

"You," I gasp.

"You've got me."

"This…" I grab his cock; I rub his head. His eyelids sag.

"Fuck me with it. Fuck me, Bear…"

I gambled correctly. His eyes open: blazing. "You want to be fucked, Piggy?"

"If you can…" I quirk a brow. I can feel Bear's tip rubbing between my lips. I don't look down; I just hold his eyes: a challenge that I pray will get me off.

I see his jaw tighten. Then I'm blinded by a hard, smooth thrust.

I cry out as stars explode behind my eyes. I hear him chuckle. Then he's got my wrists…He's holding onto my hips. His strokes are deliciously forceful. My toes curl. My legs go weak. I'm panting so hard I can't breathe.

"If I can," I think I hear him laugh.

Then I'm dizzied. I've been flipped over, and he's on top now, driving into me, lifting my legs. He drapes them over his big shoulders, finds my clit with his thumb. I can feel his balls slap my taint as he pounds me. My cries meet his grunts. It's Christmas and I'm being worshipped. *Oh, sweet sacrilege…*

I'm smiling with my front teeth on my lower lip as I fall into the abyss, and Barrett makes a soft sound, then his warmth spreads through me, and it's Christmas.

Christmas at Mom's house is overboard as always: first world at its finest, with more food than anyone can eat, enough gifts to produce five huge, biodegradable garbage bags full of wrapping paper, and two bottles of Château Léoville-Barton from Dad's wine cellar to go with dinner, which is roasted duck and truffle butter chicken, with all kinds of extravagant sides.

Mom makes Barrett feel like family. Not everyone gets a sculpture at Christmas, and this year, it's only him and me. She gives him a small bear, curled into a hibernation pose, and me a tree where a bird sits perched on a branch. If you sit the pieces beside each other, it looks like the bird is looking down on the bear.

I can tell it means a lot to him by the blank look that crosses his face when he pulls it from its hand-wrapped box, followed by a quick swallow before a very earnest "thank you." He sets the piece on his knee while we open presents, his hand cupped loosely around the little bear. I see my mom notice the way he's holding it. The whole thing makes me giddy.

Rett and Barrett talk for a long while about duck hunting, which culminates in plans to go sometime in January. By the time we leave, I'm wine drunk and Barrett is laughing his ass off because he hardly drank at all. It's started to drizzle, so he carries me to his Jeep and when he plops me down in the passenger's seat, I wrap my arms around his neck and kiss him until I'm dizzy.

"You're a funny drunk, Pig."

I smash my palm against his nose. "Am not." But I'm giggling.

"You are," he says with conviction. I feel his lips tickle my forehead. Then his arms are locked around my shoulders. He's pulling me against him. Silence throbs around us.

"God—I fucking love you, Gwenna."

"I love *you*." I love his smell, the feel of him…I'm smiling as he slides into the driver's seat. He takes my hand.

I feel him doing something with it. I look down. There's something heavy…

"Merry Christmas, Piglet."

I hold my arm up to my face and see three thin bracelets. They're smooth and dark. I sit up and flip the visor down. They sparkle.

"Oh my God. Did you—" They're bangle bracelets made of polished wood, and in the center of each bracelet is a line of tiny diamonds. My eyes fly to his. "You made these."

"Yeah." He smiles. His fingers touch the bracelets. "From a tree along our property line. Don't worry, it had fallen."

I giggle. "Like me."

He frowns.

"For you."

I throw myself at him, end up falling on the console in between our seats, and then fall victim to a minor bout of hysterical laughing.

"Barrett," I gasp. I start howling.

I can feel him laughing, too, his chest bumping into mine as his low chuckles fill the car.

"I'm sorry," I cackle. "I love them so much. And you."

By the time I pull out of his lap, I have to wipe tears from my eyes. The tears pick up steam again as I look at the bracelets. "God, they're perfect. Thank you, Bear."

I wipe my face, but that just seems to make the tears flow faster. Then I'm crying in my hands. I don't know why.

"No...Piglet." Barrett's leaning over to me now, his hands on my shoulders. "Hey...It's Christmas, and you're Santa, right? Striptease Santa doesn't cry on Christmas."

I laugh, still crying.

"You're a sad one. A sad drunk," he murmurs, wiping my tears with his fingers.

I nod.

"Better than a mad one, baby. Better than a mad one."

I settle eventually, and Barrett runs back into my mom's house and gets some water for me. I look at the bracelets, winking like a bunch of little guiding lights.

And that's when I realize: I *am* a mad one. I'm a mad drunk, and I'm mad sober. Because I love Barrett, so much. I love him, but I can't move on. I can't write a new story with Bear because I'm missing a huge chapter of my old one.

chapter nineteen

Gwenna
January 1, 2012
1:11 a.m.

I press my fingertip against the clock that sits on Jamie's bathroom counter. Isn't that what we used to do when we were kids? See a row of the same digit on the clock, and you got to make a wish. What is my wish, I wonder, as I sink my nose into the thick gray scarf.

It smells like man.

Not cologne, how Elvie smells, but *male*. Like…pheromones. And how pathetic am I, standing in Jamie's bathroom, sniffing some dude I don't even know.

I sigh, a sound that echoes. Which kind of makes me laugh. I'm still smiling as I dial Elvie.

For reasons I can't fully explain, I left the theater room, where Nic and Jamie were starting *Forrest Gump*, and went to my room to call Elvie. But I had to pee, and my bathroom didn't have toilet paper, so I came in here to—

Oh yeah. I need to use the restroom.

I sit down as the phone rings, and then stand as I realize there's no TP here, either.

I frown at myself in the mirror as the phone rings once…twice…three times before I'm answered by a male laugh.

"Elvie."

He laughs again. My lips move into a reciprocating grin, until I hear him say, "Stop, babe."

"What?"

He laughs again, and it's his slow laugh. It's his *drunk* laugh. "Sorry, babe." He hisses, "Just a second."

My pulse spikes, despite the alcohol still in my bloodstream. "Are you talking to somebody else?"

"Gwen? I can't hear you."

"I can hear you." And the other two hundred people in the background. "Elvie, where are you?"

"I can't hear you. Gwen?"

"Go somewhere else, Elvie. It's too loud. If you can't hear me, it's too loud there."

The line goes dead.

I take a deep, slow breath. My head throbs. Holy fucking hell. He dropped me. Elvie—He does this to his parents sometimes! It's the faux dropped call. I invented that, at least in our world. I used to use it when my crazy Aunt Maurine would call, when we were sophomores.

Holy fucking shit.

I'm so distraught, I sit down and pee, without *re*-realizing there's no toilet paper.

"ARGHHHH!"

So what to wipe with? I massage my temples. Sometimes there's a hand towel on the counter…Nope. Not right now. Ugh. I could use a sock. Ewwww. Gross! I spot Jamie's makeup bag. Hells yes! She sometimes has a little pack of Kleenex in her makeup bag, to blot her liquid eyeliner. I lunge up off the toilet, grab the bag, and—SCORE!

I finish taking care of business. By the time I step into Jamie's room, I'm haunted anew by what just happened with Elvie. What the hell is going on with him? Is he seeing another girl? Or is he just drunk and surrounded by fan girls and doesn't want to risk one of them saying something that would piss me off?

I wander into two other guest rooms, looking for toilet paper, then go upstairs to the home theater. I find Jamie by herself.

"Just you?" I ask, as I walk nearer to her.

"Oh." She turns to me. "Yeah, Nic left right after you did. Apparently there's some—" she drops her volume—"family drama. His mom or dad went somewhere. Something. He left in his car instead of walking next door. Which I know," she rolls her eyes, "because I watched him from the window like a stalker."

I smile. "See this scarf? I'm sniffing it."

"Ohh, what does it smell like?" She leans closer, and I hold it up.

"Nope. All mine." I inhale. "It's man-smell."

"Sweat and dirty laundry?" She arches a flawlessly plucked eyebrow.

"No." I swat her. "You're so unromantic. Man-smell like… pheromones."

Jamie, the bitch, throws her head back and actually howls. Like a wolf. At a full moon.

"Pheromones!" She points her flawless, red, bitch nail at me as if I'm naked on stage at a middle school play.

I wrap the scarf more tightly around my neck and cross my arms. "They're real, you know. I didn't make them up. This man has excellent pheromones. I can tell."

"And what's his name again?"

I blink and cast my gaze up to the ceiling. "I'm not telling," I say peevishly. And then I feel embarrassed, because maybe I really am insane, and I also don't want to fall into talking about what happened with Elvie, so I change the subject fast. "I feel like we may be out of toilet paper? Is that even possible with—"

"We are. I wiped with the hand cloth earlier."

"I looked for that."

"I stashed it underneath the sink. Nic was in my room."

"Sexxxy."

She fans her face. "I know, right?"

"So is he coming back?"

"He said he was, yeah."

"That's awesome, dude." We high-five, Jamie smiling shyly, the way she always looks when she's newly crushing on someone. It's adorable.

"So I'll go grab some? TP?"

She blinks, then frowns. "You want to? Dad could call someone."

A delivery person. That's what she means. Her parents call them any time we need something up here—sometimes in the middle of the night, even. "Nah. I'm in the mood to get out."

"Are you stewing?"

I hold both hands up and walk backward. I can't help smiling, probably guiltily. "Later, lovahhh."

"I love *you*."

"I love you more."

"Get the Cottonelle. You know how Dad is! Take his car, too."

"Yessir!"

Downstairs, the house is quiet. Jamie's parents are asleep. The family cocker spaniel, Bruno Mars, is curled up underneath the granite counter in a little red dog bed. Her ear twitches when I grab Mr. Madison's keys off the hook beside the fridge. I know they're his because they have a Wheaton keychain attached. I stare down at it for a second, then notice I left my jacket upstairs in the bathroom. Classic.

I smile ruefully at my adopted scarf.

Barrett. Jamie didn't remember his name, but I did.

I need to take the damn scarf off and give it to Nic.

Later.

For now, I decide to go full-on Mr. Madison and borrow his long, black down coat in addition to his SUV. I pull on my tall snow boots, lace them tightly, and admire the way his coat falls all the way down to my shoe soles. At least I won't be cold.

Outside, the porch stairs are slick and gritty with salt. Which is better than icy and snowy. Mr. Carmallo usually keeps the stairs and walk meticulously ice-free. Him or his wife. They live in a guest house behind the main house and keep the place up when the Madisons are elsewhere.

I walk slowly down the stairs and down the curving stone walk toward the driveway. Snow's still falling, landing coolly on my cheeks and scalp. The driveway hasn't been plowed in a few hours, so as I hit the "unlock" key on Mr. M's keyring, my boots squeak on the fine powder.

The inky black Lexus LS looks meticulous inside, save for a folded copy of yesterday's *Wall Street Journal* and the lingering scent of stale coffee. I grab the window scraper from the glove box, cleaning off the windshield as the defrost aids me from the inside, then folding down the windshield wipers. People in these parts leave them raised up off the windshield like this, I guess to keep them from freezing to the glass.

By the time I get back in, my seat is warm. The vents are blowing warm, coffee-scented air.

I fold my stolen scarf over my mouth and nose. As I back out, I inhale deeply.

So—I'm miserable.

That's the truth of things. That's my New Year's secret.

As I drive toward the little general store a half a mile away, I allow myself a moment to imagine the man's big, strong hands on my body. The way his fingers might feel stroking the soft skin of my throat. The way his beard would tickle the inside of my thighs.

I wonder if he'd love me well.

I tell myself he would. The snow pours down, a thick white curtain out in front of me, and I think it's a shame I never realized sooner: Elvie doesn't love me. I'm not sure he can.

That's what's been missing. Not just love—the possibility of finding it. I won't, not with Elvie. But he's comfortable. Elvie is easy. Warm and cozy.

What I need is fresh—and cold. A new start. Scary.

I say a silent prayer that I'm brave enough to change.

Barrett
December 27, 2015

I strap the brace on my left hand and look down at my fingers. The three that don't move on their own are tightly curled against my palm: just tight enough so they can wrap snugly around the grip panel of my .22.

Christmas from Gwenna. So goddamned thoughtful.

I unload a few shots into the bull's eye out in front of me, then use the lever on the fence to move the target back another thirty yards.

A cold breeze smacks it from the side, causing the bull's eye paper to flutter. All the better. I set my sights on the small, red dot and pull the trigger with my right index finger.

When the bullet slices cleanly through the middle, I grin and blow on my fingers.

Not bad for a leftie.

I spend another half an hour at the range. It's just three miles from our houses, but I still wouldn't be here were it not for my secret Christmas present to myself. I feel fucking bad about it if I think about it too long, so I try not to. I just watch her on my phone and see her singing in her car and get a deep, relieved breath.

She's leaving Home Depot with some bungee cords for the trip. We're leaving tomorrow. I follow along with her as she heads toward her hair place. Fuck, her voice is gorgeous. She's singing some old-school country music. Reba, I believe. Dove went through a country phase in Myanmar one time, so I know the classics.

When she exits the Mini Cooper, I'll track her phone. Be sure she gets into the hair place. If she loses the phone, it doesn't matter. All her shoe soles have been punctured, and the right shoe of every pair harbors a tiny GPS tracker.

I turn up the volume, trying and failing to muster up some guilt for listening to her sing while I finish up. Her voice is…like a living thing. It gets inside my chest. So far, I've withheld her last Christmas gift: a booking to sing at an upscale whiskey bar in Breckenridge on New Year's Eve. I was hoping it might take her mind off things.

Since Christmas night, I've asked her to sing to me as we go to sleep. So I can tell for sure: her voice is not affected by what happened to her mouth. She can hit all the notes, make all the sounds. I'm not sure why she doesn't perform anymore.

Something hot and tight takes hold of the back of my throat. I load the gun up and walk slowly back to my Jeep. She told me the other night that not remembering what happened to her is a problem. That she feels like she can't move on in the way she wants to.

I haven't been able to think about it since then, but now I do, as I drive back toward our houses.

It makes me feel ill.

I've been thinking more and more what matters most for someone: honesty, cohesion? Or love? There shouldn't be a choice between the two, but if there was? Then what?

What can I do for Gwenna? What can I give her? Everything I can, and my whole heart. Is that enough?

I get to her house before she does, and I'm so restless, I change clothes and jog up to the rock. I check her on my phone when I get to the enclosure gate. Still at the fucking hair salon. I run back up the hill again, so by the time she rolls into the garage, freshly styled and looking like a miracle, I'm dripping sweat.

So what does my sweet girl do? She takes my hand, kisses my sweaty jaw, and leads me in the laundry room, where she strips my wet clothes off and grabs me by the dick. We fuck on a blanket by the couch, Gwen riding me. She looks like an angel with her coppery hair swinging around her shoulders, bouncing off her creamy breasts.

I blow as she clenches my dick with her own orgasm, so hard I feel like I'm coming apart. I'm still hazy when she returns from wherever she went with a wet cloth. She kisses my lips before she drapes it over my face.

"Thanks," I manage.

I feel weird, so reflexively, I hope she goes. That's what I do—I realize more and more. When I have a problem, my instinct—my instinct as a former Operator—is to hide it. Hide me.

So I'm surprised how good I feel when Gwenna tucks the blanket over me and snuggles up beside me. She kisses my temple...My cheek. Her gentle fingers stroke my hair.

"I saw you awake the last two mornings."

I cut my bleary eyes at her, and find hers warm and understanding.

I roll on my side, hesitant about bringing my sweaty self closer to her. But Gwen wraps an arm around me.

"If you want to talk, you know I'm here. And if you don't, just fall asleep. I thought of doing stir-fry burgers, you know, with onions and green peppers and some sauce? I'll wake you up soon—or the smell will."

My eyes squeeze shut as my throat tightens. A tear slips out. I rest my forehead against her throat and swallow.

"Why do you love me?"

I didn't mean to ask. The words just tumbled out.

Her hand, stroking my back, goes still, then starts to make a slow, firm circle. I feel her soft laugh as it moves inside her throat. "Why don't I, Bear? I can't even think of one thing." I feel her lips move over my hair. "If I really love you, I love everything, yeah? Good and less good. Whole burrito." She laughs softly, tucking the blanket more tightly around me. "So there is no 'why.' There's 'why not', and there's no reason why not. You know what else?"

"No," I whisper.

"I'm not flip-floppy. I don't change my mind once it's made up. When I like someone, I like them. My college beau? I always kind of knew he was a prick, but he was comfortable, I think. Jamie? Liked her from the second I met her. Nic, her boyfriend? Never have. Don't even know why. You?" She strokes my hair. "Love at first kick. And you know what else?"

"What else?"

"I've been thinking about this a lot lately. It sounds kind of weird, but hear me out." When I don't speak, she goes on, "You might say you don't deserve it—and you don't—'deserve' it. Love is, by its definition, impossible to earn. It's an abundance. It's extravagant. Did Bill Gates 'earn' a gazillion dollars? That much money can't be 'earned.' He hit the jackpot for a thousand different reasons. Worthy or not. Love is like that, I think. It can't be deserved. It's given. It's a gift. And I'm giving it to you. You wanna try to give it back?"

I lay there, breathing. I kiss her throat. "You're incredible, Piglet." I would never think to say that in the way that she did, but I feel it just the same. I wish I could convey it.

"You're the best thing I've ever had. The best thing in my life."

"I'll take it," she says. "Because I want it."

She wants me. For just a moment, I savor it.

chapter twenty

Gwenna
December 30, 2015

We fly out of Nashville just a little shy of 5 p.m., on a nonstop flight to Denver International Airport. Barrett booked our tickets and surprises me with first class. I get strangely teary as we sink into our roomy, leather seats. Jamie and Nic spent Christmas in Breckenridge with her family. It's the earliest she's ever headed out to Colorado, and the first time she made the holiday trek without me. That Barrett booked us in first class—gives me all the feels. He doesn't notice, I don't think. In fact, in his fluffy new olive green down jacket—hip-length, with a sweatshirt type hood, ragged jeans, and sneakers, he looks slightly sleepy.

He's been keeping close to me all day. He had his arms around my waist in line to board, which is sort of unusual for him. He's never minded a little PDA, but he seemed downright handsy. Which I happen to love, but which makes me wonder what's up with him.

What's his mood? I can't tell. He seemed in a good mood, making French toast and bacon for breakfast before I even got out of the shower, but then he shaved his beard and sheared his gorgeous curls way down, and…I don't know. It seemed so random. He seemed tense after he did it. He still seems off.

We latch hands for takeoff, and I cover us with the bear blanket Rett got me for Christmas. It's fleece, with a picture of a black bear wandering the woods. Fitting, since Rett is staying at my place most of the nights we'll be gone.

When we reach cruising altitude, Barrett looks down at me and gives me a gentle smile. A few minutes later, he's asleep, slumped over in his seat, his cheek resting on my shoulder. Poor guy. I know he hasn't been sleeping well these last few days.

I can't help wondering if it's me. If it's this trip. He has those dreams about seeing people he knows lying dead, and this trip— It's kind of about that. About how I was hurt. About the accident. At this point, I think everyone knows that. Why I keep coming out here every year, even last year, when I played third wheel to Jamie and Nic. Because I'm seeking closure.

What they don't know is I might have found it.

Only Helga knows so far: I think I recognized the voice. The man's voice. My attacker in the bear enclosure. His voice was familiar. When I think about it, I smell beer. I feel beer slosh over my arm. I think someone called me "snowflake."

Just snippets. She said it's not unusual at all. I'll probably never remember everything on my own, not with a traumatic brain injury, but I could still remember little bits and pieces.

I knew that guy, once. Or know him now. In my dreams, I recognized his voice. I found tickets to an exclusive-ish whiskey bar where celebrities like to hang out on Main Street. Barrett wants to take me there on New Year's Eve. And that's a good thing. It's not even a block from Gemütlichkeit—where I spent my last night as my old self. Where I got a stranger's scarf and spilled beer on my shirt.

Barrett loves me, I think as I snuggle in beside him. With him here, I think I just might solve some mysteries.

"So Nic is staying next door and you're here?"

With a little side jump and one palm for balance, Jamie shifts to sit on the counter, but her butt knocks the alarm clock off.

"Oof." Her mouth is full of toothpaste. I giggle and scoop the clock up.

"You and the bathroom alarm clock." I shake my head.

"The only way," she mouths, losing a small glob of toothpaste bubbles.

"Ewww."

She makes a face at me and spits. "It's the only way," she says around brushing her teeth, "because…you know." She spits again. "You have to walk in here. It wakes you up."

I laugh. I *do* know. That's why I keep my alarm in arms' reach—so I can reach the snooze button.

"Anyway." She rinses her mouth out and sets her toothbrush in the little pewter holder. "Yeah, Nic's parents kinda have a hard Christmas, you know, so we thought that would be better."

"Will he be sneaking in your window like last year?"

She smiles. "No. We're an old couple now."

"I didn't say it."

"Pshh. Not lately. You're too busy with your own man."

I can't even help it. I start beaming like a kid with candy.

"He's nice looking, G. I mean, *nice* looking."

Cue more beaming.

"It's too soon to say, but I think my girl might have gotten lucky."

I'm giggling, even as I roll my eyes and throw my head back. Which reminds me I should pull my hair up. Which I do.

Jamie starts to wash her face, so I can talk without her omniscient eyes on me.

"I think so too," I say to her bent shoulders. "He's pretty wonderful."

"Your mother sculpted for him. That's a sign."

I nod. "She never did like Elvie."

"No. I don't think anybody did."

"Except me." I arch a brow at myself in the mirror. "Young, dumb Gwen."

She pats her face with a towel. "We've all been young and dumb, G."

"Yeah. You're right." I yawn. "I should go join Prince Charming in bed."

"I think it's kind of funny that he has a headache."

"Bitch!" I swipe at her. She laughs. "Not funny. But isn't he like Mr. Secret Agent Man. They go to mountains sometimes, right?"

"He has a brain injury, Jamie." I give her a for-shame look and shake my head.

"Well go take care of him," she says, giving me a little glare. "These men, wrecking our girl time."

"I know, right?"

"I think you kind of love it, though."

I hug her. "I so do."

"I love you, Gwennie."

"You more, Jam."

"I'll think of something for you for tomorrow."

"Yeah—you better."

We trade smiles and then I'm in the dark, quiet, second-floor hall, heading toward mine and Barrett's room, positioned at the far end of the floor for reasons not unknown. I grin.

Tomorrow night, Nic is hosting a giant costume party at his family's place next door. Jamie said it was only going to be a normal party, but one of Nic's friends is the tattoo artist who did my snowflake, and he has some Zelda costume, so they made a party around his desire to wear it. Ha.

Zelda reminds me, strangely, of Zoro. Maybe I should convince Bear to dress up as Zoro. Isn't he that masked marauder who wears all black and carries a gun? That would be so hot.

Maybe I should go as a bear. If I can find a bear suit. Which, okay, is 100 percent unlikely. I could go as a bandit. Then I could wear a bandana over my face.

In Breckenridge, I'm sort of…known. I wasn't ever really famous or anything, but enough people knew my face that when I had the accident, the papers in this area chronicled my recovery. Especially given how dramatic it was. I guess that made me all the more interesting.

I don't know. But my mouth draws attention, and with my red hair, I'm just worried people will ask about the accident. So I'll need some kind of mask.

I hear something behind me, and turn in time to see Jamie striding toward me in a black dress. "Hey, you. Hang on."

I give a low whistle. "I thought you were just going to 'some Southern place with fried stuff.'"

She shrugs. "It's a bar type place. You know Nic. He gets the invites every time a new place opens. I remembered something, though, G. Something I thought you might be interested in."

"Yeah? What's that?"

"Some guys came by here last night. Said they'd seen the snow plow toppled over near the street." The house's maintenance guy did, indeed, topple the plow; thank goodness he wasn't hurt. "Anyway. I could be wrong but I thought they looked familiar. I think we saw them *that* night."

"Really?"

She nods.

"Interesting. What did they act like?"

"Just normal." She shrugs. "You told me to tell you anything that came up that reminded me of the accident, so I wanted to try."

"Thanks. And have fun out."

"Will do."

As I turn, I realize I didn't ask their names. And strangely, I don't stop her. I don't need to know right now. Not right before it's time for bed. I just want to snuggle up with Bear and have a dreamless night.

chapter twenty-one

Niccolo
January 1, 2012
1:28 a.m.

M y motherfucking father: popular as all fuck politician, shit-head of a person. Everyone in Breck knows it. I can't imag-ine how Kim bears it. I'd have left him years ago. When I get back—I'll have to go home to Kim before returning next door to Jamie—I'm going to make another bid for that. I could move her out to California. No one would know her there. I think she could really benefit from that. It's got a lot of sun, like here, and no Dad.

Fucking perfect.

When I find that fuck, I'm going to haul him home. And then, behind closed doors, I'm going to punch him in his fucking teeth. Kim's friend Leah saw Dad at a coffee place in Fairplay with a woman who was not Kim. When she called John crying, he told me, but I asked him to handle it because I was enjoying Jamie so much. Also, I trust John not to throat-punch Dad. His temper's not as hot as mine is.

So he went. And then he texted me when Jamie and I were settled in the theater and said he'd tracked Dad's iPhone via Dad's Apple login info, and Dad and the woman were at what he thought was a ranch near Blue River. He said he needed to get back and check on one of his buddies, and he wasn't sure what he should do, anyway. Ring the doorbell?

So I told him we'd switch places.

Kim's my stepmom, but she's better to Casper and I than our own mom ever was. Rumor has it Dad cheated on her, but that's not true. Mom cheated on Dad, and after that, I guess he has a trust problem or something, because he's fucked around on Kim, the sweetest woman ever—she gave John her Nice Genes—from almost day one. It's shameful. Dad should feel ashamed, but I'm not sure he does.

I'm about to ask him. If I can find this fucking place. If I can get out of Breckenridge. It's snowing hard as hell.

Gwenna
December 31, 2015

"Barrett?"

He's sitting on the edge of the bed with his head in his hands.

"Hey…" I rub his broad, bare back. He turns toward me. I wrap my arms around him. I woke up from my own dream, and I'm so glad I did.

"Hey baby. It's okay. We're here together."

He's shivering. "I dreamed about Breck."

I rub his arms and back with my warm hands.

"He used to do this knock. This secret knock from his older brother's frat. I heard it. It seemed so real, Piglet." I take his hands. They're shaking.

I ease him down in the bed with me. I kiss both hands. "You're a good man, Barrett. Breck loved you. I know he did, because you are impossible not to love."

His eyes squeeze shut. His mouth flattens. He looks pained. I wait for him to ask me some anguished question, I can almost feel it coming. But he pulls me very close, holding me tightly, so I can feel his chest shaking a little. And I can feel it still.

"Thank you," he whispers.

As we drift off to sleep, I think I hear a knock at the window.

There's no question about it. Something is off with Barrett. I've noticed him staring into space a dozen times since we landed in Denver, staring at me more than normal, looking troubled, with his dark brows notched and his pretty lips melded into that pensive line.

I don't know what's wrong, and I don't want to ask, because after the information that he volunteered about his friend last night, I don't want to pry. So I just try to stay near him, to hold his hand.

The strangest thing is, looking out for him is making me feel better. With his hand in mine, I feel less alone here. I smile at him; he smiles at me. There's something comforting about loving on him.

We spend the last day of 2015 inside this bubble, taking fabric to a woman who works out of a little cottage north of town so she can sew Barrett a Zoro mask and alter a black blouse for me to wear with my red bandana; sitting beside each other in a small booth in a sandwich shop downtown, Barrett's arm around my shoulder, even as he eats; touring a candy factory where he buys me salted caramel fudge and I buy him a massive chocolate bear; buying cowboy boots and black jeans; picking up the rest of our costumes; and finally heading back to the Madisons' place just in time for pre-party hors d'oeuvres. I'm surprised to find Jamie eating goat cheese dip and crackers with her parents, no Nic in sight.

She's already wearing her pink contact lenses.

"Hey there, alien."

She studies the bags Bear and I are holding. "Zoro and..."

"His sidekick."

"A nameless sidekick?"

I shrug. "I thought of going as his horse."

Mr. Madison gets a chuckle out of that.

"So when are you all going next door?" Jamie's mom asks.

"I'll probably go soon," Jamie tells her. "Help set up."

"We might go soon, too."

After a few minutes of small talk, the three of us escape upstairs. Jamie tries to chat us up, but Barrett is clearly unenthused. I can tell he's trying, which makes it all the more obvious. Jamie gives us both an understanding smile. "I'm going to put on my alien gear! See you next door in a bit?"

I nod.

While Barrett showers, I sit on the bed and look out at the window he was staring through when I woke up last night. I get up and go over to it, staring down at the snow. It looks like... footprints. In between the bushes. As I tip my forehead toward the glass and squint, I hear the door creak.

I turn, then jump as Batman appears in the doorway. "Oh my God! Nic?"

He nods, removing his mask.

"Wow, you're...very Batman-like. You scared me."

"Looking out the window?" he asks.

"Yeah. I thought I saw some footprints."

He comes over to stand beside me. "Mine."

"What?"

He nods. "Jamie was in this room last year, remember?"

"Oh yeah. I guess she was. Were you trying to signal her or something?"

He smiles slightly. "Yeah. Hope I didn't wake you guys up."

"No," I lie. "Barrett hasn't been sleeping very well," I babble. "Probably the altitude or something."

"Maybe. I can always feel it when I come back up here."

He taps the window with his knuckles, then turns toward the door. "I guess my alien's not in here."

"Nope. You try her parents' bedroom?"

He snorts. "Pass."

"Yesterday she said she might make her eyebrows darker with one of her mom's pencils."

"Ahh." He lifts his brows, and something about the moment makes my stomach rearrange itself.

Even after he leaves, I feel weird. Kind of spacey, like I might dissociate at any moment. *That's normal*, I tell myself. This night is always going to be weird. We'll go next door, show face at the party, and then go to the site of the accident.

I had thought about visiting the beer bar, too, but now I'm not so sure. Maybe I don't have to find out anything new on this trip. Maybe I should just try to move on. With Barrett, I feel like it might finally be possible.

When he comes out of the bathroom with a towel wrapped around his waist, I lead him over to the bed and unwrap him. I take his thick cock in my hands and start to stroke it, while he moans and tweaks my nipples.

"Gwenna…"

"I need you," I whisper, squeezing him. "In my mouth…or pussy?"

"Let me eat this pussy. Then…" He lays me on the bed, never finishing his thought as he peels my pants and panties down and gently spreads me…Tastes me with the tip of his tongue.

I grip his arms, moaning as his tongue trails up my slit, lapping gently at my throbbing clit.

"Lay down so I can suck your dick." I pull on him, and Barrett does as I ask.

I get him in my throat, playing with his balls as he makes my body tremble from the pleasure of his tongue. I start to ride his face, taking his cock deeper with every moan. I feel him harden… tighten…swelling, and he lifts his hips. He moans against my pussy.

I can feel his hips shake as he tries to keep from thrusting at me.

I moan, and he trembles. I can taste him. His tongue circles my clit. I focus on his balls, so taut and heavy in my hands. I stroke them, stroke the base of his cock. Suck him deeper, work him with my tongue, and Barrett touches me just right, and I explode.

He holds out another second or two, and then he's pulling out. I grab his hips, so I can swallow. We end up, sometime later, wrapped up in each other as the light outside the window turns a fuzzy, indigo blue.

"Bear?" I press a kiss against his nape.

"Mmm."

I'm spooning him, but he turns around, onto his back, so he can get an arm around me.

"Scoot back over," I scold. "Let me hold you. It makes me feel good," I add softly.

He does, and I wrap myself around him.

"Do you want to skip tonight?"

"Tonight?"

"The party." I play with his now-short hair.

"Do you want to?" He reaches behind himself, rubbing his palm over my hip.

"I don't care. I'd probably vote 'go,' for Jamie. But I doubt she cares."

"Then let's go."

He turns over on his stomach and pushes up on his arms, so he can look at me. His eyes are surprisingly soft.

"Do you want to talk? You haven't…much."

"About the accident?"

He nods.

I shake my head. "Not now. Maybe later tonight. I could tell you the whole story."

He smiles sadly. "Okay, Pig."

chapter twenty-two

Barrett
December 31, 2015

The gun is at the bottom of my duffle bag. If you pack them right, the airport scanners never know.

One of those job perks they can't take away…

I didn't want to bring the gun.

I hadn't planned to.

Then Blue called.

Things have changed.

I take the gun out of the bag and unwrap it. Then I don my black costume. I say a silent prayer before I leave the bathroom, .38 strapped to the inside of my boot.

Gwenna
January 1, 2012
1:42 a.m.

"Oh my God, you're *Jessica*! From *End of Day*!"

The girl's brown eyes are huge in her freckled face. Her jaw drops in stunned elation, and I nod, casting my eyes down for just long enough to steel myself. I've had some practice with this sort of thing since EoD came out. It's an indie film, and like a lot of good indies, it's developed a bit of a cult following.

By the time I glance back up, the girl has whirled around, the knot of her work apron riding up her mid-back, revealing a dancing Grateful Dead bear tattoo.

As I set my items on the Breckenridge General Store's counter, she cups her hands around her mouth and bellows, "Come here, Silas! Jessica from *End of Day* is here, and she's buying one of your dad's gardenias!"

I hear the smack of shoes on the cement floor, then a high school guy steps out from between two aisles. He's tall, with white-blond Justin Bieber hair. He sticks his hands in his pockets as my eyes roll up and down him, keeping his gaze on his sneakers, his face cool, while the brown-eyed, brunette cashier cuts her eyes at him. When he comes to a stop beside the nearest magazine display and doesn't fall down at my feet, she gives him an incredulous look. "Seriously, Silas? You're the biggest fan. Can you believe she's fucking here?"

Never meeting my eyes, he gives her a sideways smile and murmurs, "No."

I'm betting this boy has my Abercrombie pool party stuff, or my Burberry nothing-under-the-jacket campaign bookmarked in his spank bank. Which means it's time to change the subject before we all end up embarrassed.

"Your dad grows the gardenias you guys sell?" I ask him, hoping to put everyone at ease, as well as steer the subject away from the movie. I'm a singer, not an actress—although I am proud of the movie.

The guy nods and finally, he looks me in the eyes.

"It's a kind of insanity," he says, revealing a retainer than makes his voice sound—well, like he's got something in his mouth. "They won't survive for long in someone's yard. So they're just house plants up here."

I hover a fingertip over one of the satiny white leaves, mostly so I can break the stare he's aiming at me like a laser beam.

"It's probably insanity to buy one when it's snowing this hard. I'm not even staying at my own place." I smile at them before I realize my publicist would smack my mouth for giving details.

"Jessica," the girl squeals, jumping up and down.

I tug Mr. Madison's big black jacket down around my ankles before reaching in his huge pocket to grab my wallet out.

"That's...not me," I murmur, joking.

"God, she's *famous*," the girl says to the boy, scanning my four-roll pack of toilet paper. I pass her the plant.

"You're a model too," the boys says, "right?"

I struggle to suppress a cringe. "Yep. But really I'm a singer."

"A singer?" the girl says.

I nod. "I have a record deal. My sound is somewhere between teenage Taylor Swift and old-school country. With a kind of bluesy undertone. Singing is my true passion."

"Damn," the boy says as the girl takes my cash. "You're multi-talented."

Heat tingles on my cheeks. Clearly, I'm 12.

The girl starts belting out a Taylor Swift song I recognize while the boy shuffles his feet. Thank God, I'm out of there not long after.

I step outside onto the cement walkway and am pummeled by fat snowflakes.

"Christ..."

I cross myself for taking the Lord's name in vain—a habit I picked up from Elvie—then cast my eyes to my boots and shuffle carefully toward the SUV.

Which doesn't crank.

Like, seriously. This thing will not crank.

"DAMMIT."

Just my motherloving luck.

I set the gardenia in the passenger's seat and try again a few times. Nothing.

"Ughh."

I look at my phone, even though I know already it will have no more than one bar. This is Breckenridge. My service blows here. Probably everyone's service blows here.

I could go inside, but Jamie got a new number recently, and I don't know it. I've got Elvie's memorized. And Mom and Dad's. But how will they help if they don't know Jamie's new number either?

I let out a big sigh. Then I rip the pack of toilet paper open, stuff a roll in Mr. Madison's huge pocket, and blink down at the gardenia in the passenger's seat.

I think it will probably freeze or something if I leave it here all night. The Madisons—they may not care to come and get the car until tomorrow. Cars are nothing to them. Cheap. Almost like bicycles.

With the gardenia under one arm, tucked partway inside my long down coat, I point myself toward the Madisons' place and start the trek back. I'm young and healthy. I've got snow shoes. There's a full moon, too.

What could possibly go wrong?

Gwenna
December 31, 2015

The weirdness of this night is a double-edged sword. One the one hand, it's weird. Not cool weird—awkward weird. And no one likes awkward weird. On the other hand, it's *so* weird, the weirdness occupies my mind, so I'm not thinking much about *It*.

I'm thinking about Barrett. And wondering what's up with him. Why he seems so miserable.

I'm trying not to be, but I'm getting kind of worried.

I know him so well now, I can just feel it. As we dance; he's a good dancer, but it rolls off him in waves. When our fingers brush as he hands me a glass of wine, his curl away from mine. When I sit on this little couch-like thing to take a break from dancing, he sits by me, and he sits so close. His arm around me is so heavy. And when I look up at his face, at his eyes, gray-blue orbs that peer down at me from the center of the ovals cut into his mask, they look depthless—almost pained.

At one point, as I elbow my way toward the bathroom—he's behind me, our fingers intertwined—his hand feels so damp, so still and stiff, I whisper-hiss, "Do you feel bad?"

When he doesn't look at me, I say his name.

"Hm?" His eyes find mine. They're wide, slightly intense.

We're in a long, quiet hallway now. I nudge him against the wall, then wrap myself around him. I lift our joined hands to my mouth and kiss him on the inside of his wrist. Soft, tender skin. I bite it, and his hooded eyes lose focus.

I lift my lips off his wrist, wrap my arms around his neck, and pull him down to kiss him. God, I need this. I just need to feel him right now.

His kisses feel as desperate as mine do. His mouth is hard and punishing, soft and silky, gentle, frantic. His fingers thread through my hair, tugging as our tongues and lips dance, making my scalp ache. His breath is warm and wine-sweet, puffing into my mouth on low groans. His beard is short. It stings me. I don't care.

I rock myself against his thigh and rub him through his pants until he moans into my mouth. I nip along his upper lip, then capture it between my teeth and suck. I love it when he gets hard in my hand. I love to tease his head, to torture him through fabric.

Every time my fingers trace his bulge, he breathes a little harder. His mouth on mine is ruthless. Finally he grabs me by the elbow, pulling me toward the nearest door. He opens it and we behold a bedroom, pearly from the moonlight streaming through two windows. He tosses me over his shoulder, smacks my ass, and shuts the door.

"Gwen. I have to have you now." His voice is hoarse, almost emotional. His body's hard—as if we're headed for a nameless fuck.

I'm tossed on the bed. I land with my feet hanging off the side, my legs slightly spread, the pillows vibrating around me as the mattress springs settle. Barrett stands against bedside, his cock tenting the fabric of his pants. He pulls my black boots off and quickly rids me of my pants and panties.

"Now," he breathes, and takes his own pants down. I reach for his dick, my fingertips brushing it for a second before his hand captures my arms.

His eyes are hot behind the mask. His tongue traces along his lower lip as he trails a finger through my slit.

His head tips slightly back. "Oh, Piglet…"

"Wet for you," I murmur.

"I can't wait."

"Don't wait…"

His eyes shut as he grabs me by the hips, positioning me at the bed's edge. He wraps a hand around his cock and spreads my lips, rubbing his head in my slickness, making circles till I'm crying out, my clit throbbing, my thighs shaking.

"Now," I pant.

He pushes gently at my entrance, stretching me just slightly. "God…"

I wriggle up against him, desperate to take all of him. With a low chuckle, he plunges in. He's so damn big, I cry out. He fills me so deeply, stretches me so perfectly, I can't help thrusting my hips at him…taking him so deeply I lose track of everything but him in me.

"Barrett…"

"God, I love you…Love you, Gwen. I love you."

My throat is so tight, I can't reply, so I look up at him and find his face is lifted to the ceiling. "*Jesus.*"

He fucks me like our lives depend on it. He fucks me like he's marked for death and my flesh is his last supper. He fucks me so I know I'm made for this, for him, I'm made to welcome him inside me, made to breathe with him and clench around him as I sigh and he groans.

When we're finished and he finally rises off me, his eyes glisten in the moonlight.

chapter twenty-three

Niccolo
December 31, 2015

Jamie told me about the telescope at Barrett's house. How much her friend Gwen likes it. So it's not hard to get rid of them both. My girl is more than happy to take her bestie upstairs to the mini-planetarium Kim designed and had installed a year and a half ago: a way, she told my dad, to see her son. It cost a fortune, but he has that. If he hadn't paid for it, I would have.

I've known for two days now that my team has been spotted. Since then, I've been thinking. Planning.

Until last year, I did a monthly write-up in the local rag. Hollywood insider type of shit. Fun for me, exciting for the people here, my way to give back to the community since I'm not willing to be a politician/whore like Dad.

I paid a visit to the *Gazette*'s offices the day we arrived. I took Jamie with me. It was perfect. She yakked her head off while I went into the archive room to "make copies of my work."

"For old times' sake," I'd told the editor, a flighty little lady named Sue.

Instead, I pulled an old New Year's edition. The *Gazette* is an afternoon paper, so what I'm looking for is there. I've seen this edition many times before, have piles of it in the wine cellar below my parents' place.

I step out of the archives looking troubled, hands in pockets. The article of interest is crumped in my pocket.

"Sue," I say in a puzzled voice, "I can't find something I'd like to copy."

"What are you looking for?"

I explain, with Jamie's help, her best friend's situation. Jamie has been telling me about her friend. Gwen's struggles. Her attack.

"I wasn't sure she even had a copy of the write-up." I look wide-eyed down at Jamie. She nods, and I can see the gratitude in her eyes—appreciative that I care.

"You know…" She taps her cheek. "I doubt she does. That's actually a really good idea. Might give her some closure."

The three of us canvass the archive room. Sue is shaken when she discovers that the page is missing. Jamie is more shaken.

"It could be him! The person who attacked Gwen. Him or… her, I guess. Who would take something like that? And why? I don't get it."

I shake my head. I'm glad she doesn't. Very, very glad my lover doesn't get it.

With Jamie and Gwen upstairs now, I find Barrett where I know I will: in John's room. The dude is standing by my brother's bookshelf with his arms crossed; really, wrapped around himself. I recognize his stance. In acting, it's an advanced skill set: displaying pain, appearing vulnerable, while keeping the face blank. But Barrett has it down. *Bear,* John called him.

I could pity him, but I don't let myself. There's no point.

I hear him inhale as I step into the room. When he sees it's me, he bows his head, biding his time to see what I will do. John told me some of this shit. Their secret agent mind-fuck shit. Not so much different than what Dad does, really. John was different. He was better than this manipulative shit. This guy is nothing like my brother. John died for him, and Barrett isn't worthy.

That helps.

It helps with my conscience.

"Bear," I say. I let my knowledge resonate in my voice. "I *thought* you were familiar…"

I've got to give it to him: He removes that stupid Zoro mask and looks me in the eye, and I can see he's sorry. I can see he's eaten up with guilt.

"You're my brother's friend. The one…" I start.

I struggle to keep my face neutral as his eyes glimmer. He nods, solemn. He seems penitent. I tell myself that's good. He should be.

"You were close to John," I say. "He told me you were his best friend."

I watch his teeth come down on the inside of his cheek, his throat working to keep his emotions silenced.

"He was mine," he says hoarsely.

I step closer to him. "It's a shame what happened. No one's fault," I lie. I raise my eyebrows. "If nothing else, we can know that he died doing what he loved."

Barrett nods. His jaw is tight, though. He won't look me in the eye.

"So, how long you been with Gwen?"

His eyes lift to mine. "Why?"

I can see aggression push the sadness off his face.

I hold my hands up. "Just asking."

He surprises me by stepping closer to me. "No, you're not."

I laugh, as if he's crazy, still holding my hands up.

"You think I didn't notice how you followed us around all night?"

557

"Is that a crime?"

His jaw clenches. He shakes his head. I watch his nostrils flare as he exhales. "I'm sorry." He shuts his eyes, rubbing his temples. Opens his eyes and holds my gaze. He looks exhausted. "What can I do for you, Nic?"

"I *was* watching you," I murmur.

His eyes sharpen. "Why?"

"John told me something. About you. And Gwen. He was always asking about her." I lower my voice. "He told me, Barrett. John told me."

I feel a bubble of satisfaction as the blood drains from his face.

"What do you mean?" he rasps.

"I think you know what I mean. Don't worry, Bear. I won't tell."

I can see it on his face: the distrust. He doesn't believe me. And that's exactly what I want.

Gwenna
December 31, 2015

Our rental car is a Ford Explorer: midnight blue, according to the small bottle of touch-up paint inside the glove box. Fitting, I think, as I watch pearly moonlight pool atop the hood. Snowflakes swirl in front of us, flying up over the windshield as Bear drives toward the general store.

The drive's not far—somewhere between a mile and half a mile, I know by now—but Barrett's going slow. We're supposed to get some crazy snow tonight, and he probably figures, rightly, that I'm already on edge.

Every few minutes, I feel his eyes on me. When our eyes meet, his mouth curves gently. *I love you.* I see it in his eyes, despite the darkness that's been in them since we got to Colorado.

At least I know the "why" on that now. After we came back downstairs, Jamie and I tracked Bear and Nic to a bedroom in Nic's parents' place. When they saw us, Nic went right into the hall with Jam, while Barrett stayed inside. I stepped in, and before I noticed all the military stuff, I noticed Bear: so still and tense and…shell-shocked.

He told me John—Nic's brother John, the dead brother—was his friend, Breck. He stretched out on John's bed, put his hands over his face, and just kept shaking his head.

"I fucked up, Gwen. I fucked up…I'm fucked up. I don't know what to do."

"I love you. You're not fucked up."

I tried to soothe him with my hands and words. He put his face against my neck, and I just held him for the longest time. Even now, with him beside me, dry-eyed and seemingly okay, my heart still feels a little bruised.

"Remember what I said," I tell him as we near the store.

His eyes slide to me, then back to the road.

"We can't be who we used to be. You're someone new. I'm someone new. The more I think about it, the more I wonder if it matters that I know what happened to me here. I'm here with you. I met you, and if you think about it, that's amazing. That it even happens. Two people who are right for each other meet up, in a world with billions of people. How unlikely is that? I just want to park in front of the store and go inside and then walk to the spot, and when we get back in the car, I think this will be over for me. Really. I'm going to leave it here. In Breckenridge. And when we leave, we won't come back again on New Year's."

His hand finds mine and squeezes—hard.

"I love you," he rasps.

"I love you."

The parking lot is dimly lit. The air is thick with falling snow. The place is quiet: only four cars, and all parked near the back of the small lot. Employees.

"Care to go inside with me?"

He nods, and kisses my cheek. I decide when we get back into the car, I'll do one final thing before I put all this behind me: I will tell him every detail of that night.

In fact, maybe I'll start my story when we reach the point of impact.

It can only be a good thing. Good and healing.

chapter twenty-four

Barrett
December 31, 2015

The night is dark. The road is white. The snow-caked trees that crowd the shoulder dangle icicles that click as wind dives down the famous ski slopes, somewhere in the pinkish clouds above us.

The weather radio said the snow will keep on through tomorrow night. A New Year's blizzard, maybe twenty inches. This is Breckenridge in winter. Frozen to a crackle. Cloaked in white.

Gwenna's breath and mine plume silver in the velvet dark that hangs like a stage curtain over the curved road. Snow is falling fast now, caking our jacket hoods and freezing in a sheen of sparkles. Her coat is the color of a plum—or blood. The thick down softens her form. She reminds me of an animal: one sweet and small, in need of shelter.

I must be more head-fucked than I thought, because she turns around, her cheeks red, her lashes wet with snowflakes, and I realize she's about twenty feet ahead of me.

"Bear?"

Her large brown eyes are widened slightly—in affection or alarm? Her mouth twitches, then presses into a small, red line. She doesn't speak, and there's no need. I know her so well. I can see the worry on her face, the burden of her fear and grief a notch between her brows.

"Come walk by me and hold my hand." She pulls her left glove off and reaches for me.

I oblige her. Anything she wants. With two long strides, I've closed the space between us. My hands are ungloved. I told her I forgot my gloves, but that's a lie. I need to feel the sting.

Her hand folds around mine and Gwen gasps.

"Barrett! Brr, I need to warm you up…" She pulls my hand into her jacket sleeve, gripping it tightly. "Crazy man."

She laughs, despite the somberness of our affair. Her eyes, wet ink in the moonlight, shine with love—for me.

"Hang on." With her right hand, she unzips her jacket. "Come here…"

She takes my hands and pulls them into her jacket, pressing them atop her sweater, underneath which I can feel her heart beat.

Her face tilts up to mine, despite the driving snow. "You can't be leaving gloves at home. It's so cold. You'll get frostbite." Behind her words, there is a smile—a small, lopsided smile she gives me almost all the time. A dreamy smile I love more than life.

I try my best to return it.

Her boots shuffle in the snow as she tries to step closer to me. "It's so freaking cold. Even with a-all these layers." She shivers, and I pull a hand out of her coat, tucking her close to me and rubbing my hand over her back.

"Better?"

"Yes!" Her voice trembles with cold.

I press her hood over her head and rub behind her neck, down to her shoulder blades, right where she likes.

"I love you." Her eyes peek out from behind the faux-fur lining her big hood. I see them crinkle with another smile.

"I love you too." I pull her close again, and God, I'd like to keep her here forever, locked against me like a splint.

"My Bear," she whispers.

I swallow. We're not there yet, but I'm starting to feel frozen—on the inside. A deep breath does nothing to thaw me. She rubs my arms through my jacket and smiles at me again. This smile is curious. Perhaps concerned.

"Your nose is red," she croons.

Her sweet voice doesn't thaw me either, but I still smile. "Yours too." I hug her close once more, but even that can't pierce the ice that's thick inside me.

We walk on, along the road's edge, through a deep snowdrift I worry will spill into her boots.

Somewhere miles away, I hear a lone firework.

She takes my hand again, searches my face as we walk slowly. "I'm glad you came with me. I'm feeling better than I ever have before. Just knowing that I'm not alone, you know? Jamie used to come with me, but you're different. I feel…healed or something."

My jaw clenches. I force my lips to curve up at the corners. "Good." I know my eyes on hers are earnest. "That's good," I murmur.

She comes closer to me. We are leg to leg, shoulder to shoulder. I'm walking off the road, so she seems as tall as I am.

"Bear?"

"Yeah?"

"Are you okay?"

I blink. "Of course." I stroke her hand. "I'm supposed to ask you that."

She smiles a little, tight and sad. "I am."

We're almost to the bend where the road curves into a copse of trees when pops like mortar sound above us. The clouds are too thick to see the fireworks. They glow faintly—green, pink, gold, purple, blue.

Gwen's face looks delicate and beautiful in the changing light. Her eyes hold mine, and she smiles.

"This is kind of nice."

I nod. Her gaze shifts upward, and I struggle to swallow.

Fuck.

I shut my eyes. I think about her under me tonight, about the way she leaned up when we both finished and wrapped her arms around me, bringing me down on her.

"Sweet Bear. Something's bugging you. I'm going to find out. Unless you decide to tell me. Hmm?"

A snowflake melts on my temple, and I can feel the ghost burn of her lips there.

"I love you. You know that, right? You're mine—and you will always be mine. Just because I said so."

"Bear?" Her voice is high and sharp. Her hand is on my arm.

I keep my eyes shut, even as the moisture freezes on my cheeks.

"What's wrong?" Her voice is softer now. Inviting. Understanding.

I inhale, and I can't feel my frozen chest. I still can't look at her.

"Hey…" She wraps her arms around my waist.

Don't do that.

"Is it the noise?"

I squeeze my eyes shut tighter. Shake my head.

"What is it then?"

She strokes my shoulders. I can barely feel it through my jacket. But my hands are free. My hands are free to reach into my pocket.

"It's okay, baby." She wraps her arms around my neck and pulls me lower. Her lips touch my face—ice cold. I feel her stand down off her tiptoes.

"Is it me?" She whispers. "I've been feeling like it's triggering for you. Something about this. Coming here?"

She knows me, this girl. Gwenna misses nothing.

It's an effort to open my eyes. To look at her face. Gwenna, whom I love. Gwen for whom I've waited my whole life.

That I have to do this...

That this is the end. It hurts so much. I ease my hand into my pocket, wrap my fingers around the gun grip. I look into her lovely eyes, although it almost kills me.

"Gwen..."

If Niccolo knows. If people are following me, following *us*, and Blue says they're not his father's guys...

It's not as if they'd actually tell Blue. If his father decided to pull the trigger, why would they tell Blue ahead of time?

Nic is a security risk. And I can't kill him. Not John's brother. Blue's father is a threat. A real one.

I'm a risk: to Gwen.

I squeeze the gun, not knowing what to do. I don't know what to fucking do.

Gwenna

Something is very, very wrong. That's all I know at first. Barrett is talking things that don't make sense. His hands are in his hair. His eyes are huge. His mouth is open. He looks stunned—or hurt. As if he doesn't know where he is, or what is going on.

I grab onto his hips. "Barrett! Look at my face."

His gaze hits mine, then bounces away. He whirls, looking around like someone's hunting us.

"Bear…" Above us, fireworks pop. "You're scaring me. Please look at me."

He starts to shake. Even with the heavy snowfall, I can see it in his shoulders. Hear it in his breathing. He sounds hoarse, like he can't get enough air.

I take a long second to calm my own body. Panic attack. That's what he's having. That's what I'm having. Because we're here. We're almost to the spot.

You're okay. You're not a victim here tonight. Take care of Bear. Go wrap your arms around him.

So I do.

I wrap myself around my poor Barrett. I make my way around to the front of him. His face is like a riot; I don't think he sees me.

"Bear…" I stroke his arms. "Sweet Bear. Look at my eyes. Look at me. It's Piglet. Can you look at me?" I rub his chest. "Tell me where you are, sweetheart. In real life we're right here together. Listen to my voice. Where are you, baby?"

"It's…so cold."

"You're cold?"

"The gun is cold."

"Barrett." I grab his face. "You need to look at Gwenna. Look at me. Look at my eyes."

He does, for just a split second. His gaze is gone fast, wrenched away. His hands are in his pockets.

"I had a plan," he chatters. "Gwen, I had a plan. To keep you safe. I love you. You're…the world." His voice breaks. "You could move on. The twins did. Everyone moves on." He rubs his head.

His eyes are so wide.

My heart gallops. "Barrett, I'm safe, and no, I can't move on. I'm here with you. I love you, and I need you."

"Do you?" There. He looks at me.

I nod firmly.

"I've never felt like this, Gwenna." His voice cracks on a sob, and then he's sinking down into the snow. He draws his legs up to his chest and holds onto his knees. His head hangs down and he's crying, shaking like those icicles in the trees. He seems like he's cracked wide open, and it's so fucking scary.

"Bear…" My hands: inept. All over him. His back. His arms. His chest. "Barrett…Come here, baby."

I'm crouched down; I try to hug him.

"It would scare you. I know."

"What are you talking about, sweetheart? C'mon…let's stand up." He's up. He's still looking around.

"If they hurt you…because of me. Gwen. I should go now. There's this house…I rented it."

I grab his wrist and tug him with me, moving in the direction of the store.

"C'mon, baby. I'm so cold. I want to get back in the car." My voice cracks, even though I'm trying to be casual.

"You don't want me. It's not worth it, Gwen, and I don't trust them. Even Blue says not to trust them. His dad's people, they're ex-*us*, they're…They'll do anything *he* tells them to, if there's a threat…" He stops and looks around, his gaze lifting. "They could be anywhere." His voice is dry and broken. "Come stand near me. I'll get out the gun."

"What gun?" I touch his arm. "Baby, do you have a gun? With you right now?"

My heart stops somewhere in the region of my throat. I wonder if I'm going to throw up.

"He's Blue's dad. Bluebell. Michael. Gwen…" He blinks slowly. "You met him in the beer bar. He told me he kept asking you to get a fish bowl."

My whole body ignites.

"What are you talking about?"

"That night." Tears drip from his eyes. "Breck was there. And Michael. We called him Blue. I saw you outside. I saw your snowflake tattoo. You said smoking cigarettes was lonely."

Nausea swirls through my gut. It's so intense, I have to swallow.

"What?" I choke. My head fills up with static.

"We talked that night. I gave you my scarf. You left. I didn't mind," his slow voice says, "because I really liked you."

"Shut up." I don't know why, but I can feel my body shaking. My head...goes so hot. When I blink at him, I see gold spots dancing.

"They all left...and, I was fucked up...at the bar. My brother died. I tried to get in touch with Breck—"

My arms and legs buzz—

"I tried calling him. A cab...But there was so much snow. I drove really slow but...then I kinda lost my shit."

"Barrett—"

"I was drunk." The word fades on a sob, but I don't care, I just don't care, he needs to shut up.

"I was going...so slow."

"SHUT UP!" My hands are by my ears, but I can't block the sound out.

"I didn't mean to! I—"

I slap him.

"SHUT UP, BARRETT!"

I don't know why—*I don't get it!*—I turn and start to run, and I can see the snowy road, this snowy road. *I can see it, I can see the white petals vibrate as I walk. I see the scarf. I'm thinking it's so pretty, all the white. I'm cold. I'm almost back, though, just a little longer...*

"IT WAS ME!"

I'm running, but the words are like a bullet.

"IT WAS ME WHO HIT YOU, GWENNA!" The sentence collapses, half sobbed. He steps toward me, reaching. "I didn't mean to, Gwen…"

He gasps.

Barrett is losing it, I think from very far away.

He holds his head as his whole body shakes with violent sobbing. I don't understand. Can only watch.

Barrett
January 1, 2012
3:29 a.m.

It's so damn dark. Except the road. It's white. It all smears into gray for me. I wipe my eyes and grip the wheel and try to breathe through my pathetic crying.

I called Dad after the bar closed. Waiting for a cab, the wait for fucking ever. It was stupid—I knew…but I kept seeing them. The twins. Kellan—in that doorway. Jesus Christ. I want to fucking hold him. He's my brother!

Lyon. My other brother.

So I called the doctor. On-call. I asked my shitty fucking dad if he'd seen Kellan. He laughed and asked who was calling.

"Your fucking son."

There was this pause. Long enough for the cars sloshing by on Main Street to get loud. Then he said, "This isn't Kellan."

"Dad, it's Barrett."

"So he is alive."

Tears filled my eyes. "I tried to see him. Kellan wouldn't—"

He laughed. "Did you go to him like that? Where are you? I hope there's not a terrorist around."

I try for the brakes as my eyes blur again.

"I'm in Breckenridge," I told him. I don't know why.

He laughed. "I don't care where you are. You stopped being in this family when your mother died and you forgot how she expected you to behave."

"Fuck."

"Are you really in the Rangers? These are their standards?"

"Goddamnit, Dad. I called about my brothers." My throat is tight with tears. I can't help it.

"One is dead now, Barrett. No one knows what will happen to the other. But you? You should forget about it. Take yourself back to wherever you came from and find yourself some family there. When this one needed you, you weren't around."

I curl over on my side now in the driver's seat, pressing my foot against the pedal, holding onto my throat as I weep for my dead brother. Who I'll never see again. Never again. I want to fucking break his casket open. I can't believe he's really in it. Lyon…I can feel his little hand in mine, can hear him say, "It's all right, brother." The way he laughed…

But I'm not their brother. No one's brother…No one's son. No one. I waited for an hour, I called Breck. I couldn't even get a ride.

I cry harder, and I'm by my mother's bed. I want to feel her hands, the way her fingers sift through my hair, but her thin fingers are cold and still. I talk to her. My father says she doesn't hear it. He says I should go to school.

I've failed at everything.

My foot gets lost, loses the brakes. The car creeps forward, plodding slowly over heaps of snow.

I wish I wasn't here. It's cold and white and I can't see. I'm drunk as fuck. Shoulda drank more…

Kellan said I'm not his brother. Not Dad's son.

I'm nothing, I think, as I listen to my own sobbing. My father didn't want me, so I left. The twins—I told myself that they were better off without me. Couldn't keep our mom alive…They had each other. I wanted to disappear, so I did, but I'm here now. It's so white. So bumpy. Fuck, I need to fucking breathe.

I rub my chest. I can't stop. I feel kind of sick.

Even the car…the dash is really bumpy…blurry.

I should really…hit the brakes.

My brother's dead.

A loud sob shakes the car, and my foot fumbles. Brakes…but. Oh, that was the gas. My hands grab the wheel. I can see them on it. White trails, snowflakes trailing by…Just like a snow globe.

Bump!

The car is stopped. It rocks gently back and forth, like there's a log in the road. I hit the brakes. Confused, I hit the gas.

It just feels wrong. It feels familiar, like those little fucking kids under the convoy tires.

Bile leaps into my throat as I throw the door open.

December 31, 2015

"Gwennie…"

I take a backward step, arms out to keep my balance.

"I'm so sorry. I'm so fucking sorry, Gwen. I didn't mean to. I got out and…" His eyes close. He sways and sobs. "Breck and Dove, they came…and Breck stayed. He said you were dead! When I woke up, we were on an airplane."

Panic rises in me, cresting quickly, dropping just as quickly off. My mind feels fuzzy.

"Why are you telling me this?" I murmur.

"That's the problem," he is saying wildly now. "Blue's dad, Michael's father, he's a big shot. He's the Chairman of the JCoS and he was in on it. He thought he was helping us, but since then, Gwen... They know I love you, and I'm scared now! If I tell you, Gwen—" He shakes his head. "There was no way. There was no way not to. If I never told you, you would never know...these things...that you deserve to know." His eyes squeeze shut. "It's my fault. I should just leave, but I'm too selfish. I don't know. I should be dead..."

"*I* died," a strange voice says.

"I'm sorry, Gwenna. I have to protect you. I couldn't leave and tell you nothing! You'll have to protect yourself, hide out while I—"

I tackle him. I guess I get my hand around the gun. I must, because it sails into the darkness. I go at his face, his throat, his shoulders: hitting, punching, clawing. I rip him to shreds because he's everything I love. He's everything I want.

He wrecked it...

Barrett
January 1, 2016

I don't care when I hear them come up on me. I can tell by the way their footfall sounds, even in snow: there must be eight at least. I see them moving in the trees around me. I hope they come fast. The snow's so deep, and I'm so tired...I left Gwen when she passed out. I called her friend. Hours ago—or days?

And suddenly there's Dove, and Blue, and more.

I look at their faces only.

I don't want to see the guns.

I shut my eyes and summon Gwenna's face. She'll never understand. I love her. It was all an accident. *I didn't mean to hurt her...I didn't mean to love her.*

"Couldn't help it."

My eyes shut, on their own.

"Bear?" Dove's voice; maybe Blue's hands on my shoulders.

I blink up at him and then...the sting.

chapter twenty-five

Gwenna
January 4, 2016

In darkness, light looks brighter. We keep passing all these little towns in—where? Where are we? Kansas? Oklahoma? Somewhere prairie-ish. It'll be pitch black except our headlights. I'll be half asleep, my mind wiped blank for half a second. Then that light. It looks like the beam of a spaceship from behind my eyelids. I'll open them up and it's like, two farmhouses and a barn. Blinding in the darkness. There'll be this lone horse hanging by the fence line, mane all blowing in the wind, maybe a piece of tumbleweed darting across the road, and it's just so depressing. So depressing.

It's my fault, though. This is what I told Jamie I wanted. Get back home to my bears. See Papa. I can tell she doesn't think I'm strong enough. She keeps mentioning my mom's, or Rett's house. How they want to see me. *Yeah.*

"Are you awake?" she murmurs.

"Of course." I sigh, then make a mental note to stop the sighing. Nothing says *I'm a bottomless pit of black angst* like a noisy sigh.

"You should really take an Ativan."

And be transported back to January 2012 in yet another way? "No thanks."

"Stubborn."

"Pushy," I snip.

"You're allowed to be stubborn," she says with her own sigh. "Right now, I'd say you're allowed to be whatever you want."

I don't have a reply for that. I don't have a reply for most things, so I just look at my cuticles, then at the road, lit up some ways ahead by the rear lights of what I think are several eighteen-wheelers in a row.

The truth is, I wish I could take Ativan. Or Xanax. I wish I could take anything, but these last couple of days, I've been haunted by those first few months after the accident. I don't even want to *see* an Ativan, much less swallow one and enter zombie mode. I might not have much right now, but I have my own thoughts and feelings—awful though they are.

I take a sip of my McDonald's latte, lift my gaze up to the car clock. It's 12:39 a.m. Soon, I think Jamie will want to stop.

It doesn't matter where we stop, or when, really. Even without the Ativan, I'll go to sleep at some point. I'll wake up. We'll have to find breakfast, gas the car back up, and get back on the road.

And in another day or two, we'll be back to Gatlinburg. Home. And I will see my bears. I'll keep on sleeping, eating, showering, because what else is there to do? Dig a pit and fall inside and die? I've thought of it—believe me. But giving up is pointless. Not to mention, difficult. I'm not wired that way. I never really have been. Even in 2012. I never really gave up. I got sad, but I didn't quit holding on.

That's the worst thing about life, I think. The way it doesn't stop when your heart does. It feels illogical, the way time marches on, and you walk too, slowly, surreally, feeling like a fish on land. Even when you can't make sense of it, eventually, you kind of have to. There's no other way. You do—because you have to. End of story.

I wish they wrote books and made movies about this: this helpless, numb continuum. I wish I *could* go off the deep end. Shave my hair off. Bash someone else's car windshield in. Refuse to leave the bed. But that's not real life.

What is?

I don't know.

What *will* I do when I get back there?

Will he be there?

Jamie told me "no." She said Nic's been keeping up with him through his friends. Breck's buddies. Of which he—Nic—was apparently one.

Nic says Bear isn't even in the South. I heard Jamie on the phone with him last night from where I stood outside her door, crying silently, about to go inside and cry in her bed. She was saying, "So he disappeared? Back to that cabin?"

Then her super ears picked up my sniffling and she got off the phone. But I know what she meant, I think. Bear had a cabin over the summer. He spent some of this past summer up here in Breckenridge. Before deciding to find me, I guess.

I look at the dashboard and I see us walking down that road. I know what I know about his real feelings for me because of how he disappeared. Jamie found me in some PTSD fugue, lying in the snow, but there was blood under my fingernails. My knuckles are still bruised and cut. My right elbow is sore and looks a little greenish. When I tried to talk to her that night—two nights ago, I think—I barely even had a voice.

I think I screamed at him.

I know I hit him.

I don't really remember…but I have this feeling. I remember feeling…rage. I can almost kind of see his face. Wide eyes. Red eyes. I can feel the difference in our sizes. He was solid underneath my fists. *He was mine.*

Tears pool in my eyes and start to streak down my cheeks.

I loved him!

I wanted nothing more than him.

Barrett.

My Barrett.

Made up. Fiction. Gone.

The man I loved doesn't exist.

He didn't love me. He felt *sorry* for me.

How pathetic did he think I was? The way his guilt mixed in with empathy and sorrow. Not to mention loneliness.

I was his atonement, I think. Or rather, I wonder. I heard people talking the day after: New Year's Day. Something about how he didn't mean to. Didn't mean to lose his dick inside of my vagina, I guess. Didn't mean to lie, to go to Christmas with me, didn't mean to tell me all about his life.

What happened between us was an accident. The second tragic accident featuring the us as co-stars.

Oh, how much I hate him.

Want to hate him.

I don't even know I nodded off until I wake under a hotel awning dreaming something strange, in which I'm saying, "Can't."

Barrett
January 5, 2016

"Hold on now." The woman holds one finger up. "Say that again?" She's almost smiling. It's this weird half smile that's not a smile. Her head is tilted sideways. I keep waiting for my heart to pound, but I'm steady as a stone as I say it again.

"I'm guilty of a hit and run. On New Year's Eve, 2012."

Her lips roll themselves together. I watch her grayish eyebrows tighten and her brown eyes sharpen. I can see her thinking.

"Twelve…" Her cheek indents from where her molars bite down on it, but her gaze is shrewd on mine. "I think I might remember something. Tell me more, mister…?"

"Sergeant Drake." I blink. "Sorry. My name is Barrett Drake. Retired Army."

I tell the woman everything I can, omitting every detail that involves my friends. Two hours later, I'm booked into the Breckenridge County Jail.

chapter twenty-six

Gwenna
January 10, 2016
Gatlinburg

I look funny in the bathroom mirror. Not sexy. Not pretty. Strange. I half-expect to see him standing just behind me. But Barrett is a ghost. He might have been made-up, for how real he turned out to be.

He isn't here.

He hasn't called.

He doesn't care.

Because he never really loved me.

He used me.

He was hurt, and I was here. *My heart stings to even think it.* I can feel my blood thrum with the want of him. It's like a drug. An awful drug. The kind of thing that you can never free yourself from once you've tasted it.

I know how fake it all was, really. How he came here just to tell me what he'd done. He saw me at the meeting that night, heard my story, so of course he bought the house.

Funny how I almost can't assign blame to him. It was *me* who kicked him in the head. It was me who threw myself at him.

I laugh, and hate my fucking smile. *Snarile.* I snarile wider. My eyes pulse with pressure and the mirror blurs. I snatch my phone off the counter and hurl it at the mirror. The thing doesn't even break.

"FUCK!"

I double over and can't stop the sob that bursts out of my throat.

I don't want to care, don't want to love him still. His love for me was fake and tainted. Barrett pitied me. No way he didn't.

There is no way Barrett could have loved me.

I was wrong to think he could. Too perfect...I laugh through my crying. That I could even think that kind of thing could happen to me. *I'm* what's tainted.

Bitterness hangs off me like a too-large coat, and feels like someone else's. But it's mine. This life is mine—and I don't want it.

Barrett
January 19, 2016
Gatlinburg

This town has a fucking wine delivery service. Who the hell would think? Since I got here on the 12th, I've watched that fucking fuchsia-colored van climb up her driveway, watched them stop and get out. Some guy in a fucking apron, with that little rectangular brown bag. Gwenna cracks the door open and reaches out her skinny arm and I can see her pale hand stretch out in a half-assed wave, and then the door is shut. The guy drives off.

I know she's drinking all day. I still have the cams inside her house, and I have no more shame. I watch them all the fucking time. Obsessed.

If I wasn't before I met her, I know I am now—and I don't give one single, solitary fuck.

She drinks and cries, and I watch.

Tell me why I shouldn't.

I did this to Gwenna: start to finish. Hit her. Left. And then I pushed my way into her life. I let myself get drawn to her. I knew I shouldn't—from square one. Before the meeting, even, when I heard her speak up at that podium, I was obsessed with her. Obsessed with my own guilt. That I had hurt something so precious. She was beautiful and kind. I saw her with the bears, the way she held the big one up against her like some living patron saint of wounded animals.

It was fucked up—how much I loved watching her. How bad it made me feel about myself. I wanted it. Craved it. She was everything I wanted—kind and gentle, loving, bright, soft, gorgeous. But she was guilt, too. Penance. That's what I thought I was doing when I first watched her. I watched her limp. I watched her smile. I felt my heart light up with pain and it felt right: a reason not to die yet.

Then I saw her that night, talking. Saw the way she walked down off the dais with her head held high. I could see how much she loved her business. How pissed off she was, and how tenacious. And somehow, I started thinking about her more than myself.

What I could do to make things up to her. As if I ever could.

I bought the house. To give it to her. When I told her.

I was supposed to tell her. Dove and Bluebell knew I needed it, so they covered for me—Dove especially; he was stateside, and at that time, Bluebell wasn't. We agreed that it would be okay and I would tell her. If she did press charges, I had come up with a story that wouldn't incriminate anyone but me. A cover story. Not that hard.

The General's people would find out afterward. And Blue could try to fight for me. At that point, everyone watching the situation would see for themselves that I hadn't taken anybody down with me, so why the need to kill me? And if they did, well…

Dove and Blue both knew I didn't really care.

Absolution. That was all I ever wanted. Just to get that huge weight off my shoulders and feel clean again, if that could even happen.

Then things changed. I couldn't stay away from her. I got too close. She kicked me.

Sometimes I wonder why she had the key. Why did she have a copy of my house key that day? Why did God let her get in? I still pray the things I learned at her church, but I'm not sure if there's a God at all.

He let her in. He let her touch me. I was gone. I should have known right then, I should have fucking left town, but I was weak.

I needed her. Not wanted. Needed, like the need to breathe or swallow.

Free will? I'm not so sure about that. I eviscerate myself for not leaving, but if I could have, I would have—right?

My real belief: I couldn't go. As soon as I spoke to her, as soon as she touched me, I was lost to Gwenna White.

I don't understand it. Something…fit. That thing I needed fixed inside me, it was quieter when she was around. The more I got of her, the smaller the wound became. It healed.

Magic. Who could walk away from magic?

Maybe it wasn't possible for me to get away from her. Or maybe it was, and I'm a greedy asshole.

I don't know.

What was the purpose of this?

I don't fucking know. I wish I did.

It gets dark, the house gets quiet, and I get scared. I feel it, feel the darkness. *There's* the purpose. I can feel it like an undertow, pulling me down where I can't breathe, where I can never re-surface.

Good, it whispers.

Over there, it used to speak. You would feel it in the air that day when something happened. *Die. You're going to die.*

But I don't want to die, because she's still alive. She's right next door. I can't leave Gwen. I know I ought to. But I can't. When she cries, I cry with her. I've already sold all the guns, but then there are the knives. There's a bungee cord down in the basement closet. There's a thousand ways. I know them all.

So torn...

That truck goes up and down her driveway, and I watch while my mind races.

chapter twenty-seven

Gwenna
January 22, 2016

"**G**wenna Isabella White. This has *got* to stop. Lift your head up and look at me, you little drunk!"

When I don't, she walks over and grabs me by my temples and she makes me.

"Owwww. That…doesn't feel good."

"Good. It's not supposed to."

Jamie drops my head, and through my closed eyes, I see bright light.

"Don't…"

"Oh yes. Curtains open. Veni vidi vici!"

I can hear her coming over to me, so I try to draw my shoulders in and push my face into the pillow like some kind of drunk, sick turtle.

"Oh, no you don't." She grabs my shirt collar, tugging. I bat at her hands.

"This is Stella McCartney, slutface. And it's cute." My words are croaks.

"Well that's a shame, because there's wine all over it."

A half-assed shriek escapes my lips. I lurch up.

"Huhh?"

I turn...slowly—my head throbs—to find Jamie smirking with her arms crossed.

"That's what it took. I'm not surprised."

"What?" I draw my elbows in against my ribcage, cradling my sore head in my hands. "It's bright."

"You're still as vain as you have been since college."

"I'm not vain."

"Materialistic."

"Materialistic?" My pulse pounds above my eyebrows.

Jamie smirks again. "I'm teasing, Gwen babe, but at least it got you moving. I can tell that you're alive now."

"Why are you here?"

"Because your brother came by earlier today. He couldn't get you to the door, so we were worried. He called, and you answered. You said you were sick. He asked what was the matter, you told him swine flu. I don't even think that that's a thing right now, but that was a red flag to him, I guess. Which is another way of saying you sounded drunker than Cooter Brown."

"Who the fuck is Cooter Brown?"

Through my shaking fingers, I see Jamie shrug in her crisp, light blue blouse. "I'm not sure, now that you ask. It's something that my grandma says. We probably don't want to know. You know how those old, Southern stories are."

I squeeze my eyes shut. Why the hell is she still talking?

I hear something. Crack an eyelid open.

I find Jamie by me...Sniffing. "Woman, how long since you had a bath?"

I stick my middle finger up. "Today," I lie.

I'm not sure when it was, but there's no way I smell. I wear deodorant and have a Glade Plug-In right there in the bathroom. I put it in for—

My throat seizes, and I'm darting toward the bathroom faster than I would have thought was possible. For whatever reason, my still-slightly-drunk self sees the sink as an easier target than the toilet, so that's where I throw up, a bunch of awful, streaky, slightly reddish stuff.

"I'm not sure if that's gross or impressive. It's like *The Exorcist*."

I want to hit her.

"What?" she asks, one eyebrow arched, as I wipe my face with a wet washcloth. "Would you like me to enable you and lie?"

"Enable." I roll my eyes. *Ouch.* "Get out." I wave at her. "I'll take a shower."

"Good. When you finish, we're going out to dinner."

I feel queasy at the thought.

"Don't worry. I'll be your very own bodyguard and life coach. Nic is coming, and he'll drive us."

Gwenna
January 24, 2016

"So what was the drinking about?" Helga's smooth voice unfurls through the cool, clean air inside her office.

I shrug. "I don't know." I'm looking at my feet, not even bothering to front. Because I'm lazy, I guess. "Self-pity. Or bitterness."

"Because?"

I snort, and look up at her.

"Not going to answer?"

I inhale and exhale, not too quietly.

"You know what?"

Her lips purse.

"I've come in here a thousand times, and I try every time to have a good attitude. To be honest. To be grateful. To be okay with where I am, and how I am. Because that's the 'right thing' to do. Because I want to make progress, to be better than I am, for…some purpose. Just so I can say I did my best, or something. I don't know. But let me say this now. Nobody knows what it's like to be in my shoes. To look this different from other people, to have things like this—" I point to my mouth—"that stand out. I was told, as you know, that I might not be able to have children because of the ovary I lost." A stark chill grips me underneath my throat as I think about Barrett, where my mind can never help but go.

"I've got a lot to deal with," I hear myself tell Helga. "It's…a lot." I fold my hands together, looking at them, and not at her face. "I found out my fucking boyfriend is the one who hit me that night. That he lied. He was with me out of guilt, no doubt. So that's what the drinking is about. If I'm going to be alone forever, why not be alone and drunk?" I throw my hands up. "Why not?"

Helga's eyes are kind and warm, almost omniscient. I stand up.

"I'll see you Thursday."

I have fifteen minutes left, but I don't care. I've never left her office early. Now can be the first time.

Jamie stands up in the waiting room when I come out.

"You're—"

"Early. Yes. That's not your problem, is it?"

Her eyes widen.

"Take me home, please. I don't feel like St. Jude right now."

Jamie does as I ask, and she's even nice about it. I'm still in a rotten mood when she leaves half an hour later.

"You'll be good? No—"

"No drinking. It was like, a week. I drank as much in a week or two than you did the first three days of spring break in Cabo our senior year. Lay off."

Again, the wide eyes. I roll mine.

"Sorry. Just leave me to my own foul mood."

When the door shuts, I sob.

chapter twenty-eight

Gwenna
February 14, 2016

Valentine's Day.

It's when I know for certain he will never contact me again.

How could he let me be alone on Valentine's Day? If he loved me?

I know from Nic that Bear surrendered at the jail in Breckenridge, and one of his old ACE friends bailed him out.

He's willing to serve jail time because he didn't really love me. If he loved me, he would have considered that I wouldn't want that for him. Would have never wanted that for him.

"Really?" Helga asks me, fingers steepled.

I frown. "Of course I wouldn't." What does she take me for? Some kind of savage? "You do remember I already beat the shit out of him, yeah? Nic told Jamie that, but I knew already. I had blood under my fingernails. I went at him. And Helga, he was suffering." I sigh, lean back against her couch's saggy cushions.

"That's the worst thing," I tell her, picking at a loose stich on my jeans. "It's not like I don't know him, didn't love him on my end of things." It hurts to say that out loud, so I breathe for just a second. Then I shut my eyes, because it's too private to say aloud and look at Helga.

"I love Barrett still. Maybe not as a lover. I understand that's over; he didn't love me that way. But I love him as a person. I will always love him. Because I knew him. Isn't that the worst thing about knowing anybody? I think knowing someone well means loving them. It almost always does, if they're a nice, good person, and they show you themselves. So if it goes south, for whatever reason, you have to turn it all around and cut it off. Except you really can't. You just pretend to."

And our time is up—right there. A fitting epilogue, I think as I walk back to my bike.

The days pass slowly. Cold days: gray and rainy. Winter in the Smoky Mountains. I don't think it's beautiful. I think it's lonely. My bears are still mostly sleeping. Jamie comes to visit when she can, but she's busy with work.

The only person I see with any regularity is Nic. A film has brought him here to my neck of the woods. I'm ashamed to realize I don't even know what kind of film. I just know he's staying here, at a fancy Airbnb on the other side of town, and one or two nights a week, he drops by and says "hi." We play checkers, or I cook dinner for him.

I think I was wrong about how boring he is. He's not *boring* per se…More just…very black and white. He doesn't see many things in gray, so I think that's why he's not into long, drawn out discussions. He seems to be a very surface sort of person. And what's wrong with that? It takes all kinds, as they say. I like movies. Nic makes movies. *Annnd we've got a match!*

Our conversations may not be riveting, but his little hour-long visits keep me from feeling totally abandoned by the world.

Which—*okay*—I kind of do, but not because I should or any-one's to blame. It's just, they're busy. Everyone is busy with their real lives. They can't pitch a tent in mine, and I don't blame them.

When Nic's not here, I go out sometimes into the yard again. It's not much, but it's progress. Ever since what happened, happened, and I had my little drinking binge—which Helga thinks was more serious than that: a real attempt to hurt myself—I've been more self-conscious again. And more secluded. More the way I was before I met Barrett.

I can't seem to fight the regression in my self-esteem and con-fidence, and it makes me very sad. Like somehow Barrett's touch has been deleted from my heart.

I started practicing my old Taekwondo forms at the top of the hill, just like old times, and like old times, I always end up crying before my workout is really finished.

Helga tells me this is normal. She says I'll heal the same way everyone does: a little jagged maybe, with some scars, but that my heart and soul will work again at some point in the future. That I won't feel broken anymore the way I do right now.

I don't believe her.

I'm not sure I want to.

That's the funny thing about grief, isn't it? It's like a blanket: protective. I'm not ready to drop it yet. Sometimes I think I never will be.

I've started dreaming about him. How could I not? It's not that interesting, not that dramatic, all things considered.

He and I are riding in my car together, and I'm driving. (I would be, since it was me who drove the whole relationship, who threw myself at him). We're going up a hill: a slope in Breckenridge, of course. And then the gas pedal stops working. The car slides backwards. I step on the brakes, but they don't work. I reach for Barrett, and I see his face is filled with shock and horror, just like mine. Barrett jumps out of the car. It slides backwards on the icy road. I'm all alone, and wrecking.

Almost every night.

I have moments where I think I truly hate him. That he left me this way. That he hasn't even called, he hasn't written, hasn't come by. God, I guess there's nothing he could say, but I don't care. He should have tried. He should care more.

He should care about me more.

He knew me, too. He said he loved me.

I blow my breath out, pull my hair back up, finish my form, and dry my useless tears. I start back down the hill.

I'm deep in thought, so I don't notice at first: there's a man in front of me. He's wearing camouflage and holding a huge gun.

Barrett

That fucker came into my house and went into my drawers and stole my ACE camo. He had my .338, I think—the one I pawned. The case looked dinged up in the same spots mine was.

I watched him walk up, dressed in dark clothes, waited patiently as he fumbled through the trusty bobby pin routine on my deadbolt. When he stepped inside the house, I hid, so I could see what that fucker would do next.

He went right upstairs. I followed. He's so unobservant, he had no idea I was right there, looking over his shoulder as he put my clothes on, went down to the den and put my gun together. I'm surprised he managed to get ammo into it.

Now that he's striding through the woods, I'm fucking terrified. I've got a stun gun and a throwing star—two weapons that survived my self-harm purge.

Jesus Christ, why did I sell my guns?

I know Gwenna is at the top of the hill, and that's where he's going. My whole body is ice cold. I'm shaking like I never did before this. Jesus, I'm an Operator, but I just can't stop shivering. I'm such a fucking wreck that it's a struggle to stay quiet behind him. As I stalk him, I can feel my phone vibrating in my pocket: call after call. And I know why now. Too bad for Dove and Blue: I can't answer.

I tell myself, in desperation, that he's trying to impress her. Mimic me or something. I don't fucking know.

But I can't stop shaking. I can't fucking breathe as I gain on him just a little. Up, up, up the hill. I hear her footfall on the leaves. She's coming down. Oh God, I fucking see her.

My reflexes are still fast, so even though my right hand sucks, I throw the star before he gets the gun's nose pointed at her. It flies fast and far—but hits his shoulder, not his spine.

Niccolo whirls: eyes wide, face twisted, gun raised.

chapter twenty-nine

Gwenna
February 14, 2016

*O*H MY GOD, THAT'S BARRETT!
He's so thin it takes a second to be sure, but I can feel him before my eyes identify his face and body. My heart swells to twice its size, surging so hard and fast, I almost fall right over.

I'm alight. *Alive.*

My mouth opens—I want to scream and run to him—but Barrett's eyes are not on me. His arm jerks up. I see the man in camo flinch, and then whirl. He's clumsy, teeters on his heel. He holds the giant gun clumsily, but *it's pointed at Barrett.*

Time stops as Bear holds his hands up. I can see him walking slowly toward the masked man. I can see his face go white. Just one time, his eyes flick to mine. I can read him like a book: RUN, GWEN!

I don't. I can't.

"It's okay," he says loudly to the gunman. He waves, as if nothing is the matter. "Hunting?"

"You—" The masked man shakes his head. His back is facing me now, as he's turned toward Barrett, lower down the hill. I see a crimson stain seep through his camo, near the shoulder blade, and realize Barrett must have...I don't know. Bear doesn't have a gun, does he?

The masked man laughs, wielding his own long rifle. "Did you throw a *knife* at me?"

I know that voice.

I hear it laugh.

"How many times have you played checkers? Dammit, woman. I can never win."

My stomach bottoms out.

It's Nic.

I hold my arms out, desperate to convey this to Barrett somehow. My mind spins. What is going on here?

Again, Bear's gaze hits mine. *Go!*

"It was a throwing star," he says calmly. His voice ignites my blood. "Sorry, man. Is that you, Nic? I wasn't sure. I just got home and saw someone head up this way. Guess I panicked."

Barrett shrugs, and if my brain weren't pealing with alarm bells from the strangeness of the situation, I would believe what he is saying.

"Hunting?" Bear repeats. He shakes his head and brings a hand up to his temple, like he has a headache. "Really sorry, man. I'll—"

"Quiet!" Still brandishing the gun, Nic steps closer to Bear. Then, abruptly, he whirls back around toward me. Using both arms, he raises the gun. I can see his finger fumble for the trigger. At the same time, I note the blur that is Barrett rushing toward us.

It happens so fast.

Nic fires the gun, and I can hear and feel the bullet—hitting me? I guess I drop down to the ground, because that's where I am when I see Barrett straddle Nic and wrench the gun out of his hands. He slams his hand down on Nic's throat and squeezes as his face twists violently.

"You fucking piece of shit!"

His body trembles and his face reddens. I think I make some sort of sound because Bear's eyes, again, fly to mine. Once his gaze hits mine, it softens.

And that's when it happens. That's when Nic, who's writhing under Barrett, reaches up and…I don't know what. Barrett recoils, his hand at his throat, and I can see the shock on his face. Then I hear a horrible gasp. His hand and his neck go red. His eyes widen. His mouth opens. A strange sound comes out. Blood is spilling out his throat and down his chest.

Run!

I read his lips, but I don't understand. I look from Nic to Barrett. Everything has slowed down. I feel like I'm in a movie. *Or a dream.*

The hollow gasping starts again. Barrett falls over, bracing himself with one palm against the ground as Nic rises, holding the gun weirdly now—weirdly meaning the wrong way…because he slams the butt of it into Barrett's head.

Barrett sprawls out in the leaves, but wobbles up. I hear his raspy, gurgling breaths and see the blood pour from a cut along his throat. As Barrett lunges for Nic, Nic whacks Barrett with the gun again. Bear blocks him, but the impact of the gun against his shoulder sends him rolling downhill.

Nic turns my way. "Put your head down, Gwen! Eyes on the ground!" His face tightens as he moves toward me. "EYES ON THE GROUND!"

I do, for a split second. And then I notice: Barrett isn't moving. He's lying on his side in the leaves. Abject terror tumbles through me.

My brain kicks into motion. I go for Nic with a hand move Bear taught me, striking at his jugular. Nic staggers. I kick him in the stomach. He falls. He rolls downhill, not stopping until he's lying right beside Bear.

I wrest the gun away from Nic and knock him in the face.

I see Barrett bleeding from the corner of my eye; I can hear his awful, gasping breaths.

"What are you doing? What is wrong with you?" I'm shrieking.

Nic grabs my fucked up ankle and yanks it out from under me. I land on his lap. Barrett's on us just a second later, tossing me aside and going for Nic's eyes. He gouges one of them, and blood spurts. *Oh my God, the sound of Barrett breathing…* He is lightning with the gun. It's in Nic's face so fast, for a second my eyes don't believe it.

"It was you," Bear wheezes. The words sound hollow, breathy, but I understand them.

Nic laughs.

"It was you, you piece of shit!"

Bear drops the gun and grabs Nic by the throat. "Why are you here…wearing my clothes…" he gasps, and I can see his body quiver, "with…my gun?"

"Hunting," Nic sneers.

Barrett's big hand squeezes his throat.

I realize belatedly that I should get the gun.

That's how, when Barrett passes out, and Nic springs up, it's me who shoots him. He takes one step toward me, and I squeeze the trigger. The gun kicks back so hard, I fall down. Nic does too.

I scramble up: numb, deaf, and blazing with adrenaline. I look down at Nic's maimed torso, at all the blood.

He's dead, I think. I think I killed him!

I'm sobbing as I drop down in the leaves by Barrett. His eyes flutter open. They're wide at first, and blinking blindly, like a fish; but then they focus on my face. His mouth moves. Blood spills from his lips. His eyes squeeze shut, and I see tears drip from the corners.

"Pig."

He blinks several times, squeezing his eyes shut, wheezes, choking on his own blood. I've got him in my lap, my arms around him. *Oh my God, he's going to die…*

"I love you, Bear. I love you so much."

His eyes open, leaking tears.

"I love you!"

His eyes seem hazy. Not focused.

I feel his body go heavy a split second before his head falls back. His eyes roll.

"Barrett?! BARRETT, wake up!" I'm shaking him when I hear the sound of footsteps crunching leaves.

Then there's a red-haired guy. Tall. Did I see him in the moccasin shop? That's all I have time to think before he's shoving me aside. Another guy comes, too. They're on Barrett so fast at first I'm scared. I try to force them off.

"Stay back," the black-haired man barks.

"You okay?" the red-haired one asks me as he stabs something into Barrett's leg.

I start to sob. "What's wrong with Bear?" I come closer and the black-haired one holds out his arm.

"Don't touch him!"

"Please?" The word collapses. Sobs start coming.

It takes me some time to notice that the red-haired one has got a red tube. There's a tube connecting him to Barrett.

The mean one—the one who said "don't touch him"—has his hands around Bear's throat.

Their faces are taut and furious. That's how they look to me. I can still hear Barrett's breathing, see him moving. *Mine.* I drop down beside his head.

"Barrett? I love you so much."

I'm still sitting there, stroking his hair and forehead, when the ambulance arrives at my house.

"RUN," one of them growls. "Tell them we need a trach, his trachea is torn and there's a rip in his left common carotid!"

I don't remember doing that. I don't remember any of the details. I just see Barrett's eyes, the way they open and shut, tears leaking the whole time they load him up. His gray cheeks, all wet, and his red lips stretched open, trying to get air into his lungs.

When the red-haired guy detaches himself from Barrett, I jump into the ambulance. Barrett's fingers stretch out slightly and his face folds on a sob that has the paramedics scrambling around his throat.

I grab his hand. I don't let go.

chapter thirty

Gwenna

I don't know where we are when Barrett starts struggling and moaning.

"Gwen…?" His voice is so raspy, I can barely make out my name, but I recognize the tone. He's called for me so many times before, how could I not?

"Right here." I squeeze his hand. It's cold and damp in mine.

His head presses back against the top of the stretcher, and his face twists. Then, before I know what happened, someone shoves me. "Back up!"

I hit the ambulance's wall with a hard bump. Oh my God, *are those paddles?*

"Stand clear!"

This weird, high-pitched noise whines. The two paramedics are messing with his chest and face. The woman starts counting, pressing on his chest; the man is at his mouth and looking down.

His face looks strange. His skin is gray, his eyes are rolling.

"What's wrong?"

I can only watch as Barrett's body twitches. His hand, curled up by his chest, unfurls and curls again as his back arches.

"Barrett!"

The paddles aren't really paddles—more like soft stickers. The first time they shock him, I'm staring at his face. *Please…please… please…*

When no one moves or speaks, I start to sob, get up, and try to go up by his head. The man holds out his arm to keep me away.

"I love you!"

I can tell it worked that time because the EMTs spring into motion once again. I can't even hear their words. Can only stare at Barrett's face, his bleeding throat.

Oh God, please…

I beg someone to let me hold his hand.

"Okay, but if I tell you move, you have to move back."

His face and body are so still. I kiss his fingers.

"It's okay, baby. Gwen is here. I'm here. I love you. I don't care what happened in the past. It doesn't matter to me."

This goes on for hours. Or minutes, maybe. I don't know. Someone tells me to move back. The ambulance stops. The paramedics jump out, rushing off, and someone helps me down. I guess the driver.

He directs me somewhere. I don't know. I'm numb. I just want Barrett, but they took him back.

"I'm his wife!"

The woman at the counter looks at me like she doesn't even care, and more tears come, and then the dark-haired guy is there, the one called Dove. He takes me to some chairs and tables somewhere.

"I just went back there. He's stable, Gwenna."

I don't know. The horror of it. And it's horror. Nothing less. Dove hugs me and I start sobbing. His shirt smells like butterscotch.

The other one is here, too: Bluebell. Michael, he tells me. I remember something about his dad being in the military, something about a threat, but not specifics.

"I'm going to talk to them again," Dove says at one point.

I look up at Michael and my stomach bottoms out.

"You're... *Fuck!*"

I jump up, running through the hall until I find a door and toss it open, getting sick inside the metal sink of one of the rooms. When I wipe my face, I find Michael in the door and cry again.

Because it's true. It's all true...

Michael is the guy who wanted me to share a beer bowl with him that night.

That night.

Really happened.

I don't want it to have been real—but it is.

Barrett hit me that night. *My* Bear.

I sit on a rolling chair in the empty room and put my head in my hands.

"You okay?" I hear Michael murmur.

I shake my head. I use my feet to scoot my chair over to the examination table, then I put my arms on the paper-covered table and I lean against it as my mind gallops ahead of me.

My heart starts racing.

Barrett hit me.

Nic came at me with a gun.

I shot Nic.

A sob leaks out.

I shot Nic! I shot Jamie's boyfriend! Will I get arrested?

Where is Barrett?

I want Barrett!

Someone rubs my back as I cry, hunched over the table. The hand stops. I hear someone come in and look up to see Dove. His lips are pressed together and his arms are crossed.

As his eyes move over mine and Michael's, he uncrosses his arms. "Talked to someone. Brothers. Wife," he waves at me, "we have a right to updates. Bear's in surgery. They cauterized the artery right after he got here, so the bleeding's stopped. He's getting blood. The surgery they're doing isn't major. Mostly on his trachea, they told me. And they think he's stable now."

I see him hold Michael's eyes, and even though Dove's aren't soft or emotional, I can feel that he is checking his friend over, making sure he's okay. Michael nods, and Dove's gaze shifts to my face.

"Gwenna, do you want to be here? One of us can take you home."

I don't even realize I've stood up until I notice how close my face is to Dove's. "You aren't taking me home!" My voice shakes. "You can't make me leave. I've never even seen you."

"Whoa, now—"

"I don't know you, but I know Barrett. Maybe everything is all messed up with us. I know—" my voice breaks. "I know he might have…" I shake my head as tears fall down my cheeks. "I still want him to be okay, though. And alive." I give a fragile little laugh, devoid of humor.

"I'm not leaving till I know he's okay and he doesn't want me here. I'm not going to force my presence on him—"

I hear someone chuckle and look back at Michael.

His brows wiggle. "Force." He's looking smirky.

"Yes, I said I wouldn't—"

Dove's hand closes on my arm. I look from Michael to him. "Sit down, Gwenna. You're shaking and I'm worried that you're going to fall. Barrett would kill both of us."

I end up on the exam table, my feet dangling off, feeling sick and leaking tears, looking out at Bear's two good friends.

"Sorry." I cup my face in my hands so I don't embarrass myself further. "You can leave me in here and just give me updates. I'll come out," I sob, "in just a little bit—" my body quivers on another sob—"to hear…if…he's okay."

I can feel Dove stepping closer, his hand touch down on my back. He pulls me up against him and I can't help it—I let him, and I cry into his flannel shirt. Bear's friends. If they were at his house, they know him; they love him. They're the ones he wanted with him, not me.

"It's a shame how this went down," I hear one of them say.

"You're a good person, Gwenna." That's Dove. I can tell because he's right beside me. "Staying here. You couldn't force your presence on him in a million years. He'll wake up and I know he'd love to see you. He went over there for you. He feels so sorry for what happened."

"It's okay. I'm okay. I'll get over it. I understand—his feelings…All the guilt." I lift my face and look from Dove to Michael. "I know why he came to Gatlinburg and bought the house. He got in…too far. Just like I did."

Michael steps closer, his eyes warm on mine. "How do you feel about him, Gwenna? Do you hate him?"

I laugh. "Hate him! Barrett?" I smile sadly, wiping stray tears from my cheeks. "I still love him. I get that he—"

"He loves you." Michael's eyes are heavy on my face. "Barrett loves you, Gwenna, and he feels like shit. He didn't mean to get in with you like he did. It was a group secret, and one he wasn't supposed to ever tell. He didn't want to tell you. He thought he could make it up to you. Make you love him and make your life good, so maybe that wouldn't matter. Could be in the past. Do you understand that what he told you put…" He shakes his head.

"He told you because he loves you. He was worried, and he knew that it would make you hate him, but he also knew he needed to protect you."

I'm crying again. "I don't get it." I look from Dove to Michael, suddenly afraid. "Should I be worried. Like…"

"It's settled, Gwenna. Bear turned himself in, in Colorado. It's all settled."

My pulse races. "He hasn't called me."

Dove steps in front of me. "Gwenna. Do you remember that night? The night in Breckenridge, when you and Bear—" I'm nodding, so he pauses; when I don't speak, he goes on. "He told you it was him, and you were very upset. Sliced your fingernails into his neck—" Dove points to his own throat—"cut up his face. He got in the snow and laid there so you could go at him, he let you punch him, got his nose all busted up, black eye right here…" Dove gestures to his own eye. "When we found him, he had called your friend Jamie and waited with you while she got there. I guess you passed out. We found Barrett walking through the woods. He didn't know what day it was, what time it was. He was in shock."

"He thought that we were there to kill him," Michael puts forth.

Dove's eyes hold mine. "That's what he wanted."

His words slice at my soul. My poor Bear. I try to imagine myself beating him up, but I can't remember. My chest aches. "Why are you telling me this?"

Their eyes meet for a moment. This time, Michael speaks. "Gwenna, we understand your feelings. How betrayed you must feel. Angry. No one has been in your position here but you. And we respect that. We just wanted you to understand that Barrett loves you. More than his own life. He wants you to be happy. He wants healing for you."

I shake my head. Without Barrett, I can never heal. "It doesn't make sense..." but it doesn't have to. It's my heart. "You don't get it." I put my head in my hands again. "No one gets it! I can't be happy without Barrett! He's my happy. Even if he did do something awful." I lift my face and look at both of them, his friends who helped him. "I don't care, okay! I know him, I love Barrett, I forgive him. There's no other option. I'm a human being and not some robot. I was shocked and upset." I start sobbing. "It wore off in like a day and then I realized that he didn't—I know he doesn't want to be with me."

Dove's arms are around me again, squeezing me against his chest a little hard. "Gwenna." His hands grip my shoulders. I look up into his brown eyes. "Barrett would do anything to be with you. He would have killed Niccolo in a heartbeat if you hadn't shot him."

My mind hums. I get a heavy breath. "I killed him. I killed Jamie's boyfriend." I can feel hysterics gather in my chest, a heavy wall of weight that needs to be let out. "Is Bear going to be okay? Am I going to get arrested?"

"Gwenna...Calm down." Dove's hand rubs a circle on my back. "If you can calm down, there's some things we want to tell you."

Fear pierces my heart. "What kind of things?"

The two men look at each other, and then at me.

Niccolo

It was never really my fault. Were it not for Dad's addiction to loose pussy, I would never have been on that road at that time. Who expects a person walking by the road's side dressed in black?

I was going faster than I should have been. You could say that. But I had snow tires. Again, I didn't know there would be anybody walking on the shoulder. I didn't see her face until it hit the windshield. From that moment forward, I knew my victim: Gwenna White, my new conquest's best friend. Gwenna White, the guest of Larry Madison and family. She was even in his jacket.

She was carrying a plant: a gardenia. It hit the hood of the car, the edge of the plastic pot leaving a tiny dent I never could get out.

When I left her there, she seemed unconscious but alive. I couldn't call the police. For starters, I didn't have cell phone service. Since I had to leave the scene to go get help, why would I tattle on myself? And ruin my career? And ruin my reputation? Why? Because that would undo what had happened?

I got to my brother John as fast as I could. I told him I'd seen a hit and run, and so I called it in—anonymously, of course. With our dad's reputation, why leave names? John understood.

Not long after that, something strange happened: John got a call on the same secret agent phone I used to call about Gwenna. He got a call from Barrett Drake. John rushed off, and only later did I find out why.

Months later, we stayed up over gin and tonic. John asked me about Gwenna—what had I heard about the girl's recovery—and I almost passed out. He didn't know. Thank fuck, he didn't know my secret. I was still with Jamie. He was curious, he said.

I told him the girl was living. Didn't die.

John told me about Barrett. How he couldn't eat or sleep, was all thrown off and felt so fucking terrible. Boo-hoo. But it worked out. Because John decided he'd tell Barrett that his victim had lived.

See, that's the beauty of it.

That one night, two hit-and-runs.

Mine, and Barrett's.

His victim: some nameless native woman with dementia, living in a teepee in the forest. She wasn't found for weeks due to the snow-packed ground and when she was, no obituary. Just a little news brief.

How would Barrett know Gwen wasn't *his* victim? He'd been so drunk, John didn't think he remembered the correct road name. They'd left a dead victim, but who's to say the dead never come back? That John hadn't simply been wrong? In fact, the stories in the papers later said she'd done just that: died and returned. A murder with no dead.

Lucky.

So lucky.

John cared so much for his friend, he helped his own brother. Only one of his accomplices, General Broomfield's son, Michael, known in ACE as Bluebell, questioned the location of the wreck when John told all of them the victim had survived. But Bluebell—Michael—had been drunk as well. They'd all been drinking. And who questioned John—their honest, valiant *Breck*?

Breck was a hero.

When he died and it came out that it was Barrett's fault—the pussy couldn't shoot some desert rat and so the operation that day went to shit, with John covering for Barrett—it made more sense to me. *There*, the type of man who drove intoxicated, hit a woman, ran.

Barrett—not me.

I told myself that it made sense, the way fate played things. Up until the time when Barrett tracked his victim down in Gatlinburg, it all made so much sense to me. And after that, the nervousness. The fear. The fury.

I tried hard to keep tabs on them. I tried to get Gwen to talk to me. I even used the fence-jump trick John taught me. I used his sed dart concoction. I failed, but things were still okay until she told Jamie about her dreaming. She remembered things about that night.

The team I'd hired to watch Gwenna and Barrett came in contact with another team of snoops: this one far superior, a team of ghosts. As it turns out, they had an agenda, too. They were working for General Broomfield, Michael's father, who was trying to keep an ACE scandal at bay.

Those men told mine that they weren't authorized to shoot and kill, but that's what they thought their boss wanted. A tragic accident.

Something awful.

What's worse than a veteran who's lost his mind, who kills his girl and then himself?

chapter thirty-one

Gwenna
March 30, 2016

It's something that I couldn't think about. Not didn't want to. *Couldn't.* It wasn't possible for me to think of Barrett as a murderer.

He was mine. I'd stamped my love on every inch of him. Even the damaged parts of him, I wanted. *Needed.* I was damaged too, living a pseudo-life, and loving Barrett made me real again. It made me *me* again.

How could I hate him? How was I to label something he'd done unforgivable?

Maybe in a moment I did. I attacked him in the snow. And in that moment, maybe the deepest part of me, the animal, wanted to take him out—the way he took me out. Wanted to get him back: life for a life. But conscious Gwen? Thinking, feeling Gwen? She could never, ever hate him. I just loved him. Kept on loving him. Because it's all my heart could do.

Love doesn't give choices. It's like an avalanche. It just happens. When it does, all you can do is hope you're strong enough to live through it.

Dove told me that Barrett tracked me down because he felt that we were linked. Like, karma. Somehow, ours became entangled.

What he did to me, he felt, was done to him in turn. My life was wrecked. I couldn't sing. I couldn't act. I couldn't even pursue Taekwondo semi-professionally. So, no shred of my former life remained.

And same for Barrett. His life as an Operator: over after Syria. His best friend: gone.

He tracked me down as penance. It would be the ultimate atonement. He could confess everything, release his awful guilt. He'd planned to let me decide what should be done to him. If I wanted him to turn himself in, if I didn't object to him doing so, then he would. He'd come completely clean, and maybe then, he'd feel clean too.

Except, he fell in love with me. And so it's funny, how wrong I had it at first. He traded absolution, traded guiltless living, he traded a fresh start to be with me. He wasn't with me because he thought he had to be. Being near me put his life at risk, it risked his friends' lives. But he did it until he was worried it would risk *my* life. And then he had to tell me. Had to let me go. That's what he thought, Dove told me.

It's a fucked-up story, this one. Hard to understand and even harder to accept.

There were two hit-and-runs that night. One mine, and one that of an elderly Arapahoe woman. She died and stayed dead. Breck hid her body underneath snow, so the local paper didn't report her death until a month and a half later.

I died and came back.

Another curve in the tracks: Breck telling Barrett, Dove, and Blue that the woman that he'd hidden was alive. Was me.

Breck thought this would make it easier for Bear to live with what had happened. He didn't know that Bear and I had talked that night at the bar. That we'd connected. Bear had called me "snowflake," given me his scarf. We smoked our cigarettes together, and I loved his handsome face, his pretty eyes. I remember just that one thing: smoking with him outside. In my memory, I even loved his sadness.

Sweet Barrett.

Mine.

I look at Barrett, and I want to hug him. Want to touch his hair and rub his scratchy cheeks. I want his lips on mine, his strong legs intertwined with my soft ones. I want him beside me at night so I can hold him, he can hold me.

It's the little things. That's all life is, when you really start to think about it. Little things that are your story. No one knows them—no one but you and yours—but they're what make a life. The twinkle lights I strung up on the ceiling for him. Him smelling gardenia petals. The flying pig bird bath.

It's the little things that make a life, and I've learned that they are all I need. Just Barrett in his Jeep. Just shower sex. Just my lover's smile as I lie in his lap on our rock in the woods.

All things I don't have, because I haven't even seen his eyes in forty-six days.

"Hey there, sleeping Beary…"

I climb into bed with him, the way I always do, crossing my legs before I take his big, warm hand in both of mine.

"You know, I should tell you, hibernation season's ending. I've seen Papa almost every day the last two weeks. Even Cinnamon is waddling out of her little nook some days, and you know females are the last ones to wake up. I want to let you know. As a Bear, you have a certain schedule that you need to follow."

My throat tightens unexpectedly. I look down at his hand and trace the scars on it, trying to tickle with my fingertips. Some days, I'll feel his fingers twitch a little, and my whole body goes hot, then cold—with hope he'll wake up and fear that he won't.

It's just so tricky. So confusing. So unknown. His number on the Galsgow Coma Scale is an eight. A three means totally unresponsive, and a fifteen is the best score: what I'd score. Anything over an eight would mean he's not technically in a coma anymore. If he would just say *anything*—even words that don't make sense—he'd be a nine. But…Barrett doesn't.

When the nurses or one of the therapists do something that hurts him, sometimes he'll recoil. Last week, when they re-casted his broken ankle and moved it in a certain way, his eyes opened. He drew a deep breath, and I thought I would pass out from pure joy. Then his eyes shut and his vitals leveled out again.

If he can feel pain, he's still here. That's what I tell myself. If he can feel pain, he can feel pleasure. So I spend some time each day massaging joints the PT thinks are sore, rubbing his feet, stroking his hair. I kiss his cheeks and face, his hands, even his arms. I put my own scented lip gloss on his lips and kiss them softly.

If only life were like a fairy tale. I know I would have the magic kiss that woke him up.

Nic only lived four days after the gunshot. On that fourth day, he got a blood clot. Before he died, on the third day, when he was seeming more stable, he confessed to hitting me, to leaving me there in the snow rather than taking me with him in his car. It's true, he didn't have cell phone service, and after he left, he called as quickly as he could. But I find I don't care about those details. In my mind, he left me there because he didn't give a shit whether I lived or died. I doubt that I would feel this way had he not done what he did in the woods that day.

Had he not tried to kill me. Had he not tried to kill Bear. Had he not deceived my best friend, wasted years of her life and now broken her heart and strained our friendship. Things are getting better slowly, and I know time will heal the awkwardness between Jamie and I right now. Our friendship is too strong, too old, to be severed—even by my murder of her lover.

But that doesn't mean I don't hate him for what he did to her. It doesn't mean I don't secretly, shamefully wish sometimes that Bear had killed him and not me.

Barrett threw a martial arts star at his back, aiming for a certain spot between two vertebrae. But Bear's left handed, and his left hand doesn't work, so the star got buried in Nic's shoulder. When Nic was on the ground, he somehow pulled it out and that's how he got Barrett in the throat.

I have the star—it's cleaned up, hiding in an old pot in my garage—and that thing is razor-sharp. So it's not surprising that it did so much damage to poor Barrett.

How he went from almost bleeding out and suffering a broken ankle to being in this coma...That's the part that no one really understands. He went into cardiac arrest in the ambulance. That's why they had to shock him. I'm told that happens sometimes when people get really low on blood. It's not good, but it's not rare, either.

Then they got him to the hospital, and they couldn't tell whether he was stable enough to put him under general anesthesia, so they went ahead and cauterized his artery with him *awake*. Sometime around then, Barrett's blood pressure shot up, then he passed back out. No one could find evidence of a stroke—they still can't; images of his brain look perfect—but in retrospect, they think something must have happened around then.

At the time, however, he seemed okay, so they put him under. They operated on his ankle, adding screws to keep it stable, and then they fixed his trachea and closed the torn up tissue around it.

When I got to him in the ICU, he had a temporary trach—so, a tube punched into his trachea a little further down from where the damage was. He was covered with hot blankets, because losing blood makes the body temperature drop. His ankle was elevated, in a cast, and his beautiful face looked gray.

A few times those first two days, his eyelids fluttered. Both times, I leaned in close to him and whispered to him, kissed his cheek, and told him how much I loved him. They still had him on painkillers, and after the fourth day, everyone had realized something was wrong. Maybe his old brain injury had flared up somehow. Maybe something with the painkillers. So they cut back on those. They took him for imaging of his brain, and Cleo, Kellan, Dove, and I all sat together, terrified. (Michael had to go back overseas). But everything looked fine.

And still does.

The trach is gone, and he can breathe. As of last week, every single medicine they had him on, the anti-seizure meds, a sedative, a sleeping pill…All, gone. And still, he sleeps.

I've heard the nurses talking about moving him out of this hospital. Somewhere designed for longer-term care.

Cleo and Kellan are still here, and they come every day, and we watch movies, eat dinner, talk—so Barrett knows he isn't by himself. No one is more empathetic than Cleo. She knows exactly what I'm going through. In the mornings, Cle and I go for a run together. It was her idea, or rather her insistence. She tells me it will keep my brain chemistry balanced so I don't get super depressed. As if…

Midday, while I'm here, they watch out for the bears and do their Cleo-Kellan things. They ride our bikes sometimes, which I know Barrett wouldn't mind. And in the afternoon, when I leave home to run errands, they go sit with him. I come back at dinner, and we're all there, and then "we" leave. I think it's funny they don't know I spend the night most nights. I guess because I leave the hospital at 5:30 every morning, drive back home, and shower, they wake up and see my car and think I stayed the night in my own house. I know when Cle finds out, she'll be on me about how I should stay at home in my own bed, but I'll call her a hypocrite.

Today, I watch *Fifty Shades of Gray* and giggle with Bear's nurses as they come in and out. When it ends, I pull the covers down and climb in bed with him. I can't always do this, but one of my favorite nurses is on, and she doesn't care. There are some tubes and wires, but I know how to rearrange them so there's room for me. Right after Shayna checks on Bear and leaves, I duck under the covers and rub my finger over his pig tat. Dove told me that he got it two weeks after New Year's: a pig flying through a snowflake storm. It's done in gorgeous color, just over his left pec. The tattoo means a lot to me, because without it, I'm not sure how I'd have known for sure that Barrett really wanted me. Not out of guilt, or out of loneliness, but out of love.

I try not to think about what Dove and Michael told me, about how Barrett only had some bear spray and the throwing star because he'd moved all of the knives and guns out of his house. And *why* he did that.

I like to imagine when he wakes up, all of that will be forgotten. He will say my name first thing, and we will hug. I'll get under the covers with him and we'll snuggle. I can give him water, wash his hair...

I'll shave his beard and kiss his lips all night. And I won't care that we're still here. It doesn't matter. Nothing matters but this man beside me. His warm skin, his old familiar scars and tattoos. I know everything about him now, every mark and curve of muscle. I will see him sleeping in my dreams for all my life and think how beautiful he is, and want to wake him up and see his eyes.

How much have I fantasized about that moment? Seeing his eyes open, focus on me. God, I want it more than life itself. Barrett wakes up, and we can talk. We can move forward. We can heal together. I know things like walking will be hard because he'll be weak, so I can take him to my house since it's a one-story. I'll do what his physical therapist here does to help his muscles stay active. He'll regain his strength, and I'll cook all the best foods for him. They'll take out the tiny yellow tube that's threaded through his nose into his stomach, because he'll eat my food. He won't need that. In my fantasy, he won't need anything but me.

And so, of course, it has to happen that he wakes up on a Wednesday night—the first night I've been booked to sing at the Bluebird in almost five years.

I get the text when I dig in my purse for my car keys, after. I'm already sweaty and exhilarated, so when I see Cleo's words, I nearly pass dead out.

Barrett's awake!!!!!!!! Don't come back yet though. They have to do a few things first. I'll keep you posted!!! :D

What the fuck?

Just…what the fuck?

I drive straight to the hospital. Cleo can sit on a cactus. When I get near his room, I bump into Kellan on his way out. I know something's wrong the second his gaze touches mine.

"…Gwenna."

My knees are so shaky, I'm forced to grab his arm. Compassion overtakes the weirdness in his eyes. He leads me not into Bear's room, but over to a hallway chair.

"Sit down."

"I don't want to sit down! *Kellan…*"

"He's okay. He's doing great. Ray the PT was in there and Barrett didn't like the way Ray moved his left hand." Kellan's eyes widen. "He could feel it."

"His left hand?"

He nods. "Not sure if it's all the way or what. He's pretty sleepy, but he said some things to Ray and asked 'What's this shit in my nose?' and tried to pull the NG tube out." Barrett chuckles. "He did pull it out. It's gone. He's drinking juice."

My pulse surges. "What's the catch?"

Kellan's eyes dart down to his feet. I see his jaw flex. "Gwen... He asked where Lyon was. He remembered when I told him. He asked how I got cleared to come to Germany."

"He thought he was at Landstuhl."

"Yeah."

"Is that a problem? Does that mean—"

"After a few minutes, he remembered what happened. With Nic."

"You're scaring me! What aren't you saying, Kellan?"

"He called you Snowflake. He said, 'that girl. The snowflake girl.' I started to ask him what that meant and he said the one with red hair. I told you you were okay, and he tried to ask about the accident. We kept telling him you were okay, but he got upset. They weren't going to give him anything but they ended up giving him a small amount of Xanax. When we asked if he wanted to see you, to see Gwen, he told us no. I'm so sorry, Gwen. It might be different tomorrow. But tonight, they want us all to go. He's very tired, he's sleeping. I've woken up after a long sleep before, and trust me, he's not going to be looking for us. I doubt he's even quite that with it yet. They think that this is big for him. Hell, it's amazing. They just want us to leave him starting now until sometime in the morning. Let the nurses and the doctors check him over. See if he'll wake up in another few hours and say more then."

My throat is so tight, when I try to speak, nothing comes out. "You would leave him?" I manage.

618

Kellan's face goes gentle. "He's my brother, Gwen. I'm not saying we go far. We can stay at that hotel across the street. If he wakes up again and asks for us, we come right over."

I open my mouth and try go get some air into my lungs. "Did he remember you?"

"He did."

"Cleo?" I rasp.

"Yes. He remembered Cle."

My voice wavers. "He didn't ask for me?"

"That's why I didn't want you to go in just yet. He had the Xanax, now he's sleeping. If you get upset Gwen, Barrett might, too."

"No he won't! Not if he doesn't remember me. He called me Snowflake New Year's Eve! In 2012." I grab onto Barrett's wrist. He wraps his arm behind my back. "If he didn't call me Gwen or Pig, he doesn't know me! Kell, I have to know! I have to know if he knows who I am…" Against my will, I start to cry.

He pulls me close. "You want some Xanax too?" He makes a sound like a chuckle, but it's darker. His face, when I draw away and look into his eyes, is tight and pale.

"I don't want Xanax. I don't want your help!" I run blindly down the hall, and I don't stop until I'm outside in the parking lot.

chapter thirty-two

Gwenna

Kellan is crazy. You couldn't pry me away from Bear right now to save the planet. Also, it's not true what Kellan said. What he implied. That we can't see Barrett right now.

We can if we want. Even I can. All the doctors are saying is they want him to have a solid night's rest because sleep is important for healing of the brain, and if we want him to stay conscious, he needs to sleep.

Did Kellan think I would run into his room and make him more upset? The thought fills me with fury until sometime in the wee hours when I'm dozing in the waiting room—and I realize that if Kellan hadn't kept me away, maybe I *would* have burst into Bear's room and made a fuss.

So what?

I can still be mad at Kellan.

I can still be mad.

I look out the window in front of me, out at the Smoky Mountains, green hills wreathed with blue-gray fog, and I wonder what I'll do if he doesn't remember me. Doesn't remember *us*. How will I cope with that?

How is this even happening right now? After everything...

I shut my eyes and think of myself up there on stage last night at the Bluebird. How good it felt. And how I thought of Barrett the whole time because I knew how proud he'd be of me.

Once his friends told me how he felt, and I saw that pig tattoo, everything shifted back to normal in my head. Even if it had been me he hit...It would have been weird, yeah. Of course. A sensitive subject. But I think we'd have learned to joke about it. I think we could have gotten through it.

What kind of universe—what kind of God—takes that kind of love and just...erases it?

Tears fill my eyes. I need to get up. Walk around a little. Breathe, before I go into hysterics and the woman at the waiting room security desk makes me leave.

She's talking on her phone as I elbow through a one of the double-doors, bound for the cafeteria. I give her a tight smile.

"Ma'am?"

I look over my shoulder.

"Gwenna, right?"

I nod.

"They need you down the hall."

My stomach flips. "Which hall?"

She laughs. "The other way." She waves across the room, toward the other double-doors. "The one with all the patients."

I push through that set of doors with clammy hands. Is something wrong? I'm met mid-hallway by Nancy, one of the nicer nurses. When I see her face, my head goes airy.

"Gwenna." She looks troubled. "I'm glad you're here."

"What's going on?"

"I'm not exactly sure."

I grab out for the wall, leaning against it as her dark brows draw together. "Barrett is awake, which is phenomenal, but he's..."

"What?" I snap.

"He's very upset. We can't seem to get him calmed down. The charge nurse, Sue, is in there now and has paged the on-call, but...I think it's psychological rather than physical. Honestly? I think he's having some kind of flashback."

I suck a deep breath in and start off toward his room. "I'll know what it is."

Nancy trots along beside me. "He *has* said your name a few times."

I burst through the door to find the room still dark. Barrett's on his side, curled up and shaking with soft, muffled sobs.

"Barrett?" I reach his bed, then freeze. My head is spinning so hard, I almost feel dizzy. I reach out for him, my hand touching his arm. "Bear? It's Gwenna."

I can't breathe as I lean there against his mattress. *So surreal...*

I see his shoulders shake a little, and the shock of seeing him in motion wakes me back up.

"Beary...Hey, it's Gwen." I squeeze his shoulder. "You all right?"

With a knot in my throat, I look behind me at the nurses, and then climb carefully up on the bed.

"I do this at home," I murmur to them as I move in close and wrap an arm around him. He's so thin. He's shaking. God, *my Barrett*. It's so weird to feel his body moving...

My clumsy hands sift through the sheets, feeling the smoothness of his shoulder, then his neck, his face...His throat still sports a small bandage. I stroke alongside that, the way I always used to when I'd try to wake him up.

"Bear? It's Gwennie." My voice cracks on my name. What if he doesn't know it? I inhale as his head comes to rest against my shoulder. "Bear." Tears fill my eyes. I cup his warm neck. "We're okay..."

I can feel his face against my shoulder, feel his body pause…

His forehead tips back, eyes rising to mine. "Pig?"

A little sob slips out, mixed with a crazed laugh. "Yes."

Bear's arms come around me, pulling me to him. It's the sweetest thing I've ever felt.

epilogue

Barrett
May 28, 2016

It's hot today, but I don't care. Gwenna likes to hold my hand, and I like holding hers. We've taken Brian to the enclosure, into Piglet's house, and now we're walking to the open-roofed gazebo behind mine. I squeeze Gwen's hand as Brian climbs the step and takes a seat on the wooden bench that wraps around the inside of the octagon.

Pig and I sit down across from him. Brian takes out his tiny, black recorder, and Gwenna draws my arm into her lap. Her free hand starts to stroke the inside of my forearm.

I can't bring myself to be bothered by the PDA. Three weekends ago, we sat in Gwenna's living room while Brian heard her side of our story. She and I sat leg-to-leg and hip-to-hip, my arm around her shoulders, while she talked for four and a half hours, taking breaks to wipe her eyes and blow her nose. As we served Brian dinner, she found small moments to peck me on the cheek and rub my hip and whisper, "Good?"

I smiled for her, just like I always try to, even when it's not all good. Because she smiles for me. Because, now that she has my mother's emerald on her left hand, I've vowed to make her life the best that it can be, to be her strength, her shield, the second heart that keeps her breathing when she can't.

Brian's a cool guy, and I like him. If I didn't, or she didn't, we wouldn't be here. We don't have to be. It's not because we need the money. It's because, if Brian does make the movie, our share of the profits and one fourth of his will go to veterans. I get to choose the charities myself.

So when Brian smiles at us, and Gwen looks at me, I take a slow, quiet breath and think about my buddy Breck. And all the guys I've been getting to know with the veteran's group, the guys who will work with me in a few months, when I'm back in fighting form and the building is remodeled, and I open the doors of Freedom Martial Arts.

I give Brian a small nod.

"So we'll do just like we did with Gwenna. Trying to get notes on you for the actor, and for me, of course." He smiles, his glasses shifting on his face. "Let's start off with something lighter. Tell me how you felt when you woke up that night and Gwen was there."

I shift my eyes from Brian's to the bench beside him. Gwen's hand squeezes my wrist. What do I tell him? They don't make words for it, not for something like that. The way it felt to have her arms around me, just her smell...

I inhale deeply. My throat aches.

"Surprised." It comes out a whisper.

"Why?" he asks.

I feel Gwen's forehead press against my bicep. Grit my teeth. A prickling hive of anger washes through me. I don't even know at whom. *Myself.*

I'm still not over this. Doc says I will be. But I'm still mad, for now. At me.

I bite the inside of my cheek and shake my head. "Didn't think I'd see her there."

"But Gwen said her feelings didn't really change."

I raise my right hand to my forehead, rub; I stretch my fingers to my temples and press down. "Well, I didn't know that," I say into my hand.

I'm going to fuck this up.

I think of Breck. And Gwen. If the movie is made, Brian, one of the writers who helped the author of *End of Day* turn it into a script, will have some pull with who gets cast as Gwenna. It could even be her.

I let my gaze wander to her face. She smiles sadly. I smile back.

Another deep breath, more a sigh, and I force my gaze back to Brian's. "Because I hadn't seen her," I tell him evenly. "After my confession that night, her getting upset, I called her friend Jamie and like Gwen said, they came back here. I thought my friends were there to kill me when they found me in the woods. I wasn't…" In my right mind.

Brian nods.

"Remember," I say sharply, "that part has to pass review. The part about my friends."

"I know." He smiles. "In this business, I'm well-versed in the NDA, and yours was ironclad."

Gwen's nails stroke my arm. I have to work to keep my eyes from sagging shut.

"I'm sorry," I mumble.

"This is sensitive material. I understand that. And it's hard to talk about."

"I was surprised to see her," I say, going back to what he asked. "I didn't know she…Damn." I shut my eyes and grab a deep breath.

"It's okay," Gwen murmurs.

I shake my head. I need to spit it out. Quit hedging. Even if my voice cracks. Which it does when I say, "I didn't realize she would still...want me."

"And love you," she whispers.

I wipe my eyes, then stroke her hair. "I was surprised," I repeat quietly.

"Just as long as you aren't in the future." She kisses my arm, and I try to bring the emotion level down while Brian asks more questions about the weeks after I woke up.

Gwenna finds a way to keep things light and teasing, joking with Brian that she had to wipe my ass. When my face heats up and I swat at her, she cackles.

I grab the recorder. "That's a damn lie. Nobody loses that much muscle in a month. I was walking around in a couple of days. Not far, and Piglet held my hand." I give her a tender smile.

"We're hand-holders."

"And your hand worked? The left one?"

I nod. "Not perfect, but yeah. More than it did." I flex it for Brian. "I broke a rib back there: the second one from the top, here on the left side. The nerves to this hand were never damaged beyond repair, they just had pressure on them. That's how they explained it to me. Something about that rib breaking gave the nerve more room to breathe."

I put my hand down, and Gwen laces her fingers through mine.

She ends up helping me describe our coming home, on tax day, as it were. "We both filed for extensions." She smiles.

"So tell me what you're doing now."

I tell Brian about the studio, the renovations we've got going. "Gwen's still singing, so we go to Nashville once a week, like she told you."

"How's that going?"

She beams. "I'm in talks with a small label about a record deal."

I can't help grinning, too.

We talk about the bears—all doing well—and I go through Kellan and Lyon's story, and Kell and Cleo's. When I think I've given all the facts and have started thinking about peeling Piglet's little jean shorts off, Brian says, "Just a few more things. I need more details for the character sketches."

Gwen takes a swig from her water bottle, passes it to me. I take a long swallow.

"I'd—Can you tell me more about when you first came here?" he asks. "You were watching her. What was that like?"

I look down at my boots. It's something Gwen and I have talked about, of course. But I don't want to share it.

"You liked her right away?" Brian prompts. "Were drawn to her in some way?"

"Yes."

"What was it?"

"Obsession."

Brian blinks and glances down at his recorder, then looks up at me intensely. "That's what you would call it?"

"I just did."

"Obsessed with the outcome?"

"With her fate, and mine. Obsessed with her. I wanted her from the first time I saw her. When she kicked me, though…" I shake my head. "When we talked in the woods…I—Left. I tried to get away from her because," I rasp, "it scared me. How I felt for her. It felt…out of hand. I couldn't stop."

I wrap an arm around Gwennie and pull her close to me. "I can't stop loving her. I tried," I tell him quietly.

"Oh, I tried too," she chimes in. "After he told me on the mountain. And he left." I hear the pain in her voice as she remembers the night I hurt her so badly by leaving her with Jamie. Leaving just like Elvie did. It's on my long list of regrets.

"I'm so sorry," I tell her again now, because I need to. Every time. If there's an audience or not.

"I don't blame you, B. You know I don't." She strokes my cheek. "Our situation is unusual," she says to Brian. She smiles. "I guess that's why you came to me about it."

He nods. "But what I like the best is how you are together. Not the facts, but you, the people. Characters sell movies. Love stories like this one…People see it as redeeming."

"It is." I'm surprised by my own quiet words. I didn't plan to speak. It happens more since I woke up. I'll just…say something. Doc says it's a good thing. That I'm moving further from my old self and becoming more like a civilian.

"Tell me more about that," Brian says.

I arch my brows and kind of want to kick myself. But I know what he wants. I think I know what he needs more of. I decide to give it to him so he'll leave and I can fuck my fiancé.

"I did a lot of bad things. Some for the job, and other things because I fucked up as an individual. Like the hit and run."

"Which you've paid a fine for."

I nod. "And I'll be doing some community service there before the summer ends."

A gentle summer breeze drifts through the trees, and I feel Gwenna's hair against my shoulder. For a second, my eyes close. It's so damn strange. That this is my life.

I felt so damn dirty when I tracked Gwen down those months ago. So wrecked and ruined. Like I would never, I *could* never, be clean again. Every time she smiles at me, I feel like I've been baptized. Her love cleanses my soul, restores me, in a way I had no fucking clue was possible.

"I have a perfect life," I tell the man in front of us. I look at Gwen. "One that I don't deserve. But you can't earn somebody's love. It's given or it isn't love to start with. I don't know why this happened to Gwen and me. If it was God or something like that. But it's one of hell of a coincidence." I smile at Gwen. "We're going to spend our lives together, and this—it's just the start. It's just the first chapter of *our* story," I say, giving Brian a funny look, then smiling back at Gwen. I can't help it. "After the movie is over, our story will still be going. Just the two of us."

And when Brian goes, I show her what I mean. Pig and I walk to her house, still holding hands, and when I get her in the door, I toss her on the couch and peel her clothes off—shirt, then bra, sucking her nipples, wriggling her jean shorts down. All she's wearing is a small, white thong. I drag it off and part her legs, tasting her sweetness.

Gwenna moans and pulls my hair. Inside my jeans, my cock throbs.

"Mmmm," I rumble as I stroke her up and down her slit, and ease a finger into her heat. "So warm and wet…"

"I've been waiting!" She laughs. The sound is husky. Beautiful.

She wraps her legs around my neck, lifting herself up to my face, and my balls tighten. "Jesus, woman…I'm not gonna last…"

"Oh yes, you are…" She tugs my hair and moans as I kiss between her lips and slide another finger into her. "You're going to last forever." She laughs, rocking against my face again. "I need you, too…please!"

I flick her clit with my tongue. "What can I do for you, Piglet?"

"Your cock…" She pouts. "Put it inside me!"

Leaving my fingers in her, sucking on her clit, I take my jeans down with my right hand, then jerk myself off while I smirk down at Gwen. "You want the whole thing?"

"Yes...Oh, please," she moans as I swirl my head between her lips. "Please...Bear."

She spreads her legs wider. I draw my fingers out and tease my way from her clit down to where she wants it. "Please...right there." I work my way inside, just the tip, and Gwenna groans so loud I feel it in my balls.

She pushes against me, trying to take me deeper. I pull out a little.

"Barrett!"

I grin. "Okay." I curl down over her and kiss her chest, and then I shove inside, a little rough—the way she wants it.

"OHHHH!"

"Like that?"

"Oh God...Again!"

I draw myself out, shuddering at how fucking tight and hot and good she feels. I push back in.

"Ahhhh...Love you, Barrett."

I hold her gaze. "You more."

She grunts—and arches up against me. I know what she's asking for. I stretch out just a little, ignoring the ache in my back as I roll my tongue over her nipple. Gwenna likes it when I bite them, as I fuck her—hard.

I can tell when she's getting close, because she gets so slick and stops saying my name, just panting as I fill her up and leave her empty, gasping as I fill her up and moaning when I leave. I fucking love the way her body starts to shake. My muscles tighten and I feel myself get even fucking harder. Pleasure spins out from my cock all down my legs, making my lower belly tighten, too. It's like a roller coaster. I hold onto her.

"Love you, Piglet..."

"Love you."

Our moans blend together in a symphony of need, and this time, like some others, we come at the same moment. Afterwards, we lie there in each other's arms and hold on tight.

And Gwenna cries.

"What's wrong, baby?"

"Happy." She smiles as she wipes her tears. "Tell me you are too."

"Oh fuck, there's no one happier than me."

"You love me lots."

"And lots."

"Forever? And ever?" She giggles.

"And ever, and ever, and ever. With everything I have, and everything I am."

"Can we write our own vows?" she murmurs as her sleepy eyes sag shut.

"I'm all yours, Piglet. Tell me what you need, I make it happen."

She yawns, smiling. Her hand reaches for my face and cups my scratchy cheek.

"Just you."

I top it off with dinner while she sleeps. Some of her favorite wine—a strict half glass, and none for me—and then I go into the laundry room and bring out a gardenia. I put it in the center of the table before setting plates for us. I guess she's tired from the day, because she sleeps while I serve chicken parm and asparagus for both of us, and even find and light a pair of candles.

When she wakes up, she smiles until her eyes are wet. "This was really sweet."

I shrug.

"You're really sweet." She kisses my chin, pulling on my neck so I lean down. We share a slow kiss.

"For you," I whisper.

"Mine."

We eat in near silence, just smiling, while the small white flowers look down on us.

"You look hot in my apron."

It says *Hers*, and it's right. *This* is right. No matter how hard the road here was—for both of us—the destination is where we belonged.

That night, as we fall asleep under the twinkle stars, I send up a thank you for our long, sad, perfect fucking story.

Gwen and Barrett. Pig and Bear.

There are almost no dreams now: only our two warm bodies, curled together underneath the rainbow.

THE END

I'm planning to write *Covet* next. It wasn't next in my lineup, but it's pushed its way to the forefront of my mind because the characters are amazing. You can add *Covet* to your Goodreads bookshelf and see the beautiful cover by Mae I Design here: https://www.goodreads.com/book/show/25867615-covet

If you want to stay in touch, you can sign up for my newsletter here: http://www.ellajamesbooks.com/newsletter/

You can follow me on Facebook at www.facebook.com/ellajamesauthorpage

I have an amazing readers' group called Ella's Elite, which you can join here: https://www.facebook.com/groups/EllasEliteTeam/

For my email address and other social media links, check out my web site at www.ellajamesbooks.com

Made in the USA
Middletown, DE
13 August 2016